TWO CROSSES

A NOVEL

ELIZABETH MUSSER

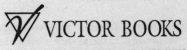

VICTOR BOOKS

A DIVISION OF SCRIPTURE PRESS PUBLICATIONS INC.
USA CANADA ENGLAND

All Scripture is from the *Authorized (King James) Version.*

Cover Design: Paul Higdon
Interior Design: Scott Rattray
Editors: Lora Beth Norton, Barbara Williams
Cover Illustration: George Bush
Maps: Andrea Boven
Production: Julianne Marotz
Book Flow/Electronic Production: Elizabeth MacKinney

Library of Congress Cataloging-in-Publication Data

Musser, Elizabeth.
    Two crosses : a novel / Elizabeth Musser.
    p.   cm.
    ISBN 1-56476-577-6
    I. Title.
PS3563.U839T88   1996
813' .54–dc20
                                                            96-15646
                                                               CIP

1 2 3 4 5 6 7 8 9 10 Printing/Year 00 99 98 97 96

This book is a work of fiction. Names, characters, places, and incidents are either the product of the author's imagination or are used fictitiously. Any resemblance to actual events or locales or persons, living or dead, is entirely coincidental.

This story is dedicated to my beloved grandmother, Allene Massey Goldsmith, with
prayers that we will have many more afternoons together, sitting on the wicker love seat
on your porch.

For as long as I can remember, you have listened, encouraged, cared, and believed. You
are one of God's greatest gifts to me. Thanks
for finding a face in each pansy. I love you.

Acknowledgments

It seems all of my life I have been writing stories in my head. To have one in book form, after all these years, is a testimony to the Lord's goodness and timing. "Faithful is He who calls you, and He will also bring it to pass."

To my parents, Barbara and Jere Goldsmith, I owe a lifetime of thanks for encouraging me and allowing me to pursue my dreams. You are truly two of the most generous people on the face of this earth.

To my grandmother, Allene Goldsmith, I say again thank you for caring and spending time with me.

To all my friends here in France who so willingly gave me information about events that were often painful memories, *merci mille fois!*

To all of our prayer partners on the other side of the ocean who have read my letters throughout our years of ministry in France, thank you, for your prayers and for encouraging me in my writing.

To Dave Horton, my friend, editor, and fellow French enthusiast, I am deeply grateful to you for making this book happen, for giving patient advice, and for reminding me of the intrigue of the Huguenot cross.

To Lora Beth Norton, for your careful editing and expert eye, I am glad to have had the opportunity to work together.

To Trudy Owens and Cathy Carmeni, for reading and rereading the manuscript and offering helpful advice, I appreciate it.

To my teammates, Howard and Trudy Owens and Odette Beauregard, who have been cheerleaders, babysitters, soulmates, and family away from home, *je vous embrasse avec tout mon coeur.*

To Andrew and Christopher, my precious sons, who have been so patient while Mommy sat at the computer and who have served as role models for the children in this book, I give you a heart full of hugs.

And mostly, to my husband, Paul, who has laughed and cried in all the right places year after year, I can never say it enough: *je t'aime.*

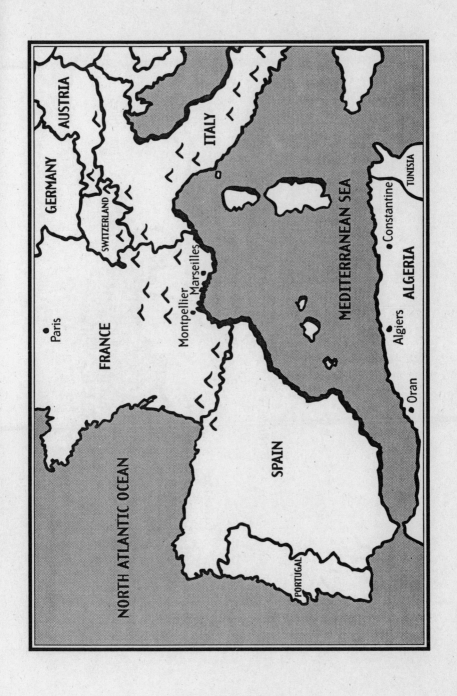

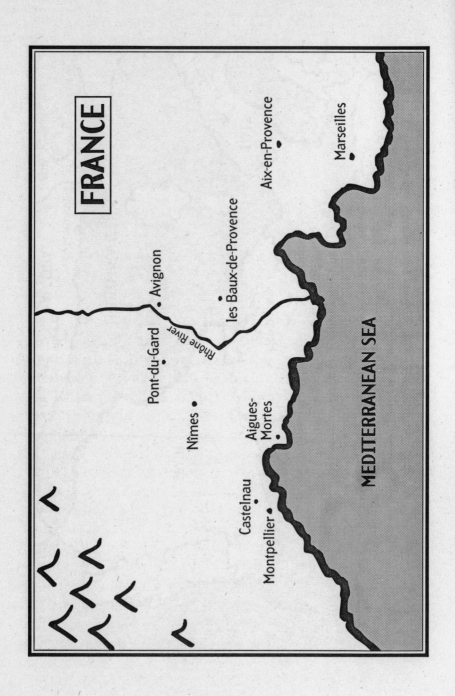

PART I

Chapter One

SEPTEMBER 1961

Gabriella Madison stared out the window as the sun rose softly on the lazy town of Castelnau in southern France. She slipped out of bed, stretched, and ran her fingers through her thick red hair. The tile floor felt cool to her bare feet, but she knew the day promised to be blistering hot. Peering down from her tiny room, she watched the empty streets begin to fill with people. Having observed this daily ritual for two weeks, Gabriella was not surprised that Mme. Leclerc, her landlady, was the first to enter the *boulangerie* just in view down the street. She'd be buying *baguettes* and *gros pain*, as she did every morning—bread for the breakfast of her three boarding students. A little boy about six raced up to the shop door next, his shoulders heaving from having apparently run all the way.

Gabriella watched a moment longer, until a lanky young man in his mid-twenties walked briskly up the street. There was no mistaking the third client who entered the *boulangerie*. Gabriella had recognized him several days earlier from the description of Mme.

Leclerc's other boarders. This was David Hoffmann, the American instructor who taught at St. Joseph's. A mysterious man they had whispered to Gabriella playfully. She strained to get a closer look at him.

A pleasant town, Castelnau, she thought as she moved away from the window. She pulled the comforter up from the end of the bed and lightly fluffed her pillow. *Not a bit like Dakar, or like anything in Senegal, except of course, there is the beach and ocean not far away.* She corrected herself. *Actually, the Mediterranean Sea.*

She tied back her unruly hair with a ribbon, then washed her face in the small porcelain sink that stood in the corner of the room. Opening a large oak armoire, she removed a freshly pressed blouse and a simple, straight-lined navy skirt. The skirt hung loosely around her waist. *I thought one gained weight in this country of bread and pastries.*

Gabriella had come to Castelnau only two weeks ago, excited and confident, ready to discover a new land and people. But gradually, as the days between her and her family lengthened, the gnawing pain of homesickness would surprise her in the midst of a walk through town. She'd notice a woman with hair like Mama's, or two lithe, tanned girls, carefree and laughing, like Jessica and Henrietta. She found herself pushing away a creeping fear on this morning so bright and crisp, with the hint of autumn in the air. At home, there would be no fall smells. At home, she would not yet be starting her first day of university. But here, in this small village separated from her African world by a sea, Gabriella knew she must push away thoughts of how things had been. *It is no use to be homesick on the first day of class. There's nothing to do but get going and see what the day brings.*

She reached for the large leather-bound Bible on

her wooden nightstand and held it close, like a dear friend. Her long fingers leafed familiarly through the pages until she found the place she was looking for and began to read.

Ten minutes later, as she placed the Bible carefully back on the stand, a letter fell from inside the book to the floor. Gabriella reached down to retrieve it. But before she replaced the letter in the book, she paused to read a few of the words: "... I give you this cross, which has always been for me a symbol of forgiveness and love. Perhaps one day, you too will need to be reminded of this. ..." A shadow of concern swept across her face as she pushed away a hazy memory from her past. Instinctively she reached to touch the gold chain that hung around her neck. Then she knelt on the floor and propped her folded hands on the side of the bed. Unaware of the cold, hard tile on her bare knees, she moved her lips without a sound escaping. It was only later, as she rose to her feet and smoothed her skirt, that she saw that her hands were wet from her own hot tears.

* * *

Gabriella finished her breakfast of bread, butter, and jelly dipped into a huge bowl of rich hot chocolate. She did not yet like the strong coffee that the French drank in their wide bowls for breakfast. Since the first disasterous morning when she had choked down her coffee, diluting it with plenty of cream and four cubes of sugar, kind Mme. Leclerc had offered her hot chocolate instead. Smiling as she recalled her embarrassment, she swept the crumbs of bread from her skirt, cleared the table, and set the dishes down with a rattle in the small sink.

"Go along now, Gabriella, please. You are always the last one, helping an old lady like me. But today you mustn't be late. *Allez!* Go on with you and catch up with Stephanie and Caroline." Mme. Leclerc shooed her out of the house. The two other boarders had already hurried off, and Gabriella appreciated Mme. Leclerc's friendly dismissal. She grabbed her small green backpack that lay by the door of the apartment. Opening the door, she turned back to say *Au revoir* and place the expected quick kisses on each cheek of her landlady. "And *merci!*"

She made her way down the dark, narrow staircase where a massive oak door opened onto the street. On a good day, Gabriella could descend the stairs two at a time, race back up, and come down again before the automatic light in the stairwell went off. It was her little game, childish she knew, but nonetheless amusing. But today she did not press the shining orange button. She needed these few seconds of darkness to collect her thoughts.

As she stepped out into the sunlight of the early September day, she blinked from the sudden rush of light. Quickly she trotted down the sidewalk, past the *boulangerie* with its tempting smells of fresh bread and pastries. She passed the *café* where paunchy men were already sipping an early morning *aperitif*, and women chatted noisily as their dogs strained on leashes. She had grown fond of this short walk through the small village that led her to the imposing church of St. Joseph. The church was not big, yet its architecture was Roman, and it seemed to Gabriella that it stood like a benevolent father guarding a houseful of children, saying nothing but ever present and knowing.

She stepped through the red-washed wooden side door of the church down the steps into the hollow nave where flickering candles testified to the early morning fidelity of a few parishoners. The church was slowly filling up with young women. Gabriella took a seat on one of the wooden pews near the front, next to Stephanie.

"You made it," her housemate said too loudly. "I thought you'd be late."

Gabriella smiled. "Fortunately it's a short walk."

"I've heard the first day is a little boring," Stephanie whispered. Her husky voice echoed in the hollow room. Gabriella nodded and put a finger to her lips.

By now, many young women were scattered throughout the twenty rows of pews. A small woman wearing a black nun's habit walked up the aisle and stood before them. Gabriella had heard that Mother Griolet was over seventy, but the nun's green eyes were lively. She spoke in English, with a heavy French accent. "Good morning, girls, and welcome to the church of St. Joseph's. I am Mother Griolet, the director of the program. As you have already discovered during your week of orientation, this church is where you will meet each morning at 8:30 for announcements, after which you will go to your morning classes.

"As you may also know, this is my fourteenth year of working with the Franco-American exchange program here in Castelnau, and by now, I have . . . shall we say, gotten used to the ways of American women." She lifted her eyebrows, and muffled laughter echoed through the church. "We try not to have too many rules, for we want you to soak up this region of France and learn the language. *However*"—again a scattered bit of nervous laughter—"we do expect you to act becoming of your age and remember that you are representing your country.

"As is my custom, I will give you a little history of St. Joseph's. Do not worry. I will be brief." She winked. "This church dates back to the thirteenth century. The parsonage, as you call it, was added in the eighteenth century along with the classrooms, refectory, and dormitory. At one time St. Joseph's was used as a parochial school for French women. I came here in 1917 as a teacher and later stepped into the role of director. I also opened a small orphanage at that time. I'm sure you have noticed the children.

"During World War II, the school was abandoned, though the church and orphanage remained open. I found my work reduced to part-time. Of course, one can always find work, especially in the church." A slightly suspicious tone played in her voice, and again she raised her eyebrows, but no one laughed.

"After the war, with the help of some wealthy businessmen from America, St. Joseph's was transformed into a school that offered classes in both French and English—a type of exchange program for these men's daughters during their junior year of education.

"And so in 1947, I stepped back into my old position as director, only this time I had to brush up on my English a bit. You understand." She emphasized her last phrase with an exaggerated accent, and the girls laughed.

"As I like to tell your parents, who are paying, as you say, 'through the nose' for you to be here, the school's location on the Mediterranean offers an ideal setting for the cultural advancement of their daughters. Several excursions are planned each quarter to historical sites of the region. And there is, of course, springtime in Paris. Two weeks to soak up the charm of the city, lose oneself in the museums, and join the students from the Sorbonne in a *café* on the Left Bank. Doesn't it sound grand?" The girls nodded at Mother Griolet's romantic description.

"This year, there are forty-two of you representing seven different universities and three countries. As in past years, many of you are taking *demi-pension*, living with a French family and eating your meals there. The others are housed at the University in Montpellier, only fifteen minutes away by bus. I hope you have already begun to meet one another.

"I would now like to introduce our professors." She looked down at the three men and one woman seated in the front row and addressed them. "If you will please stand for a moment after I introduce you."

Then she focused again on the women. "First Mr. Claude Brunet, who will teach all three levels of French grammar, as well as the conversation class." A thin, tall, middle-aged man with an enormous mustache and heavy eyebrows rose and nodded slightly.

"He's the one who had the affair with the girl from Rhode Island last year. A real playboy," Stephanie whispered. Gabriella gave her a look of disbelief.

"It's perfectly true—my last year's roommate's sister was in the program."

Gabriella rolled her eyes at Stephanie as Mr. Brunet sat down.

"Next, Mr. Jean-Luc Vidal." A balding man who looked at least sixty, with wire glasses and a generous stomach, stood quickly, a slightly flustered expression on his face. "Mr. Vidal will teach you European history—in French, of course."

"Boring," was Stephanie's comment.

Mother Griolet continued, "This year we are privileged to have a professor from the *Faculté des Lettres* in Montpellier to teach two classes. Madame Josephine Resch will teach eighteenth-century French literature and twentieth-century French novels." A woman of about thirty-five with black blunt-cut hair stood.

"She's supposed to be tough but good," came the running commentary from Stephanie.

"And finally, Mr. David Hoffmann, who will be teach-

ing a course he first presented at St. Joseph's last year:
'Visions of Man, Past and Present.' Mr. Hoffmann will
teach in both French and English, since his course deals
with art, history, and literature from both countries."

When David Hoffmann rose to his feet, every eye in
the church followed him. His frame was tall and athletic, and his hair and eyes were jet black. He appeared
calm and sophisticated for a man in his mid-twenties.

Stephanie jabbed Gabriella in the ribs. "He is one
charming man, I hear. But very distant."

When he sat down, a hushed appreciation filled
the church.

Mother Griolet thanked the professors, then turned
her attention once again to the young women. "We are
delighted to have you with us for the school year. I
believe you have all received your course schedules and
know where the classrooms are. I will end by saying
that I am an old woman and have seen many things.
Young ladies can get into all kinds of trouble. I cannot
prevent it, but my office is open for a friendly chat if
you should happen to need it. You are dismissed."

She left the podium, her face a picture of joviality
dusted with friendly concern. There was a smattering
of polite applause before the girls stood up and filed out
of the church and into the adjoining building.

Gabriella liked the firm yet humorous style of the
director. *I know why Mother grew so fond of her,* she
thought. Then she hurried after Stephanie to find a
place in the classroom of Mr. David Hoffmann.

* * *

Mother Griolet closed the door to her small office
and sat down behind the rich mahogany desk. She
picked up the list in front of her, cursorily reading the
forty-two girls' names. These were mostly girls she did

16

not know, but whose faces would become as familiar to her as her own in the next few months. Then she let her eyes rest on one name: Gabriella Madison. At once she saw this young woman with the fiery hair as a child of six, trembling and sobbing, her face dirty as she clung to Mother Griolet's black skirts.

Mother Griolet did not cry often, but the memory of that scene brought an unexpected sting to her green eyes. A chill ran through her small frame.

"Dear child. Dear, dear child. How could you come back here? Why did you come back here?" She was sure it was a mistake. She was equally sure that she would pray night and day that Gabriella Madison would never discover the story that an old nun had kept to herself for so many years.

Chapter Two

David Hoffmann stood confidently before his class, the hint of a cynical smile on his lips. He looked forward to the first day of classes at St. Joseph's. The young women scurried excitedly into the room, polished and poised, giggling nervously in spite of their efforts to look mature and appealing. He knew their thoughts well. The rumors had been the same last year: he would be a perfect match for one of these up-and-coming debutantes.

"Ladies," he said sternly, "please be seated. You may powder your noses later." More giggling, and a few raised eyebrows. "As I hope you are aware, I have the distinct pleasure of presiding over this most fascinating course, entitled 'Visions of Man: Past and Present.' It is a composite of several subject areas and will test and tax your pretty little brains in the areas of French and English literature, poetry, the history of art, and the psychology of learning. You will soon see how marvelously these subjects flow together. Is that not right, Miss Loudermilk?"

An impeccably dressed blonde in the third row

looked up, surprised, and then beamed back. "Of course, Mr. Hoffmann. It sounds enchanting."

Everything is going as planned, he thought. *They aren't quite sure what to think of me.* But his eyes kept focusing on a girl sitting like a statue on his right. He had noticed her immediately: mounds of red hair curling wildly about her head; bright, clear blue eyes, with an innocence and luminosity that shone like an angel from one of Raphael's paintings. There was nothing pretentious about her. In contrast to the other girls, she seemed childlike and fragile. An angel, he laughed to himself. A Raphaelite angel.

He realized then who she was, so out of place among these sophisticated socialites-in-training. Yes, this must be the daughter of those missionaries who lived on the west coast of Africa. A wealthly relative was paying her way for her junior year abroad before she continued her education at a college in the States. That was the story, anyway. *Poor girl*, he laughed to himself. *I bet she's scared stiff.*

Clearing his throat in an ostentatious manner, he came around to the front of his desk and sat lightly on it. His dark eyes flashed rich and powerful as almost impulsively, yet with a depth of passion, he began to recite:

> Know then thyself, presume not God to scan;
> The proper study of mankind is Man
> Placed on this isthmus of a middle state,
> A being darkly wise, and rudely great:
> With too much knowledge for the skeptic's side,
> With too much weakness for the Stoic's pride,
> He hangs between; in doubt to act, or rest,
> In doubt to deem himself a god, or beast;
> In doubt his mind or body to prefer,
> Born but to die, and reasoning but to err;

19

Alike in ignorance, his reason such,
Whether he thinks too little, or too much:
Chaos of thought and passion, all confused;
Still by himself abused, or disabused;
Created half to rise, and half to fall;
Great lord of all things, yet a prey to all;
Sole judge of truth, in endless error hurled:
The glory, jest, and riddle of the world!

He calmly returned behind his desk and stared at the mesmerized girls, who seemed not to have understood a word of his soliloquy, but nonetheless appreciated his charm and talent. "Ladies, please! Who can tell me the poet's name and work?"

Forty-two heads looked around nervously, laughing and rolling their eyes. *Sure*, their faces said. *He's got to be kidding*.

Then a hand went up. David Hoffman almost didn't see it, it was so unexpected. "Yes, Miss . . ." His voice trailed off as he searched the roll for the missionary kid's name.

"Madison. Gabriella Madison." Her voice was soft but calm.

Gabriella! Even the name of an angel!

"Why, it's from Alexander Pope's 'Essay on Man'!" she exclaimed excitedly, as if she were delighted to find someone else who shared her enthusiasm for the poet.

David Hoffmann blushed for a second, then regained his composure and began his lecture. But after class, his thoughts returned to the angel on his right. Worth investigating, this Gabriella Madison.

*   *   *

Everything in France closes between noon and two, thought Gabriella as she picked up her books from the desk and started out of the classroom. She had observed

20

the daily routine: store owners covered their windows with corrugated aluminum and locked their doors, and workers from all over town passed one another on the cobblestones in the center of town as they headed toward their homes.

The main meal of the day lasted two full hours, eaten in leisurely fashion with plenty of bread and wine accompanying each of the four courses. Gabriella blushed slightly as she remembered her first taste of wine at Mme. Leclerc's dinner table. *"Mais, bien sur,* you must try a little red wine, *ma chère,"* the proprietor had insisted. "What is a French meal without wine?"

To be polite, Gabriella had lifted the glass to her lips and sipped the rich red liquid that was previously forbidden to her. It had burned her mouth and caused her eyes to fill with tears, and she had coughed uncontrollably. Mme. Leclerc, Stephanie, and Caroline had laughed loudly at Gabriella's innocent entry into the world of wine.

"The first sip is always surprising. But do not worry, *ma chère.* You will come to appreciate it, I assure you."

So far, all that Gabriella had come to appreciate about the red wine and copious noontime meal was how hard it was for her to keep her eyes open the rest of the afternoon. She did not want to fall asleep in her first European history class. She had met the history teacher several times during her week of orientation. Mr. Vidal's slow, droning voice would lull even the staunchest teetotaler into dreamland, Gabriella suspected. If only she had Mr. Hoffmann after lunch! No girl in her right mind could have heavy eyes in his class.

She had found it hard to concentrate on his lecture this morning. He seemed discerning and profound, but his dark, deep-set eyes made her uncomfortable. Were they dark blue or coffee brown or jet black? In any case, they were penetrating, perhaps even ridiculing his class of students. The other girls called him handsome and mysterious, but Gabriella saw something different. Brilliant and sad, was her conclusion.

"Miss Madison! May I have a word with you?"

Gabriella turned to see the self-confident form of Mr. Hoffmann striding toward her. A feeling of panic swept over her as her cheeks turned crimson. What could he want with her? Had he read her mind? She considered ignoring his question and hurrying toward the door of Mme. Leclerc's apartment. Instead, she slowed her step to let him catch up. The brightness of the sun combined with her own embarrassment made her feel suddenly lightheaded and weak. She tripped on the cobblestoned street and stumbled awkwardly until Mr. Hoffmann's strong hand grasped her arm and steadied her. *If only I could disappear,* she groaned inwardly. Every girl at school was longing for a *tête-à-tête* with David Hoffmann, and she, at this golden opportunity, could only conduct herself like a clumsy adolescent.

He seemed not to notice as he matched her pace. "Where are you going? You don't eat lunch at the cafeteria in town, I suppose?"

"Oh, no. I'm boarding with Mme. Leclerc. We eat our main meal at her house at noon. Actually, we eat all of our meals with her. She says we keep her company. It's always quite delicious, but the wine and food make me sleepy." She was babbling, saying more than she needed or meant.

He chuckled. "Bring some toothpicks, then, for Mr. Vidal's class. You'll need them to prop open your eyes!"

Although Gabriella disapproved of Mr. Hoffmann's cutting remark, she nevertheless felt her lips curling upward into a grin, which only added to her embarrassment.

Again Mr. Hoffmann seemed oblivious to her uneasiness. "I was impressed that you knew Mr. Pope and his poem. I didn't expect anyone to have knowledge of or interest in my opening statement."

"Oh, I'm sure everyone was interested; they just weren't familiar with the work. My mother used to read to us all the time—classics, poetry, any books she could get her hands on. I mean, it was sometimes hard to have books ... where we lived ... in English." Rambling again, she finished lamely, "Anyway, I really like Pope's poetry."

"You're from Africa, I hear. What do you think of St. Joseph's and her charming ladies?"

"I think it will be fine, interesting. Oh, dear, there's Mme. Leclerc looking out the window for me. Good-bye." With that, she left his side and hurriedly walked toward her smiling landlady. Racing up the stairs and entering the apartment, she caught a glimpse of her flushed face in the mirror in the entranceway. Her heart was pounding so loudly that she was sure the other girls would notice.

* * *

The first day of classes was over at St. Joseph's, and Mother Griolet slumped quietly into the black-cushioned chair behind her desk. *Things progressed well for a first day,* she concluded, satisfied. *Not a bit like the old days, with all the nuns scurrying about.*

Now St. Joseph's exchange program had, if anything, a Protestant aura to it. To Mother Griolet, the religion of the school did not matter, though she wore her nun's habit with pride. She had grown tired of the hypocritical, reluctant sisters who left the school after hours and slept with the butcher's sons. Religion was dying in France. Everyone was Catholic, and no one was Catholic. Like their last names, their Catholicism stayed with them forever, but only to a few did it mean something.

Now all the professors were bilingual, and most of them were male. At times she had wondered if hiring each of them had been a mistake. Mr. Brunet was a womanizer and everyone knew it, but he taught grammar better than anyone else and left Mother Griolet alone. Mr. Vidal had needed a job when he applied four years ago. He spoke a pitiful English, but his knowledge of European history was vast, and she allowed him to teach in French. He had rendered a favor for Mother Griolet long ago during the War, and one great favor deserved another. A position at St. Joseph's would pay his bills, if he managed to stay away from the *café-bar* on his way home after class.

But it was not Mr. Vidal's drinking habits that bothered Mother Griolet today as she sat reflecting at her desk—it was the baffling personality of Mr. David Hoffmann. She had hired him on the spot eighteen months ago. His references had been impeccable; a brilliant young man with an Ivy League education, twenty-three years old, the son of an ambassador. Well-traveled. Charming. He had come to her confident in his ability to assume his first teaching position. And Mother Griolet had not been disappointed. Though he did not have the degrees to match the professors, he was a gifted teacher. She had been especially impressed with his desire for this job, when she was sure he could easily have found something more prestigious. He seemed to feel that he *needed* to be here.

But Mother Griolet suspected that David Hoffmann was not teaching at St. Joseph's as an end in itself. He spoke beautiful French; his manners were polite, though aloof. But his eyes searched for something, and she feared it had to do with the war across the Mediterranean.

The bells in the chapel chimed five o'clock. She stood up, smoothed the black robe that had been her daily wardrobe for nearly fifty years, and carried her small frame out the door and down the hall.

* * *

David Hoffmann walked briskly down the street through the darkness, the click of his heels reverberating on the deserted cobblestones. He slipped into a phone booth, plunked a franc piece into the open slot, and dialed a number.

"It's me," he whispered. "Yes, I'll be there. And listen, I'm bringing a girl." He waited for the response, then continued. "What? No. Don't worry—it will work out beautifully." He smiled into the phone receiver, listening to the angry reproach from his unseen conversationalist.

"No, I promise. She doesn't know a thing. Trust me." He paused again, intent on every word coming through the phone line.

"We'll be in Aigues-Mortes in two weeks. Oh, and my friend has red hair. Lots of it. *À bientôt, mon ami.*" He placed the receiver back on the hook and said to himself, *Yes, I will see you very soon, my friend, and wait til you meet the angel I'll be bringing with me.*

He wrinkled his brow as if not quite convinced of his plan. Then he turned and walked back up the street, deep in thought.

Chapter Three

In the streets beyond the Seine on the Left Bank of Paris, a young child played alone while her mother looked on from their third-floor apartment. "Be careful, Ophélie!" called the woman, glancing down the street to where three men waited at the corner. *Students from the Sorbonne, foreigners perhaps,* she thought as the men began to move in her direction.

"Dinnertime, *ma chère*," called the worried mother. "*Vite!* Come upstairs quickly."

"But, Mama," the child protested, "you said I could play awhile longer. The sun has not yet closed his eyes. A few more minutes, please, Mama."

The young woman coughed weakly. Her face was pale and thin, but her beauty was obvious. The dark, almost black eyes, framed by rich, thick lashes, mirrored intense pain. Again she coughed and pleaded, "*Now*, Ophélie, you must come now." The three men drew closer, and she recognized their faces. Fear erased the pain in her eyes. "Now!" Her voice, not loud but nonetheless insistent, betrayed her concern.

* * *

Ophélie glanced over her shoulder at the men half a block away. For a moment, a look of hatred registered on her innocent face. Then she replaced it with a carefree smile as she tossed her long brown hair over her shoulders. "*Oui*, Mama. I'm coming."

Like an actress poised before her audience, she turned to face the shadows of the strangers. Ophélie would play her part well. For the sake of Mama, she would not be afraid. She would know nothing, no matter what they asked. If, of course, they came to the door, as so many others had done before in her short life.

"You must leave at once, *ma chère*," whispered Mama as she pulled Ophélie inside the apartment and bolted the door. She handed her daughter the precious little blue sack that had been stored away, waiting for this fateful day. "Go out the secret way, Ophélie. Run fast to Mr. Gady's shop. Tell him you must stay with him until I come. He will understand. Now go quickly." As Ophélie prepared to leave, her mother caught her up in her arms and hugged her fiercely against her breast. "Always you know that Mama loves you. Always. You are a wonderful girl."

Mother and child ran to the back bedroom and opened the window. Ophélie perched on the sill for only a moment, like a baby swallow before its first flight. Then, with the small sack crossed over her neck, she grabbed the thick rope that her mother had tied to the outside railing months ago. The rope fell to the ground, and she shimmied down quickly, just as she had done in their many "secret practice sessions," as Mama had called them. Ophélie had felt a sense of adventure and excitement as she practiced for some unknown day. But as dusk settled in and she touched the cement of the street below, she knew that tonight's performance was not a practice. She looked up for one last glimpse of Mama, who pulled in the rope and closed the window.

"*Au revoir*, Mama. *À bientôt*," whispered Ophélie as she rushed down the side street and lost herself in the teeming crowd of the Left Bank of Paris at sunset.

* * *

Anne-Marie Duchemin could hear their footsteps as the three men rushed up the stairs to her apartment. "Oh, God, this is it." She longed to escape down the rope as Ophélie had done, but love held her back. She would not let them find her daughter. She would delay them for the precious few minutes Ophélie needed to reach Mr. Gady's shop. They would never find her there…unless they forced Anne-Marie to talk.

She had no doubt that she might talk if she were tortured. It had happened before. But this time she was prepared. Her life did not matter anymore. Her experience had left these words engraved in her mind, "From here on out, you must regard your life as totally dispensable for the sake of a much greater cause."

Yet Anne-Marie would not die for a lofty cause that, however important, was very flawed. No, Anne-Marie had discovered that there was only one cause worth dying for—that of love. She smiled peacefully through her tears. *What irony, ma chère, Ophélie. To keep you close to me forever, I must leave you for right now.* She felt the tiny bottle sewn inside her sleeve. If she needed, she could slip a pill under her tongue, and she would reveal nothing.

Hurriedly, Anne-Marie untied the rope and ran to the kitchen where she opened the small metal trash chute. Silently she let the rope fall through it into the dumpster in the basement of the building.

By now the men were banging on the door, cursing loudly in Arabic. Anne-Marie stood frozen in the hall-

28

way. *Just a few more seconds, and she will be safe.* Again with trembling fingers, she unbolted the brass lock and put her hand to the door. Immediately three dark-skinned Arab men rushed in upon her. Anne-Marie stepped back, stumbling and catching herself on a small table in the hall.

"Moustafa!" she whispered.

The young man was no more than twenty-one, and as she said his name, he lowered his head, a look of guilt and sorrow in his eyes.

She read it easily. *I am sorry, my friend, I had no choice.* She knew it was true.

"Where is the girl? Bring her here now." The tallest of the three shoved the second man, whose young face was badly scarred, toward the kitchen. Moustafa stood riveted in his place, dark panic in his eyes.

"You coward! Help Rachid! Go find the girl!" He pushed Moustafa toward the open bedroom.

Anne-Marie followed Moustafa as obediently, like a whipped puppy, he walked toward the back of the apartment and briefly glanced around the sparse bedroom. It held an old mattress and springs with no headboard, two chairs with worn material, a cheap armoire, and a small bedside table. He stopped by the window to look out at the street below. The curtain fluttered slightly, and he quietly pushed the window shut and turned the handle to lock it.

Thank you, Moustafa, Anne-Marie thought.

He went back to the doorway. "There is nothing back here, Ali. She is not here," he reported.

Ali turned his rage-filled face to Anne-Marie and demanded, "Where is your daughter? We have seen her. She is near."

Anne-Marie said nothing, terror in her eyes. She remembered too well Ali's penchant for sadistic pleasure.

He reached for her face, grabbing her chin. "Tell me, woman." His voice was filled with hatred. "I can make you tell me." He swung his other hand and hit her fiercely across the cheek.

Anne-Marie cried out as she fell backward, and Moustafa caught her.

"Please." She was on her knees. "You do not need her. I will go with you! She is nothing to you." She was sobbing and Ali pulled her to her feet. He looked as if he might strike her again, but Moustafa interrupted.

"Ali, sir, I have seen them often at the meat stand, as I told you. The girl is only six. She knows nothing."

"And have you lived with them?" He turned angrily to stare at Moustafa, relaxing his grip on Anne-Marie. "Have you heard every conversation? Of course not! You do not know. There is a war on in your country. Algeria will be independent! And you would protect a disgusting whore and her bastard child instead of the cause. You will die with them. Fool."

Finishing his search of the small apartment, the other young man called Rachid came into the hall. "Ali! Calm yourself. You will kill her, and then we will never find the others. Moustafa is right. What would a scared kid know? Bring along the woman. She will talk. She has talked before."

* * *

Ophélie waited until well past dark at Mr. Gady's shop for her mother to reappear. Each time a customer entered through the doorway, pushing aside the long strands of colorful beads, Ophélie glanced up hopefully. But Mama was never there. They came and bought flour and *couscous* and rice from Thailand and hot little peppers. They laughed and joked with the stooped, graying shopkeeper. He winked back and shuffled

30

behind the counter. Ophélie sat on a small stool and watched each face and grew angry that they could laugh and joke while her life had stopped abruptly. She wondered when Mr. Gady would close the store. Her stomach rumbled, and she knew it must be past dinnertime.

As if reading her thoughts, the shopkeeper said, "Ah, little Ophélie, we will lock the store soon and have our supper, *n'est-ce pas?* Come now, little one. Do not worry. Oh, such sadness in your big brown eyes! No, dear child. Mr. Gady will care for you. And Mother will come soon. You will see."

But Ophélie read the fear in his tired eyes. She had seen the lines of concern too often on the face of her mother. No, something was wrong and she knew it.

The small blue velvet bag still hung on the white cord around her neck, hidden beneath her dress. She found an excuse to leave the watchful eye of Mr. Gady and go out the back way, up the narrow steps that led to his apartment. Mama had said she should give the bag to Mr. Gady immediately, but she had not. What if he took it and never returned it? Then all that mattered would be lost, and she would not even carry the memory of her mother with her. Quickly she removed the bag from around her neck. Reaching inside, she fumbled through two folded envelopes until she touched a thin necklace at the bottom of the bag. Bringing it out, she examined the small gold cross that hung on the chain. She lifted it to her lips and kissed it gently, putting it away.

Ophélie crept back down the stairs as darkness closed its heavy curtain over the busy city. Out in the dust of the street behind the shop, she bent down, and with her finger drew a crude picture of the cross she had just held. It was a thick cross, with a dove hanging below the lowest branch. "For you, Mama," she whispered. "For you. Here is hope." Then she stood and brushed away the picture with the sole of her shoe.

* * *

At forty-six years of age, Ali Boudani looked more like a man of sixty. His face was weathered, and his teeth shone crooked and broken when he smiled, which he did often. He carried his tall, lean frame with steely confidence, a look he had acquired through thirty years in the armed service. He was a military man to the core, like his father. The spitting image of his dad. With pride he had watched his father's military progress at the end of World War I, when he was only four. He had decided then and there that he would make his father proud.

He smirked with an angry thought. *You would be proud of me now, Father, if you only knew. You would be proud.* The musty basement where he paced back and forth on this night was occupied by a handful of somber men, several of them dark-skinned Arabs like Ali. Two others were unmistakably French.

"Today, here in Paris, we have found the woman we have been hunting these months. Anne-Marie Duchemin." The face of a woman, delicate and beautiful, appeared on a screen at the front of the room. "We must thank our new friend, Moustafa, for this prize." Ali chuckled cruelly as he pointed to the young man seated in the back of the small smoky room.

"Some of you remember Anne-Marie. She was of great help to us at the beginning of the war. A foolish woman, a disgusting *pied-noir*. Her parents were killed in the massacre of 1958." A self-assured smile played around his lips. "A most unfortunate accident, of course. And she came with us. She did not know. She had the little child and was alone ... and Jean-Claude was so kind to her." There was quiet laughter, and heads nodded. A few of the Arabs patted a handsome young Frenchman on the back.

"Very helpful, this woman, until she left Algeria six months ago. She wanted to protect her daughter, you understand. Perhaps she has succeeded in that for now. We did not find the child." Another picture flashed on the screen: a young girl, fine and graceful, an image of a younger Anne-Marie, her brown hair pulled back in a long braid and a carefree smile on her face.

"For now we do not know where Ophélie Duchemin is hiding. But, of course, we have little use for her.

"We believe the mother has information about the disturbing smuggling activities we have recently learned of. She has had close ties in the past with several informers. We will have this information soon. We will take her back to Algeria with us." Again he chuckled, a mad glaze in his eyes, as a man with a turban around his head clicked off the projector. The men rose to leave the smoke-filled room, muttering amongst themselves. Ali called back the two Frenchmen. "Jean-Claude and Emile. You will stay in France. There is work for you here."

* * *

Moustafa Dramchini sat a moment longer in his chair in the back corner, touching the scars on his wrists. Anger burned in his eyes as he watched Ali huddled with the two Frenchmen, whispering and planning their unspeakable deeds. "You are mad with power and hatred, Ali. You use this war for your own revenge," he whispered.

Moustafa crept out of the room and into the shadows of the night. Ali's men were watching, he knew. He could not get away. The warm wind of September rushed him along as the stars winked down at him and seemed to say, "Do not keep silent. Do not keep silent."

* * *

Rajib Karel crept through the streets of Algiers as the sun yawned and left a shimmering whisper across the face of the waters in the port. Its fading brilliance caught the silver on the sailboat *Capitaine* and sent a sharp glare out from the boat. Rajib crouched in the shadows of the dock and waited impatiently for darkness.

He glanced down at the slip of paper grasped tightly in his hand. A strange cross was scribbled in the top left-hand corner of the paper. It was a thick cross, with four arrows pointing inward and a bird drawn from the bottom arrow.

Rajib did not contemplate the cross. Instead he reread the message scrawled on the paper: *vendredi20h15*. Friday, 8:15 P.M. Tonight. It was time.

He stiffened as he heard a slight noise in the shadows. Heart pounding, he pulled himself behind a small sailboat and watched. Silence. Only ten more minutes, and he would climb aboard the *Capitaine* and head to France. Ten more minutes to safety.

The boy had prepared the speech in his head. *My father served your army well in the second world war and Indochina. Now he has been killed by the FLN here in Algeria. They called him a traitor. He was a* harki. *I am his son. We are on your side in this war. Please. I only seek escape. No one is left in my family. They have all been murdered. I am fleeing Algeria with only the clothes on my back. I was told by a friend that here I would be safe.*

He remembered the warning that the French did not want refugees, especially Algerian ones. They only wanted out of the war that was claiming their sons' lives. Twenty years of war had taken its toll on France. First the Second World War, then Indochina, and now Algeria.

But someone will understand, he thought. The

months of hiding and terror would soon be over, and he could start a new life in France. He looked at the sky. Black. Now was the time!

Slowly Rajib left the cover of the small sailboat. Crouching, he hurried along the dock. Four hundred yards to freedom.

Out of the darkness another form appeared, blocking Rajib's way. A low laugh echoed in the stillness of the night. "And where do you think you are going, Rajib?"

The boy froze, looking frantically about him. Then he dashed toward a small fishing rig. *Jump in the water.* There was safety. But even as he moved, a shot rang out. Pain seared through his chest as he fell back onto the planks. Still conscious, he pulled his body toward the water. Another shot was fired. One foot from the edge of the dock, he stopped. Rajib Karel never moved again.

* * *

The dark form of a man bent down over the body. "Fool! No one escapes Ali! Now your whole family has paid for the traitorous act of your father. And many others will pay. The sons of the *harkis* will run, and so will the European filth. Run from a free Algeria! But those whom Ali has picked will never escape."

He searched the body and found nothing of importance in the pockets of Rajib's pants. He unpried the dead boy's closed fist and smiled.

"Thank you, Rajib. This is exactly what I was looking for. Ali will be most pleased." He shoved the body into the cool waters in the port and walked back toward the lights of the city, while the *Capitaine* waited and waited in the dark.

Chapter Four

The second bell rang out from atop the church of St. Joseph as the young women hurried to the stone house behind the church. Gabriella slowed down when she reached the steps leading to the classroom on the second floor. Recalling her brief conversation with Mr. Hoffmann after yesterday's class, she felt embarrassed to see him again.

She took a seat next to Stephanie, who was stuffing the last of a *pain au chocolat* in her mouth and giggling in the process.

"Did you read that poetry stuff for today?" Not waiting for Gabriella's reply, she continued, "It's pure nonsense to me. Analyzing John Donne! Insane."

Mr. Hoffmann entered the classroom, striding smoothly to the podium, where he placed his notes and book. "Ladies, please open your anthologies to page 1,182. We will be considering the poetry and prose of John Donne, one of the wittiest and most spiritual men of the early seventeenth century. From him we carry such phrases as 'for whom the bell tolls,' 'no man is an island,' and 'death, be not proud.' A fascinating man, at once a scandalous young cavalier and a passionate, intellectual preacher.

"Miss Madison—" The teacher turned his dark eyes toward Gabriella. "Could you please tell us your impressions of a man who could write both sensual love poems and profound sermons?"

She was petrified. *And he is pleased,* she thought. *He wants to prove he knows more than I do. So let him.*

But Gabriella was too proud to let this man defeat her in a battle of wits. Without another thought, she began. "Donne possessed a genius that was fully appreciated some 200 years after his death. His poems ring with colloquialisms which resonate in our minds. His sermons are passionately human, more concerned with displaying the drama of sin, guilt, repentance, and faith than theorizing on Christian dogma. His poetry and prose are filled with images that shock and delight...." She had almost forgotten where she was as she continued expounding her thoughts on a man who happened to be one of her favorite poets, Mr. John Donne.

* * *

"You were great, Gabriella," Stephanie enthused after class. "Next thing you know, Mr. Hoffmann will be asking you to teach." She scurried out of the room as the teacher approached.

"Miss Madison?"

"Yes?" Gabriella looked up at him without smiling.

"Would you care to join me for a stroll on the Place de la Comedie in Montpellier this afternoon after class? It's a wonderful spot for people-watching. I'm interested in what you can tell me about Africa."

"This afternoon? Well, I suppose I could, for a little while. I need to get some studying done and, of course,

37

I couldn't spend all day, but—"

David Hoffmann chuckled and interrupted her. "My dear young lady. It is not a date. Just a few questions in broad daylight. There's no need to worry about my intentions." He winked slyly at her and bent down to retrieve his leather briefcase. "I'll meet you outside the church at 4:30."

He left her standing in the middle of the empty classroom, fuming. *Arrogant man.*

* * *

David led Gabriella through the tiny back streets of Montpellier until suddenly they entered a vast, open square, surrounded by majestic old buildings. In the center of the square, a fountain of the Three Graces sprayed water around students who hovered by it.

"It's beautiful!"

"The center, with the fountain, is called *l'oeuf,*" said David.

"The egg? Because of its oval shape?"

"That's right. La Place de la Comedie is a favorite gathering spot for students. They waste their days away at little outdoor *cafés.* Speaking of which, will you join me for a drink?"

The sun was high and the sky a fierce, bright blue. Gabriella felt beads of perspiration on her forehead and wished she had tied back her hair.

"A drink would be great," she said enthusiastically.

David strolled across the great square, stopping to observe a collection of knives displayed on an oriental rug.

The black African vendor smiled, his white teeth lighting up his face, and followed them down the Place. "Beeutifuwl knives for thees leetle lady with the long red hair."

"Montpellier has been called the 'Oxford of France,'" David commented, ignoring the African. He touched Gabriella's arm and guided her through the square. "The university has been around since the thirteenth century. The medical school is especially renowned."

Gabriella nodded, enchanted by this huge gathering spot of multicolored youths. Beside a movie theater, a violinist played, his open case collecting franc pieces from appreciative pedestrians.

"Vivaldi's 'Autumn,'" reflected Gabriella, charmed by the poignant melody.

"Ah, this missionary is not only well read, she also knows her classical music," David exclaimed, in feigned astonishment. "Have a seat, my dear." He offered her a chair at a small round table overlooking the Comedie. To her right Gabriella saw more spewing fountains and a wide, long tree-lined park where people walked slowly beside gardens overflowing with impatiens and begonias.

Following her gaze, David commented, "That is the Esplanade, a lovely little plot of earth filled with centuries' worth of history and splattered in years gone by with the blood of your beloved Protestants."

"What do you mean?"

"Ah, you are here in this town with such rich Protestant roots, yet you do not know its history? She quotes Pope and Donne and dances to Vivaldi, but the poor little missionary cannot explain her roots. 'Tis strange methinks." His tone was theatrical, but Gabriella knew he only was looking for a friendly argument.

"If you mean the history of the Huguenots, I am quite aware of the courageous stand they took after the revocation of the Edict of Nantes in 1685. I know they hid in the Cevennes mountains north of here, and I hope to see Aigues-Mortes where the women Huguenots were imprisoned. But if you mean, do I know what happened right here where we sit, Sir Historian, I am all ears. Please enlighten me."

"Well said, Miss Madison!" David replied, seemingly pleased that she was not afraid to stand up to him. "During the time of Louis XIV, Nicolas Baville was overseeing life in this region. He ordered many French Protestants killed. They were martyred for their faith right here on the Esplanade, where we sit, and thousands turned out to watch the bloody deeds. Awful, isn't it?"

A waiter hovered impatiently, interrupting David's sordid tale.

"Yes, I'll have a *pastis*, if you please, and the lady..." He looked inquiringly at Gabriella, who blushed and said, *"Un citron pressé, s'il vous plaît."*

"Wonderful!" David laughed. "A lemonade for the lady."

Gabriella squinted up at David. "Do go on with your story."

"Ah, with the bloody deeds? Yes, well you must know of Claude Bresson. He was a very famous and brilliant lawyer who was also a Protestant pastor. He was torn apart alive on the wheel, right here on the Esplanade." He paused as if to let the gruesome words sink in. "And why? Because he didn't agree with His Majesty and the Pope. And then there was Pierre Durand. He was hung from the gallows as people like us stood and watched.

"It's a terrible waste, wouldn't you say? These intellectuals who came to study at the great university of Montpellier and were killed for what they believed."

Gabriella did not reply.

"That's why I don't believe anything, Miss Madison. You would tell me there is a God up there? What was He doing while His people argued over petty doctrine and ripped each other apart because one group didn't believe the Pope was infallible? A pure waste, religion.

A curse for those who are born under its roof." David spoke with passion now, continuing his soliloquy.

"Look at Algeria today, with its Muslims and Catholics and Protestants and Jews. They lived together in peace until somebody thought Algeria needed its precious freedom. Then suddenly they started hating each other and killing and torturing their neighbors, because they were forced to take sides. The war is over independence, but still, religion divides. It is pointless."

Gabriella looked up as the waiter placed their drinks on the table, spilling a bit of the *citron pressé* and rushing off to another table with two frothy mugs of beer.

She spoke with mock admiration. "My, you know a lot about history. But with your cynical views, why are you so concerned with the Algerian War? Which side do you pick to win?"

"That's a very good question, Miss Madison, and one I am not prepared to answer. It's rather complicated, after all. You have the FLN on one side—the Algerian extremists who launched this crazy war in 1954. They want Algeria to be independent of France. A rather fanatical group. Of course, they have their reasons. Most of the Muslim population of Algeria, which numbers near ten million, now agrees with the FLN, desiring their independence from France.

"Then you have the *pied-noirs*—the French citizens born in Algeria. Many of these families trace their heritage in Algeria back to when it first became a French colony in 1830. There are maybe a million of these. They, of course, do not want to leave what they consider their homeland.

"You also have the French Army in Algeria, who originally came to keep Algeria French and ward off the FLN. In military power, they have all but won this war. But politically, no one is satisfied, and the FLN, though

41

small in numbers, is strong in persuasion through fear."

Gabriella wrinkled her brow, trying to keep up with this man who was suddenly lost in a world of his own. David did not seem to notice.

"Back in 1958 the whole country, both Muslim and French, demanded that General de Gaulle return to power in France, seeing him as the only man capable of settling this gory war. But many in his army, and the *pied-noirs*, now see him as betraying them, as it becomes more apparent that he will give Algeria its independence.

"So now there are those in the French Army, some very important men, who are against de Gaulle and have formed the OAS, France's own secret terrorist group, who resort to the same barbaric measures as the FLN. They are determined to keep Algeria French.

"Perhaps the most pitiful group are the *harkis*—the Muslim military who have remained loyal to France. They are, of course, seen as traitors to their country, and the FLN takes great delight in slitting their throats from ear to ear if they are captured.

"And in the middle of this complicated mess, a lot of innocent people are being killed. It is the same in every war." His voice betrayed a deep-set bitterness and hatred that startled Gabriella.

"It sounds, as you say, terribly confusing," Gabriella admitted, although she was still thinking of the Huguenots.

They sat without speaking for a long time as Gabriella stared down the Esplanande and pictured the men of yesterday screaming their pain and love to God as they were martyred. She reached up to touch the small cross that hung around her neck beneath her blouse.

David broke the silence with a question. "Miss Madison, do you not agree that religion only brings despair? If there were a God up there, why would He sit silently by while His devoted followers tear each other apart?"

"I believe that God looks after His children," she replied.

"His children! Ha! I love it! Aren't the Jews His children? And didn't your God look after them well as they were marched off to death camps and put into the gas chambers. What a great father!" David's eyes flashed anger. "Tell me about your father, Miss Madison. What is he like?"

Gabriella looked puzzled for a moment, and then brightened. "My father is a very kind, wise, loving man. He gets along great with all kinds of people. He's not pretentious. He's . . . he's humble but smart. . . ." Her voice trailed off as she noted the anger in David's eyes.

"You have a nice dad, so you believe in a nice God—a Daddy God. Well, I'm not interested in a God who will be my dad. The one I have just about killed me."

"I'm sorry. I didn't know you had had such a terrible experience." She was flustered by his self-righteous anger.

"No, Miss Madison, I'm not interested in your God. David Hoffmann believes only in David Hoffmann." He scowled at nothing in particular, then his face softened and for a moment, he seemed to want desperately for her to understand. "You were raised in a family that believed in an omniscient, loving Higher Being. It is easy for you to believe as your parents do. You Christians say something is an answer to prayer. I take the same circumstance and interpret it differently; I say it is coincidence. It simply depends on how you look at it. Prove to me a prayer was answered in your neat little religious way. I will show you it was not."

Gabriella said nothing for a while, contemplating his dare. Why was this man she barely knew, challenging her with such anger, such intensity? Finally she spoke. "Mr. Hoffmann, I can't prove that prayers are answered or that God is above if you don't want to believe it. But that isn't my business anyway; it is God's. He's the one who changes hearts. Ask Him to prove Himself to you. I dare you to ask Him."

David laughed loudly, too loudly. "Miss Madison, you are rarely at a loss for words, are you?" He reached out and touched her hand.

She met his gaze and pulled her hand away. She could not think of anything to say and so again they sat in silence.

David was studying some unseen object. Presently he recited, " 'I will lift up mine eyes unto the hills, from whence cometh my help. My help cometh from the Lord which made heaven and earth. He will not suffer thy foot to be moved; He that keepeth thee will not slumber. Behold He that keepeth Israel shall neither slumber nor sleep.' " He quoted eloquently, full of feeling.

"Aren't you impressed, Miss Madison? I know that psalm and many others by heart. But you will wait a very long time if you hope to hear me claim it as my own prayer. Just a little warning."

Gabriella had been put on the defensive long enough. "I thought you asked me here to talk of my life in Senegal," she said coldly, "not to criticize my religion."

"Ah yes, that was my original intention. Forgive me. It was thinking of those poor Huguenots that got me on another tangent. And now I'm afraid it's time to go back. I wouldn't want your landlady to disapprove." For a fleeting moment, he seemed genuinely disappointed. "But never mind. We shall see each other often, Miss Madison. You will have plenty of time to tell me all about your life on the dark continent." He got to his feet, then took Gabriella's arm to help her up.

She brushed away his hand. "If you don't mind, I think I'll stay a little longer." With a touch of sarcasm in her voice, she added, "And don't worry about my getting home. I'm a big girl."

David's eyes flashed, but he kept his composure. "As you wish. Good afternoon, Miss Madison." He walked across the open square and turned down an adjoining street toward the bus stop.

If he asks me again to do something, I will say no, Gabriella promised herself. But she knew it was a promise she wouldn't keep. The heat of the sun began to fade and shadows spread out along the Comedie, but Gabriella did not move from her seat at the *café* until she was sure that David Hoffmann was a long way away.

* * *

Gabriella sat at the small wooden desk in her room, books spread out in front of her. In her mind she saw again David Hoffmann's dark eyes taunting her on the Comedie and heard his rich, deep voice reciting Psalm 121 with all the conviction of a true believer. *He is so angry,* she thought. *I don't know why, but he is very angry.* Still, Gabriella was convinced that there was more to David behind his cynical eyes and proud exterior. Something worth discovering. She had felt it there this afternoon, below the surface of harsh words and sarcasm.

She imagined again the French Protestants being tortured and killed for their faith, and she pulled the Huguenot cross out from under her blouse. Holding it gently in her hand, she traced its outline with her fingers. The points of four thick arrows turned inward toward the center, with four *fleurs-de-lis* embedded within the corners of the cross. A small dove dangled below the bottom arrow. "Here in Montpellier is where the people lived who wore this. And wearing it, these people lived and died for their faith."

She opened her Bible and leafed through the pages until she found Psalm 121. In the margin, Gabriella had scribbled the words, "This is Your promise to me, God." *How ironic,* she mused, *that he would quote the very psalm I claimed for myself as I left Senegal to come here.*

I hate David Hoffman for his arrogance and his blatant disrespect, she thought as she undressed for bed. Yet he fascinated her, and she found herself eager to see him in class the next day. "Is he an evil man, Lord? Or only bitter?" As she climbed into bed, she let her eyes fall back onto the page and began reading the psalm where David had left off. "The Lord is thy keeper; the Lord is thy shade upon thy right hand. The sun shall not smite thee by day." She thought of the brilliant heat as they had sat at the *café.* "Nor the moon by night. The Lord shall preserve thee from all evil; He shall preserve thy soul. The Lord shall preserve thy going out and thy coming in from this time forth and even for evermore."

Gabriella did not fall asleep until long after the moon had risen. The warm wind of September teased the olive tree outside her window, causing its leaves to brush against the pane and whisper a taunt of love and hope.

Chapter Five

A boat lurched wildly on the waves of the Mediterranean. Dawn had not yet come, and the wind blew cool in the early morn. Far off Anne-Marie could see the flickering lights of the shore. Her eyes gazed out from a face swollen and bruised.

She groaned in agony, not so much from the wounds as from the thought of returning to Algeria. "Oh, Ophélie, I am glad you cannot see Mama now. It is better that you think I am dead. Dear Ophélie. God be with you, darling. The God of Papa be with you!"

The sheets rustled on the bunk above where Moustafa sat in a crouched position, his head skimming the ceiling of the compartment.

"We will be there soon." His voice was gruff, and Anne-Marie felt the anger and bitterness in his words. Moustafa would not help her now. He had been beaten into submission, and he was theirs. *I do not blame you, Moustafa*, she thought. It was her life or his. Of course, he would choose to save his own. Only for love did one give his life for another, and there was no love in this war. Only wild extremists who sacrificed everything for the cause of independence. And a crazy man who sought a terrifying revenge.

What had happened to the Algeria she had known and loved? She could barely remember the joyful days of her childhood when she had played with friends in the street: French and Algerian, Muslim and Catholic, Protestant and Jew. Perhaps, after all, it had only been a dream.

"Get up, Anne-Marie! We will not be the last to debark."

He climbed down the ladder and waited for her to rise. She stood shakily, and for a moment thought she would faint. His hand steadied her and firmly led her through the door and down the dark corridor. Ali and Rachid waited impatiently by the door.

"Here, put this on," Ali hissed, thrusting a white lace scarf into her hands. "Welcome back home, little tramp!" He laughed wickedly, pushing her toward the railing as the boat lurched again and made its way into the port.

* * *

Anne-Marie stepped from the crowded bus into the streets of Algiers. Before her loomed rows and rows of buildings, stacked like a deck of cards on a hill of the city. No one needed to tell her where she was; she knew all too well that she was entering the part of town known as the Casbah. This was the old part of the city, named for the Turkish-built sixteenth-century fortress that dominated the quarter. It was also the Algerian slums and the headquarters for the FLN— the Algerian extremists.

They walked past countless stalls where merchants sold fruits, vegetables, and other wares in front of the row of low arches that marked the beginning of the Casbah.

She pulled the scarf tightly around her face so that only her eyes were visible. It was a death sentence for a French *pied-noir* to enter this neighborhood. Even in France she had heard of the young *pied-noir* girl who had been raped and beaten to death here a few months back. She slowed her pace and felt her body stiffen against her will.

Keep walking or they will kill you right here, she told herself. Her skin was not as dark as the Algerians, but with her black hair and dark eyes and the typical Algerian scarf covering her face, she hoped to conceal her identity.

Moustafa was by her side, pushing her along in front of Ali and his henchman, Rachid. They began to climb the hill toward the mountain of apartments that stretched out before them in haphazard fashion.

"It is a labyrinth. Once you are inside, it is impossible to find your way out unless you live there." She recalled the gossip of the *pied-noir* women in her community. Ever since the war began in 1954, they had whispered the treacheries of the Casbah in the late hours of the night after the children were asleep.

Now as Anne-Marie started up the gradual embankment toward the maze of tiny, narrow streets, she knew it was true. Would she ever leave this place alive? Her throat was parched and she wished desperately for a drink of water, but she dared not ask. The sound of her dry cough echoed again and again as they continued up the road.

She glanced over at Moustafa and pitied him. Her danger in the Casbah was great, but what about his? He was twice a traitor; nowhere would be safe for him. He did not look afraid. His young face was set in determination and hate, so different from the face of the young man she used to know.

Only days ago she had talked to him as a trusted friend. She had run her comb through his tight-curled black hair, admonishing him affectionately to care for his appearance. Eight months ago he had crossed the Mediterranean with her and Ophélie, escaping from Algeria. A *pied-noir* woman, her fatherless child, and the son of a *harki*. *Harki!* It was an explosive word in these days of war.

Anne-Marie shivered as she thought of the Algerian military men who fought for France. They were despised by the FLN. If found, the FLN slit the throats of these traitors. It had happened to Moustafa's father. She remembered the day Moustafa had come to her, his eyes wide with fear.

"They killed my father, Anne-Marie. Those madmen cut his throat yesterday." He wept before her. "Ali knows about our plan, I am sure. I must leave or they will kill me. You must leave too. It is much too dangerous for Ophélie...and for you."

She had known he was right. Life in Algeria was dangerous enough for a son of a *harki* and a *pied-noir* who had given information to the FLN at one time. If only their crime stopped there! But it was much worse. So they had fled from their homeland in the middle of a bitter night in January in search of safety in France.

"We are here." Moustafa's voice interrupted her thoughts. "This is where you will stay." While Ali and Rachid looked on, Moustafa shoved Anne-Marie into the darkness of a drab cement building.

"Touching, isn't it, to see these friends reunited in their lovely Algeria," Ali crooned sarcastically. He entered the dark room and grabbed Moustafa's shirt, pulling him around. "You explain the rules to her carefully. Remind her of what happens to beautiful women who do not talk! To disgusting *pied-noir* trash! Although

I would be surprised if she has forgotten so soon." He let go of Moustafa's shirt, pushing him back into the darkness. "We will be back shortly."

Anne-Marie touched her lips to silence the sobs escaping from her mouth, but she could not stop the tears. She felt about in the blackness and found a chair. As her eyes grew accustomed to the dark, she sat down. She did not look up at Moustafa, who was pacing back and forth in the small room.

"Stop crying!" he whispered angrily. "I cannot think if you cry."

She turned her tear-stained face toward him. "You will not betray Ophélie, Moustafa?"

"You are foolish, Anne-Marie. We all do what we have to. You will talk if you wish to survive! They will bring Ophélie back here with the information. There is hope that you may both live, if you will only talk. Otherwise, you will die. And they will still find Ophélie, and it will be much worse for her."

Anne-Marie held her head in her hands, saying nothing, wiping away the tears. She did not believe Moustafa. She felt certain that he too would be eliminated as soon as Ali had the information he wanted.

By now Mr. Gady would have the little blue bag, she thought with relief. He would know, and Ophélie would be safe, hidden away. All she had to do was reveal a part of the truth. Ali's men would go to Mr. Gady's shop and search, but no one would be there.

She turned to Moustafa, a soft, hopeful tone in her voice. "Do not worry, Moustafa. I will talk." But in spite of her resolve, she touched the tiny bottle sewn into her sleeve and smiled to herself. *You will be safe, Ophélie.*

* * *

Ophélie sat on a mattress in the upstairs office of Mr. Gady's shop. She could hear the old man breathing as he slept. She was glad he was asleep. Twice that day he had questioned her. "You are sure you have nothing for me, little one? Nothing from your mother?" Each time Ophélie shook her head. How could she trust him? There was no one to trust.

The old man's eyes had looked disappointed and concerned. He had hovered by the radio all day and grumbled to himself, cursing and repeating, "Crazy war, crazy war."

Now, in the quiet of the night, she carefully switched on the lamp on the desk and emptied out the contents of the blue bag. The cross fell lightly onto the desk, as well as a worn photograph and two small, sealed envelopes. Ophélie reached for one envelope. On the front was one simple word written in Mama's hand. She knew what it said. *Ophélie.* Quietly she unsealed the envelope and spread the letter before her.

Three pink pages, written in the smooth script of Mama. At the top of the first page she again read her name, "Ophélie." She turned to the last piece of paper and saw "Mama." These two words she knew. But the rest of the letter lay before her, a mysterious blend of lines falling up and down.

"Oh, Mama, how will I ever know what you wish to tell me if I cannot read?" She began to cry. "I need to know, Mama. I cannot tell Mr. Gady. Please do not be mad, Mama, but I cannot give him the bag."

She reached for the cross and slipped it around her neck, fastening it in the back. "You said it was good luck, Mama. I will wear the cross, and then Grandpapy's God will bring me good luck." She placed the letter and the other envelope back into the sack, pausing only to look at a small photo of Mama holding her in her arms. "Please,

Mama, do not die. I will learn how to read, and then I will know. Wait for me, Mama, wherever you are."

* * *

Rachid El Drissi watched as Ali walked easily through the maze of buildings in the Casbah. The night was black, but Rachid knew that Ali could find his way through this neighborhood blindfolded.

Ali slipped onto an outside stairwell and climbed it, crouching like a cat waiting to attack an unsuspecting sparrow. On the second floor, he stepped into a window, pulling it closed behind him. The September air was heavy, suffocating, even at this late hour. Soundlessly he walked into a bedroom and switched on the light, nodding to Rachid. He seated himself at an old, worn desk and took out a manila folder filled with papers. As he worked, Rachid hovered beside him.

"The work must be done on Tuesday night. Look." Ali put his finger on a hand-sketched map of several areas of Algiers. "Monoprix is here at the corner."

Rachid nodded. Everyone knew where the large department store was located.

"The bomb must go off here." Ali drew a red circle around the street that ran in front of the store. "Everyone will be asleep, but word will travel quickly nonetheless. They will panic and run, and then BOOM!" He laughed sadistically. "It will be no doubt very convincing, yes?" His hand grazed the jagged scars on Rachid's face.

Again Rachid nodded, the sleepiness gone from his eyes and in its place, a passionate stare. Tuesday he would test another of his little bombs. Small but effective. "Do not worry, Ali. It is no trouble. Quite easy."

Ali turned to leave. As he closed the door behind him, Rachid brushed his fingers through his coarse hair and whispered, "Boom," chuckling softly to himself.

Chapter Six

A lone swallow flew low to the ground outside Mme. Leclerc's apartment. From her second-story window, Gabriella watched as other birds joined the first in weaving up into the air and swooping down almost to touch the ground.

Quand les hirondelles volent bas, il y aura de la pluie ce soir. She thought of the French proverb she had learned in her childhood in Senegal. *There's sure to be rain if the swallow flies low.* But Gabriella wished desperately that the rain would not come. Not this Saturday.

Today David Hoffmann had asked her to join him for a picnic on the beach with perhaps a ride on horseback through the marshes afterwards. "The Camargue ponies are sturdy and surefooted, even if you've never been on a horse in your life," he had told her.

Gabriella had not mentioned that she had once had a horse in North Africa, she had only replied that she would go. She had wanted to refuse, after their miserable afternoon on the Comedie, but she could not. She felt drawn to him, as if he somehow needed her. "But I will watch what I say," she told herself.

David arrived at the apartment promptly at eleven o'clock, seemingly oblivious to the sky rumbling cantankerously in the background. Mme. Leclerc buzzed him in at once, looking jovial and pleased.

"*Bonjour, Madame.* Is Mademoiselle Madison available?"

"*Bien sur.* I will fetch her."

As Gabriella entered the hallway, she tried to ignore the giggling of Stephanie and Caroline who had rushed into her room every five minutes all morning long to debate about the weather and the probability of Gabriella's date. Caroline had predicted, "He will come, no matter what. I don't think a hurricane could stop Mr. Hoffmann once he has decided to do something."

Caroline was right, Gabriella thought as she joined her teacher at the front door.

"*Enchanté,* Miss Madison," he greeted her, his dark eyes mocking. He hurried her along the cobblestones to his car, an old pale blue *deux chevaux* which, he commented, did fine on flat ground, but could not climb a hill. If he was aware that his every movement was being observed, he didn't give even a hint of it to the girls and woman watching from the boarding house windows.

* * *

The sun poked its face through the disturbing gray clouds as David spread out an old sheet on the sand and motioned for Gabriella to sit down. He placed a heavy basket beside him and took out sandwiches, cheese, fruit, fresh vegetables drenched in vinaigrette, and a bottle of red wine.

"I wish you would have let me fix something, Mr. Hoffmann," Gabriella stuttered nervously.

"Ah, my dear, don't think that I am the preparer of

such a feast. Mme. Pons, with whom I board, is determined to marry me off, and insists on fixing everything *comme il faut* for a proper picnic. Quite good, actually. Can't beat a ham and Emmenthal cheese on a French *baguette*."

He opened the wine bottle and set it in the sand. "And you may call me David ... out of class." For a moment he stared so intently into her eyes that she wondered what he was trying to see. She blushed and turned her head quickly away to gaze out on the Mediterranean Sea.

"But I don't want to talk about myself today. I want to hear about you. It must be quite a shock to find yourself among these prim and proper socialites after being raised among the savages."

She gasped at his words and turned back to look at him, anger and indignation sparkling in her eyes. "How dare you—" she began fiercely, only to stop when she saw the amusement in his eyes.

"Forgive me, Miss Madison. I can't resist getting a reaction whenever possible. I'm glad to see that our missionary has a bit of fire in her character!"

Gabriella did not mean to start crying; it just happened. Tears burned her face as she stood to her feet and glared at him. "Why did you invite me out today? Didn't you criticize me enough on the Comedie? If you just want to make fun of me and anyone else you can possibly think of, I'd rather go back to Mme. Leclerc's. Right now!" And after a moment she added, "Please." *I was wrong to come*, she thought to herself.

In the midst of her confused thoughts, she felt David's strong hand holding her own and pulling her back down beside him. "I'm sorry, Miss Madison." His voice sounded genuine for the first time. "You're absolutely right. Rather bad form to invite a girl out and criticize her from the start. It's nothing personal, just my style, you see.

Please don't cry." Reaching into the pocket of his khaki pants, he pulled out a clean, white handkerchief. "Here. Dry your eyes. And please stay. I can't eat all this food alone, and Mme. Pons would be furious to know that I had ruined my chances with yet another lovely lady."

Gabriella looked at him reluctantly, wiped her eyes, and removed her hand from his grasp. "I'll stay," she stated flatly. "But only for the sake of the food and Mme. Pons. And, of course, because I don't want to get on the bad side of my distinguished professor." She was surprised at her own biting tone.

"*Chapeau,* Miss Madison. I stand rebuked. Now let's move on to a more interesting subject. I would like to know about a young woman who can quote Pope and Dryden and who has lived such a different life from the other girls at St. Joseph's. They only want to talk of shopping and marriage and sex." He emphasized the last word with a smile playing on his lips.

Gabriella's eyes met his without blinking. "Trying to get another reaction, sir?" But this time she was smiling too.

She looked again toward the dark blue of the sea and spoke as if to the rolling waves that lapped upon the fine, dusty sand. "I loved my life in Senegal. My parents moved there years ago, before I was even a thought. They gave up a lot of luxuries like transportation, a clean home, a life free from malaria, because they believed in what they were doing.

"I grew up with the nationals and felt quite at home as the only white-skinned child besides my sisters. I learned several tribal languages because we moved four times. And I learned French, the trade language." Vibrancy returned to Gabriella's voice as she forgot about her present circumstances and envisioned again the life she had left only a month before.

57

"I loved galloping down the beach on my small mare, looking behind to see her hoofprints in the white sand. I could ride for hours on the beach without being disturbed. And always when we turned around to ride back home, the hoofprints were gone. Washed away like a forgotten memory. Once I came home and told my dad that the prints had vanished. He smiled and whispered, 'Let it be a lesson to you. Some footprints never disappear. You must leave footprints that are worthy of being followed.'

"I often think of Daddy's words, because I'm not sure anybody would want to follow in my steps."

David was staring at her with the same fixed gaze that had caused her to feel uncomfortable when they had first arrived at the beach. But now she understood what she read in his eyes. It was admiration. He leaned foward, almost touching her hands with his. "What do your friends call you, Miss Madison?" he asked.

Instinctively she shifted her weight back, away from him. After a moment, she replied, "I'm always introduced as Gabriella. I love long names, and I don't want to give mine up. But friends can call me whatever they want. That's the privilege of friendship, isn't it?"

"Then I shall call you Gabby."

* * *

The lunch was finished, and David swallowed down the last sip of wine in his glass. "Are you sure you don't want any, Gabby?" His tone was casual as he pronounced her name.

"No, thank you, really. I'm not used to wine; I don't like the way it makes me feel." She raised her eyebrows and waited for his reaction.

He chuckled. "You are delightful. Did your mother warn you of what dashing young intellectuals might try to do to a beautiful idealist when she came to France?

You are right to be on your guard."

"I have a question for you, the wise teacher."

"Go ahead. I can't wait to hear it." He scooted closer to her, then stretched out his long frame on the blanket, resting his chin in his hands. He looked up at her, the sun behind her head making him squint. "From this position I have the feeling that I'm in the presence of an angel. Your hair is magnificent." He paused, then said softly, "You are magnificent."

"Please stop," she replied, hesitant to use his given name. "You're only trying to embarrass me, and it's working. I know your game. You are afraid of my question, so you try to divert my attention. It won't work.

"Tell me this. You admire the poets who had such great faith, like Pope and Donne and Herrick. How can you admire their work and yet deny their God?"

David was sifting sand through his fingers. He did not answer immediately. "I have a question for you. How can you admire a 'wise teacher' and deny his advances?"

He reached toward her, but she turned away, disappointed in his refusal to answer her seriously.

The clouds had returned. Gabriella stood up and said, "It is time to go home."

"It is indeed, my dear. We'll save the Camargue ponies for another day." Quickly they filled the picnic basket with leftovers as the sky grumbled impatiently. Heavy drops of rain began to fall, and David took Gabriella's arm, pushing her up the beach until they passed the dunes and came to the road where the *deux chevaux* was parked. By the time they reached the car, they were drenched. David laughed heartily, holding his arms out to catch the rain.

"Wonderful, Gabby! Isn't it wonderful!"

Gabriella smiled and brushed the rain off her face as she stepped into the car. Her hair clung to her like a mass of wet noodles. She wrinkled her nose. "I'm afraid your poor car is in for a treat."

"Never mind, my dear. This old beater has seen worse." He looked over at her and winked.

Gabriella did not speak on the way home, but she counted the rushing beat of her heart and wished with all her might that she were safe in her small room behind a closed door, where David Hoffmann could not read her tumultuous thoughts.

* * *

David's face was set in a look of intense concentration, and beads of perspiration ran down his forehead. He studied the hand-drawn map that had arrived in the mail, carefully examining the directions, and cursed lightly to himself. "Right in the middle of Aigues-Mortes. Just as he said."

He absent-mindedly began rolling up the sleeves on his light blue Oxford shirt. The rain had stopped, and the air was muggy and thick and unbearably hot.

He sat lost in thought for a full five minutes. A look of anger and then pain registered on his handsome face. What did he feel this time? The months of planning might at last bring results. Vital results—the kind that could perhaps touch even David Hoffmann's hard heart. Yes, he felt excitement, anger, and that old enemy—fear.

He thought of his afternoon with Gabriella on the beach. He liked the innocent redhead. *So why must I drag her into this*, he argued with himself. He could do it alone. Still, he wanted to take her with him.

"It is time to show Gabby the charming town of Aigues-Mortes," he whispered to himself.

Chapter Seven

Mme. Monique Pons brought two cups of steaming coffee into the parlor where Mme. Yvette Leclerc sat at the table, bending over to peruse her basket of fruits and vegetables. "The pears were not a bit pretty today at the *marché*, quite a pity, but the price of tomatoes was down twenty *centimes!* And such tomatoes. The last of the season, to be sure."

She accepted the *demi-tasse* of black coffee with a smile, sat back in her chair and relaxed. There was simply nothing better than coffee and a chat at Monique's house! It had been their daily custom for over twenty years. After the morning trip to the *marché*, she would arrive at 10 o'clock for the ritual *rendez-vous*, a time to catch up on the latest news before hurrying home to fix the noon meal. She never stayed long, but there was so much news to give and receive. The latest prices on tomatoes, the newest recipe from that cocky French chef who had crossed the ocean to make his fortune in *Amerique*. The nerve! The most recent report on grown children and grandchildren and all the extended family.

Castelnau was a small town, but oh, the news!

But today the two graying women had much more interesting tidbits to exchange. How fortunate that the two of them kept boarders who were now entangled in what would surely be a love story.

Mme. Pons was babbling along. "Oh, yes, he came back from the beach simply drenched. But he was happy. That man is strange, that Mr. Hoffmann, but I can tell when he is happy. Very rare that he smiles, you know. It's been that way all the time he's boarded here."

She chuckled and leaned forward, her cheeks rosy from the fresh air, the loose skin jiggling under her chin as she described the encounter. "But that afternoon, he was all smiles. Gave me a kiss on each cheek, he did, when he came in. Kissed me," she blushed at the memory, "and stood there dripping on my floor. *Ooh la la!*" She shook her head in disbelief.

Mme. Leclerc raised her eyebrows with glee, and her eyes danced. "And what did he say, Monique? What did he say?" Could it be that the dashing young American had finally decided to court a woman properly? They had been waiting for this moment for over a year. Other Monday mornings, when they compared notes about Mr. Hoffmann's weekend activities, Mme. Pons had sad reports. "He said she's just another uppity, rich snob. All looks and no brains. The whole picnic basket was empty, wine bottle too. They just ate and drank and didn't have a thing to say to each other. Bored stiff, that poor Mr. Hoffmann."

But what extreme luck today. Not only had Mr. Hoffmann smiled after his date, but the young lady was Mme. Leclerc's beautiful American boarder! Why, when this romance blossomed, Mme. Pons and Mme. Leclerc would be practically related!

"You know what he said? Oh yes, Yvette, listen! He

said he was sorry that they hadn't eaten everything, but that they had been so busy talking. He said she thought the food was delicious, nothing against it. But how they must have talked. You would have thought a bird had been nibbling at my basket. Only a bird." Her eyes glowed with excitement. "And the wine bottle was still half full. Imagine! He said she didn't drink a drop. No wine to make the heart gay, and still they talked and talked. It is surely a sign."

Madame Leclerc was smiling and nodding. "She doesn't touch the wine, that Gabriella. She's an interesting girl. Smart as a whip, I tell you. As smart as that American *professeur*, I'm sure. She's different all right. Not looking for a free party in France with all the wine and . . . you know, how the other girls are sometimes."

Their eyes met, and the two women laughed heartily. My, did they know. Oh, the troubles they'd had with some of these American girls. Oh, the scandals. But the two aging widows had each other to confide in and commiserate with. In truth, they would admit occasionally, they loved the American girls and the extra revenue they gave to a widow's pension.

They were still laughing when suddenly Mme. Leclerc stopped abruptly and shook her head. "I can't imagine what Gabriella is doing with the likes of your Mr. Hoffmann. Really! He is not her type. You know," she bent forward and lowered her voice, "she is very religious." Religion was fine, the women agreed—if it was the Catholic church and Mass. But this Gabriella Madison was Protestant. "And not a Protestant like the other Americans I've seen. She reads her Bible! Every day, I think. And once I caught her praying on her knees! Now what would a girl who prays on her knees see in your cold *professeur*? She's a fine girl, that Gabriella Madison. A strange, fine girl." When they really thought about it, neither Mme. Leclerc nor Mme. Pons could figure out why Gabriella Madison had gone to the beach with Mr. David Hoffmann.

* * *

Mother Griolet's small office was cozy and inviting. The bookshelves were stuffed in random order with antique books in French and English by the saints of old. Gabriella lightly touched the worn volumes of Thomas Aquinas' *L'Imitation de Christ* and Paul Bunyan's *Pilgrim's Progress*. Interspersed among the old classics, she noticed, were books on psychology, children, education, and theology. Remembering the reason for her visit, Gabriella left the bookshelves and settled into the chair that sat before the mahoghany desk of Mother Griolet.

The old nun looked up from the papers on her desk and smiled at Gabriella. "Ah, Gabriella Madison. You've grown up to be a very lovely young woman. Your parents must be quite proud of their oldest daughter."

Gabriella blushed. Not knowing how to respond, she changed the subject. "Mother Griolet, I've come to see you about a ... a problem. I mean it's not really a problem, but a question. Well, it's just an idea and ... and I want your advice."

Mother Griolet waited patiently for Gabriella to explain herself. "Yes, my child. I'll be happy to help you in any way I can."

"It's about your work. Well, not exactly this work, but ..." She paused awkwardly, then began again. "I just wondered if you ever really wanted to do something great—not for yourself. I don't mean that, but to do something that mattered, that helped others."

Mother Griolet crossed her arms and settled back into her large office chair. Her green eyes twinkled while she considered Gabriella"s question. "Ah, yes, I suppose when I was your age, I dreamed of doing something great for God and man. We all have dreams. And sometimes the dreams are selfless and good..."

"Yes. I mean, I know some of my thoughts are wrong," Gabriella interrupted. "I just wish I knew for certain what I should do with my life. Mother and Father were so sure. They were sure that God had called them to Africa, and they were no older than I am. But I am not sure. I can't really think where I belong. Is Africa home? Is America? I barely know America. Or perhaps it doesn't matter."

"Dear child, you are wondering what the future holds? I wondered too at twenty-one. But I already had my orders as a nun. My friends were all getting married. They thought I was quite strange and devout."

"And did you not want to marry, to have a family?"

"How can I explain?" She leaned forward and rested her arms on the desk, fingers intertwined. "It was not so much that I didn't want a husband or a family as the conviction that I must do something else. This." Her arm swept around the room, and Gabriella followed her movement. "I chose this life, and it didn't seem heavy or full of sacrifices at the time. I loved teaching the children. We had just come out of the Great War, and there were so many orphans. So we started a school and orphanage right here. I didn't have time to worry about a family. I had my hands full with these children."

"And that was enough? You never wanted to do something else? A higher position? A different town?"

"Ah, Gabriella, there were opportunties to leave Castelnau for something that sounded better. But I could not. God was working here. I found myself quite busy. And of course, when the Second World War came and France fell in 1940, we had even more orphans.

And we hid many Jewish children."

Gabriella was impressed. "It must have felt good to be helping like that. I mean...it was dangerous."

"We each did our part. It was war, and we were not looking for honors, just survival. War doesn't make sense. In the end, nobody wins. Death rips apart families. I do not take sides in war. I prayed, and God showed me whom to help. Most of the time it was children. By God's grace some children survived who would not have otherwise. I keep in touch with many of them. You see, I do have a large family." She nodded to the far wall, which was covered with old photographs of children. "Once, we even hid a German officer here."

She laughed at Gabriella's horrified expression.

"It was either that or watch him be slaughtered in the courtyard with the children looking on. Just a poor terrified boy who was trying to serve his country. He now serves Another," and she winked and pointed skyward. Gabriella laughed, imagining a captured German attending Mass with a group of Jewish orphans.

"And how did you know all this was from God?"

"God is always at work around us, child. You have doubtless seen that in Senegal. The question each of us must ask is, will I join Him or will I ask Him to join me? One way works, the other does not. I found out long ago, and the hard way, that God did not need my lofty plans. His were much better."

She paused for a moment, lost in some memory, and Gabriella regarded her with amazement. This woman who was over seventy had such a zest for life, such a sparkle and assurance. And a faith that was real. She didn't mean to ask it, but without thinking, she blurted out, "And did you always agree with the Catholic church?"

Again the elderly woman smiled. "I think I should rather say that they did not always agree with me. I seemed to be running ahead of them and teaching things that got me into all sorts of trouble. And kept me right here in lowly Castelnau." Another mischevious grin.

"It didn't bother me in the least. I knew I was obeying the Master, and I got my marching orders from His book. Ah, well, it is not up to me to judge. Have you noticed that it is usually easier to judge than obey? Religious people are especially good at it. I tried not to get caught up in that destructive little game. God works. I obey. Not an easy life, Gabriella." She leaned forward again and looked the young woman full in the face. "It is never easy to take orders from Him. But I can assure you, I have never been bored. And my, all the adventures I've known!"

Gabriella contemplated Mother Griolet's words. "Mother says the same thing about her life. It is true. Our days were full and hard and exciting . . . and terribly painful . . ." she let her phrase dangle, and Mother Griolet nodded, understanding.

"But if only I knew that here was right and how I could help. I see you with the orphans, and I feel as if that is what I want to do. Pour my life into children who have no life. To give them a future and a hope, as the verse in Jeremiah says." Now Gabriella's eyes were dancing, and an enthusiasm filled her voice. "I am not too good at much, but I am good with children. I've taught lots of things in Africa—Sunday School and crafts and sports and . . ."

"Gabriella, are you asking if you can help me with the orphans? Is that your question?" She seemed amused at Gabriella's roundabout way of getting to the point, and Gabriella blushed. "Because, my child, I will certainly not tell you no." Mother Griolet's eyes were soft, and her wrinkled face a picture of compassion. "There is a verse in the Bible that greatly influenced my choices when I was young. Perhaps you know it. 'Pure religion and undefiled before God is this, to visit the fatherless and widows in their affliction and to keep himself unspotted by the world.' I suppose I have tried to do just that." Her voice trailed off as if she were thinking about her past.

"If you want to be God's, Gabriella, He will take you. It is not every girl who cares. Do not worry. I can use you here, happily. And you may start tomorrow if you wish."

"Thank you, Mother Griolet. Mother was right. You know how to encourage others." Impulsively she stood up, bent over the desk, and kissed Mother Griolet vigorously on both cheeks.

* * *

Gabriella picked up her books and notebooks off the desk and hurriedly placed them in her backpack. She left Mr. Vidal's classroom without waiting for Stephanie and Caroline. Today she would not be going back to Mme. Leclerc's after class. Today she would meet the orphans. She had awakened with that thought. It had carried her through David Hoffmann's class, so that she did not blush when he called on her to read George Herbert's poetry aloud. The morning had flown by with this thought: *Today I meet the orphans!* The thought had even kept her wide awake in Mr. Vidal's history class as he droned on about the splendors of Louis XIV and his court and the palace at Versailles. Now at last it was time.

"Come to the basement after your last afternoon class," Mother Griolet had instructed. "I will show you around and then introduce you to the children." Now Gabriella skipped down the steps of the parsonage to ground level. Not pausing, she continued down another flight into the basement of the large old stone building. The corridor was narrow and dimly lit. It smelled vaguely of mildew, but Gabriella was undaunted.

She remembered the smiling black faces of the little ones in Senegal. She heard in her mind their excited chatter as she led them to the large thatched-roof pavillion her father had built. "Hello, children," she had addressed them in their tribal tongue. "Today we will learn about Joseph." And they had stared up at her, the whites of their eyes shining in their ebony faces.

She had missed the children these past two years. Attending the university of Dakar, eighty miles from her tribal village, she had missed the voices of children.

*   *   *

She entered the large classroom behind Mother Griolet. The children were seated in rows of wooden desks, their hands folded neatly on the tops. *"Bonjour, mes enfants,"* Mother Griolet cooed happily.

"Bonjour, Mère Griolet," the children responded, happy as well.

"Today I want you to meet a friend of mine." She motioned to Gabriella. "This is *Mademoiselle* Madison. She will be working with us several afternoons a week."

The children said nothing, but twenty-three pairs of eyes looked admiringly up at the new teacher. *"Elle est belle,"* whispered a girl of about five to her neighbor.

"Yes, she is very beautiful," replied the other with a giggle.

Gabriella pretended not to notice their wonder. "Hello, children. I'm so glad to be here and meet you. I can't wait for you to show me all around your school. And perhaps I could see your rooms?"

"Oui, oui, Maîtresse," the children chorused enthusiastically.

"But first, I must know your names. Who will be the first to tell me?"

Immediately small hands flew into the air. *"Maîtresse,*

Maîtresse, ask me first."

Gabriella laughed. "One at a time. We'll start with you." She indicated a smiling little girl with black hair pulled into a long braid. "And we'll go down each row. One at a time, please."

Mother Griolet watched, pleased, as one by one the children stood and introduced themselves to the beautiful new *maîtresse* with the long red hair. The old nun chuckled as Gabriella charmed them with her smile and warmth.

"Yes, dear Gabriella, this is your place. Among the orphans. It is as natural for you as a mother singing to her baby." No one noticed as the small woman in black skirts left the room.

* * *

Two hours later, Gabriella had had a royal tour of the basement of the parsonage. She knew almost every child's name, and she was winded after their game of *un, deux, trois soleil* in the church garden. Now she took the chubby hand of little Christophe. Barely four, he was the youngest at the orphanage. His blue eyes danced with joy and pride as he held the hand of the new teacher. Gabriella could not resist bending down to kiss his round, rosy cheeks. He might be four, but he still had the appearance of a toddler.

His six-year-old brother, André, came beside Gabriella on the other side. He was tall and thin for his age, a sharp contrast to his pudgy brother. André said nothing, but stared at Gabriella, his hazel eyes surrounded by long, delicate, brown lashes. His eyes held a depth of longing that made Gabriella stop and gently brush his face with her fingers. These brothers knew hurt and solitude. All of these children knew. In their eyes she saw it. A painful wisdom beyond their years.

And a hope and longing that maybe, just maybe, this new *maîtresse* would have enough love to soothe their hurting hearts like a lullaby at bedtime.

* * *

The story of the bombing in the street beside Monoprix made the front page of every Algerian newspaper. "Seven killed in midnight madness," the caption read. This time the victims were all French *pied-noirs*, although the previous bomb had killed two Algerians. The nationality did not matter so much to the FLN. The point was well taken: terrorism. No one was safe. Watch out. And underneath the terror, whispering in the night to all those who still favored a French Algeria, were the words, "Get out! Leave us alone! Get out while you can, or it will be too late."

Ali was quite pleased with the front-page report. "Good work, Rachid," he complimented. "With results like this, you will soon have more important jobs. Perhaps a position in the new future government! Independence is not far away, I tell you. Algeria will be free! The senseless *pied-noirs* will see soon enough what their holy General de Gaulle meant when he said, 'I understand you!' " He laughed dryly. "He meant he understands *us!* He understands that it is hopeless for the French. They can never win this war. Give up! We will be free!"

Rachid regarded his crazed leader with fear and admiration. It was true, he felt sure. The war that had already cost hundreds of thousands of lives as it dragged on for seven years was nearing its end. But the death toll would surely climb, faster and faster, like a man escaping a fire on a misplaced ladder, only to find that the ladder led him nowhere except to thicker smoke and death itself.

71

The French had their own group of extremists who launched a campaign of counter-terrorism against the FLN and their own French authorities. The brutality of the Secret Army Organization of the French matched in every way the cruel schemes of the FLN. Rachid smiled at Ali. The end was in sight, but the war was just heating up.

"Anne-Marie has talked?" he questioned, hoping that he would soon have an opportunity to use his vivid imagination to eliminate this woman and her *harki* friend.

Ali shook his head. "No. We have asked nothing of either of them yet. There has been more important business to handle. It is satisfying enough to see them huddle in fear in that stinking room every time we enter. But do not worry. Their end will come soon enough. And the child will be found. We have someone watching. His eyes are very good." Again a low chuckle.

"I am not in a hurry to kill the woman. You remember our first encounter with her in '56? The FLN came calling on the beautiful daughter of the slain captain of the French army. She had so much to tell us then! A delicious woman." He caught Rachid's eye, and the young man blushed at the memory of their lust and cruelty.

"I am sure we will find that little list of names. She cannot flee to France and think she will be safe. Never! The *pied-noirs* will be crushed and run for their lives. And the children of the *harkis!* The traitors will die like their fathers! Every one of them!" He pulled his finger across his throat in demonstration of their fate.

Rachid nodded. He understood. Ali had his own plans, his own personal grudges. He aimed to fit them in with the FLN's terrorist activities. After all, what would a few dozen more dead women and children mean in a war that had already claimed the lives of so many? Who would be left to mourn the extra carnage?

* * *

Anne-Marie listened from her seat on the floor as Moustafa described the bombing of Monoprix. "It happened at two yesterday morning. Half the block was destroyed. Three women and four children were killed, several men are missing. All *pied-noir.*"

"Of course. I know the neighborhood well." She sighed. "What is the point of so many innocent deaths?"

"The point is fear, Anne-Marie."

She nodded. Her question was only a cry in vain. She knew the point too well.

"Fear," Moustafa continued. "So they all pack up and leave, as we did. Ironic that we are right back where we started from. Only worse off."

She glanced up at him. "We will never be free of them, will we, Moustafa?"

He looked away. "No. They are convinced you have more information. More than I have. Or that we both know about the little operation in the south of France." He met her eyes.

"Yes, we know something. But only the names of the *harki* children leaving. Thank goodness I cannot tell anything else. How or where, I do not know. Ophélie is surely gone from Mr. Gady's shop. I have no idea where the bag is now."

"We must escape. It is the only way. They will kill us soon, or worse." His eyes were tender again.

Anne-Marie knew what worse meant. She looked down. "They will not torture me, Moustafa. Not like before. They will not have me." She shuddered, remembering the horrible night five years ago when they had come to take her. Seven Arab men. In the end Jean-Claude had saved her from being killed. How was she to know that he worked for them too? How was she to know what he could do to a beautiful *pied-noir* girl

73

who helped the French army?

"We were so foolish, you and I," she said. "We thought Algeria would stay French. We thought it would never change. Now everything will change."

"You tried to help, Anne-Marie. You did what you thought was right. The *pied-noir* and *harki* children must flee to France. They must leave. Ali murders for pleasure and revenge. His war is not only Algeria's war, his war is personal. And we are in the way. It is not good, my friend."

After a moment, Anne-Marie reached for the bottle inside her sleeve. "Here. There are two. Cyanide. If we die now—" Her eyes were desperate.

Moustafa turned away. "Suicide! Your religion does not permit it, nor does mine! It is wrong."

"You know that I have no religion, Moustafa. My father was Protestant, my mother Catholic, but I follow neither one. The Church will not have a stained woman. A woman with a child and no husband. A woman who has slept with the enemy to save her skin. A woman who is *pied-noir* and has betrayed her heritage. My sins are too many for the Church and its God. I am not ashamed of suicide. Ophélie will have a different life. I will save her by dying before they force me to talk."

"No!" Moustafa grasped her shoulders. "Not yet. Our fathers have died at the hands of a murderer. We cannot be cowards. Their blood runs in the trenches. Perhaps mine will too. But I will die fighting, not by my own hand. Give me another day. Another day to live. For both of us to live." He held Anne-Marie in his arms as she wept.

Chapter Eight

Jean-Claude Gachon stepped off the train in the small town of Aigues-Mortes, his frame rippling underneath the shirt he had chosen that morning. The color brought out the intensity of his hazel eyes. His thick brown hair touched the shirt's collar.

The scent of fish greeted him as he walked along the platform and out into the late September sun. He stared across a canal to where a stone tower rose imposingly before him, then walked toward the entrance to the fortified city. The stone wall that totally encircled the city with its towers and drawbridge looked like a life-size replica from a fairy tale. But Jean-Claude was no stranger to the history of his country, and he knew this city had existed long before the Grimm brothers penned their first story.

He chuckled to himself as he walked briskly across a bridge and made his way through the city gates. Feeling in his pocket, he brought out a scrap of paper, which he held with care. The picture of a cross was crudely scribbled on it, a strange cross with a dove dangling from the tip. Underneath, written in a hurried manner, were the words, "Found on body. What does it have to do with the operation? Something is going on in Aigues-Mortes on the 30th, our friend Moustafa has kindly revealed to us. Find out what it is."

As a *porteur de valise*, Jean-Claude had been working clandestinely for the FLN ever since the war began. There were many other French who, like him, supported the Algerians' desire for independence, giving their time, money, and brains to the cause. Jean-Claude was proud of his ability to help the FLN. That was how he had met Ali, the brilliant, driven military man, whose personal mission had intrigued Jean-Claude. It was a violent plan, and it paid well.

Jean-Claude stared at the slip of paper and laughed, remembering when Ali had given him the note back in Paris after Anne-Marie had been captured. So Ali was searching for crosses now. In his four years of working with this madman, Jean-Claude had never had such an easy assignment. He knew all about the Huguenot cross. He remembered seeing it sparkling around Anne-Marie's neck every night when she had lain close to him. And he could still hear her words, *"It was my father's. He was a Protestant, a descendant of the Huguenots. He told me stories of how their pastors were tortured and killed and the women imprisoned in a tower in Aigues-Mortes."*

If something was happening in Aigues-Mortes today, Jean-Claude knew just where to look: a tall tower that once confined Huguenot women. He walked into the early morning *marché*. At last he had something to do. Another assignment to keep him busy on this side of the Mediterranean, until he could cross the sea and celebrate Algeria's victory with his friends.

* * *

"You see, Gabby. It's not a long drive at all," David remarked as they rumbled down the road past a small marker that indicated "Aigues-Mortes: five kilometers."

"This is real swampland around here," she mused, observing the white gulls flying *en masse* toward the open sea far in the distance.

"Yes, well, we've followed the Mediterranean since we left Montpellier twenty minutes ago. You know what Aigues-Mortes means, don't you?"

"Dead waters?"

"Exactly. It's totally surrounded by lagoons. The city was built in the thirteenth century under Saint Louis, France's crusading king. He hoped to attract trade, making this a port. Later, after his death, his son Philippe the Bold built the walls. You'll see them in a minute—they are almost perfectly preserved. Quite impressive. The Tower of Constance is ninety feet high and sixty feet in diameter, with walls eighteen feet thick."

Even as he spoke Gabriella gasped. A perfect walled city, complete with the massive tower he had just described, came into view, rising like a mirage on the flat horizon. "It's amazing! Like something out of a dream from childhood."

David agreed. "It's one of the most handsome and well-preserved monuments from the Middle Ages. The tower is where the Huguenot women were imprisoned over a span of eighty years, from 1692 to 1768, I believe. We'll park the car and have a look around."

They pulled into town, and David found a parking spot just outside the city walls. They got out of the car, walking past the vendors selling their wares.

"Saturday morning is always busy. But the city is nothing of what it was back in the Middle Ages. Fifteen thousand inhabitants then, a mere four thousand now. Marseilles, of course, became France's great port, and the silt from the Rhône River eventually cut off access from the river to the town of Aigues-Mortes.

"We enter here by the Porte de la Gardette." David took Gabriella's arm and guided her through the heavy wooden doors into the cobblestone streets of the city. He looked at his watch. "It's eleven o'clock now. You'll have plenty of time to visit the tower and walk on the ramparts before lunch." He grinned. "But be careful. The ramparts aren't protected. Don't slip off into the home of some squire in the village."

"You mean you won't come with me?"

"My dear, I've been here five times and been through the tower and ramparts as many. After a while, even fascinating history loses its luster. No, I'll leave you alone to contemplate the fate of your Protestant counterparts. This little book will provide all the details you are lacking." He handed her a copy of Samuel Bastide's *Les Prisonniers de la Tour de Constance*.

"You're sure you won't come, then?"

"No, you run along and enjoy. I'll meet you at the main gate in an hour. No, let's make it 12:30. Ah, but yes. We should get the bread first. The *boulangeries* all close at noon. Here." He put ten francs in her hand. "Get a *baguette* and a *ficelle*. There's a good little store with a green-and-white awning right on the next road. Do you mind? I'll slip out to the *marché* and get us some fruit and cheese. What will you have?"

"A pear," she laughed, "and some Morbier. I'll see you back here in a sec."

Gabriella turned down the side street David had indicated and found the bread store with delicious smells escaping from its door. She slipped inside and waited behind two customers.

"*Bonjour, mademoiselle,*" the hearty baker greeted her when her turn came.

"Bonjour. Yes, I'd like a *baguette* and, and a ... now what did he say ... Oh, yes, a *ficelle!* Yes, that's it." She brightened as the man dusted in flour reached behind him to where loaves upon loaves of bread of all shapes and sizes stood lined neatly in wire racks. He retrieved a very long narrow one and placed it on the counter. "A *ficelle,* you said?" His heavy eyebrows rose.

Gabriella blushed. "Yes, a *ficelle.* And a *baguette.*"

"You are sure?"

"Yes, quite." She placed the ten francs on the counter and waited for the change before picking up the loaves of bread, which had been wrapped together around the middle with a thin piece of tissue.

"Bonne journée."

"Good day to you, too, *Monsieur."* Her accent was perfect. *It did not give me away,* Gabriella reflected. *But somehow they always know I am not French. And they tease me.*

She and David met in the open square, both grinning with their purchases. "Wonderful, Gabby! Enjoy yourself, and when you return, I'll have the most delicious sandwich that your mouth has ever tasted waiting for you."

"I'll be ready." She waved and headed for the imposing tower to her right.

"Don't forget to tip the custodian when he lets you out," David called after her.

* * *

Gabriella walked across the drawbridge that had obviously once led over a moat and passed through the heavy gates of the tower. The main floor was empty except for a young man in a dark green shirt. He stood in the center of the circular room, looking up at the tall vaulted ceiling. Gabriella leafed through her book, which was filled with illustrations of the Tower of Constance. Reading to herself, she walked around the room and felt the cool stones. *A prison.*

She found the narrow spiral stone stairs to the second floor and made her way up, letting her imagination take her back several centuries. *What if I were coming to this prison because I was a Huguenot?* The thought made her shiver as she arrived on the landing of the second floor, which the book called the Salle des Chevaliers. She had seen the evocative painting in the medical school in Montpellier of the Huguenot women prisoners huddling together on the roof of the Tower; standing here, it all seemed more real.

This room looked to Gabriella like an exact replica of the one below. In the middle of the room, on the stone floor, was a round opening covered with steel grating. She sat down on a curb of raised stones surrounding the hole and ran her fingers along the top of the curb, noticing what seemed to be writing on one particular stone.

Straining to make out the word, she let out a small cry. "So this is it!" This was where Marie Durand had scratched the famous word *"Résistez"* with her fingernail in the stone. *Don't give up, hang on, endure to the end!* Taken prisoner when she was nineteen years old, Marie Durand lived in this tower for thirty-seven years, standing firm in her faith and encouraging the other women to do the same.

Gabriella marveled at the Durand family. Marie's brother, Pierre, was a brilliant pastor who was hanged on the Place de la Comedie. Her father died in another prison for his faith. And Marie Durand carved out her faith with a single word in a stone that would outlive the cruelty of kings who tortured and killed their subjects.

After a while, Gabriella looked up and saw an old worn banner hanging against the rounded wall. In the center of the banner was a print of the Huguenot cross. Instinctively she moved near it, pulling her own cross out from under her blouse and holding it delicately in her hand to inspect it.

It was the same, the thick sides of the cross turning inward like four arrows pointing to the center of a target. In between, touching the sides of these arrows, was a *fleur-de-lis*, the symbol of royalty. A dove hung from the southernmost arrow. Suddenly Gabriella felt a rush of emotion, standing in this cool, damp tower where women who wore this cross had suffered and died, many of starvation and insanity.

So engrossed was Gabriella in her own thoughts that she did not notice the young Frenchman until he stood inches behind her, peering over her shoulder at the cross she held in her hands.

"Interesting," he whispered in French. Gabriella turned and let out a sharp cry.

"Oh! You frightened me!" she said, embarrassed. "Excuse me, I should not have screamed."

"On the contrary, *Mademoiselle*, it is I who need to ask your pardon. I thought you heard me in the room." They stood for a moment in awkward silence until the young man ventured, "I couldn't help but notice that you wear the same cross as the one on the banner. Such an unusual cross. What does it mean?"

"Oh, yes, it is the Huguenot cross. Perhaps you do not know the history of the Huguenots? They were hunted down, and many either killed or imprisoned in this tower after the Revocation of the Edict of Nantes in 1685."

"Yes, our king decided everyone should be Catholic. And these Huguenots, what did they believe? I hope you do not mind my questions, *Mademoiselle?*"

"Not at all. I'm afraid I don't have all the answers myself, but I do know they believed much the same as the

Protestants of today. They were followers of Calvin and
the Reformation. They believed in Jesus and the Bible."

"*Mais, oui!* I see. And you have come from far away
to visit this tower? A pilgrimage for your faith?"

"Oh, not so far. I just came over for the day from
Montpellier. I mean, that's not where I'm from originally...I'm just studying there."

"And why do you wear this cross, if I may ask?"

Gabriella looked surprised. "Me? It was a gift to me
from my mother. We are Protestants, and I suppose she
knew of its history and wanted me to understand its symbolism." When she said the word *symbolism*, the young
man raised his eyebrows and moved closer.

"It is symbolic of what? Forgive me, but could I look
at it?"

Suddenly Gabriella felt uneasy and stepped back
from the young man, tripping on an uneven stone. "Oh,
it is the same as the one on the banner. Nothing unusual. I...I must be going now."

She shifted her weight and walked toward the steps,
but he caught her arm. "Please, *Mademoiselle.* I only
wish to know a few things about this history. Perhaps
we could have lunch together? My treat."

"Oh, no. That is quite impossible, thank you. I have
a friend who is waiting for me for lunch."

"This friend did not wish to visit the tower?" he
asked, seeming suspicious of her excuse.

"Oh, no, I'm afraid he doesn't have much interest in
Protestants and Huguenot crosses." She laughed nervously, feeling, as she often did, that she had said too
much. *Just another flirtatious Frenchman,* she thought.

"Well, I think I will have a look around upstairs on
the terrace—it gives a magnificent view of the village,
I'm told. You're sure you won't join me?" He moved
toward her again.

"No, I need to be going now." Gabriella turned and walked quickly down the winding stairs until she came to the same large room on the ground floor. She paused to listen for the young man, but he did not follow. Again she touched the cross around her neck, and then carefully placed it back under her blouse.

She glanced at her watch. Eleven-thirty. There was still plenty of time to visit the ramparts. As Gabriella stepped across the drawbridge, she turned to her right where a sign indicated the way. Several flights of stone steps, worn lower in the middle through centuries of use, led to the impressive walls of the city. She climbed the stairs until she stood on the narrow walkway at the top of the wall. Looking to her right, Gabriella could see a canal filled with fishing boats and happy sailors proud of their catch. The canal twisted its way out to the Mediterranean Sea barely visible on the horizon. She stared for a moment at the scene, the quiet of the marshes and the white gulls that flew toward the sun in search of an unknown destination.

The walkway along the wall was interspersed with many thick towers, much smaller in size than the Tower of Constance. Gabriella walked along, enchanted as she looked to her left into the interior of the city. From the ramparts, she had a bird's-eye view of the town and its red-tiled roofs, which protected the streets from the sun like a large sombrero over the face of a Mexican. Occasionally the roofs would open to reveal a beautiful garden, perfectly manicured, with geraniums cascading down the walls of a house. Olive, cedar, and magnolia trees rustled their leaves to applaud an ancient city constructed with the same elaborate planning as the yards in which they stood.

Taken by the scenery, Gabriella barely noticed that she had walked almost a third of the way around the ramparts. She stopped to peek inside a small vaulted room that contained an ancient fireplace and three windows giving a view onto the marshes and the water. She gathered her skirt under her and perched herself by a small open window to read more about the history of the city.

* * *

From the terrace above the Salle des Chevaliers, Jean-Claude Gachon could see for miles in every direction. A small plastic map erected for tourists indicated that Paris was eight hundred kilometers to the north and the great port of Marseilles only an hour to the east. Jean-Claude smiled as he looked to the west, back toward Montpellier and what he knew to be the Cevennes mountains, where these strange Huguenots had hidden as fugitives for years. He laughed at his luck, having met the red-haired beauty downstairs. Wearing the same cross! Surely it was not coincidence.

He walked beside the turret to look down and out to the south and the sea. Eight hundred kilometers away, if he looked with his imagination, he could see the city of Algiers and the fighting men and the explosions and the bodies. Algeria was where the action was . . . and Jean-Claude Gachon wanted to be in on the action.

Still looking south, he had a complete view of the walled city that spread out below him like a huge parallelogram enclosing neat lines of streets and buildings. He reached into the small leather shoulder bag that he carried, like every proper Frenchman, but he was not interested in the documents and money it contained. He pulled out a small pair of binoculars and put them to his eyes. Red-tiled roofs, baking in an undulating pattern in the warm sun. A few haphazard antennas thrusting skinny arms to the sky, testimony to modern technology. An old man with a *casquette* kneeling on a roof, repair-

84

ing a broken tile from a recent windstorm. A red-haired girl on the ramparts climbing several stairs and disappearing into one of the towers in the wall.

The girl! So she was out on the ramparts. He laughed again at his good luck. There was no way for her to escape. She must either retrace her steps or continue around the walls. Either way, he had plenty of time to reach her. Perhaps a subtle warning would do. Yes, Ali would appreciate that. A subtle warning to the girl with the flaming hair, who wore a Huguenot cross around her neck. Jean-Claude Gachon replaced his binoculars in the leather sack and hurried down the winding steps, eager for the action that awaited him on the ramparts.

* * *

Gabriella left the window and walked back through the room toward the ramparts. She stopped before leaving the small room as she noticed a small flight of steps on her left leading upward. Curious, she took them. The curving stairwell, dark and damp, was barely wide enough for one person. After climbing twenty steps, Gabriella found herself in the open day on a small terrace. She walked toward the south wall and stared again at the Mediterranean, which twinkled in the distance as the sun kissed it.

"Mother, here I am in this city of prisoners. You gave me this cross because it reminded you of something. But what?" She felt a chill run through her, and she wished that she could see her mother: the kind face, the wise eyes. "You would smile, Mother, to see how interested others are in this cross. And I don't even know why you gave it to me."

She stood for a moment longer before glancing at her wristwatch. "Time to go," she said out loud and headed back toward the narrow stairs.

* * *

It took Jean-Claude no more than five minutes to reach the tower where he had seen the girl disappear. The room was empty, but he was sure she had not come back out onto the ramparts. Then he saw a small stair-case that wound upward, and again he smiled. He moved silently up the narrow case, placed his leather shoulder bag on a step, tiptoed back down the steps, and waited just outside the room on the ramparts.

Soon he heard the sound of footsteps above him. The girl was skipping down the dark stairwell with ease. Jean-Claude smiled, pleased. Suddenly with a scream she slid down the remaining steps and lay dazed and silent at the foot of the stairwell.

Jean-Claude waited a moment longer before coming into the room. The girl lay still, and he silently stooped to retrieve his leather bag before coming to her side. Bending down in the shadows, he feigned concern and said, "*Mademoiselle*, I heard you scream from where I was on the wall. Are you all right? What happened?"

She took a moment to answer. "Oh, yes," she grimaced as she sat up. "I think I'm okay. I just tripped on something coming down the steps." She glanced toward the stairs.

Jean-Claude walked to the steps. "These steps are narrow and uneven."

"Yes, I suppose. I thought I stepped on something. You don't see anything?"

"Nothing, *Mademoiselle*."

"Well, you are right. It is dark and the steps are uneven. Careless of me."

Jean-Claude helped her to her feet, but as she tried to stand, she stumbled and reached out for his arm. "Oh, dear, I think I've sprained my ankle."

"Then I will help you back around." She hobbled

next to him as they retraced their steps.

"My friend will be here soon," the girl assured Jean-Claude. "Thank you for helping me."

"It is nothing." He smiled and whispered, "You must be careful, *Mademoiselle*. Huguenot crosses seem to bring bad luck to those who wear them." He disappeared down a side street, grinning to himself. It was nothing, indeed. A small accident. There would be others.

* * *

David found Gabriella sitting on a step beside the entrance to the city. "There you are, Gabby! I was beginning to worry. Thought you might have fallen off the ramparts."

She squinted, looking up at him. "Don't joke, please! I've done something nearly as stupid. I think I've sprained my ankle."

David bent down and inspected her swollen leg. "Good grief. I'm sorry! How did you do this?"

"Clumsy. I'm just clumsy. I was walking on the ramparts and went into one of those towers over there." She pointed. "There was a neat little terrace up above. Beautiful view of the Mediterranean. But the steps are narrow and uneven, and it's pitch-dark, and coming back down, I tripped and fell. I'm quite embarrassed.

"If it hadn't been for a nice young Frenchman, I don't think I would have made it back."

David perked up. "A young Frenchman? He was with you?"

Gabby laughed. "I met him in the Tower. Actually, I thought he was trying to pick me up. Asking lots of questions. You know, flirting. Anyway, I left to walk on the ramparts. He must have come out there a little later because when I fell, he heard me scream and came to see if I was hurt. He helped me get back here. I had to assure him I had a friend who would take care of me, or he would have carried me off with him, I'm quite sure."

"Yes, I imagine . . ." He did not question Gabriella further. There would be time later for that.

"Here, let me help you up. I suppose we should get you home. You'll need some ice on that ankle. We'll just have to enjoy the sandwiches in the car."

"I'm so sorry for my bumbling. We can still picnic if you wish." But she winced as she stood.

Impulsively, he picked her up in his arms and carried her back to the car. She laughed, embarrassed.

But David did not talk much on the way home. He thought about the young Frenchman and the pretty redhead and the information tucked in the pocket of his leather jacket. It had turned out to be a very interesting day after all.

* * *

Gabriella sat on her bed, holding a pack of ice on her swollen ankle. Ice on the ankle! How Mme. Leclerc had balked at the idea. And where would they get ice in this heat? But she had placed some water in the tiny freezer that hung inside the refrigerator, and they had made a pack. Now she stood over Gabriella like a conscientious nursemaid.

"*Ooh, la la. Ma pauvre petite fille!* This is not good. You will need crutches to walk. Such a pity, this accident."

"Really quite stupid of me, Mme. Leclerc." Gabriella tried to sound cheery. "I'll be fine, I promise. You have plenty of other things to do."

After several more *Ooh, la las*, the jolly woman left the room. Gabriella was glad to be alone at last with her thoughts.

"You are so clumsy!" she scolded herself out loud.

"Can't you do anything right? You always spoil everything."

She was angry that David had not been more sympathetic. He seemed distant and worried, but not worried for her. She was furious with herself for stumbling down the steps. And she felt uneasy when she thought of the young Frenchman, helping her to her feet and whispering that strange phrase about Huguenot crosses. What an odd thing to say. Again she thought of Mother and longed to talk to her.

"What have I done? I've come here and gotten mixed up with this crazy intellectual who doesn't give two hoots about me. And I have no idea why I'm here or what is next." Just last week she had felt so sure about the orphans, but now everything seemed confusing and pointless.

She could hear her mother's voice reaching out to her as she had hugged her that last morning in the Dakar airport. *There will be a time in your life when your faith will be tested. It must be so, otherwise it is not your faith. You have had the privilege of living in a family who knows God. And because you love your father and me, it has been easy to believe. But if God is truly God, He is big enough to show you, and you alone, that His Word is true, that He loves you, and that Christ is indeed His Son. Go out now, Gabriella, with our blessings and our prayers.*

"But I don't want to be tested this way! I know God loves me, but I just keep messing up. Maybe He can't even use me. Maybe it isn't my faith at all."

The ice pack fell to the floor and slowly melted on the tiles as Gabriella turned over and cried herself to sleep.

Chapter Nine

September had closed its door to let October open its own, and with it the weather became cooler in the city of Paris. Ophélie stared out the window of Mr. Gady's apartment and grew impatient. Fall was in the air, and all the other children raced to school, giggling and chasing one another down the narrow streets. But school was forbidden to Ophélie.

"My dear," Mr. Gady had explained lamely several weeks ago, "it is not wise right now for you to be at school. Soon things will change. Soon."

But Ophélie knew that things would not change. Mama had promised the same, and yet their life had always been one of flight and fear. Mama had called it adventure. She had tried to help Ophélie be brave. But Ophélie had known. It was not a child's adventure now.

School! First grade! How she longed to run to class with the other children, to sit in the wooden desks and learn to read. It was time. She knew she could learn fast, if only someone would help her. *She had to learn how to read.* The blue bag was tucked inside the pillow case this morning, and the letter in Mama's handwriting lay there, still a mystery.

"It isn't fair," she cried to the silent room, turning away from the window with its picture of happy schoolchildren. "I want friends. I'm tired of playing alone!" When they had arrived in France, Mama had said that she shouldn't go to school at first. But the days had become long for a six-year-old stuck in a tiny apartment with a beautiful mama who coughed all the time and looked at her with weak, tired eyes.

"Things will get better, *ma chére*," Mama had promised.

"But they are not better, Mama!" Again Ophélie spoke out loud. "They are worse, much worse. Why don't you come back? Why won't you tell me where you are? I miss you, Mama." Ophélie hid her face in the pillow to muffle her sobs.

"Ophélie! Ophélie!" Mr. Gady's loud voice boomed up the stairwell and startled her. Usually she knew when he was coming. He talked in an animated way to all his clients downstairs in the *épicerie*, and she could hear every word. But today she had been crying and hadn't heard his footsteps on the stairs.

She wiped her eyes and came to the door. "*Oui*, Mr. Gady?"

"Ophélie, come down and see, my child. Mme. Soliveau has brought us flowers!"

Slowly Ophélie descended the stairs, her long brown hair tousled.

"You are still in your bedclothes, little one. You do not feel well?"

Ophélie shook her head but did not look at the old shopkeeper.

"It is the school again, *n'est-ce pas?*"

Another nod.

"I know it is hard for you to stay cooped up with this old man, like a chick with its mother." He reached out a wrinkled hand and placed it under Ophélie's chin, gently pulling her face up until their eyes met. "It is not easy, my child. I am only trying to do what is best." He looked away and then seemed to remember his initial reason for summoning the child.

"But look. Today we will plant pansies! Aren't they lovely? Mme. Soliveau has brought them for us to plant in windowboxes and hang on the balcony. You will help me?"

Ophélie looked at the flowers. Delicate and velvety. White and bright yellow, deep purple and amber with a dark purple center in each flower. "They are pretty."

Suddenly she had an idea. She looked up at him hopefully. "I will help you plant the flowers. But will you help me, Mr. Gady? Will you help me learn to read?" Her eyes were bright and intense and convincing.

Mr. Gady's face broke into a relieved smile. "Ah, so this is it? This is why you miss school so much? Yes, yes of course. A little girl must know how to read. Then she can travel many places, even if for now she must stay in an ugly apartment with an old man. Yes, yes. I will teach you to read." Then his enthusiasm wavered, and he rubbed his forehead with a gnarled hand. "Hmm. Yes, but I will have to find the right books. But do not worry. Mr. Gady has many friends. I am sure someone will know just the right books for a little girl like you." Again he looked worried. "But it must be our secret. No one can know that I am teaching you, that you do not attend the *école primaire*. It will be our secret, *d'accord?*"

Ophélie brightened and nodded vigorously. "Oh *oui, oui, Monsieur!* I will not tell anyone. And may we start today? After we plant the pansies?"

* * *

Lunch was over, and Mr. Gady was snoring loudly on the couch in his little *salon*. The store would not open for a while, Ophélie knew. He always closed up, like everyone else in France, so that people could go home and eat. Ophélie was not sure how much time she had, but she tiptoed down the steps. What luck. Today he had fallen asleep teaching her to read!

Today she would slip out the door and go to the meat stand where Moustafa worked. Surely Moustafa would know about Mama. And she could be back before the old man ever opened his eyes or stumbled down the stairs to open the doors to the clients who would bustle in, jolly and full after their noon meal.

* * *

Emile Torrès walked down the three floors of stairs and stepped into the bright October afternoon. He followed the same narrow streets through the Left Bank that he had traveled every day of the previous three weeks. He was not in a hurry. "Find the girl. She cannot be far away." The instructions from Ali had been simple. So simple to pay the rent on Anne-Marie Duchemin's vacant apartment, to sleep on her sagging bed, and to walk three times a day down the street, past the *boulangerie* to the *tabac* where he bought a pack of cigarettes and the *Le Monde* newspaper. Simple to turn from Rue Boucher onto Rue de l'Echaude in the sixth arrondissement of Paris and find the meat stand where the now-captured Moustafa had worked. Simple to wait at the *café* across the street and read of the world, as he puffed a *Gitane*.

Today the news on the third page brought a smile to Emile's young, hardened face. Seven *pied-noirs* killed in an explosion outside of Monoprix in the French section of Algiers. That was fine news. The FLN continued on its path of terrorism. Emile relaxed in his chair in the smoky *café-bar* and watched the people hastening by on the sidewalk. Mostly students at this hour, laughing and hurling insults at one another, munching hot crêpes bought from the vendor across the street. Not a bad job, to wait and watch.

A small girl came into view as she hurried into the *boucherie*. Her long brown hair looked unkempt, and she wore a plain blue dress that came above her knees. Emile sat up immediately. He reached for an envelope from inside his jacket and pulled out a small photograph. *It was the same girl.* Ophélie Duchemin had walked into the butcher's store in plain daylight for all the world to see. Emile chuckled as he stood up, folded his newspaper under his arm and left ten francs on the table beside his empty cup. He put out his cigarette in the ashtray and left the *café-bar*. So very simple after all.

* * *

Ophélie's face was pained as she talked to the heavy-set man behind the counter who was slicing *Jambon de Paris* for another customer. "You are sure he is not here? I must find Moustafa!" Ophélie blinked back the tears as the butcher shook his head.

"I am so sorry, Miss Ophélie, but I have not seen Moustafa for three weeks. He has taken a long vacation without warning the boss. Not very good etiquette, I would say!" He laughed, but Ophélie could see the same worry lines in his face as she saw in Mr. Gady's.

He leaned over the glass that enclosed the raw meats, and lowered his voice. "Your mother, she is all right? I have not seen her either lately. You both have been sick, maybe?"

Ophélie did not want to talk about Mama. Surely he would know she was lying if she said all was well. But she could not think of anything else to say. Her eyes pleaded with him to understand. "We are fine ... only ... I wanted to talk to Moustafa. I need to see him. You will tell him when he comes back?"

"Of course, little Ophélie. I will tell him. Now you take care of yourself and your mama."

Ophelie left the store before he could question her further. She did not notice the little man with the thin mustache who followed her as she stepped out onto the sidewalk and ran all the way back to Mr. Gady's shop, letting the tears fall as she went.

She opened the door to the darkened store and closed it quietly behind her. Standing on the chair she had used earlier, she once again bolted the lock shut. She tiptoed back upstairs and past Mr. Gady, who continued to snore peacefully.

Once again Ophélie buried her head in her pillow and cried. She touched the blue bag and whispered, "Mama. Moustafa is gone. Gone like you. But Mr. Gady is going to teach me to read."

* * *

His class was over for the day at St. Joseph's. Jean-Louis Vidal packed up his worn-out briefcase and left the parsonage. He looked more than his fifty-five years, and everyone said it was because of the alcohol. His cheeks were a continuous deep cherry red, with little veins spreading across them like tiny roads on a map. The girls often whispered and giggled about his mismatched clothes with their pre-World War II styles, but he did not care.

The *café-bar* at the corner of rue Bastide had not changed much in twenty-three years. Jean-Louis knew all the other men who congregated there in the late afternoons. Often, after a refreshing *pastis*, the men would head to the nearby sand court for an invigorating game of *petanque*. Two teams tossed heavy metal balls toward

a *cochonnet,* which resembled a Ping-Pong ball in size
and weight. The physical exercise involved in the game
was minimal, but Jean-Louis enjoyed the company.

"*Bonjour,* Henri," he greeted the bartender, who
nodded without looking up. A few minutes later, Henri
placed a tall glass of *pastis* diluted in water in front of
the history teacher. Jean-Louis sipped it thoughtfully.
The licorice drink was a specialty of the Languedoc-
Rousillion region of France. And he for one wanted to be
sure that the supply-and-demand curve stayed balanced:
an occasional nip of wine in the morning, a half-litre of
the table *rouge* at lunch, and four glasses of *pastis* in the
afternoon, with some good red wine for supper.

A jolly, graying man, thin, with a prominent nose,
took a seat at his table. Jean-Louis greeted the man,
Pierre, a *boulanger* who occasionally slipped away from
his bread store in the afternoons, leaving his wife to
tend to the customers.

"*B'jour,*" Pierre mumbled, shaking hands with Jean-
Louis. "*Tu vas bien?*" His accent was thick and his
words strung out, typical of the region. Jean-Louis had
never adopted the southern French drawl, though he
had lived in Castelnau for twenty-three years. His
French was purely Parisian.

They chatted about the weather and the Mistral,
which had picked up the night before and blown tiles
from the roofs of several houses in the village of Teyran,
ten minutes down the road. "Must've been 100 kilometers an hour, that Mistral. Mighty fierce I tell you, rushing down that Rhône valley and spilling out to blow us
away. First bad wind of the season. Calmed down a bit
since yesterday. Right pleasant outside now."

Jean-Louis agreed with his table mate, and they
talked on.

"You'll be joining us for a game of *pétanque* this

afternoon, Pierre?" Jean-Louis questioned.

"Don't mind if I do, don't mind if I do." The two men walked out of the *café-bar*, nodding and gesturing, and somewhere in the course of the afternoon, Jean-Louis Vidal put his hand in his tweed jacket pocket and touched an envelope that had not been there that morning.

* * *

Every evening at 6:30, Mother Griolet took a stroll around the courtyard that lay within the walls of the church. It was her time to breathe and relax. In the summer, when the sun was still high, she sometimes sat in a wicker chair and read from the Gospels. She imagined herself in Jerusalem in the first century as she sat in the shade of the olive trees. Very peaceful. Now in the early days of October, she pulled her navy cardigan over her nun's habit as a crisp breeze played in the leaves.

She walked for twenty minutes, time enough to make five laps around the courtyard. And as she walked she always prayed out loud. On the south side of the church and parsonage, she prayed for some of the forty-two girls in the Franco-American program. "Thank you, Lord, for sending me Gabriella. I was wrong to be afraid for her. You always know best. I am getting old, and I need help with the children. She is so good and gentle with them. Please help her discover who she is in You. I'm afraid it may be painful ... but alas, You know best." She was quiet for a moment. Then as if adding a postscript to a letter, she addressed the Lord again. "And do help her be wise about Mr. Hoffmann. Oh yes, Lord. Open her eyes."

She passed the refectory, where soon the children would be eating dinner. The quiet in the hall would be shattered by happy little voices and clanking silverware. And singing. That was the best part, when the children sang the blessing in a round.

"Pour ce repas, pour toute joie
Nous te louons, Seigneur. Amen."

She drank in the melody even in the stillness of the
late afternoon. The innocent, sweet voices of children.
For all the heartache and trouble of the orphanage, she
thanked God for the cherubic voices. "And do please,
Lord, take away little Christophe's rasping cough. It
worries me, though he looks quite healthy. And you
remember, Lord, of course, that little Anne-Sophie has
lost her *nounours.* You know how much that teddy bear
means to her. She is having a dreadful time sleeping at
night. And Jérémy. *Ooh la!* What will we do with
Jérémy? He is so angry in that little heart of his...."

By the time she had reminded the Lord of the special
needs of each of the orphans she was on her third lap,
and just passing the dormitories. "And thank You, too,
dear Lord, for Sister Rosaline and Sister Isabelle.
Forgive me for taking them for granted. They have been
faithful to You and me all these years. Help them now as
they prepare the evening meal. Give them laughter as
they work. May they remember the verse we read this
morning, 'Inasmuch as ye have done it unto one of the
least of these My brethren, ye have done it unto Me.'"

She leaned against the stone wall at the north end of
the courtyard. The back of the church and the parsonage stood in front of her. To the left, the lights in the
refectory shone into the courtyard. The dormitory lay
dark on the right. Together the buildings joined to hold
hands, making three-quarters of a square, while the
stone wall against which she leaned completed it. She
loved this piece of earth. For forty-five years, she had
called this abbey her home. She ran her fingers over
the warm stones. She knew this place well. "And Lord,
you know this new little adventure that I'm involved in.
Well, it is a bit worrisome. I am getting older. Help me

do my part well."

She walked straight across the courtyard and let herself in the back door of the parsonage that led into her modest den. The ground floor of the parsonage held her living quarters, a bedroom, office, den, dining room, and kitchen. Years ago she had transformed a second bedroom into a student lounge. It made for less privacy, but gave the exchange students a place to gather and talk between classes. The second floor was reserved for classrooms and a language lab. The orphans had their schoolrooms in the basement. The old building had served the church well for over a hundred years.

Mother Griolet walked down the hall toward her office. She unlocked the door and stepped inside the dark room. She sighed as she switched on the lamp on her desk and surveyed the walls. Her desk faced the south wall with a large window that looked onto the courtyard. On either side of the window were bookcases lined with aging volumes. The other walls were literally wallpapered with framed photographs. It was Mother Griolet's home. Her family. She settled into the large chair behind her desk.

A lone white envelope sat on the desk. There was no writing on the outside. She flipped it over and opened the seal. A small piece of paper slipped out. In the top left-hand corner was scribbled the image of a cross. A Huguenot cross, Mother Griolet knew, by its Maltese shape and the dove hanging beneath. In the middle of the page was typed *14h30JeudiSNCF*.

She breathed out heavily. "So, Lord, You answer an old woman's prayer quickly. But will I be ready? Thursday at two-thirty. It is less than a week away."

She picked up the paper, tucked it into the pocket of her dress, and switched off the light. Closing the door behind her, she locked it and walked down the hallway back into the courtyard and across to the dining hall. The children's voices were singing the blessing as she slipped in the side door. She closed her eyes and soaked in the sweet sound. "Yes, Lord, for this food we give You thanks. And for the grace to meet each day's challenges."

By the time she had taken her tray and was seated with Sister Rosaline and Sister Isabelle at the head table, her face radiated peace, warmth, and composure. Someone else was looking after Mother Griolet's problems. That was good enough for her.

Chapter Ten

By mid-October every girl in the exchange program thought of Gabriella Madison and David Hoffmann as a couple. It was their delight and pastime to examine every look or word that passed between the couple in public and to dream of what passed between them in private. They wrote the script down to the last detail. *Homely missionary kid meets dashing young American professor. She is transformed into a radiant princess and will be making her debut this summer in New York City....*

Everyone except the couple itself. Gabriella knew that David Hoffmann did not consider her his girlfriend. Sometimes she wished it different, but that did not change matters at all. David Hoffmann's heart was not up for bids. Of that she was quite sure.

She could not take her eyes off him in class as he talked eloquently about the Impressionist artists. Gabriella marveled that David had jumped over two centuries since the last class, and yet had kept the feeling of the beauty and intensity of art, from Delacroix and Gericault's flashing social statements to the peaceful painting of sailboats that now appeared on the screen. He was speaking in French at the moment, and his voice was passionate.

"...Of course, Monet became the leading member of this expression of art, known around the world as Impressionism. This term was first used by an art critic to ridicule one of Monet's paintings, called *Impression of Sunrise*, which was part of the first Impressionist exhibition in 1874. Now the Impressionists' works are some of the favorites of art lovers the world over.

"It is just that—the impression of an image—that Monet leaves you with. The goal is to capture the moment and reveal it with dots or streaks of color that the eye will blend into detail from a distance. A master of light, Monet uses the sun to brighten and emphasize the changing effects of daylight on his subject matter. Note the difference in detail from the painters we studied last week. Whereas for Claude Lorraine the true subject in his paintings of seaports is the light of the sun in the background, reflected in the sea and contrasted in shadows and lights, Monet uses the sun to give a pleasant impression, a wisp of wind on the canvas, a silent air in the sails of the boat. The depth is present in a different way. A sharp contrast to the fundamental classicism and lyrical idealism of the early seventeenth century. But it still involves light, the artist's child, to be observed and nurtured until by its presence the painting is revealed."

He continued to flash slides on the screen. Gabriella jotted down the names of the paintings in her spiral notebook, *The Boats at Argenteuil, The Painter's Garden at Giverny, The Poppies Near Argenteuil.*

David spoke again. "Look at the poppies, with the artist's small son lost in the field of wildflowers. The contrast of colors, the rich variety of the landscape. Nature and human life, blended together in a vibration

102

of light. Poppies in spring. Their bright red garment that suprises and delights the eye. Beautiful."

Gabriella could feel his eyes on her, and she tossed her hair over her shoulders self-consciously. Hope and spring. But fall was barely in the air, and Gabriella did not want to think beyond one day at a time.

* * *

"It is lovely this afternoon, Gabby. Why don't you come for a ride through the vineyards with me? It will certainly beat hobbling around on those crutches." David nodded toward her foot, wrapped in heavy bandages. "How much longer do you have to wear that thing?"

"Another week at least, the doctor says."

"Poor you. You will join me then?"

Gabriella could think of no excuse to turn him down. She was not helping with the orphans today. "Sure, why not?"

The car left the limits of Castelnau and headed north. Before them on the smaller roads lay field after field of vineyards. "The migrant workers and starving students have finished picking the grapes now. Nothing left on those vines. But look at the colors."

He had chosen the late afternoon as the sun was slipping down, and its reflection on the vines was brilliant. "See there, the bright red ones. And the yellows and oranges. It is my therapy in fall, to drive among the vineyards and watch their colors change. The nearest thing I can find to fall in Princeton."

"Princeton? In New Jersey, right?"

"Yes, I was in school there for four years. A magnificent part of the world. Cold and frank and bold. The maples are fiery red and crackling orange and bright yellow. Your hair would fit in perfectly." He smiled as he said it. "Striking."

"I can hardly imagine it. Senegal's vegetation doesn't change at all during the year. There's the rainy season and the dry season and not many trees."

"Do you miss Africa?" He changed the subject as smoothly as he had advanced the slides in the tray that morning. A simple flick of the finger.

"Yes. I miss it a lot. Sometimes more than others."

"When do you miss it the most?"

She gazed at the blue sky descending on the vines with purple and pink hues mixed in. "I guess when things get hazy where I am. When I can't see what's ahead. Then I picture myself back there, comfortable in my little niche."

David was staring at her, his eyes barely on the road. "What are you wearing around your neck?" he demanded, intrigued.

"Oh, you haven't seen it before? I wear it all the time. I just usually keep it tucked inside my blouse. But surely you can't mean that you don't recognize the Huguenot cross?"

"No, I don't mean that." He spoke in a far-off way. "I just didn't know you wore it."

His statement begged a reply. "My mother gave it to me before I left Senegal. Symbolic of my faith. She told me to find out more about the Huguenots while I was here. I never expected anyone else to be interested in the cross."

"It is unusual."

"I suppose. She got this cross in Montpellier. She was here, you know, after the Second World War. Dad sent her here with me and Jessica and Henrietta for a few months' break. That's when she met Mother Griolet."

"Ah, I see." His eyes were on the road, but occasionally he would glance again at the shining chain around her neck. "Do you remember Montpellier? You were how old then?"

"Five or six. No, I don't remember anything. Hardly anything."

"What made you come back?"

She fiddled with the cross, sliding it up and down its chain. "A family member wanted to pay for the rest of my college education. He suggested I start with a year abroad, 'abroad' meaning Europe. I thought this program sounded safe. Mom knew the town and the director. Really just circumstances and . . ." She let the phrase trail off.

"And what?"

"Circumstances." Her tone signaled the end of her revelations. "Do you miss Africa, David?"

"And why should I miss it, Gabby?"

"Because you lived in Algeria for a year, before this war broke out."

He laughed and gave her an inquisitive look.

"Mother Griolet told me, from your resumé. I help her with the orphans now, and she was filling me in on the school and its professors."

"I see. A fine woman, Mother Griolet. No wonder you came back." He seemed a million miles away.

"Well, yes, I mean it was more because my Mother knew her. She spoke so highly of her. I don't remember much about that time. . . . But we were speaking of Algeria." Gabriella gently urged him back to the subject she wanted to hear about.

"Yes, I lived there briefly. A lovely spot, before the war. Of course, I could see trouble coming fast."

"Where did you live?"

"Algiers. The capital. Lived in the *pied-noir* neighborhood."

"Was everything segregated then?"

"No, not really. The *pied-noirs* were friends with

Arab merchants and the Jews. Everyone got along pretty well."

"Where did the name *pied-noir* come from, anyway?"

"Oh, there are lots of explanations. The most colorful is that after France colonized Algeria in 1830, the first French *colons* or citizens who settled there came as farmers. They wore big black boots to work the land. The Algerians had never seen boots; they worked the land barefoot. So they started calling these foreigners *pied-noir* or black foot. Now it simply means a French citizen who was born in Algeria."

"Mmm. Interesting. And now all the *pied-noirs* will be leaving Algeria?"

"Most likely. Of course, the large majority don't believe, even now, that France will lose the war. They are staying because they have nowhere else to go. Algeria is their home, their roots for over a hundred years."

"But wouldn't they be welcomed back to France? After all, they are French citizens, you said."

David had been talking easily, more easily than she could remember. But with her last question, he grew silent, brooding.

He pulled off the road, slowing the car to a stop, and looked at her with what she was sure was pain in his eyes.

"Don't you understand, Gabby?" He spoke rapidly, with anger in his voice. Then he shook his head. "No, of course, you can't understand. Nobody wants the *pied-noirs*. Algeria will kill them if they stay there. France wants Algeria's oil, but the *pied-noirs*? As far as France is concerned, they can go to—" He started over. "There's no place for them. Just one more burdensome minority."

"But you care about them, David?"

"Hah! You know me better than that. I have already told you. I care about me, my skin. But you are right. Somewhere in my troubled soul, I have a soft spot for minorities. I understand the Algerians who long for independence from their strict mother, France. But I have lived among the *pied-noirs* who only want to keep their land. They are perhaps idealistic and naive, but I understand them.

"They both have good reasons, Gabby. Good reasons to fight and to want what they want. It's too bad that war is so complicated. Too bad that we can't always tell who are the good guys and who are the bad." He looked out toward the vineyards. "Like a bottle of wine—you don't know the quality of the vine until the fruit is picked and fermented and tasted. And sometimes, we would judge too quickly."

Gabriella reflected on David's words, appreciating the silence and the scenery. She focused on the vineyard in front of her. Each knotty plant, no more than four feet tall, twisted and held out its branches, which now boasted only variegated leaves. Presently she said, "I am the Vine, ye are the branches: He that abideth in Me, and I in him, the same bringeth forth much fruit: for without Me, ye can do nothing."

"That sounds rather biblical to me. Where's it from?"

"The Gospel of John. Jesus talking to his disciples." She smiled. "Jesus was probably sitting near the vineyards with His disciples, contemplating their beauty just as we are doing, when He said that 2,000 years ago."

"Could be. I don't follow the teachings of Jesus, you remember."

"Never mind. It is true, what He said. No matter the minority, the position, the color of the skin. In Him the fruit is good. You know what the next verse says?" She did not wait for an answer. "If a man abide not in Me, he is cast forth as a branch, and is withered; and men gather them, and cast them into the fire, and they are burned."

"You're getting theological, Gabby. And very narrow. Sounds like a lot of bad fruit to me."

"There is. But the good fruit does not depend on where you were born or your society. It just depends on God and you. He won't throw you out because of a troubled past."

"That is good news indeed. Amazing what we can learn from the vineyards."

Gabriella caught the sarcasm in his voice and suddenly had no desire to say anything more.

David started the engine and pulled back onto the road. They drove for a long time between the tall plane trees that lined the narrow country roads like rows of soldiers saluting their advancing general. Gabriella relaxed in the beauty of the setting sun, playing its light across the canvas of the landscape. *Monet would have enjoyed this ride*, she thought. She was determined to enjoy it also, even seated beside David Hoffmann, who kept his heart locked away in some painful past.

* * *

Saturday morning Gabriella had promised to help Mother Griolet plant pansies. She arrived at the stone house at nine o'clock, exhausted after maneuvering through the cobblestoned streets on her crutches.

"You are sure you feel up to this, my child?" Mother Griolet asked skeptically.

"Oh, yes. Quite sure. It will do me good to be outside in this gorgeous weather."

"Very well, then. Come along." She led her through her apartment and out the door that opened from her den into the courtyard. "I always like to plant my pansies early. The middle of October is just right. Gives them time to get used to the soil before it gets too cold. And before the Mistral sweeps down in all its fury."

Mother Griolet had purchased three trays, each

filled with ten plastic cups of flowers of all hues. She took one cup out and pushed the loose earth through her fingers. "I usually plant them on each side of the courtyard. One-and-a-half trays in front of the dining hall, and the other one-and-a-half in front of the dormitory. Unless, my dear, you have another thought." She smiled. "I'm always open to new ideas."

"Oh, no. I'm not much of a gardener. You decide."

"All right then." Mother Griolet handed Gabriella a trowel and a tray of pansies. They walked toward the dining hall. The old woman knelt on the cool soil with the agility of someone who was quite used to kneeling. She held a bunch of yellow pansies in her hands. "I love the feel of the earth on my hands, the dirt under my fingernails. It is so ... so therapeutic, you know."

Gabriella watched and nodded.

"And what have we here?" She was talking to the flowers. "My, but aren't you splendid in that bright yellow frock! A regular sunflower in disguise, I'd say." She laughed and held the flowers toward Gabriella. "You see, there is a face in each flower, delicate and full of promise." She pointed to the dark velvet interior of the pansy.

Gabriella gasped. "Why, that's just what Mother used to say, 'A face in each flower, delicate and full of promise.' We didn't plant pansies, but Mother has an art book, and in it there is the most wonderful still life of pansies by Fantin-Latour. That's what she would say about the pansies."

"She said that, did she?" Mother Griolet was amused. "I'm surprised she remembered."

"What do you mean?"

"Many years ago, your mother knelt in this very courtyard with me and planted pansies. I suppose I told her the same thing."

"You and Mother were good friends, then?"

"I guess you might say circumstances drew us together." A cloud passed over Mother Griolet's face, then she brightened. "A lovely woman, your mother. Such a woman of faith. And so smart! I believe she must have memorized half her Bible. You know, there are few people who can find Scriptures quicker than I, but your mother—she had me beat."

"Tell me about when we were here in Montpellier. Mother always speaks so highly of you, but she never speaks directly of our time here."

"Well, there really isn't that much to tell. You were staying in the mission house over on the west side of Montpellier. I believe it was a break for your mother. Your dad could not leave Senegal at the time, so they postponed their furlough to the States, and your mother brought you and your sisters here for three months.

"We met by accident." Then the old nun looked up at Gabriella with a far-off smile. "Not by accident. It cannot have been a simple coincidence when I see you here with me, helping a silly old lady who won't retire. No, it was just another thread in the tapestry of God's work. She was here, and now you are here. Another instance of God weaving our lives in and out to bring about His good will."

"But how did you meet?"

"I was at an interchurch seminar. Very radical in that day, but I went. And there was your mother, sitting strong and tall in the pew beside me. She spoke easily—like you, my dear." The old nun winked. "And it was like a flower, our friendship; it bloomed so quietly and simply. I missed her a lot when she left."

"And you knew us too? What were we like?"

"Precious, absolutely precious. You had that curly red hair, and Jessica was a little towhead. The French had never seen anything like it. Henrietta was just a baby. She crawled around this courtyard more than once, that little rascal. Quite a handful."

Gabriella laughed and nodded, but her eyes were wet with tears.

"Oh, my! I've made you homesick, I fear."

"It's nothing," Gabriella said, brushing away the tears. "Just remembering. We must have been so happy then." She fought back the tears again. She did not look at Mother Griolet when she spoke. "You know we had another sister. She was born the year after we returned from Montpellier."

"Yes, your mother wrote me about her. Ericka, *n'est-ce pas?*" she pronounced the name with difficulty, a knot catching in her throat.

"Ericka. Beautiful little Ericka. Henrietta was all mischief, but Ericka—an angelic baby. The biggest blue eyes you ever saw. And black hair. Jet black. She didn't look a thing like the rest of us. Thick black hair and long eyelashes and ...." But Gabriella could not go on. She dropped the trowel and buried her face in her dirty hands and cried.

Mother Griolet knelt beside her, arms encircling the young woman's thin shoulders. "There now, Gabriella. It is too hard, too sad to remember." She pulled Gabriella close to her, and the girl sobbed on her breast.

"It was hard ... so awful. She was my favorite sister. My favorite sister for six years. And then she was gone. The sickness took her in four days, and she ... she was gone."

"There now, my child. You go ahead and cry. Sometimes it is the only thing that helps. We can plant the pansies later."

Mother Griolet led Gabriella into her small apartment and to the bathroom, where she left her alone to wash her

111

face. Then she walked slowly down the hall to her office.
In the bottom drawer of her desk, she took out a faded
photograph of herself as a much younger woman. Beside
her stood a tall, attractive woman of about thirty, holding
a baby, with two little girls at her knees.

"Rebecca. Rebecca Madison. How I have missed
you. Forgive me for not knowing how to tell you how
very, very sorry I was when I heard about Ericka." She
replaced the picture and sat for a moment longer at the
desk, wiping her eyes with a clean white handkerchief.

Chapter Eleven

Malika Abdel was short for her eleven years of age, but
what she lacked in height she made up for in common
sense. Streetwise, they called her. She knew everything
about what men and women did together in bed, and
she knew other things that happened behind closed
doors when an angry argument was followed by a slap
and then a fist, and later a bruised eye. Her father had
taught her well through his actions. So Malika grew up
fast and stood tall between her cruel father and her
younger sisters.

Daddy was always mad about something; these days
it was about Algeria. "Someday we will go back home,"
he promised his girls.

Malika knew that money was one thing that appeased
her father's temper, at least for awhile. Now she could
make money. The skinny Frenchman with the thin mous-
tache had approached her ten days ago with a simple
request. Make friends with the little girl who lived with
the old man above the *épicerie* down the street.

Four hundred francs he would pay her to bring the

girl to him. But Malika had not yet met the child. Every day she made up an excuse to go to the shop. She browsed for fifteen or twenty minutes each time, but the girl never appeared. Now the thin Frenchman was getting impatient.

"You will have nothing if you do not bring her soon! I cannot wait forever! Tomorrow night there is a march to the prefecture. Bring her along, and you will have your four hundred francs." The man had grabbed her arm this morning as she left for school. Malika did not show her fear, but she shivered as she left the school building at noon to walk home.

Once again she stopped by the *épicerie*. The old shopkeeper looked up from the counter. *"Bonjour, Mademoiselle.* You are back again today?"

"Yes, I brought some marbles for your granddaughter."

"My granddaughter?" He looked at her suspiciously.

"Yes, the little girl who is sick. I have seen her, but she never goes to school. She is sick, your granddaughter?"

"Yes, yes, she is sick."

As if on cue, the child came down the back stairs coughing loudly. She smiled sheepishly as the old man turned toward her. "Ophélie. What are you doing downstairs?"

"I wanted a *pastille*, please."

Malika caught her eye, and the girls smiled at each other.

"A cough drop? Well, here you go. Now go back upstairs."

"Please, *Monsieur.* May I give Ophélie these marbles?" Malika held out her hand and displayed the small glass balls.

"Oh! They are pretty!" Ophélie came around the

corner and stared at the shining gift.

The shopkeeper cleared his throat. "Ophélie."

"Yes? May I have them please, Mr. Gady?"

She reached for the gems, and Malika took her hand. "I will teach you to play, okay? Tomorrow afternoon, when I get back from school, I will come over and teach you to play."

Ophélie took the marbles and placed them in her pocket. With an eager look in her eyes, Malika left the store before the man called Mr. Gady could refuse her offer.

* * *

"Would you care to join me this weekend in Aix, Gabby?" David asked nonchalantly as he joined Gabriella in the gardens in the interior of the old school building. The bright afternoon sun caught the red in Gabriella's hair and made it glisten like sparks flying from a soddering iron.

Her head had been bent over a book, and she gasped with surprise upon hearing his voice. "Oh, David! You startled me. I'm afraid I'm quite overwhelmed with Mr. Donne and his beautiful prose. What did you say about Aix?"

"I've got to go to Aix this weekend on some business. I thought you might like to come. We'd leave early Saturday morning and be home in time for you to get your studies done on Sunday."

"I, I don't know. Let me think about it, and I'll let you know tonight. You are coming to eat at Mme. Leclerc's, aren't you?" A flush crept onto her cheeks.

He sat down beside her, his arm brushing hers lightly, seemingly unconscious of his proximity. "Dear Gabby, you know me well enough to know that I would never pass up a free meal, especially with such delightful company as Miss Stephanie Thrasher and Miss Caroline Harland." He touched her hand. "And you, of course."

Gabriella blushed, but she was careful to keep her head buried in her anthology of English literature.

"Listen, dear. I am leaving on the night train for Paris immediately after dinner. I'll be there for a few days. Mr. Vidal has kindly agreed to take my classes this week. But please come with me to Aix on Saturday. It would give me something to look forward to while I'm away. You'll be off those crutches by then. We can celebrate."

Gabriella's heart was thumping like a bass drum. She liked the feel of his hand on hers. She longed to gently close her fingers around his, but she did not dare. For a brief moment she imagined his lips brushing hers in the vibrance of the fall afternoon. Then she shivered. "I don't know, David."

"You needn't worry about the arrangements for the trip. You'll be staying with a friend of mine. She's quite nice and would love to meet you."

So that's it, Gabriella thought. *He's going to Aix to see a woman.* "Why in the world do you want me to go with you?" She had not meant to blurt the question out loud, but the damage was done.

David removed his hand from hers, the spell broken. He laughed. "I for one would be bored to death if I had to spend every weekend in this silent town. It's a chance to see a little of this great country. You'll love it, I guarantee."

"I was just reading here what Mr. Donne has to say. You know: 'No man is an island.' We all need each other to make one big happy family. Sure, I'll go, just so you won't be alone." There was a hint of a smirk on her lips.

"I'm not sure you've interpreted Mr. Donne correctly, Gabby," said David, joining in the game of matching wits. "Nonetheless, if he has convinced you to come along, then I'm delighted. Bring some comfortable clothes." He stood to leave, then turned around to face her. "One more thing. Bring along an appropriate dress for Mass. I'm sure you wouldn't want to miss it. My friend will be glad to go along with you."

"And what about you, David?" Her voice was soft and penetrating.

David shrugged. "Me? I wouldn't be caught dead in a church!" Then he laughed. "Or maybe I should say, that's the only condition in which you'll find me there."

He was gone before she could reply. As she watched him disappear into the doors of the parsonage, she shook her head. *He is the most tactless, cynical man I have ever met.* Yet she laughed out loud, thinking about his last remark.

* * *

Gabriella turned off the hallway light, leaving the basement of the parsonage dark. The last orphan had slipped out the door into the courtyard, where Sister Isabelle was waiting to lead them to the refectory. They marched in single file, stealing glances back at Gabriella, waving and smiling. Gabriella waved too. She stood there a moment longer, satisfied. A feeling of joy danced inside as she thought of the afternoon they had spent together. Mother Griolet had let her start teaching the orphans, and Gabriella loved it. Sometimes she would throw in a detail from one of David's lectures. Never too soon to introduce the children to history and culture.

She glanced at her watch. Seven o'clock. Just enough time to hobble home and get ready for dinner. *David is coming to dinner.* The thought brought a rush to her heart as she limped back through the hall toward the front stairs.

She heard a squeak, like a chair being pulled across

the floor. *Now what child is hiding out in the classroom?* She was sure she had counted twenty-three children leaving for dinner. Gabriella turned into the empty classroom and flicked on the light. At first she saw nothing. Then there was a slight noise again. "Who is there?"

A young boy of about fourteen stood up behind a row of desks. Gabriella had never seen him before. He was thin and his skin dark olive. Gabriella knew immediately that he was North African.

"May I help you?" she asked softly.

The boy said nothing, but stood trembling before her.

Gabriella tried to calm the fear mounting in her mind. *He is only a boy. He will not hurt you.* Still, she suspected he was Algerian, and Algerians and French were not on good terms right now, even in France.

"Do you need something?" she ventured.

He raised his eyes from the floor and stared at her sullenly. Then, quite unexpectedly, he moved toward her, reaching his hand toward her throat.

Instinctively Gabriella backed up, bumping a desk and tripping with her crutches. She scrambled to regain her balance.

The boy observed her silently. He reached out again and spoke. "The cross." A look of understanding was in his eyes.

"Oh," Gabriella mumbled awkwardly. "Is that all? You like my cross?" A wave of relief swept over her. *Good grief! This cross. It will cause me to have a heart attack someday.*

"You wear the cross. Hugo?"

"Yes, the Huguenot cross."

"Hugo," he repeated again.

Gabriella stared at him blankly. "What do you want?"

He reached in his pocket and pulled out a scrap of

paper and held it out to her.

Gabriella cautiously took the paper and looked at it. Scribbled in one corner was the crude drawing of a Huguenot cross.

"Where did you get this? What is it?"

He looked at her again, silent and hopeful.

"I'm sorry," she said. "I don't understand what you want. Is it my cross?"

There was a sound in the hall, and suddenly Mother Griolet appeared in the room.

"Oh, my! Hakim! Well, Gabriella. I see you've met our newest boarder." Mother Griolet looked slightly flustered as she laughed nervously. "Hakim will be staying with us briefly. He arrived last Thursday. I'm sorry I didn't have a chance to introduce him to you over the weekend. He's been working with me. He will join the class tomorrow."

"It's quite all right. I'm afraid we surprised each other, that is all."

"Yes, I'm sure. Come along with me, Hakim. It is time for dinner. I will see you tomorrow, Gabriella. Thank you for letting the children out."

Gabriella left the classroom and slowly climbed the steps to the ground floor as Mother Griolet hurried Hakim down the hallway and out into the courtyard. The young woman touched the cross around her neck and wondered, for an instant, what the old nun could be planning to do with an Arab child at St. Joseph's.

* * *

David placed a stack of neatly folded clothes into the small, hard vinyl suitcase lying open on his bed. Then he added several books and a map of Paris to the stack before closing the case and latching it. Then he walked across the room and leaned over the small oak desk. His eyes fell on the letter he had received in the mail two days earlier.

Algerians plan peaceful march in Paris on 17th. Possible information from E. Torrès. Meet him at Pont St. Michel, north side at 21h30.

David folded the paper. His hands trembled slightly as he put the note inside his wallet. At last, possible information from an FLN informer. This was good. Six months of waiting might pay off tomorrow. Six months! Or was it seven years? He did not dwell on the thought.

His hands steady, he set the suitcase by his bed and left the room, locking the door behind him. Paris was still a long way off. First there was dinner at Mme. Leclerc's house.

* * *

"Mr. Hoffmann is coming to dinner tonight!" Stephanie danced around her room, and Caroline joined in the fun.

"Woo wee! He's coming to see Gabriella. Lovey dovey."

"Really, you two," Gabriella admonished. "That is the most childish thing I've ever heard. It was Mme. Leclerc's idea to invite him. You know she and Mme. Pons are always scheming." She left their room, but Stephanie ran after her.

"Gabriella. Don't act so nonchalant. How many times have you been out with him now? Three? Four?"

Gabriella did not mention his recent invitation to take her to Aix. That would really send the rumors flying.

"Do you think he'll like what she's fixing? I saw the recipe," Stephanie jabbered. *"Fricassé de laperau avec des tomates fraîches."*

"Rabbit in tomato sauce. Why not? Anything Mme. Leclerc cooks is delicious." Even then the odors from the kitchen drifted back to their rooms to entice them.

"Don't I know it," retorted Stephanie, patting her hips which were squeezed in a tight-fitting skirt. "If she doesn't quit feeding us so well, I'm going to have to get a new wardrobe."

"Wait till we go to Paris," replied Caroline, who was brushing her shiny golden hair in front of the mirror. "Mmmm, wouldn't that be nice? A new wardrobe straight from the designers on Rue St. Honore."

Gabriella heard David ring the doorbell at precisely 8 o'clock. Mme. Leclerc pushed the buzzer inside, which allowed him to open the door. After a moment, they heard him knock lightly on the door.

"*Entrez.*" Mme. Leclerc invited him in with a wide grin on her face. "*Ooh la la,*" she added as David presented her with a bouquet of flowers. "*Merci,* Monsieur Hoffmann."

The three boarders stood obediently behind their landlady, taking in the scene with delight. Mr. Hoffmann looked stunning, his black hair combed back from his face. A few wisps tumbled over his forehead, giving him a carefree, rugged appearance. He smelled vaguely of some rich aftershave. He wore a pale yellow Oxford cloth shirt and tweed pants, and his leather loafers were polished.

"Mademoiselle Thrasher," he said softly, as Stephanie approached and smiled. He took her hand and kissed it lightly. Stephanie's eyes grew wide, and her face turned crimson.

"*Enchanté,* Monsieur Hoffmann," she stammered.

"And Mademoiselle Harland."

Caroline, who was wearing a red dress that set off her perfect curves, came foward and lifted her eyebrows. "*Enchanté,* Monsieur Hoffmann." She winked at him as she offered him her hand, and he kissed it also.

Gabriella felt a tiny pang of jealousy as she noted

Caroline's flirtatious ease. She felt embarrassed to meet David's eyes.

"And my dear Mademoiselle Madison."

Gabriella hobbled forward on her crutches and extended her hand in mock obedience.

Ignoring it completely, David bent down and held her shoulders gently. Then he kissed her softly on each cheek, starting and ending with the left one. He whispered, "If I am not mistaken, it is three times on the cheeks here in Castelnau."

Gabriella felt lightheaded and at a total loss for words as she met his eyes. They stood there, he gazing down at her with his hands on her shoulders, until Mme. Leclerc cleared her throat and Gabriella stuttered, "Oh, *enchanté*, Dav...David...I mean, Monsieur Hoffmann."

* * *

Mme. Leclerc busied herself in her kitchen, humming contentedly to herself. The meal was progressing fabulously, and Mr. Hoffmann was behaving like a charm. So gracious and smooth and seductive! *Ooh la la!* She could not wait to report every detail to Monique tomorrow.

The first course, avocado halves with shrimp sauce, had been appreciated by everyone. She laughed as she brought the steaming plate of *gratin dauphinois* to the table. Americans always liked her scalloped potatoes. She went back to fetch the green beans in garlic butter and placed it before her guests.

One more trip to the kitchen, and she brought out the specialty of the evening. Young rabbit cooked in the typically rich tomato sauce of the region.

"It all looks wonderful," Stephanie exclaimed. "Delicious!"

Mme. Leclerc busied herself with serving the plates as they were passed to her. She was pleased with the picture, the blend of yellow and red and green. Such a pretty table, with her fine china and the bright colors of the food. Such a perfect evening.

She announced the names of each dish, as was her custom with her American boarders, who often wanted the recipes.

"Tonight we have *gratin dauphinois, haricots à l'ail et fricassé de lapereau avec des tomates fraîches.*" She beamed as the four young people nodded approvingly and the steam rose from their plates. *"Alors, bon appetit!"*

* * *

For several minutes the conversation stopped as everyone tasted the food that Mme. Leclerc had placed before them. David, who had been talking with ease during the first course, stared at his plate with a pained expression on his face. He gingerly ate the potatoes and the green beans as Stephanie and Caroline questioned him about an artist they had been studying in class. His reply was curt.

Gabriella noticed immediately that something was wrong, and tried to change the subject. "The rabbit is wonderful, simply delicious, Mme. Leclerc."

"Oh, yes," chimed Stephanie and Caroline.

David Hoffmann's silverware lay on his plate, and a far-off look was in his eyes.

"Mr. Hoffmann, you are all right?" Mme. Leclerc inquired. "The food is not good?"

David shook himself out of his thoughts. "It is superb, Mme. Leclerc. Only . . ." He lost his composure for only a moment. "I am afraid that I cannot eat the . . . the *lapereau*," he said the word with difficulty. "I am sure it is delicious. It is just that . . ." Again his voice trailed off. The girls stared at him, shocked. David Hoffmann had fallen from his pedestal. His face was red, and Gabriella noticed drips of perspiration on his forehead.

"I am allergic." he finished lamely.

Mme. Leclerc was standing and nodding sympathetically. "*Ooh la la.* It is nothing! If only I had known." She whisked the plate away. "I will fix you something ·else. It will not take long. You like chicken? *Poulet cordon bleu,* perhaps."

David wiped his face with the cloth napkin. He had recovered. "Please, no, excuse me. It is all fine. Do not bother. A nervous reaction, I am afraid. Please, I will have some more of the delicious *gratin dauphinois* and *des haricots verts*. That will be delightful."

It took five minutes for the conversation to resume. David spoke once again with charm and dry wit. The main course was cleared away, the rabbit forgotten. The cheese course was served, followed by a tray of fresh fruit and then Mme. Leclerc's rich yet light *mousse au chocolat*. It was 11:30 before the coffee was drunk and the table cleared.

David Hoffmann thanked Mme. Leclerc profusely for the meal and kissed her on each cheek before he left, causing her to roll her eyes with glee as she bustled toward the kitchen.

He took Gabriella's arm and pulled her into the hallway.

"You will come to Aix with me, it is sure?"

"Yes, David, I will come." She wrinkled her brow. "Are you all right?"

"Yes, I am all right. I must go now. I have a train to catch. Good-bye, Gabby." He brushed her cheek with his hand, but his eyes were far off. He descended the steps without looking back. Gabriella watched him go, and wondered about a smooth-talking teacher who had become unnerved over a dead rabbit.

* * *

Moustafa awoke to the sound of Anne-Marie's incessant coughing. He wiped the sleep from his eyes and sat up. The sole window in the room, small and barred near the ceiling, revealed no light. The middle of the night.

"Anne-Marie," he whispered. "There is a little water left. Take it. It will help calm the cough." He handed a bottle across to the mattress where she lay.

"Thank you," she rasped. After a long drink, she said, "We will die here, Moustafa. I will not wait any longer."

Moustafa did not reply. *Yes, we will die here. She is right. Take the pill and be done with it. They are slowly starving us to death.* Three and a half weeks they had been locked in this room. He had made a mark on the wall at the same time each day, the time when a skinny hand unlocked the door and pushed in a plate of stale bread and a bottle of water.

"Anne-Marie. Do not give up. We will have our chance. You will see. And when it comes, we must be ready. Please. It is not over yet. Be sure you know what to say. I know you can be convincing. You have more information that you must present to Ali. I have forced you to talk. This is what we have planned."

"I will try," she moaned, lying back down and curling up like a kitten, desperate for warmth.

He reached out to touch her, but he stopped himself. How he longed to hold her and love her, even in the filth of this basement. He could keep her warm. But he would not. An impossible love! A *harki* and a *pied-noir*. So he had listened to her cough and had watched her grow weaker by the day. And he had often thought about the two pills that she kept in a small bottle, sewn in her sleeve.

* * *

Ali lit a cigarette and stamped the match out. A small group of men sat in metal chairs, smoking also.

"Emile has found the girl. He is a bit slow about his work, but he always gets it done. We will have the information by tomorrow night." He smiled. "Of course, we all know what an important night that will be in Paris. I am told it will be a peaceful march to the prefecture. But the French police will understand. Power to the Algerians. Freedom at last!" He paused, transfixed in a type of daze.

Then he resumed, "Of course, our little matter of concern will go on quite unnoticed. No more of these *harki* children will escape. None! Nor the *pied-noirs*. We will have their names, and they will pay for the sins of their fathers. Ali will have the revenge he is due. My father did not die in vain! Blood is the only revenge. Sweet red revenge! They will pay! Do you understand? They will pay. And you will bring me the proof. A coat of many colors stained with blood. Their blood!"

He had worked himself into a fury, and the men shifted nervously in their chairs. "Leave! Go on with you. I will call for you when we have the news."

The men shuffled out into the pitch-black night. Only Rachid stayed, at Ali's command. "What of the prisoners?"

"There is nothing to report. They are surely half dead with hunger. Do you wish for me to talk with them?" Rachid eyed his leader hopefully.

"You are too eager, Rachid. Time. A little time. Emile will have the girl, and then we will see fear in the eyes of the Duchemin woman. She will talk and talk. She will beg to tell us everything."

"And the *harki* son?"

"Moustafa is a swine. And you know what happens to swine! To the butcher! It will be soon. Do not worry."

Chapter Twelve

Gabriella knocked softly on the door of Mother Griolet's office.

"Come in," came the woman's gentle voice.

Cautiously Gabriella entered and took a chair. "I think I've gotten myself into a real mess, Mother Griolet," she began. "Could I talk to you about something ...something personal?"

Mother Griolet nodded.

"I just feel ... I feel ... well, how can I describe it?" She searched for the words. "I feel unpeaceful. That's it. As though I've made some mistake." She leaned back in the big chair and sighed. "I hate making mistakes. What do you think God thinks about our mistakes? I know He is forgiving, but I've been so pigheaded."

"What exactly is the problem, my dear?"

"It's David—I mean Mr. Hoffmann." She blushed. "I'm not sure what he's up to, but I'm involved with him, and I don't know what to do."

Mother Griolet waited patiently for an explanation.

"It's just that he's an atheist. He doesn't believe in

God. Have I messed up everything?"

Mother Griolet settled back in her chair, a kind smile spreading over her wrinkled face. "My dear child, I am sure you are familiar with the Scriptures, *non?*" She nodded toward the large Bible on the corner of her desk.

"Yes, of course. I read my Bible," Gabriella stammered.

"Good. Yes, and I am sure you are familiar with the stories of Abraham and Joseph and Moses and Paul and Peter and many other of the patriarchs and saints?"

"Yes, I know about their lives." A baffled expression came over Gabriella's face.

Mother Griolet smiled. "I have always found great comfort in the fact that our Lord worked with extremely human humans. They were always bumbling around and getting themselves in the worst trouble, even when they knew better." She raised her eyebrows and looked at Gabriella, who reddened and smiled and looked down.

"Yes, fortunately for us, the Lord kept picking them back up and forgiving them and helping them get on with the business He had them about. It seems that most of them had to learn some lessons the hard way. I can't recall a one that was perfect. But the smart ones, ah, there's the difference. They recognized when they had 'messed up' as you say, and they came before God and asked forgiveness and got back on the right track. Wonderful isn't it, how forgiveness works?" She winked at Gabriella.

"We're free to sin, and for some things we'll suffer the consequences all our lives. Think of Moses missing out on the Promised Land because he struck a rock instead of speaking to it, as God commanded. Or David. His adultery with Bathsheba and murder of her husband was forgiven, but their baby died. And St. Paul, how many years did it take him to convince those he'd been persecuting that he was now a convert?

"But when Christ forgives us, we're freed to start over again in His power. And little by little we learn." She stopped for a breath, but Gabriella said nothing.

"Oh dear, I'm afraid I've quite babbled on. Perhaps I've not answered your question."

"No. I mean yes, you have. Yes. It's true I need to get on with things. It's only that . . ." her voice trailed off. "It's just that I'm in love with him." This she said so softly that Mother Griolet strained to understand, though Gabriella knew that she had already understood.

"And this is a problem? To be in love?"

"Well, you know. He doesn't believe. We are so different."

"And you would be the same? That is your wish?"

Gabriella smiled as she fumbled for words. Dear Mother Griolet, playing the devil's advocate. "You will have me spell it out, won't you, Mother Griolet?"

The old woman smiled and nodded.

"I find myself having very strong feelings for him, but I think I shouldn't because he mocks my God. I know it is dangerous to love someone who does not share your beliefs. It is clear throughout Scripture. But the problem is this: I don't want to stop caring for him. And I don't know what to do."

"So you would ask me to approve what your conscience forbids? I cannot do that, Gabriella."

"No, of course not. I would not ask that of you. You do not like Mr. Hoffmann, do you?" Her eyes begged for mercy.

"Gabriella, professionally speaking, he is an extremely intelligent young man who performs his role as teacher without flaw. But you want my feeling here?" She pointed to her heart. "He scares me. There is a war going on, and it is not a pretty thing. People do strange things in war. Perhaps he is not involved in the least; I could be wrong. But there is something about him that bothers me. Very secretive, he is. I cannot forbid you to see him. We no longer have rules like that at St. Joseph's. But for your own good, Gabriella, I beg you to be careful." She was quiet for a moment, searching for the right words. "I would not want you to mistake what you think is love for something else. He has a certain way with ladies, and perhaps his interest in you is not merely sentimental."

Gabriella was crying now. "He is using me. That is what you think. I am afraid too, but I cannot stay away. It is too strong. Will you pray for me, Mother Griolet?"

The old woman came around to the front of her desk and knelt beside Gabriella. She took the young woman's soft creamy hands into her gnarled ones. Then she looked at Gabriella with her bright green eyes that did not betray her age. "Our God is not a God of confusion. You must trust. He gives strength to do what we cannot do on our own. But Gabriella, you must let Him do it. Even if it breaks your heart." She looked off into the distance and for an instant, Gabriella was sure that this wise woman knew what it was to have her heart broken.

* * *

David made his way through the first few rooms in the Jeu de Paume Museum on the Right Bank of Paris. The museum was crowded for a Tuesday afternoon. He pushed past two women busily chatting in front of Fantin-Latour's portrait of the eight well-known Impressionist artists. David had admired most of the works in the small museum many times before, but today he felt an urgency to find one certain painting and then leave.

Van Gogh's sunflowers caught his attention, but

could not keep it. "Sunflowers turning their faces up to the sky, searching for light. Like me," he laughed dryly, remembering Gabriella's comment of the other day.

"But David, we are all seeking something. I believe you want to find truth."

"Perhaps," he had countered. "Yes, truth. But you, dear girl, claim there is only one Truth. That is not the truth I am seeking."

Entering another room, he walked quickly toward the back wall and stopped. "*Les Coquelicots*. The poppies. Monsieur Monet's field of poppies." And then he whispered, "Gabriella."

At once he saw her before him, laughing, lighting up the classroom or the courtyard or the beach. A shocking picture of hope. A lone poppy in a field of sunflowers.

"They take over the field, you know, and the farmers hate them. Just a weed really. A wildflower. You start with one and it spreads like wildfire, those blasted poppies." David remembered Mr. Vidal reproaching him last spring when he had commented on their delicate beauty.

Delicate beauty, yes. That was Gabriella. Shocking with life and yet delicate and fine, with an enthusiasm and charm that spread out and spilled over, infectious in its winsome spirit.

"Gabriella," he whispered again, and with one last glance at the poppies, he turned and left the museum.

* * *

David walked briskly through the Tuileries gardens that led from the Jeu de Paume to the Louvre. The bright October sky of an hour ago now grumbled menacingly. And something grumbled even louder within the soul of David Hoffmann. It was October 17, a dark day for history. The day the French King Louis XIV had signed the Revocation of the Edit of Nantes in

1685, abolishing religious liberty in France. And with that quick release of ink, the blood of thousands of Protestants flowed through the caverns and mountains of the Midi. They ran and hid; they prayed and cried out to the heavens. Still the blood flowed and mingled with the mud and was forgotten. David wondered, was the cause worth the price of blood?

Yet the Huguenots had stood firm in their faith through the persecutions and tortures and spilled blood. He could not deny it, even though he would not show Gabriella how deeply it moved him. A people who believed that their faith was worth dying for.

He listened to the wind and he could almost hear its mournful warning, *Blood will flow again*. Tonight, he knew, once again a supressed minority would raise their angry fists and cry "Liberty!" But who would answer back? Who in fact knew the answer for Algeria? Who could truly see past the passion of political parties into the soul of the people?

David shook his head as he walked through the gardens. He would observe the march tonight, and perhaps get the information he needed to appease his conscience. But he knew there was no answer to appease both Algeria and France, the FLN and the OAS, the *harkis* and the *pied-noirs*. No answer would satisfy, and so the blood would continue to spill onto white pages not yet written, which would someday fill the history books.

* * *

Ophélie slipped out of the apartment, rushed down the stairs and out the back way. Malika waited for her in the late afternoon, her eyes glistening with excitement. "Tonight we will march for freedom! Tonight France will understand that Algeria must be free and

132

independent. We will be strong and powerful like the other nations of the world!" Her voice lifted and swelled with feeling, a young girl reciting her poetry into the afternoon air.

"Will you still teach me about the marbles?" Ophélie asked innocently.

"Marbles! Ha! I am talking about freedom. Come march with us for freedom!"

"I may come with you, then?" Ophélie longed for excitement and the taste of the wind on her face.

Malika bent down to Ophélie's height and looked her in the eyes. "Do you believe in a free Algeria?"

The young child's face clouded. What did Mama think? They had left Algeria, of that she was sure. But she could not remember if Algeria was good or bad. She did not care. Tonight she would escape with this big girl.

"I believe what you believe! I want to be with you."

"Then come along, Ophélie. Tonight you will be part of history!"

*   *   *

The sky was black when Ophélie finally heard Mr. Gady snoring in his room. She gathered up an old sweater the old man had found for her when the weather had turned colder. Before she left the office, she stopped. *What if Mr. Gady wakes up? What if he looks for me and finds the blue bag?* Quickly she pulled the bag out of the pillowcase and put it around her neck, tucking it under her shirt and sweater. The cross lay safely in the bottom.

Ophélie tiptoed down the steps and let herself outside with the key that Mr. Gady kept on a hook near the door. She had practiced locking the door with Mr. Gady. Now she pulled the door closed, locked it from the outside and dropped the key into the blue bag.

Malika was waiting for her. "You are late. We must hurry."

"Is this an adventure?" Ophélie asked.

"Yes, yes. An adventure, little girl. You will see. Now come on!"

Masses of Algerians crowded through the streets along the Seine. Ophélie struggled to keep up with the moving tide of human flesh. Men, women, and children hurried silently along, their eyes burning bright. All was quiet. No angry, bitter words. But she could see the look of determination on their young faces. "To the Prefecture," they whispered in Arabic.

Ophélie searched for Malika, suddenly feeling afraid. The other girl was running ahead, laughing with youthful extremism. She did not hear Ophélie's cries.

By the time the crowd reached the Prefecture, Ophélie felt she could walk no farther. She wished she had stayed with Mr. Gady. "I think this is bad, Mama. I want to go home. Mama." She was crying as she ran, pushed along by the stream of Algerians. "Mama!"

Suddenly a shot rang out. Then another and another, until it sounded to Ophélie like the celebrations when the sky lit up with beautiful fire. But this was not a celebration. People were screaming and running. "Malika! Help me, Malika!" Ophélie stood terrified as the mass turned and fled down the same streets they had just come up.

Someone grabbed her arm and pulled her along. "Ophélie, you must run fast. It is not safe."

Ophélie looked up to see Malika beside her, eyes filled with terror. "Run, Ophélie. Come with me."

The night had erupted into a nightmare. Ophélie shivered and cried, remembering the times she had run with Mama when they lived in that other country that now wanted to be free.

Mama, you said we would be safe in France. But we aren't. You are gone. And now I must run. But Ophélie did not know what she was running from. Who was bad? And where could she hide?

Another burst of popping sounded out. Sharp, quick, like the beating of the drum before an important person appears. *But no important person is coming. We are running.* Suddenly, Malika screamed and then went limp, falling to the ground. Ophélie tripped over her body and fell beside her. Malika's eyes fluttered. "Run, Ophélie, do not stay with me," she moaned. "I am okay."

Ophélie touched Malika's head. It was wet. She looked at her fingers in the light of the lampposts on the Seine. A thick, dark liquid stained her small hand. Ophélie stood up and began to run, looking over her shoulder and screaming "Malika! Malika!" Other shots spat through the sky. Something sharp stung her leg and she fell again, screaming with pain.

"Help me! Mama! Malika! Someone help me. Mr. Gady. I must find you, Mr. Gady." She crawled on the wet pavement, dragging her left leg behind, until she sat in a cluster of bushes close to the large bridge they had just crossed.

She sat for a long time, sniffling back her fear as men in blue uniforms and tall hats picked up the bodies of the fallen and threw them into the river. The men in blue, they were good, she knew. They were police. But they were shooting and beating and throwing these people into the river. Only Ophélie's terror kept her from crying out. She waited and watched until the dark-skinned men with gleaming eyes and the men in blue uniforms with guns and sticks had left the bridge, screaming their angry words at each other in the dark.

* * *

It was nine-thirty and the sound of gunshots rang out as David walked toward the Prefecture. In the dark of the Pont St. Michel, he heard the screams of Algerians as the Paris police beat, kicked, and shot at the protestors. He hung in the shadows, sickened. Mr. Torrès would not show up tonight in this scene of slaughter. His plans were not the only ones to run awry.

Not again! David cried within. *More blood spilled.* In his mind, he was back in Paris, in 1941. *The blood of Jews.* He saw the Nazi guards standing before him, the shots, the blood. "Why did you think we would be safe, Mother!" He spoke out loud, and the sound of his voice startled him.

Tonight in Paris, it was the same hatred for another race that had spilled blood on the pavement of the bridge. And once again, no one came to their defense. Only the Seine, running swift and smooth, knew the count of those who were killed. Again and again, the *gendarmes* threw the lifeless bodies of beaten Algerians into the river and watched as they sank below her slow-moving current. And the sweet river, which had seen before the bitter birth of hatred, once again closed her sad eyes and was silent.

* * *

"Mama! Mama!" The screams of a young girl pierced the stillness of the bloody Paris night, and David could not ignore them.

"Where are you?" he whispered, running toward the left side of the Seine, even as the Paris police charged off in another direction.

"Here, please, *Monsieur,* help me."

David stooped to see the crumpled form of a sobbing young girl. Instinctively he picked her up, turning away from the bridge and the river, which groaned with her heavy secret. He ran until he reached the safety of a small square down the road from the Pont Neuf. He slipped down a side street that was now in complete darkness. Far away, other cries rang out, and gunshots echoed through the night. But here there were no police.

Carefully he placed the small girl on the sidewalk and bent close to inspect her wounds. Her breathing was shallow and forced, and her eyes glazed as she stared up at him, helpless.

"Mr. Gady? It is you?"

"I am a friend. Where is Mr. Gady?"

"Take me to Mr. Gady. He will help me," she rasped, frantic for breath.

"Do not worry. I won't leave you, little one." He removed his jacket and then his shirt, ripping it and tying it around the wound in her leg.

The child was murmuring incoherently. "He is near the big school, by the *beaux arts*. Such a pretty red-and-white awning. The little store . . . yes, Mama, I know. Rue de Beaux Arts . . . yes, I can get there from our house." Her eyes fluttered and she fainted.

David picked up her lithe form and held it close. "Don't die, little girl. Don't die! Not like Greta. This time I will help." His strides lengthened as the moon alone witnessed the tall American racing along the sidewalks of the Left Bank of Paris, in search of rue des Beaux Arts and a shop with a red-and-white awning.

* * *

David knew many cities of the world, but none better than Paris. He was not far from the Ecole des Beaux Arts. He hoped that this child did indeed live nearby. Moments later in the dark, a storefront with an awning of red and white came into view. By the streetlight, David read the word *Epicerie* across the top. As he approached the door, he stepped on broken glass. The windowpanes were gone. He did not need to ring the bell, for the wooden door stood ajar. Entering the darkness, he waited in the shadows for several minutes, but there was no noise. Nothing moved. Slowly he made his way toward the back of the shop and through the doorway that led up a flight of stairs. He walked into a small room where a mattress lay on the floor. A small desk and couch were the only pieces of furniture in the room. The desk had been overturned and every drawer emptied. The mattress and a pillow had been slit, and stuffing littered the floor.

David walked out of the room and into the hall. The door to the adjoining room stood ajar, and David walked in. There he halted abruptly.

"I am glad you cannot see this," he said to the unconscious child in his arms. An old man lay slumped on the floor with a bullet hole through his head.

* * *

Emile Torrès cursed himself as he crossed over the Seine on the Pont St. Michel. He had lost the girl and he had missed the informant. He knew the rules well enough. Whatever information this man had, he could not wait around to find out. The whole night had exploded into chaos. The child was gone. *She will return to the shop if she can,* he reasoned. He cursed again. But he had already searched there. The old shopkeeper had told him nothing. Terrified and shaking, he could only repeat, "The little girl did not have the bag. Her mama told me there would be a bag."

Emile had torn the place apart, but the old man was right. No bag. The night had been a failure. Only a ransacked apartment and a dead old man. But surely the child knew something. What a waste. Emile's head would roll, too, if Ali did not have the information. God forbid that the child lay at the bottom of the Seine with the Algerians.

He headed back toward the Left Bank and the little *épicerie*, where the waiting game would continue. And if he did not find the child, he knew his next step: an obituary in the paper and a changed name. He could start over. He had done it before.

* * *

David left the *épicerie* immediately. One thing was obvious: the child was in some type of danger. He carried her back through the black streets of Paris, covering her with his jacket. He arrived at his hotel around 11. Ignoring the puzzled look of the concierge, he carried the little girl up two flights of steps and unlocked the door.

Carefully he laid her on the bed. Removing his jacket and the ripped shirt, he inspected her leg. The bleeding had stopped. The bullet wound was clearly visible, having entered the child's left thigh, just above the knee. He saw another small hole on the other side of her leg and shook his head in relief. The bullet had gone straight through. Perhaps he could avoid the hospital. Elevating the leg, he washed the wound with warm water. From his small suitcase, he took out a white T-shirt. As he bent over the child to wrap her leg, her eyes fluttered open.

"Mr. Gady?" she whispered.

"Mr. Gady isn't here, little one. I found you by the bridge. You were hurt. What is your name?"

"Where is Mr. Gady?"

"I cannot take you to him tonight. It is not good for you to move, with this wound."

Tears welled in the child's eyes. "Mama! I want my mama."

"Of course you do," David softened his tone. "Where

is your mama? We will find her tomorrow." He looked at the child's fine features. *A beautiful child,* he thought. *Such striking features.* But he pushed away the memory.

"My mama is lost. The bad men took her away." Suddenly the little girl looked up at David with new fear in her eyes. "Are you bad? Do you want to kill me too?" she asked.

David smiled. "No, I am not one of them."

Relief spread across her face. "I am not trying to be mean, *Monsieur,* but ...it is just that I cannot tell who is good and who is bad anymore." She clutched the bedsheet in her small hand, wiping her eyes with a corner.

David patted her hand. "I do not know your mother or the bad men, but I will try to help you. Perhaps you can tell me where your father lives?"

The child wrinkled her brow and sniffed. "I do not have a father. It is only Mama and me. But now she is gone. You will have to ask Mr. Gady. Tomorrow ask him. He will tell you."

"Of course. Now try to sleep. What is your name, little one?"

"Ophélie."

"What is your last name?"

"My name is Ophélie. That is all." She closed her eyes, and David covered her with the bedspread. Soon she was asleep.

He sat wearily in the room's lone chair, wiping his hand over his brow. The night had been a fiasco. The riot, the missed contact, the police, the shootings. Now he was stuck with a little girl whose mother was gone, who had no father, and whose sole friend was an old man who lay dead in his apartment. As he relived the nightmare again, he heard the child's soft voice in his mind. *"It is just that I cannot tell who is good and who is bad anymore."*

140

"Neither can I, little Ophélie," he whispered to the sleeping girl. "Neither can I." He held his head in his hands for a long time. Finally he pulled his jacket around his shoulders and nodded off in the chair.

* * *

David carefully cleaned Ophélie's wound, applying the ointment and covering it with a bandage. The pharmacist had kindly explained exactly what to do. The leg had not become infected. This was a good sign. But the other signs were bad.

E. Torrès, whoever he had been, was no more. An obituary in this morning's paper had announced the fact, stating *cause of death unknown.* David scoffed at that. Of course, the papers would not reveal the truth. He did not know what had really happened to Mr. Torrès, and he was sure he would never find out. A wasted trip to Paris.

David watched the sullen, small girl as he taped her bandage in place. The child refused to talk. David was only *Monsieur* to her, and this he preferred. Yet he could not simply abandon her in the streets of Paris.

"I will have to take you to the police," he said, exasperated. "They will find your mother for you."

Ophélie burst into tears. "No! No! Please, *Monsieur.* Not the police. They will kill me. They have already tried. Only Mr. Gady. He is the only one."

"Mr. Gady is dead." David said it flatly, tired, forgetting whom he was talking to.

Ophélie stared at him with wide eyes, brimming again with tears. "He is dead? No. It can't be. How do you know?"

"I found him in his apartment. He . . . he was shot." David held her hands. "Little Ophélie, I am so sorry to tell you this. But you must understand. I do not know

how to help you. I do not live here in Paris. Already
you have been in this room for two days. Tomorrow I
must leave to go home. What will I do with you then?"
He was sure she did not understand.

He tried again. "Listen, do you know why bad people would take your mother and kill Mr. Gady? Think
hard. Do you know?"

Ophélie turned her eyes away. She shook her head.
"No, I do not know. I only know that I am scared."
Suddenly she grabbed his hand. "Take me with you,
Monsieur. Please take me with you. I am afraid to
stay here."

He shook his head, bewildered. "Ophélie, I can't
just take you with me. I can't keep a little kid." He
sighed and thought of Gabriella. She would know how
to talk to this child. He was getting nowhere at all, and
he had a train to catch in twelve hours.

"Gabriella," he whispered. An idea came to him,
and he smiled. "No, I couldn't . . ." He watched the
pretty child with the long brown hair and the dark eyes
that held so much fear.

"Maybe," he said.

"What?" Ophélie asked, hopeful.

"Nothing, little Ophélie. Just thinking out loud. Let
me think for a moment."

After a while he smiled down at the child on the
bed. "Don't you worry, now. Everything is going to be
all right. You will see."

Chapter Thirteen

Gabriella pulled a lightweight V-neck sweater over her white starched blouse. She looked at her reflection in the small mirror above the sink in the corner of her room. This morning she liked what she saw. The pale blue cashmere sweater brought out the blue of her eyes against her creamy white skin. She patted a little blush across her freckled cheekbones and began to brush her thick hair.

The sky outside was a bright cobalt blue. It seemed to Gabriella the perfect weather for a day in Aix with David. She wanted to look mature and beautiful. She wanted him to stare at her and smile and approve. Especially when she met his *friend*.

Even as she readied herself for the outing, a nagging voice played in the back of her mind. *Don't go*, it warned. She pushed the thought away as she tied back her hair with a soft blue ribbon that matched her sweater. *I really look like a debutante now*, she laughed to herself, remembering Caroline's enthusiasm when Gabriella had asked if she might borrow one of her sweaters.

She must have tried on seven of them, all cashmere, before Caroline had announced, "The blue one is perfect, Gabriella. You look smashing. He'll be all over you." She had eyed Gabriella slyly and then changed the subject. "I have a ribbon that matches, for your hair. You know, you really should wear it in a French braid. It would look great."

But Gabriella had decided against the braid. Too many changes at once would have David mocking instead of admiring her, she was sure.

She stood back from the mirror and on her tiptoes, but she could not see past her waist. Climbing onto the bed, she stood up and looked toward the mirror again, this time catching the reflection of her lower half. The sweater fit nicely, enhancing her curves. It gave new life to her plain navy skirt. She felt thin and graceful and feminine. She could not recall feeling this way before. She could not even remember caring. But today she cared.

Now she heard the voice of Mother Griolet in her mind. *His interest in you is perhaps not merely sentimental. . . . God gives strength to do what we cannot do on our own. But Gabriella, you must let Him do it. Even if it breaks your heart.*

She was suddenly mad at herself for having confided her love for David to Mother Griolet. "You always talk too much," she chided herself.

Gabriella sat back on the bed and reached for the Bible, but could not bring herself to read it. She did not want any advice today. The sunlight seeped in through the windows, and her thoughts returned to David. The clock by the bed showed the time at eight-thirty. He would be here soon. "I'm twenty-one, and I deserve to have fun," she said in a whisper, arguing with her subconscious. No one answered. Gabriella glanced in the

144

mirror again and then left the room. The Bible lay unopened on the table beside the bed.

* * *

David's *deux chevaux* was quite unreliable for trips longer than fifty kilometers, he had explained to Gabriella as he bought them round-trip train tickets to Aix. Seated together on the two-hour trip, Gabriella had noticed that his eyes were both surprised and approving as they talked.

"You look lovely, Gabriella. Absolutely radiant."

At once, Gabriella felt embarrassed and offered an excuse. "Well, it was Caroline who loaned me the sweater. I mean . . . I don't have anything cashmere; it's so expensive." She could feel the heat mounting in her cheeks.

"Cashmere or not, you are lovely." He touched her hand and gently pulled it to rest on his leg, stroking her fingers as he talked.

"You will love Aix, Gabby. It has the reputation of being one of the most elegant of all French cities, with its twenty-one splashing fountains and its thermal waters, which people have flocked to for their *cure* for two thousand years.

"The old part of town is quintessential charming. And of course, we'll visit Cezanne's studio. He lived and died at a little house in the city. But he would go to his studio outside Aix every day to paint."

"I feel as though I already know this region, from all the slides you've shown us of his work."

"Yes, it is a moment of bliss to discover the city and the surrounding areas after having seen it through Cezanne's eyes. He caught it all. The whitish blue of the mountains, the green shrubbery of Provence, the sun-bathed houses with their red-tiled hats."

He took her arm in his as the train pulled into the

station, and they stepped out onto the platform. As they walked into the sunlight, a gust of wind slapped against their faces.

"Yes, Mr. Mistral is here, too." He pulled her close as she shivered and fumbled to button her dark blue pea jacket.

They walked briskly through the small streets to the center of town. Gabriella relaxed with his strong arm around her. She almost dared not breathe, so intensely did she wish for this moment to last forever.

David seemed not to notice as he excitedly pointed out a historical landmark, a bubbling fountain, and the elegant seventeenth-century facades on the *hôtels* of the city.

"I'm not walking too fast for you, am I?" he questioned suddenly. "How is your ankle holding up?"

"Fine. It's fine." She wanted to add *as long as you keep your arm around me.*

"We'll drop off our bags at my friend's house. It's right off the Place de la Liberation."

For a moment, Gabriella tensed up. She had no desire to meet his friend.

They walked toward a huge three-tiered fountain flanked by bright flowers. A round point encircled the fountain, with cars dodging in and out and careening to take one of the four side roads that turned off the Place like spokes on an enormous wheel.

"She's right down here on Boulevard de la Republique." The road was wide and stately, and David strode confidently past the shops on the left side of the street. "She lives above the *pâtisserie,* on the third floor."

He stopped in front of a heavy door and pressed the buzzer with the name *de Saléon* written beside it.

"You ring twice, pausing in between. That's our signal." He laughed, not noticing Gabriella's suddenly sour expression.

Immediately a window three floors up flew open, and a woman's head appeared. *"David!"* she squealed in French. *"Quel plaisir! Allez! Montez."*

Gabriella squinted in the sun to see the woman's face, but she could not distinguish anything about her.

A loud buzzer sounded, and David pulled the door open, motioning to Gabriella to enter first. "The button is on the left, just there." He pointed to the shining orange button that Gabriella knew to be part of every French stairwell.

They climbed the marble winding staircase slowly. David, always the teacher, told her of its noble eighteenth-century origins. As they reached the third floor, a door opened and a smiling woman of about fifty-five bustled out to greet them. Her auburn hair, pulled back in an elegant chignon, was flecked slightly with gray. Her gray eyes sparkled, and she was dressed in a sophisticated green tweed suit, the perfect fashion of the day.

"Madeleine, so good to see you!" David set down the bags and warmly embraced her with kisses on each cheek. "Let me introduce you to a friend of mine. Gabriella Madison."

"Enchanté, Mademoiselle Gabriella. My, but you always pick the pretty ones," she laughed and winked at David.

Gabriella's face showed every sign of relief as she beamed back at the attractive woman. *"Enchanté, aussi."* Was she ever pleased to meet her. So there was no lovely young mistress after all.

"Well, do come in. I'll show you to your rooms. I'm sure you're anxious to be out and about Aix, but you will have a drink? Something light? The trip was easy, *non?* And the change of trains in Marseilles? No problem?" She threw up her hands and touched her hair, "But of course, with David there is never any problem. Such a fine young man. And *trés beau, n'est-ce pas?*" She leaned toward Gabriella, who nodded, blushing.

They sat in her *salon* for a few minutes drinking a *sirop*. "She speaks such beautiful French, David," Mme. de Saleon commented. Then directing her gaze at Gabriella, asked, "Where did you study?"

"I grew up in Senegal. My schooling was in French."

Mme. de Saleon nodded and talked on, making pleasant conversation. Ten minutes later she shooed them out of the apartment. "To the Cour Mirabeau, you two. David will tell you all about it. Now on with you. I'll expect you for supper at seven-thirty."

* * *

By eleven-thirty the biting chill of the Mistral had calmed, and the sun began to warm up the Cours Mirabeau. David directed Gabriella to a chair at one of the outdoor *cafés* on the north side of the wide, straight boulevard, lined by four rows of magnificent old plane trees. The trees on either side of the avenue stretched their limbs toward the center, forming a type of rustling canopy above the street and the pedestrians.

"This road is named for the eloquent general who sowed enough discord in the *Etats généraux* in 1789 to bring about the French Revolution."

Gabriella eyed him suspiciously. "Mirabeau caused the Revolution? Come on, David. That sounds rather simplistic. There were a number of reasons."

"Yes, you are right. But he had a powerful influence. Anyway, he lived here in Aix, and was elected as their deputy in the *Etats généraux*. Good old General Mirabeau. But I'll leave his story to Mr. Vidal to recount.

"And down there, at the end of the road, is the statue of *le bon roi René*. He was the exiled king of Naples, who lived and reigned in Aix as Count of Provence from 1442 until 1482. The statue holds in its hands the famous muscat grapes. René is the one who originally thought of harvesting them into the well-known *aperitif*. You should try it. Quite sweet and pleasant, if you don't drink too much."

"I shall try some then. Later. At Mme. de Saleon's."

"After lunch I'll take you to the spot where Cezanne painted many of his finest works. You'll be surprised," David said.

"A view of Mt. St. Victoire, right?"

"How did you know?"

"I've been reading my art books to keep up with my distinguished professor."

David laughed, a hearty carefree laugh that she had not heard before. Leaning closer, he whispered, "And what may your distinguished professor offer his most illustrious pupil?"

For a moment Gabriella thought she would reach out and touch his face with her hand. He caught her look and held her gaze with his eyes, then he reached his hand across the table and interlocked his fingers in hers.

"I'll have the usual," she whispered, afraid to look away, afraid that a simple blowing of the wind would destroy the magic of Aix on the Cour Mirabeau.

Their drinks consumed, they sat for a moment in silence. Then David stood up abruptly and said, "It's time to eat."

As if on cue, she was standing too, as he fumbled for the francs and let them jangle on the table.

"I know. I'll get the bread." She laughed to think of how he was so adamant that she try every different type of bread and cheese France offered. Turning to look back at him, she said, "I remember: only *pain de seigle* for us today."

"Hurry on with you, girl," he waved to her smiling. "They close in five minutes."

Along the cobblestoned streets of the *vielle ville* she walked until she reached the *boulangerie* that David had indicated earlier. The best *pain de seigle* in town, he assured her. As she entered, a short, dark-haired man standing behind the counter greeted her cautiously. *"Bonjour, Mademoiselle."*

"Bonjour. A pain de seigle, please." He turned quickly to retrieve the loaf, but Gabby stopped him.

"Oh, no. Wait a minute. I think I'd rather have the *pain de campagne.* It looks delicious."

"You are sure, Mademoiselle?" he questioned, replacing the other loaf.

"Yes, sure." She was pleased with the thought of surprising David and immediately prepared her excuse. *But David, we haven't tried this kind either. I've heard it is very nutritious.*

She placed five francs on the counter as the plump man wrapped a piece of thin tissue around the brown loaf and taped it in place. He then handed her the forty *centimes* of change.

"Au revoir, Mademoiselle."

"Bonne journée," she replied and trotted down the cobblestones and back to the Cour Mirabeau where David waited with the straw bag Mme. de Saleon had filled with rice salad, *pâté,* cheeses, and wine.

"Where shall we eat, David?"

"How about by the Fontaine des Quatre Dauphins? There are a few *hôtels* on the road that I'd like you to see."

"Sounds perfect to me."

She followed him across the boulevard and onto one of the streets behind the Cours. Sitting down beside a fountain of four dolphins, Gabriella began talking,

"You know, David, I never realized that Cezanne was a contemporary of Gaugin—they lived together and were good friends." Her chatter was interrupted by David's harsh demand.

"Gabriella? What have you done? This isn't *pain de seigle!* Why didn't you get the *pain de seigle* as I told you?" He grabbed her arm and clutched it almost fiercely, so that Gabriella gave a quick jerk back.

"For goodness' sake, David, you're hurting me! What is the matter? What could possibly be the difference in a loaf of bread? Don't look at me that way. I only thought it might be fun to try something different."

Immediately David relaxed his grip. "Of course, you are right. Excuse me, Gabby." He composed himself and said softly, "Look, I know it sounds nuts, but I'd really like the *pain de seigle.* Could you please run back and get me a loaf?"

"But they'll be closed, David."

"Maybe not. Go."

He sounded urgent and firm, and she did not hesitate. Back across the Cours Mirabeau and up the cobblestoned road she ran, feeling like a rebuked child. *He is impossible, demanding, cruel,* she thought. Somewhere in her mind she heard again a piercing reminder: *Don't go!* Once again she wanted to push the voice away, but it kept chanting in her mind until she felt cold fear run down her back. *Something is wrong here, Gabby. Something is wrong with this dashing young American. Get away!* But she continued on.

As she reached the store, the little shopkeeper was just pulling down the corrugated siding and locking the door.

"*Monsieur!*" Gabby cried loudly. "Wait! Could I please have a *pain de seigle?*" She slowed to a walk, out of breath.

He seemed to pay no attention, not even looking at her, but quietly he muttered, "How dare you come back? It is not safe. You must leave now! Tell your friend the neighbor's bread is better. Now leave!"

Bewildered, she turned to go. What did he mean? Why was he suddenly so angry, just as David had been? And then the chanting words: *Something is wrong. Get away!*

Gabriella had never had a vision from heaven, but she believed God communicated in an inaudible but real voice to His chosen people. And she knew it was this voice she was hearing. *But where do I go, Lord?* The sounds of the open market and pedestrians' feet on the cobblestones suddenly seemed magnified, and she realized her heart was racing.

Then David was there, walking toward her with a look of fear on his usually inscrutable face. He did not slow down as he passed her. He whispered, "Leave Aix, Gabby. I do not know you. Take the train. Go home."

That was all, but his tone conveyed an urgency that struck new fear in her heart. Quickly she began brushing past the vendors in the *marché*, slipping beside the man selling cheese as he cried after her, "*Mademoiselle,* come try the St. Paulin!"

She limped past the butcher with the dead chickens hanging upside down from the awning above his table. She grazed the table displaying an array of pigs' hooves and weaved wildly between the fruit and vegetable stands, hearing again and again, "*Mademoiselle!*" She never looked back, but she could feel the eyes of someone, unknown and unnoticed by the busy scene at the *marché*. Someone was following and the knowledge of that had shattered David's cynical, confident air.

"The train station," she panted as she reached the Place de la Liberation. "Five more minutes and I will be there." Gabriella did not look back to see a handsome man with hazel eyes and thick brown hair deftly stepping around the vendors in the market, following the bright flash of red hair far in front of him.

* * *

David continued walking away from Gabriella, but as he turned down a small side street, he paused to watch the beautiful American with the wild red hair twisting in and out through the market. Farther behind, a man followed in her steps.

David groaned, "It is hopeless. She stands out like the first red poppy in a field of sunflowers. He will find her. And she will not know what to tell him, and then..."

He shook his head angrily. *What have I done?* he thought. *I've brought an angel into the devil's world.*

Gabby the innocent scapegoat. It would be so easy to let her carry it, and he could go free. But David Hoffmann could not. The hatred and bitterness and revenge were pushed aside in his mind as he ran down the side street and mingled in the crowd of the *marché*, far behind the fiery blaze of Gabriella's hair and the dark-haired man who followed silently behind her like a long shadow in the afternoon sun.

* * *

Jean-Claude Gachon knew the red-haired girl was scared. With his small pocket camera, he clicked several pictures of her limping through the street.

"You think you can get away so easily? Hop a train, and I will leave you alone?" He jogged on behind her. "The train will not leave for thirty minutes, and that is plenty of time for another small accident. Or perhaps you will be more helpful this time. I know more than you think."

He paused at the corner of the road by the post office, watching the young woman continue her frantic flight to the train station. He heard a slight noise behind him and turned to see a bottle of wine lifted above his head. Too late he raised his arms to protect himself. The bottle crashed down, and the glass shattered on his head, spraying the dark red liquid down over his face so that it mingled with his own blood. He sank to the ground and lay there motionless.

* * *

The train ride from Aix was without incident. Gabriella got off the train in Montpellier and walked along the Place de la Comedie all afternoon, embarrassed to return to Mme. Leclerc's and Stephanie and Caroline's inquisitive stares.

When she went back to the apartment, it was dark. The girls had gone out for the evening, and Mme. Leclerc discreetly prepared her a bowl of soup, asking no questions. Every time the phone rang, Gabriella started, hoping it was David. Surely he would check on her. But David did not call.

The night seemed like an endless dark tunnel to Gabriella, offering no sleep, no soft bed of thoughts, but only a hovering fear and a heavy heartache.

Again and again she rehashed the events of the day. The enchantment of the train ride with David and their walk through Aix, her relief at meeting Mme. de Saleon, the pure pleasure of sitting with David on the Cours Mirabeau.

Then the stupid mistake with the bread. The bread! Something had been terribly wrong in Aix, and she was sure that it concerned more than a misplaced *pain de seigle*.

Then the terrifying wait in the train station, wondering who would appear to snatch her away like a quick burst from the Mistral. But no one had come.

She thought of that subconscious warning that had haunted her on and off all day. "I should have listened to Mother Griolet . . . to You, Lord." She twisted and turned throughout the night.

Heavily she picked herself up off her bed, surprised to see a glimmer of sun streaking through the tiny gap in the closed shutters. Her head throbbing, she slowly pulled on her skirt and a warm wool sweater. The blue cashmere lay in a heap on the chair, reminding her of the way her day had ended.

It was past nine, and Gabriella realized that she must have finally fallen asleep near dawn. Sunday morning. The whole weekend spoiled. Immediately she decided to go help Mother Griolet with the orphans at the church.

"Perhaps it is better this way. I won't think about yesterday. . ."

She leafed through her Bible to the Gospel of John, chapter 15. "I am the Vine, ye are the branches; he that abideth in Me, and I in him, the same bringeth forth much fruit, for without Me, ye can do nothing."

She closed the Bible and sat for a moment with her eyes closed. "Nothing, Lord. You are right. So please come along with me today."

* * *

Gabriella found Mother Griolet sitting in the hollow echoes of the church alone.

"*Ah, ma fille. Bonjour!* I was not expecting you." She reached up to kiss her softly on each cheek. Then she held her face away and stared into Gabriella's eyes. "You are not well today, my vivacious redhead. Look how swollen are your pretty eyes!"

"Homesick, that's all. It is nothing. It will pass. Give

me work to do and it will pass."

"Ah, and work I have today, Gabriella. A new child has arrived from out of the blue, as you Americans say. Her mother is missing, presumed dead. No father. She is terrified and grieving . . . I am sure of it. But that is not what you will see on her face. I cannot make her talk, so it is best that she grieves in her way.

"But perhaps you could take her to the beach for a walk. I'm sure she will like you. I'll handle the others this morning with Sister Isabelle and Sister Rosaline."

Mother Griolet rose from the bench, her long black robes silently sweeping the church's stone floor. Gabriella followed behind, wiping a tear with her sleeve and turning to focus on a new challenge.

As the old woman opened the peeling wooden door to the parsonage, she turned back and whispered, "Her name is Ophélie."

* * *

The child had said nothing since the moment they met. Gabriella felt a slight uneasiness. "Here we are at the beach at Carnon. This is where we get off." She stepped down from the bus and held out her hand for Ophélie, who descended without taking it.

They made their way off the road and down through a path leading to the beach. The rich scent of wild thyme reached out from the dunes that rose up as if protecting the beach from the noise of the road.

"I like to come here by myself, just to think." Gabriella offered, but Ophélie did not turn her head up to look or listen. They walked in the quiet of the late morning, the chilly sea wind stinging their ears. The beach was deserted. Ophélie's long, sleek brown hair flew in wild wisps behind her, pulled by the wind. Her coat was unzipped and her nose red with cold, but she said nothing.

"Would you like to go back? Are you too cold?" A definite shake of the head was Ophélie's only response. A seagull swooped down in front and cried mockingly out to other invisible birds who would soon appear on the horizon. The froth of the sea settled dangerously close to their feet. Gabriella moved away from the approaching tide, but Ophélie continued walking straight in the same direction.

"Do you mind if we sit for a moment on those rocks over there, Ophélie? I am going to tie my hair back. It is such a mess in this wind." Without waiting for what she knew would be silence, Gabriella walked up the beach and sat down on a cluster of smooth rocks that were embedded far away from the reach of the tide. Ophélie followed.

Gabriella quickly untied the bright blue handkerchief from around her neck, placing it between her teeth as she gathered her mass of hair into a single thick strand. As she tied the hair into place, pulling wisps out from under her collar, the lightweight chain and cross came out from under her shirt and settled on her chest, shimmering in the sun, like a child blinking in the morning light.

"There. That is much better. It drives me mad to have my mane dancing about in every direction. I should have pulled it back before we came, but I didn't think of it at all."

Gabriella babbled on, making conversation over nothing, but Ophélie did not seem to hear her. The child's gaze was held by the shimmering cross that hung lightly around Gabriella's neck.

Slowly Ophélie reached behind her neck and unfastened a chain, then with both hands brought the chain in front of her and placed it in the folds of her skirt.

She fingered it delicately, with a soft, tender passion.

A moment later she turned a tear-streaked face toward Gabriella, with a hopeful smile on her thin lips. The woman and the child stared for a long while at the two crosses.

As a knowing look came to Ophélie's eyes, she whispered with choked emotion, "It was my mama's cross. A gift from her papa before he was killed in the war." Her gaze was fixed on the golden treasure in her hands. Then again she straightened and looked at Gabriella, full in the face. "I am not an orphan. I don't believe Mama is dead. She is missing. But she has been missing before."

Gabriella gently took Ophélie's hand in hers and fingered the cross. "And now your mother has given it to you. It is a beautiful cross, isn't it?"

"It is hope for Mama."

"Yes, it is hope. Does your mother believe in the God of this cross?"

A shadow crept across Ophélie's face. "I do not think so. But my grandfather did. Mama said he used to sing me songs about God when I was a baby. But then he died. Mama tried to sing the songs, I think, but she would always cry. Poor Mama. She was always so sad. She didn't think I saw."

"She was sad because of her father?" Gabriella pressed cautiously for more information.

"Yes . . . and because of the bad men. There were bad men who came for her."

"Why would bad men come after your mother, Ophélie?"

Ophélie did not meet Gabriella's eyes with her own, but lowered her head further so that her hair hung limply over her face. Her voice was almost inaudible. "She is not bad. My mother is not bad!" This she said passionately. And then slowly, "But people might think she was bad because of those men. They were not nice to her."

Ophélie lifted her face toward Gabriella. Her eyes were liquid and dark and filled with a hurt too deep for a child so young.

Gabriella pulled Ophélie closer, enfolding her in her arms. "Of course she is not bad. She must be a very wonderful mother indeed to have a little girl like you."

She kissed the child softly on the forehead and held her for what seemed a long time. In her mind she had a flash of another little girl whose mother was not bad. And farther out, the peaceful Mediterranean watched the wordless embrace of the young woman and the child, and the sun danced its rays through the mingled strands of red and brown hair and dried the unseen tears that they shared.

Chapter Fourteen

Jean-Claude Gachon nursed the large bump on the top of his head with a pack of ice. The headache was still there this morning, but not as fierce as yesterday. He wished the children in the streets below would not make such a racket, nor the baby upstairs that cried at two A.M. He noticed more with this headache. But these were the slums of Marseilles, and he had not come here in search of luxury. This apartment fit his needs well on most occasions. He cursed as he thought of the wine bottle crashing on his head.

He held a roll of film in his hands and slid it into a thick envelope, mumbling to himself, "Your information was right, Ali. Something was going on in Aix on October twenty-first. Something with the redhead." He laughed cynically.

But she wasn't alone. Now I've got a lump the size of an orange on my head, and this is all I have for you, right now. There are some good slides, I assure you. And do not worry. It is only a quick train ride from Marseilles to Montpellier. I will find the redhead again.

I have good eyes. And I will find out the next time she goes on a little trip. It is a simple matter of knowing the right place to wait. There are not so many choices.

He licked the flap of the envelope and sealed it tightly, still holding the pack of ice to his head.

* * *

Yvette Leclerc shook her head as she sat at Monique Pons' kitchen table, her morning purchases from the marché at her feet.

"It is such a pity, Monique. She was just devastated. Couldn't say a word. Would not even look at me with her sad blue eyes. The whole weekend a total disaster. I just have no idea what could have happened."

"Yes, it is a dreadful shame. He was quiet when he came in Sunday night. I was already in bed. I can't tell you what the hour was. Imagine that poor young woman coming home early from her weekend away!"

Mme. Leclerc leaned closer to her friend, almost knocking over the cup of coffee. "I hate to say it, but I was a bit shocked to think that *she* would go away with him for the weekend! Young girls these days. *Ooh, la la!* Still, I am sorry for her."

"Well, life goes on," stated Mme. Pons matter-of-factly. "I'm sure she will get over it, that Gabriella."

Yes, the two women were sure that their boarders would be fine. But what of their plans for this blooming romance? *That* was the shame. The two friends would simply have to find another interesting tidbit of news to share for their coffee break tomorrow.

* * *

David caught Gabriella's arm as she was leaving class on Monday morning. "May I have a word with you, Miss Madison?" He waited for the other women to

161

leave and then escorted her downstairs and through
Mother Griolet's apartment to the steps that led outside
to the courtyard.

"You are all right? You made it home without trouble? I have your things. I am sorry."

Gabriella was too angry to hear his excuse. "You are
sorry, David. But not for me. You are sorry that I
botched your plans. I do not know what they were, but I
got in the way. You could at least have the decency to
tell me what you are dragging me into."

David did not flinch. "Yes, you are right. It won't
happen again."

"And that is all you have to say to me? You put my
life in danger, and that is all you will say?" She stopped
for a moment and looked away, brushing her long hair
over her shoulders. The late October chill made her
shiver as she watched the last leaves clinging to the
branches of an old gnarled plane tree.

"You won't tell me, will you, what you are up to?
You are not just a professor for the program. You pretend not to tell me for my safety. But it is not that. It is
something else."

He said nothing, so Gabriella continued. She never
had been able to keep her thoughts to herself. "Is it
the war?" she blurted out. "Are you involved in the
Algerian war?"

David laughed and sat down on the steps, motioning
her to do the same. "And what would I, an American,
have to do with the war over there?" He nodded his
head in the direction of the sea.

"I don't know. You tell me."

He leaned toward her, his eyes taunting. "Do you
really want to know?"

"Yes, of course." She squirmed in her place, suddenly ill at ease, as if he were about to reveal a secret that

162

she had no business knowing.

"Revenge," he replied.

"Revenge? Revenge for what?"

"Revenge for a helpless little boy who watched his mother and sister die. Revenge for a Jew."

He whispered with a vengeance that scared her, "This war is about minorities. Algerians who feel oppressed by the French. *Pied-noirs* who want to keep their land and possessions. *Harkis* who are faithful to France. They are all pitiful minorities.

"So I was too, in the other war. My people were killed because of our heritage. I was in a camp for a year. And I was the only child to survive. The only one."

He turned to Gabriella, but she was sure he was not seeing her. "Yes, I survived, but I died doing it. You cannot know! You have no right to know!" He stood up abruptly and walked away, then stopped.

Gabriella felt pity for him, but she was too proud to say it. "And so now you take out your hatred on others? Is that it? You are such an angry man, David Hoffmann."

"I deserve to be angry, woman! What right do you have to accuse me, you who lived in the shelter of your mother's skirts? Do not judge me in your pious way!" He cursed as he turned back and sat down beside her.

Gabriella said nothing for a moment. Then she spoke, reaching for her words, as the sun glimmered through the near-leafless plane tree and a simple breeze chased several tenacious leaves to the ground.

"You think you are the only one in the world who has suffered? You think that because I call myself a Christian, life has been easy for me and my family? You think we are immune to pain? That nothing touches us? If this is what you think, then you are wrong."

She looked away from him suddenly, her eyes wet with tears. "I have two younger sisters, but at one time there were three. Ericka was only six. I was twelve. She became terribly ill, and Father was away in the bush. Mother had some medicine with her, but as the fever rose and Ericka became delirious, Mother knew she must get her to a hospital where there was penicillin.

"We had no car, no means of transportation. We had been in this village for two years, living among the people, but they still seemed hostile and removed. Mother was frantic. Even though she always seemed calm, I knew. She radioed to the closest mission station, two hundred miles away, but it would be three days before they could get to us. And so she prayed. For two days and nights she didn't sleep. She bathed Ericka and put compresses on her, but my sister only grew weaker.

"And then I saw her dying. Her skin turned yellowish, and bluish, and she coughed up blood. And then she was gone. Mother sat beside her cold body for another day. She spent all her tears there.

"Then she put on her black shawl and the other traditional mourning clothes of the Senegalese people. She opened her home and received the women of the village. They embraced her and wailed and held her. For suddenly she was like them, in her grief.

"We buried Ericka, Mother and I, with the tribespeople looking on. And when Father returned five days later, it was all over."

David touched her sleeve, as if to touch the pain, but Gabriella's head remained bent, oblivious to his gesture.

"And how did you get through your pain?" he asked.

"I cried a lot. I cried in my bed every night, and I yelled at God. I thought I would never get over the searing pain. But the pain went, and then there was something even worse. It was hate."

She brushed her eyes and continued, "I was mad. Mad at anyone whom I could blame. Mad at Daddy for being away. Mad at the mission for not coming quickly enough. Mad at God for letting her die. He could have stopped it!" The pitch in her voice relived the emotion of the past hurt. "Yes, I was even mad at myself for standing by and not being able to do anything. I could do nothing but watch Ericka die."

David nodded, as if he understood the feeling of helplessness. "And are you still mad?"

Gabriella thought for a moment. "No, I am not mad. Mother watched me grieve, and she told me and my sisters that it was okay to be mad. I could read in her eyes that she felt anger too. So senseless! In America she would have had the penicillin!

"But little by little, she said, we must forgive. Forgive those who didn't help, forgive ourselves. Forgive God. I will never forget it. She told me that anger is a wound that festers and rots and turns to bitterness unless we let it go. Unless we forgive."

Gabriella looked up at David. "She said forgiveness is freedom. It is letting go. It is not so much for those I'm angry at, as for myself. If I don't forgive, I will live forever with the hatred until it destroys me."

"And so you forgave and everything was fine?" His voice held sarcasm.

She was suddenly afraid of his question, of her vulnerability. "It wasn't easy."

"You are wrong, Gabriella. You and your mother are wrong. Forgiveness is weakness. It is not power or strength. It is kneeling before the enemy and forgetting. I do not want to forget. The memory of their wrong spurs me on! It fuels me to live! Forgiveness is to relinquish, and David Hoffmann will never give up. I will win my private wars, Gabby. You cannot stop me, and neither can anyone else."

The doors from the basement of the parsonage flew

open, and twenty-five vivacious children spilled out
into the courtyard. Gabriella got quickly to her feet,
waving to the children.

"I must go," she said to him. "Good-bye, David."
As she pronounced those words, she felt the distance of
an ocean between them, and she rushed away, chilled
by his icy stare and the whipping Mistral.

* * *

Ophélie sat on a lower bunk in the dormitory. *"Un,
deux, trois, quatre. . . ."* Slowly she counted the bunk
beds in the room. There were eight of them. That made
sixteen beds. Most of them had little girls sleeping in
them at night. And now this bed belonged to her. The
old nun that everyone called Mother Griolet had said so.

The first night she had barely slept at all. She had
awakened three times screaming "Mama!" with the
sound of gunshots in her ears. Sister Isabelle had come
rushing in. The second day had been different. The
woman with the long red hair had taken her to the
beach. And she wore Papy's cross. Ophélie smiled to
think of it. She was a pretty woman, and she smiled a
lot. And she had understood that Mama was not bad.

For the first time in as long as she could remember,
Ophélie felt safe. The tall man who had rescued her
had disappeared the moment the train had stopped in
this town. But everyone else had been friendly.
Friendly with a sad, pitiful look in their eyes.

But it did not matter. The red-haired woman named
Gabriella wore the cross and told her that her mama
was a wonderful woman to have such a good girl.

She hugged her knees to her chest and smiled again.
She heard the sound of the other children's voices
laughing in the courtyard, and again she felt safe. She
did not know where she was. But it was a good place to

166

be, she was sure. A place where adults were kind and children laughed.

And best of all, there was school! Today she had gone to the classroom. Today she had gone to school!

She recalled the old lady's words when she had whispered that she did not know how to read. *"Ah, Ophélie! Reading! It is a gift. You are a bright child. We will have you reading in no time at all!"*

Ophélie took the blue bag out from under her pillow. She could not leave it there because the Sisters changed the sheets every week. This was important for cleanliness, Mother Griolet had explained. No, they might take off the pillowcase and find the bag.

But now she had a little chest of drawers all to herself. It sat at the head of her bed. When she had opened the drawers the first day, she had not believed what she saw. Clothes! Two long-sleeved white blouses, two black wool skirts, and a bright pink sweater in the first drawer. And more treasures in the second: five pairs of white underwear. On one pair there was even lace! And two pairs of tights. The warm wool kind. A robe and a warm flannel nightgown and slippers. They were all there. A miracle.

She liked looking in the bottom drawer the best. There was a pink plastic brush and comb. All her own! And two sets of pink barrettes for her hair. But the last treasure she found had made her cry with delight. A doll. A doll with black hair that reached to her waist and fancy little eyes that opened and closed when she was rocked. And a pretty blue dress.

The old nun had explained that the clothes were not new, nor the brush and comb nor the doll. Kind people gave these things to the orphanage. But Ophélie did not care. These were her treasures! Hers!

It is a miracle, Mama! I have a doll of my own. And lots of little girls to play with. And Mama, very soon I will know how to read.

Ophélie pulled the pair of blue tights out of the second drawer. Carefully she slid the blue bag down into one of the legs. Then she placed the tights back in their place, beside the white ones and the frilly panties.

I will be safe here, Mama. I will stay right here until you come to get me. Don't worry, Mama.

* * *

Mother Griolet watched the children playing in the courtyard from her chair behind the old mahogany desk. Through the closed windows, the muffled noise of their laughter rose like a faint melody, reaching into her office. Little Ophélie stepped out from the dormitory into the sunlight. She stood on the edge of the grass, hesitating before she ran out to join the other children.

"This little one is a mystery to me, Lord. Oh, I know You know her well. She is one of Your precious sparrows. But I do not know. And, Lord, You understand that there are certain papers I must have. Certain regulations for the orphanage."

She leaned back in her chair, chuckling to herself. "Why is it, Lord, that I get the feeling You are testing me again? Do You like these verbal wrestling matches with such an old lady?" She shook her head and peered down on the children.

"Yes, I know. They are warm. They are fed. They are happy. You have always provided."

Hakim stood off alone, leaning against the far wall of the courtyard. He was taller than the other children, his skin darker. "This one too, Lord. He is here now. I am counting on You for the next step. I am perhaps a bit rusty in my old age, *non?* So please speak clearly. I will wait. That is one thing You have taught me over the years. Your timing is best."

She reached down, pulled out the bottom desk drawer, and lifted out the faded photograph of Rebecca Madison standing beside her, with all the children. "And one more thing, Lord. Darling Gabriella. You know she wears her mother's cross. You saw it long before I did. It is only that I find it a bit ironic, don't You? And confusing? This too I am sure You can handle. Nothing is too difficult for You. You see all; the past, the present, the future. Please prepare me for the next step. That is all I care to know. The next step with You."

Settling back in the big chair, she held the old photograph in her hands for another minute. Then she closed her eyes and began a soft chant that flowed from her lips with the ease of years of repetition. Yet the emotion in her voice testified to her assurance as she prayed, *"Now unto Him that is able to do exceeding abundantly above all that we ask or think, according to the power that worketh in us. Unto Him be glory in the church by Christ Jesus throughout all ages, world without end. Amen."*

* * *

Rachid waited until the middle of the night to trace his way through the maze of streets in the Casbah. At last, he could make the lovely *pied-noir* talk. He had such an effective way with women!

Ali was angry now. He wanted the information. Emile had let the girl get away, and Ali's fury was raging. The girl had disappeared. Emile had disappeared too. But Rachid could not disappear. Ali would find him in Algiers. So he must make the woman talk. He was ready with his story, ready to watch Anne-Marie Duchemin squirm and scream.

He let himself into the tiny brick basement that smelled of mold and sewage. For almost a month the two hostages had been locked in this room with no facilities and no light except for the small windows with bars at the top of the walls. He laughed at how easy his task would be. Bread and water and filth for a month. They would talk now.

He entered the room where Moustafa and Anne-Marie lay asleep on the two thin matresses. He knelt beside Anne-Marie and softly brushed her hair with his fingers. She reached for his hand in her sleep, and woke with a start. She screamed, sitting up quickly.

"Now my dear, why do you scream? I am only feeling your hair. It is so nice to the touch." He moved closer, pressing his body down softly on Anne-Marie's.

* * *

Moustafa awakened to the sound of Anne-Marie screaming. He scrambled to stand up, but before he could get to his feet, Rachid had his gun pointed toward him. "Sit down, you fool. Fool! You do not know a lovely woman when you see her? We have left you here for so long together, and still you have not shown her the tenderness she deserves?" He laughed. "If you cannot show it, then I shall. I am very convincing."

"Leave her alone! She is ill. She is very sick, this woman. You cannot bring her anything for her cough? It drives me crazy. She will die here, and then this place will reek even more!" Moustafa searched desperately for a way to divert Rachid. His head spun. He was weak from lack of food. "What do you want anyway, Rachid? You have not asked anything of us."

Rachid turned away from Anne-Marie for a moment. "It has not been necessary. You see, we have found your daughter." Anne-Marie gasped. "Yes, she and the old shopkeeper. 'Tis a pity the old man was not more helpful. But your daughter. Yes! She too coughs a lot, our friend tells us."

"Where is Ophélie? You have not hurt her?"

"Do not worry so, Anne-Marie. She is a very cooperative child. She does, after all, have the information." He watched for the mother's reaction.

Anne-Marie said nothing.

"So you see, we have no need of either of you, after all." He toyed with the gun. "Unless there is something else you wish to tell us. Something that could help Ali?"

Anne-Marie turned to Moustafa, her eyes filled with fear. He read her thoughts. *Ophélie! They have Ophélie! Something has gone wrong, and they have found her.* Moustafa shot her an angry look.

"Yes, Rachid. I think Anne-Marie has some very vital information for Ali. It would be a pity to kill her now. I have discovered several things she knows. As you say, it pays to be tender." He met Rachid's eyes and smiled. "She trusts too much, this woman. Tell Ali that she will meet with him. With all of the men together."

Rachid struck Moustafa hard across the face. "Idiot! You will never leave here alive. You tell me now, woman, or I will kill your tender friend." He held the gun to Moustafa's head.

Anne-Marie spoke, forcing a cold, harsh tone into her voice. "Kill him if you wish. He is worse than the rest of you. Get his stinking body away. But I will not talk here. Take me to Ali."

"I can make you talk, you trash." He swerved angrily, the gun now pointing at her. In a flash, Moustafa grabbed him by the neck. Rachid lashed back with his elbow, striking Moustafa full in the stomach, but the young man held on. With one hand he gripped Rachid around the neck and with the other he grasped for the gun, which Rachid circled wildly above him.

"Anne-Marie!"

She had grabbed the old chair and now brought it down on Rachid's skull. The gun went off. Moustafa fell backward with Rachid on top of him. Again Anne-Marie brought down the chair on Rachid's back. With a scream Rachid pulled himself off of Moustafa, waving the gun madly about his head. "You!" he moaned and fell at Anne-Marie's feet.

Her hands trembling, she pulled the gun out of his grasp. "Moustafa? Moustafa? Hurry!"

The young man slowly pulled himself from the ground.

"You are hurt?" Panic was in her voice.

"Not bad. He shot himself when you hit him with the chair." Moustafa crouched beside Rachid.

"Is he dead?"

"No. Give me the bottle."

Anne-Marie did not move.

"The bottle. The pill. Now!"

"I cannot."

Moustafa was standing, grabbing at her sleeve. He ripped the little bottle out. "Leave if you do not care to watch. I am coming."

Still Anne-Marie did not move.

Moustafa took a tiny pill and slipped it under Rachid's tongue. "Rest in peace, you coward."

He watched Anne-Marie run out into the night air and heard her gag. Again her body was racked with dry heaves as she sobbed. Moustafa was by her side instantly. He locked the door with Rachid's keys, and tucked the gun in his belt.

"Come now, Anne-Marie. Do not give up now! To life!"

End of Part I

PART II

Chapter Fifteen

"In the later years of his life, Coleridge was reconciled with his friend Wordsworth. After Coleridge's death, Wordsworth declared that he was 'the most wonderful man that I have ever known.'" David Hoffmann finished his lecture comparing the literature of Samuel Taylor Coleridge and William Wordsworth.

It was one of his favorite lectures, but today he felt dissatisfied as the women left his class. Gabriella politely addressed him as Mr. Hoffmann when she spoke in class, but otherwise, she avoided his eyes. She did not linger after class to talk with him. Such had been her behavior for almost a month now, and November was coming to a close.

It was his fault. He knew it. She had not understood what he had tried to tell her that day in the courtyard after Aix. "If only you knew, Gabby," he whispered to himself. "But I cannot tell you the truth. I cannot show you what would only hurt you more."

So David played the game of silence with his red-haired student. In class he did not change his composure.

He laughed and winked and surprised the women with his witty comments. But he never reached out to touch Miss Madison after the other women were out of sight. Only in his mind did he reach out to the poppies and long for the laughter that haunted his dreams.

He left the classroom, briefcase in hand, and walked away from the parsonage through town, toward Mme. Pons' apartment. The fruit stand outside the entrance to his apartment did not tempt him with its polished red apples and thick orange *clementines*. He quickly let himself into his room and closed the door, leaving his briefcase by the bed and seating himself at the small desk. Opening his lap drawer, he brought out a stack of papers. An old photograph sat on the top of the stack, and he brushed it with his hand. He had not looked at the picture for four months. Not since Gabby had come to St. Joseph's. But today he looked.

"My God, I wish I knew where you were. I have given up hope, you know. I do not know where to look any more. For a while, I thought I wouldn't care. But after all, I am here for you. It was you who needed my help!"

His eyes flashed, and he dropped the photograph and covered his face with his hands. Gabby's silence was not the only quiet he feared. There was no more news. None! It was becoming too complicated and hopeless.

Yesterday's paper lay on the floor. He reached down to retrieve it and reread the headlines. "Twenty Killed in OAS Terrorist Attack at Casino in Algiers." The article continued, "While dozens of young students laughed and danced at the city's popular casino, a bomb exploded in their midst, instantly killing twenty and severely maiming many others. Sobbing parents and friends looked through the carnage, horrified to find body parts strewn amongst the rubble...."

He picked up the photograph again. "I don't know

what to do now. If only you would tell me! I need you. I need someone." He brushed the photograph with his fingertips as if he could touch the face of the young woman who stood beside him, frozen in place, smiling out of the picture without a care in the world.

* * *

Gabriella hardly touched the delicious noon meal that Mme. Leclerc had prepared. Her stomach growled, but she could not make herself eat. Stephanie had already asked for seconds while Gabriella played with the noodles and meat in the *boeuf bourgignon*.

"My dear Gabriella, you have lost your appetite lately. Do you think your parents will be happy to see their daughter so thin after her year in France? *Ooh la la!* You will ruin my reputation as the best cook in Castelnau."

Gabriella smiled as she set down her fork. "Now Mme. Leclerc, you know it is nothing to do with you or your cooking. Surely you have had other boarders who were homesick?"

"Homesick? Yes, my dear. But for a whole month! You have hardly eaten a thing for all of November. It is not right!"

Stephanie laughed. "Yeah, Gabriella. Think of it this way. The less you eat, the more is left over, and I always seem to find room to have seconds! Imagine what *my* parents will say!"

Caroline did not comment. She only eyed Gabriella with a mixture of pity and satisfaction.

Gabriella nodded, smiled, and ate the *boeuf bourgignon*. No one said a word about David Hoffmann. But she knew what they were thinking. *She's lovesick for him, and it isn't working out.* They were right.

* * *

Mother Griolet noticed Gabriella's quiet restlessness more than anyone else. She prayed daily for the private battle the young woman fought with her God. She watched her leave the parsonage quickly after classes and return only when she had work with the orphans.

Today Mother Griolet shrugged her shoulders. "You still know best, Lord, *non?* She stays away from the American and clings to the children. Especially Ophélie. One life to fill up the hole left by another. It is not so bad."

Gabriella appeared in the doorway of her office, interrupting the old nun's thoughts. *"Bonjour,* Mother Griolet! I am ready for the afternoon adventure. Is Ophélie here?"

"Yes, my child. She's quite thrilled to have the afternoon alone with you. She's been brushing her hair now for half an hour." The nun laughed. "It's a joy to see the way that child is coming around. There's a sparkle in her eyes. And the way she eats! *Mais alors!* Soon I'll have to find her a new skirt."

She looked at Gabriella and said softly, "You have been so good for the children, my child. You are like the pansy in winter, bright and delicate to the sight but strong and tenacious in spirit. They last throughout the winter, the pansies do, you know." She met Gabriella's eyes. "You are a blessing to those children. An example. You are hope for Ophélie. You see it, *non?*"

Gabriella's face reddened, and Mother Griolet added quickly, "I am not telling you these things for you to get a big head. God has gifted you with the children. He has done it to help a stubborn little old lady in an orphanage. You are strong, Gabriella. Remember that." She grasped Gabriella's hand and held it for a moment. "Do not be afraid. He is with you. Thank you for being with Him."

She pronounced the last phrases with great care, and

Gabriella raised her eyebrows. "I get the feeling you are trying to tell me something, Mother Griolet. But you do not dare. It is more than a simple encouragement for a lovesick girl, is it not?"

"I do not know what I can say. Go on now. Show little Ophélie the house you lived in when you were here as a child." She placed two bus tickets in Gabriella's hand.

Gabriella left the office, pulling the door shut behind her.

* * *

The bus ride from Castelnau through Montpellier to the west side of town took thirty-five minutes. Ophélie chattered excitedly as Gabriella pointed out different landmarks. "I love riding on the bus! Oh, it is such fun! So big!"

Gabriella smiled at her. "We're almost there now." She glanced down at the directions Mother Griolet had scribbled for her when Gabriella had asked how to get to the old mission house. At first the old nun had balked at the idea. "There's no need to go back over there. I'm not even sure the mission still owns it." But at Gabriella's insistence, she had telephoned and arranged the visit.

"The next stop is ours," Gabriella said.

The bus came to a halt and the glass doors parted, opening to release an eager little girl and her *maîtresse*. The air was cold as woman and girl stepped onto the sidewalk, but the wind was not blowing. "It is just a short walk from here," Gabriella said.

She fumbled in her coat pocket and brought out a five-franc piece, which she handed to Ophélie. "A treat from me. You can buy a pastry at the first *patisserie* you find."

"Oh, thank you, Gabriella!" Ophélie's eyes danced

177

with anticipation, searching the street for a store. "May I try that *boulangerie* over there? Look, there are pastries in the window. See?" She tugged on Gabriella's coat, pulling her toward a window front filled with delicate looking confections.

"Now which one should I choose?" Ophélie looked up at her *maîtresse*. "What would you choose if you were me?"

"Well, that is a good question, Ophélie. Let me see. Look, there is an *éclair*. It's a pastry filled with cream and topped with chocolate. Or look at the *mille-feuille*. You know what that means, *non?* See all the thin layers of pastry with cream in between each layer and a chocolate-vanilla swirled icing. Absolutely delicious, I guarantee."

"And there, look at that one. It looks like a person." Ophélie pointed to two balls of pastry stacked on top of each other, like a snowman with a chocolate hat.

"Oh, now *that*. That is what we call a *religieuse*. A nun! Can you see it, Ophélie? It's like a nun with her black scarf and robes. And inside the pastry is that same thick, delicious cream."

"That's what I want! Yes, yes! A *religieuse!* Like Mother Griolet. I am sure it will be the sweetest pastry in the whole wide world!" She hugged Gabriella tightly before she ran into the store, her long hair, braided in two pigtails, flying out behind her.

Moments later she returned to the sidewalk, beaming as she held the little *religieuse* in its paper doily. "You know, Gabriella, this is my first pastry. Mama never had the money for pastries."

"She is wise, your mama. You mustn't waste money on pastries. Just this once. It is a special treat for a special girl on a special day. Come along now."

* * *

The mission house looked much the same as the other houses that faced the busy avenue. Its facade was sturdy, built of cement blocks and then stuccoed in the light coral color typical of the Midi. Four pairs of heavy wooden shutters had been painted a grayish blue. They stood open, displaying the large single-paned windows that blinked back the sun's reflection.

Gabriella rang the doorbell by the street entrance. Moments later a tall, blonde young woman, holding a baby in her arms, opened the door.

"Gabriella Madison! Welcome!" the woman said in English. "And this must be your little friend, Ophélie. *Bonjour!*" She reached out with her free hand and stroked the child's head.

"Oh, dear. I hope we didn't wake the baby," Gabriella said.

"No, no. She had just gotten up. Now let me introduce myself; I'm Barbara Butler. Do come in. Mother Griolet phoned yesterday to say you'd be coming. Did you realize that my parents know your folks, Gabriella? They met at a training conference with the mission years ago in the States. Your parents are in Senegal, is that right?"

"Yes, that's right. And your parents are in the Belgian Congo, I remember. Mother didn't tell me that you would be here in Montpellier."

"We are just here briefly, on our way to the Congo ourselves. Can I get you something to drink?" She smiled at Ophélie. "It looks like you've already had your *goûter*, from that chocolate mustache you're wearing."

Ophélie nodded happily. "Yes, Gabriella bought me a *religieuse!*"

"Oh, my, those are good. Well, come on up and have something to drink. Water, a *sirop* perhaps? We have strawberry and lemon."

179

Barbara Butler led her guests through a large open room, its walls lined with books. "This is the meeting room for the students who are here to learn French and African culture—you know all about that, I suppose. Our apartment is upstairs." They walked through the room and up a winding flight of stairs.

"Have a seat in the den." Barbara welcomed them into her apartment. "I'll just put little Alice in her playpen here."

Ophélie and Gabriella stepped into the den. "I hardly remember this place at all," Gabriella called out to Barbara. "Did Mother Griolet tell you I was here with my mother and sisters when I was little?"

"Oh, no! How fun to come back!" Barbara called back. She came into the den with three tall glasses of lemonade, which she placed on a coffee table. "Oh, there's the phone! Excuse me for a second."

As she bustled out of the room, Ophélie took one of the glasses and moved toward the cooing baby.

Gabriella smiled and watched the little girl bending over the baby. Suddenly an image flashed before her, like a photograph. *A little girl with curly red hair bending down over someone. Not a baby, but a woman.* "Mommy!" Gabriella whispered.

Ophélie turned to look at her. "What did you say, Gabriella?"

Gabriella shook herself. "Nothing, dear. I was just remembering. . . ." She closed her eyes to wipe away the picture, but it flashed before her again in the darkness. *The little redhead was looking down at her mother, whose face was bruised and bloody. She was shaking her frantically and crying.*

"No!" Gabriella cried out loud.

Ophélie came over to her. "What is wrong, *maîtresse?* You look so scared. What is the matter?"

180

Gabriella knelt down and hugged Ophélie to her chest. "It is nothing, sweetheart. I'm sorry if I frightened you. Go back and play with little Alice. I am fine."

When Barbara entered the den a few minutes later, Gabriella excused herself to find the bathroom. She walked down the hall and opened a door, instinctively knowing that the bathroom was there. She closed the door behind her and leaned over the sink, crying. Another picture flashed through her mind. *Water was running from the spigot. Water and blood.* "Lord! What is this?" she whispered, turning on the water. Again and again she splashed cool water on her face, washing away the memory.

Five minutes later Gabriella dried her face on a towel that hung by the sink, and emerged from the bathroom. Baby Alice was giggling loudly along with Ophélie, and Barbara was enjoying the show.

"Ophélie is wonderful with babies," Barbara gushed as Gabriella entered the den. "Alice is delighted."

Gabriella picked up her drink and patted Ophélie on the head. "Yes, we are so happy to have Ophélie with us." Her voice caught.

"Would you like to see the rest of the house?" Barbara asked.

"No," she replied quickly. "No, this is just fine. We can't stay too long anyway." The two women sat down on the couch. "Tell me exactly what you will be doing in the Congo, Barbara," Gabriella said.

For almost an hour, the women talked of Africa while Ophélie played happily beside the baby. No other pictures flashed through Gabriella's mind, but she breathed a deep sigh when they stepped outside and waved good-bye to Barbara and Alice. Ophélie held Gabriella's hand, swinging her arms jubilantly as she matched the young woman's brisk gait.

"It has been a wonderful afternoon. I have had so much fun," Ophélie exclaimed. "Thank you, Gabriella. Thank you for one of the happiest days of my life!"

Gabriella squeezed her hand and forced a smile on her face. "One of the happiest days in your life . . ."

* * *

The bell in the church chimed seven o'clock. Ophélie waited until all the other children had left the dormitory to open her middle drawer and pull out the little blue bag from inside her tights. She shook the contents out of the bag.

"It has been the most wonderful day, Mama! I rode a big bus and ate the yummiest pastry and held hands and laughed with Gabriella." She furrowed her brow. "I don't want you to think I have forgotten you, Mama. It is only that Gabriella is so nice. And she teaches me things. Important things. And I know she likes me." The child picked up the small photograph of her mother and herself. "I still miss you, Mama. I still love you the most. But when I am with *her*, I sometimes forget how much I miss you."

The envelope with her name on it lay wrinkled on the bed. Ophélie removed the thin pink sheets of paper. "See, Mama. I can read some of it now. *Mère Griolet* writes the same way you do. *Des lettres attachées.* She is teaching us. Gabriella says that the children in America do not learn this way first. Not cursive, but print, she says. But I am glad this is what we learn in France. See, I can already read some of it."

She took the first sheet of paper and began sounding out the words. "It is like this: D . . . dea . . . dear! Dear Ophélie. I lo . . . love y . . . ya . . . you. I love you. Oh, see, Mama! I can read! You love me! Yes, I know it. And I will read the rest later."

182

She folded the letter with the other sheets of paper and then tucked the picture into the bag with them. Back into the dark blue tights went the blue velvet bag. Back into the middle drawer. Ophélie stood up and pulled the cross out from under her blouse. She kissed it softly. "Mama, Gabriella talks to me about God. And His son, Jesus. I don't think you will mind. I'm sure you would like to hear about Him too." She ran out of the room and across the courtyard to the dining hall.

* * *

Ophélie was still eating her dessert when Mother Griolet sat down beside her in the dining hall. "How was your afternoon in town?" the nun questioned.

"It was really, really fun, *Mère Griolet*. Gabriella even bought me a pastry—a *religieuse*—that was as sweet as you are! And I played with the baby and rode on the biggest bus."

"My child, I am so glad you had such a lovely time." An expression of concern registered on her face. "What is that you are wearing around your neck, little Ophélie?"

"My cross? It was my Papy's cross that he gave to Mama. Then Papy died." She touched the necklace, her face sad. Then immediately her face changed. "Did you know that Gabriella has the same cross? We wear the same cross! She says it was the cross of the Huguos . . . the Hunots . . ."

"The Huguenots."

"Yes, the Huguenots. They were brave people who lived in France a long time ago when a mean king ruled. He wouldn't let them pray to Jesus. He locked them in prisons and killed all the men. But they were so very brave. And they wore this cross to show who they were!"

"I see that Gabriella has taught you much about history."

"History?"

"Yes, the events of the past. Well, it is a lovely cross. And what did you say your Mama's name is, dear?"

"Are you going to find her for me?" Ophélie's eyes held hope in them.

"I hope we can find her. But not if you don't tell me her name. Surely you see now that we only want to help you?"

Ophélie considered Mother Griolet's words carefully. "I suppose it would be okay to tell you. Her name is Anne-Marie. She is the most beautiful lady in the whole world. Anne-Marie Duchemin."

"Thank you, my child. What a pretty name she has. Now at least we will know who we are looking for." She patted the child's hand as she rose to leave the table.

Suddenly she turned back around. "Did your mother ever tell you anything that was special about the cross? Did she tell you why she gave it to you?"

"Oh, yes! She said that I should wear it so that the God of Papy would be with me. That is why!"

"A good reason. A very good reason indeed."

* * *

Gabriella sat up in her bed, sweat streaming down her face. Her own screams had awakened her. Caroline knocked on the door and peeped in.

"Are you okay, Gab? Bad dream? Boy, did you yell!"

"Yes, I'm fine, Caroline. Thanks for checking. Just a bad dream. Sorry to wake you." The door closed, leaving Gabriella in the darkness. She switched on the lamp beside the bed.

"Oh, Lord, what can this be? Is it real or only a dream?" This time it was not a single image she saw, but a whole scene played out before her. *A dark-skinned man kneeling over her mother, a little red-haired child*

184

hiding behind a door. Her mother's screams. The man reaching and touching ...

"No, Lord, it can't be true! Not Mother!" The house was quiet. Gabriella climbed out of bed and walked over to the window. The pane was cold to her touch. She shivered, watching the shadow of the olive tree. Its leaves, still intact in winter, moved silently. She closed her eyes and saw Barbara Butler smiling at her with the baby in her arms. Then she saw Ophélie laughing. Immediately her mother took the place of Barbara in her mind, she too holding a baby. "Ericka!" Gabriella cried. "No! No, God! Oh, no. Not Mother, not Ericka." She leaned against the pane and strained to see through the darkness. But all was perfectly black.

* * *

Ophélie woke in the middle of the night. She sat straight up in bed, bumping her head on the top bunk. "Mama!" she said out loud. She smiled to think of the wonderful dream. She was walking hand-in-hand with Mama, laughing, running in the sand at the beach.

Then she covered her mouth with her hand. "It wasn't you, Mama. It wasn't you after all." The woman in her dream had had long red hair.

Chapter Sixteen

Ali Boudani held the thick manilla envelope in his hands. "At last it is here. We have waited these weeks for the slides from our friend in France. The mail is slow. Or perhaps someone else has tampered with the envelope first?" His piercing eyes glared at the five men seated around him.

"Do not be too eager for news! It is dangerous. You have seen what happened to our brother Rachid. Too eager. And he went alone to have his way. Fool! Another martyr for the cause. But he has tarnished his father's name. Dying at the hands of our prisoners!"

He handed the envelope to a rugged old man who wore a turban around his head. His tanned cheeks were drawn tight over his bones.

"Mohemmed, prepare the slides." Ali circled the room like a wolf instructing his pack.

"Idiotic! As you know, the *pied-noir* escaped last month with her *harki* boyfriend. *But they will never leave Algeria.* Perhaps they have rotted here in the

Casbah, under our noses. Do we not smell the stench? We will find them again, and how they will howl in pain. I will make these friends regret that they wished to see another day. For the honor of Rachid's name, their tortured bodies will be displayed for all to see and remember. They cannot hide forever. And Ali has eyes in the back of his head." He laughed, and the men nodded with a low, nervous laughter.

"The slides are ready, Mohemmed?"

"Yes," the old man whispered.

With a click of the switch, a slide spread across the screen. A woman with long, curly red hair was walking away, her back to the camera. She wore a dark blue pea jacket.

"Go on," Ali instructed.

Another slide appeared of the same woman, this time half-turned to face the camera.

"Jean-Claude has met this woman twice, as he waited for information. He is quite sure that she is involved in the smuggling activities. She lives in Montpellier. Jean-Claude has not found out her name, but he believes she is a student. And most important of all—" He motioned to Mohemmed to advance the slides. A close-up of the woman's head and shoulders flashed on the screen. "She wears the cross."

The men murmured as they squinted at the slide to see a small cross hanging around the neck of the red-haired woman.

"Jean-Claude will find her again soon. We have lost the mother and her daughter and their *harki* slime. We will not lose anyone else. It is only a matter of time. We will find them all!" He screamed with wrath, leaving the dingy basement of the Casbah and walking out into the night air.

He whispered to the stars, "Now you, too, will be

avenged, Rachid. With my father." His eyes glistened with passion, and a lone tear escaped down his cheek.

* * *

It was barely dawn when Gabriella appeared at the parsonage. Mother Griolet opened the door slightly, peeking outside to see her unexpected caller.

"Gabriella! My dear child. What in the world ... *Entre, entre.*" She pulled the young woman into her apartment, shutting the door as several dead leaves blew into the corridor. Gabriella stood before her, trembling, her hair tangled and eyes swollen and red. A thick gray wool sweater covered her flannel nightgown, and her feet were bare inside a pair of thin bedroom slippers.

"Child, look at you! You'll catch your death running around in the wee morn dressed like that. *Mais alors!* Come back to the den!"

The old nun scurried through the hallway with Gabriella following behind. Once in the den, she said, "Here now. Take a seat on the couch. I'll bring you a quilt and some coffee."

Mother Griolet stepped quickly back into her room. She smoothed her silver hair, unfastening several pins so that it fell down well past her shoulders. She gathered up a thick quilt in her arms. Her Bible lay open on the bed.

She hurried back into the den and surrounded Gabriella with the quilt. "The coffee will be ready in just a moment, dear. There are tissues in the bathroom if you need them."

Gabriella sat quietly on the couch. She uttered no words as she huddled there like a wounded puppy.

"Here, now." Mother Griolet set a small tray with two steaming bowls of coffee on a low table in front of the couch. The rich, enticing aroma of the hot drink filled the room. The church bell chimed six times.

Mother Griolet pulled up an old wicker rocking chair and sat in silence beside Gabriella. Minutes droned by, broken only by the sound of Gabriella's sniffling. She wiped her eyes with the sleeve of her sweater and curled herself up more tightly on the couch. Her eyes stared at the black coffee and the swirling steam.

Finally she spoke, her voice choked with emotion. "She was raped! Raped! Mother was raped, and you knew!" Her voice exploded with a vengeance. "You let me go to that house to remember! You have known all along. Why?" She turned, her eyes streaming with tears, to look at the old woman. "Why didn't you tell me? Did you think I would never remember?

"It was a cruel scheme. You and Mother! She sent me back here to relive her nightmare! Why? Why did no one tell me?" Gabriella sobbed uncontrollably, covering her mouth in a desperate attempt to regain her composure. Her thin body shook violently under the covers. Mother Griolet came to her side, cuddling her in her arms like a wailing baby.

"Dear Gabriella. I am so sorry. Yes, you are right. I knew about the ... the accident ... the rape ..." She squeezed her lips together and closed her eyes. Tears lined her wrinkled face. She tried to speak again. "It is hard to know, sometimes, what is best."

Gabriella sat up, pulling herself away from Mother Griolet's embrace. She spoke softly into the air. "A burglar. An Arab. He surprised Mother nursing Henrietta in the den. I don't know where Jessica was, but ..." Her voice quavered. "But I hid ... I hid behind the door."

Suddenly Gabriella seemed not to be with Mother Griolet. She screamed, "No! Stop it! Stop it! Mother is yelling, she is screaming. 'Gabriella! Get help!' She is screaming, and then she is not screaming anymore. And the man . . . the man picks himself off Mother. He tucks in his shirt and zips his pants. And he leaves. He leaves." She turned to face Mother Griolet.

"I saw it all. And I never said a word. I couldn't scream. I hid and watched the man. . . ." Her sobs increased. She stood quickly, letting the covers fall to the floor, and ran toward the hall.

Mother Griolet listened as Gabriella heaved and sobbed in the bathroom. The nun cried and rocked herself, whispering softly, "My God, my God. Come Lord Jesus, and comfort us now."

* * *

Sunlight streamed through the windows in Mother Griolet's den. The bell had long since chimed seven times. Mother Griolet sat beside Gabriella, praying and crying with the young woman. Gabriella's tears had finally stopped.

Now Mother Griolet spoke. "Gabriella, your mother did not know you saw, nor did I. A neighbor found your mother. She heard the baby wailing on and on and came over to see. She called me immediately. She knew that I was a friend of you mother's.

"When I got there, your mother was already at the hospital. The neighbor had Henrietta. Jessica had been playing at a friend's house. And you . . ." Her eyes met Gabriella's. "You were in the garden, playing in the mud. That is where the neighbor found you. When you saw me, you hugged me. You had been crying. We thought you were afraid because of the police. Dear child, we did not know that you saw it all!"

"Why didn't Mother ever tell me she was raped?" Gabriella accused.

Mother Griolet massaged her temples and sighed. "The doctor here advised against it. He said you were too young to understand. She was trying to do what was best for you."

"But later. She could have told me later. Years later. I was not too young! Not too young to know what happened. To understand that Ericka ... that Ericka ..." She could not continue.

"She would have told you, Gabriella. But things turned out differently. You were only twelve when ..."

"When Ericka died. I could see she was not like us. But I never once thought— I did not remember! I had no memory of the rape until yesterday. No idea!"

"That is quite normal, dear. Such violent abuses are often hidden away until a woman is grown. Locked away in the memory." Mother Griolet paused. Then looking out the window, she continued, "Afterward, it was too painful for your mother to speak of Ericka. She could not see how telling you everything would help."

"Father knew?"

"Of course. There was never any question that she would keep the baby. He knew.

"You see, Gabriella, it was really this terrible circumstance that bonded your mother and me. We had only known each other a month when the rape occurred. I helped her through the grieving process. And then, when she found out she was pregnant ..." She sighed heavily. "Such a very difficult time.

"But you all left soon after. Back to Senegal. Of course we corresponded." The nun reached for Gabriella's hand and squeezed it. "She loved Ericka just like the rest of you, Gabriella. And she knew what a jewel that baby sister was for you. She did not see what good it could do to bring up the past." Mother Griolet rubbed her forehead.

"And then Ericka got sick and died, and it didn't matter any more," Gabriella said sarcastically. "And I never would have known if I hadn't decided to come back here. That is why Mother was worried. She was afraid I might remember. That is why she gave me this cross!" She yanked it out from under her nightgown with such force that the chain snapped, and the cross fell to the floor.

"Now, dear, calm yourself...."

"I will not be calm!" Gabriella yelled. "I cannot sweep away a nightmare ... a nightmare I never knew existed. Do you expect me to get over it? Just like that?"

"No, no. You could never just get over it. It will take time. Much time." She reached out and touched Gabriella's sleeve. "I will be here to walk through it with you. As I did with your mother. If you want." She hugged Gabriella to her breast and let her cry until the young woman closed her eyes and slept in the old nun's lap.

The church bell chimed eight o'clock, and Mother Griolet quietly slipped out of the room. Gabriella slept peacefully on the couch as the sun seeped in the window and caught the fallen Huguenot cross in its rays, sending a shimmering shadow across the ceiling of the room.

* * *

By the time Mother Griolet returned to her apartment later in the morning, Gabriella had gone. The quilt lay in a heap on the couch, and the coffee bowls were still full of black liquid, but the steam had disappeared. Mother Griolet collapsed on the couch, breathing heavily.

"Dear Lord, it is a shock. A shock to see such anger on lovely Gabriella's face. I did not know." She massaged a leg and then pulled it up with difficulty to let it rest on the small coffee table. "I am an old lady, after all." She took a deep breath, wincing with pain. "You see, Lord. Even after all these years with You, I still do not do well with these tragedies. I am afraid that Gabriella will have a hard time with this, with forgiveness.

192

"She has that temperament, fiery like her hair. Oh, I know she deserves to be angry. To rage. Life is so unjust! Only, please, *Mon Père*, give me the strength. And the words. And the ears to hear."

Her eyes fell to the floor where the Huguenot cross still lay, the chain half hidden under the couch. Mother Griolet reached down to pick it up. She held it in the palm of her hand, fingering the dove that dangled from the end of the cross.

"You have come back to remind me, haven't you?" She spoke to the treasure in her hand. "An unconventional Catholic nun once bought you for a grieving friend. 'Come to the cross,' that nun said. 'That is the only way. There is forgiveness.' And now that same old nun must remember her words. Remember for a very scared young woman. And remember for herself." She touched the cross to her lips and closed her eyes.

"Lord Jesus, I come to Your cross today as every day. And I say, forgive me. Forgive me if in keeping this secret, I have brought unnecessary pain to Gabriella. You know that was never my intention. I am a stubborn old woman, but I am trying, Lord. Trying to take up my cross daily and follow You."

The cross hung from its broken chain, swaying back and forth in Mother Griolet's hand as she prayed. A burst of sunlight invaded the room. Suddenly hundreds of spots of light danced and shimmered across the wall. Mother Griolet opened her eyes, staring at the jubilant dance of light surrounding her. At first she did not detect the source. Then she touched the cross. Immediately the bright spots of light twirled through the room, imitating and expanding the soft movement of the cross.

A sparkle returned to Mother Griolet's eyes as she watched the play of light against the shadows. She chuckled softly. "No, I have not forgotten what You said,

193

Lord. 'I am the Light of the world: he that followeth Me shall not walk in darkness, but shall have the light of life.' I have not forgotten." She slipped the cross into the pocket of her robe and pulled herself off the couch.

The gait of the vivacious nun was slower that day. "Old age," she winked to Sister Rosaline, who inquired after her. "Don't you worry about me. Our Father has not finished with me yet. *Ooh la la!* Such plans He has!"

* * *

Gabriella skipped all of her classes. She wandered through the streets of Castelnau, restless and angry. The two *pains au chocolat* that she had bought after changing her clothes at Mme. Leclerc's grew stale in their paper sack. She caught a bus to Montpellier and rode all the way back to the west side of town. She walked to the mission house and stood outside across the street for two hours, numbed by the biting chill of the wind. The cold stung her eyes, but no tears flowed.

She took a stone from the sidewalk and threw it forcefully into the road. It hit the pavement, yards shy of the house. A bus stopped down the street, and she ran to jump on. For another hour the bus roamed the streets of Montpellier. Gabriella never got off. She did not know where she was, and she did not care.

Suddenly she thought of David's words, *"Yes, I survived, but I died doing it."*

"I did not understand you then, David," she whispered. "But now I do. It is a living death. A living death to survive." She closed her eyes and dozed off.

Sometime later, the bus driver gently shook her awake. *"Mademoiselle, c'est la fin de la ligne.* It is the end of the line here. You must get off."

Obediently Gabriella descended from the bus. Children were shouting gleefully in a nearby school playground. Cars lined the street in the late afternoon traffic. Gabriella stepped into the road, and an angry horn blared. She looked up to see the driver gesticulating and cursing as he swerved to miss her. She stepped back onto the sidewalk and walked until she came to another bus stop.

Much later, Gabriella Madison opened the door to Mme. Leclerc's apartment and disappeared into her room.

* * *

The comforter was pulled up around Gabriella's neck, but still she shivered in her bed. The lamp on the nightstand gave the only light in the room. Somewhere in the apartment the telephone rang, and Mme. Leclerc bustled to answer. Her voice was muffled, but Gabriella knew that Mother Griolet was calling to ask about her.

The Bible on the nightstand caught her eye. Turning on her side, Gabriella let the book fall open to where a letter lay within its pages. She lifted the letter out of the Bible and unfolded the single page.

Dearest Gabriella,

You are my firstborn and my delight. How proud your father and I are of you! And now it is time for you to go off on your own.

I am giving you this cross, the Huguenot cross. It comes from France, where we lived years ago when you were only a child. Now you are returning to France, to Castelnau, to that same city that was dear to me so long ago.

Life is not easy, Gabriella. You know this, but perhaps you will know it more now, on your own. I give you this cross, which has always been a symbol of forgiveness and love to me. It was a gift to me when I was suffering. Wear it and know of my love and constant prayers for you.

God has always been faithful to me and your father, Gabriella. He has taught us to reach past the hurt, to forgive when our hearts are breaking. To love Him and to hold on. Someday you may need to know this too.

Go out with our blessing. Learn and enjoy. Discover a new country. Read about the Huguenots. And may your faith be strengthened in so doing.

We love you,
Mother

Gabriella closed the sheet of paper and wiped her eyes. "I thought there were no more tears for today, Mother." She felt for the cross and remembered breaking its chain at Mother Griolet's.

"I am sorry, Mother. It will take time. To forgive as you say. I am so sorry that I said nothing. I was so afraid, Mother. I didn't know what to do. I was so afraid."

196

Chapter Seventeen

The middle of the afternoon found the streets of Algiers deserted. Fear hung on every street corner, blood stained each sidewalk, and no amount of washing could erase the horror of the war.

The FLN's terrorist activities were rivaled in every way by the violent action of the OAS. Every day this new military organization, determined to keep Algeria French, resorted to new methods of barbarism.

Some *pied-noirs* joined the camps of this underground organization. Others hesitated. It was certain that de Gaulle had betrayed them. The French president was clearly pushing for an independent Algeria. Ever since the botched *putsch* of last April, the discontent French leaders had plotted and planned from their hideouts. Now it was time to act. So the daily papers announced murder after murder. Hatred bred and fermented and spread throughout the neighborhoods of Algiers.

Only the week before, an important member of Algiers' socialist party had been murdered during what was being called the OAS's bloodiest week yet. Nowhere was safe. This war would not simply fizzle out with a victorious FLN. The OAS planned on plenty of fireworks right up until the gory end.

Anne-Marie was almost too tired to care, as she stared numbly out the window of the small bedroom in the slums of Bab el Oued. This was the neighborhood of the *petits blancs*, the poorest of the Europeans in Algeria. This was also the headquarters of the OAS. Fifty thousand Europeans were crammed into the space between the Casbah and the Mediterranean. These *petits blancs* stood to lose everything if Algeria gained independence. They had nothing in France, and what work could they find under angry Algerians if this country was granted its freedom? So they joined the OAS to register their desperate cry for an *Algérie française*.

But Anne-Marie had grown weary of political games. Forever hiding, always on the run or worse, seeking to escape. She knew she should feel thankful to be out of the Casbah and relatively safe. The memory of their frantic race through the tiny streets of the Casbah in the dead of night was still fresh enough to make her heart pound. Only the night had hidden the terror in Moustafa's and Anne-Marie's eyes from one another. Terror that the sun would rise and they would still be trapped within the arches of the Casbah, an easy prey for a throat-slitting member of the FLN.

But miraculously, Moustafa had found his way through the labyrinth, and they had stepped through the low arches of their prison before the first streaks of light played through the sky. Later that morning they had slipped inside the small apartment of Marcus Cirou in Bab el Oued. The middle-aged *pied-noir* had welcomed Anne-Marie. He was short and lean and his gray hair glistened, not from the sun, but from grease.

Marcus Cirou's respect for her father during the last

198

war was great. It was only natural, he had told Anne-Marie, that he would shelter Captain Duchemin's daughter. He had eyed Moustafa suspiciously at first, but Anne-Marie soon convinced him that this *harki's* son was indeed on the *pied-noirs'* side. A reluctant part of the FLN when tortured, a loyal *harki's* son once free.

Marcus shared his humble provisions with his two unexpected guests. He even found a bottle of precious medicine for Anne-Marie's cough. But after a month she was still weak, her eyes dull, even when the sound of bombs reverberated in the night.

What she heard in her mind echoed louder than the bombs that exploded routinely around the neighborhood, louder than the angry shouts of the *pied-noirs* on the square in front of the Prefecture. She heard it in the early morn and throughout the day. At night, it woke her troubled sleep.

We have found your daughter. Rachid's voice repeated the simple statement incessantly in her head. She had not wanted to kill him. She had not wanted to run. The fault for his death and their escape had fallen on Ophélie, she was sure. She shuddered, afraid to imagine what Ali's anger could do to her daughter. Nothing mattered at all if hope for Ophélie was lost.

"Anne-Marie, please, you must eat this." Moustafa had entered the bedroom with a plate of rice and beans. He sat beside her, gently stroking her back and neck. "My dear, do not worry so. We are not even sure that they have Ophélie. Three times I have been back to the Casbah. Three times I have watched these men. They have not spoken of Ophélie. Please, you must eat."

It was the same argument he had used for the past month, but Anne-Marie was not convinced. She doubted that Moustafa could even convince himself.

"It is a miracle that we are alive," he continued.

"Surely this is not in vain. Soon we will leave Algeria. You must remember that we are not alone in our fight. We are helping others. I have reached three of the families in Algiers. Soon we will set up another *voyage* for the *Capitaine*. You will see. The children will escape. All of the children. Ophélie too!" He shook Anne-Marie's shoulders, but she stared at him blankly.

"I am sorry, Moustafa. I am trying to believe. What can I think of in this room? What do I see day after day, week after week? I see the face of my daughter. I live for that face. And I fear."

He held her in a tight embrace, her head buried against his chest. Gently he took her chin in one hand and stroked her face with his other. He kissed her lightly on the forehead. "Live for Ophélie, my dear. Live for her, of course." Now he looked into the depths of her sad eyes. "But live for me, too. I need you. I need you very much."

His lips brushed hers, softly, then with passion. Immediately he pulled himself away. "I must leave." He rose to his feet, touching her lips with his fingers. Anne-Marie smiled, a weak, tired smile.

"Thank you," she whispered as he left the room. She covered her mouth with her hand and cried.

* * *

Bus 11 left the cobblestoned streets of Castelnau and turned into the large *rond point* that connected this village to the east side of Montpellier. It veered onto Avenue de la Pompignane, stopping beside a nursery that advertised a sale on chrysanthemums, two pots for forty francs. The front of the nursery was lined with hundreds of pots of the orange, yellow, and burgundy flowers, offered at a special price ever since the first of November, All Saints' Day, when the mums were bought by the dozen and adorned each tombstone in Montpellier.

It was now the 28th of November. Gabriella had promised Ophélie another outing in town, explaining that she needed to get the chain for her Huguenot cross fixed.

"Mother Griolet showed me where to go in town. It's the same jeweler who sold her the cross years ago." She did not mention why the cross was broken or the nightmares of the past week. She watched Ophélie bouncing happily on the cushion of the bus seat, singing an old French melody they had learned in class that morning. *"Oh clair de la lune, mon ami Pierrot..."*

Gabriella caught Ophélie's attention. "Look there, at the fountains spraying water. See all the mums they've planted there?" The bus swerved around another *rond point* that encircled a small green hill, topped with a replica of an ancient Roman house. Rows of crysanthemums outlined the green grass. A fountain of water ran down from inside the Roman ruin.

"The flowers are *belle! Belle, belle comme toi,* Gabriella! You are so very pretty." Ophélie bounced higher in her seat, laughing and hugging Gabriella as she sang. "And look, Gabriella! One of my teeth is loose. Look." She wiggled her top front tooth back and forth. "Do you think *la petite souris* will come to the orphanage when I lose my tooth?"

"Well, of course she will. The little mouse can get in anywhere that a child has hidden her tooth under a pillow. I'm sure she will come to see you." Gabriella touched the tooth. "But it won't be for a while, sweetheart. Not for a good while."

Gabriella watched Ophélie beside her, but she was somehow suddenly back in Senegal holding Ericka on her lap, and giggling with her little sister as she twisted her hair into braids.

Closing her eyes, Gabriella tried to shut out the racing images swirling before her. *A little girl sobbing, hiding her face in Mother Griolet's black skirts. A black-haired child lying desperately still and yellow in an African hut. A bright-eyed six-year-old raising her hand in class and beaming back at the red-haired teacher.*

She opened her eyes and asked, "What do you like best about being six years old, Ophélie?"

The child wrinkled her nose and thought. "What do I like best? Hmm. I like learning how to read. *Oui!* That is best." Again she bounced up and down, up and down, pigtails swishing back and forth behind her. *"Non!"* she cried joyfully. "That is not even the best thing about being six! Not even reading. The best thing about being six years old is getting to know you!"

Impetuously she grabbed Gabriella around the neck and kissed her cheeks. The bus stopped abruptly, and the woman and child held each other tightly, bracing themselves against the sudden motion.

They burst out in laughter together. "Six years old. You are glad, then, Ophélie, that you are six?"

"Oh, yes. So very glad."

The bus pulled to a stop across the street from the Montpellier train station, beside a park where another fountain spewed and children climbed onto jungle gyms and slides.

"Time to get off, *ma cherie.*"

"May I play in the park, Bribri?" Ophélie pleaded, using the name she had adopted for her friend.

"Yes, go ahead for a moment."

Gabriella followed behind Ophélie, who dashed through the park toward a swing set. Higher and higher she pushed herself, pumping her legs vigorously against the wind. "Look at me! Look how high I can go, Bribri. Look!"

Gabriella nodded from the bench where she sat,

watching the joyful six-year-old and countless other children playing enthusiastically. She waved to Ophélie and whispered to herself, "Live, Ophélie. And laugh and love. That is what you should be doing at six years old."

* * *

Gabriella and Ophélie walked up the street from the bus stop to where it opened onto the Place de la Comedie. Hundreds of people mingled around the outdoor cafés, huddling together in the brisk chill of the afternoon. Ophélie skipped along, swinging Gabriella's hand with hers. "Look! Another fountain." She giggled. "With three naked ladies standing in the middle." She squinted in the sun as she turned toward her *maîtresse.* "Isn't that funny? Naked ladies in the fountain!"

"Those are the Three Graces. They represent beauty. You will study about them one day. Come along, now. The jeweler's is somewhere behind la Comedie."

They twisted through the narrow streets of the *centre ville,* Ophélie straining like a dog on a leash to peek inside a toy store, a *boulangerie,* and a store lined with rows and rows of children's shoes. On the sidewalk a man was drawing a picture of the Virgin and Child in bright pastel chalks. Ophélie planted her feet and refused to budge.

"Ooh la, regarde ça!" she chirped, tugging on Gabriella's hand. "Have you ever seen such a pretty picture? And on the sidewalk. That is too bad. It will wash away when it rains."

"The artist wants you to give him some money." Gabriella handed Ophélie a franc. "It is people like you who make him happy. See? Go put this in his hat over there."

Cautiously Ophélie tiptoed over to where the man's hat lay overturned with a few francs and centimes sparkling like real treasure inside. The young man looked up and smiled at Ophélie. *"Merci, jeune fille,"* he murmured, before returning to his work.

A vendor was selling *châtaignes* at his stall a few feet away. The smell of the roasting chestnuts enticed Ophélie. "Oh, Bribri! May we buy a *cornet* of those? Oh, please!" She jumped up and down with excitement.

"Ophélie, come on with you. I won't have any money to pay the jeweler if we stop and buy everything we see. Just observe. And on our way home you may pick one treat. Only one. *D'accord?"*

"Oh, yes. Thank you." She planted a kiss on Gabriella's cheek.

* * *

It was four o'clock when Jean-Claude Gachon stepped off the train and walked out into the sunlight of Montpellier. He strode across the street and up the wide avenue that was flanked on both sides by waiting pedestrians and stationary buses. When he arrived at Place de la Comedie, he found a chair at a *café* that gave him a good view of the open square.

"Un pastis," he mumbled to the waiter, unfolding a newspaper and settling back to read it. If one had to waste his days, this was not a bad way to do it, he mused. Hundreds of students milled around the center of town, gossiping and laughing as they walked with carefree spirits. At this time of day, la Comedie belonged to the students.

He had spent the month at la Comedie, watching for a red-haired woman to appear. Each day he sat for two hours at a *café*, observing the gathering of youth that played out like a movie before him. Then he strolled along the Esplanade and through the old part of town to the Place de Peyrou, an immense park with an ancient water tower at the end, a hexagonal building standing majestically over the pond at its feet. Long arches of an ancient aqueduct spread out behind the park, running through the city as a silent witness to days gone by. But never did the red-haired woman appear.

Today Jean-Claude was restless and impatient. He decided he would not leave the *café* until long after dark. He needed news to send to Ali. He needed a little bit of luck today.

* * *

Mr. Edouard Auguste was one of the best-known goldsmiths in Montpellier, Mother Griolet had confided to Gabriella. She had also said that he was an encyclopedia of information if Gabriella wished to question him about the Huguenots. At the time, the idea did not strike Gabriella as very interesting. But now, standing in his store, surrounded by gold and silver jewelry, she began asking questions.

Ophélie squatted down to see the treasures locked behind glass cabinets. She touched the glass with her fingers as if she could feel the jewelry inside.

Mr. Auguste spoke with the thick accent of the Midi. His eyes were deep blue and lively, and he had the dignified air of a true gentleman, tall and proper. A silk scarf was tied smartly around his neck. His gray flannel suit matched the color of his hair and mustache.

"Oui, oui, Mademoiselle," he nodded, as Gabriella inquired about the origins of the cross. "The Huguenot cross strongly resembles the medal of the Order of the Holy Spirit that was created by Henri III in the sixteenth century. This medal consisted of a Maltese cross with a dove in the center. It was used as a military decoration to distinguish excellent French warriors in the cavalry. But, of course, Protestants were forbidden to receive it, despite their military prowess.

"It is thought that a goldsmith in Nîmes created the first Huguenot cross around the year 1688. It differs from the medal in that the Huguenot cross has the *pendatif*—the dove—hanging from the lower branch with its wings spread and head pointing down. It is likely that this dove symbolized the *Saint Esprit*, the Holy Spirit, who descended upon Jesus at the time of His baptism in the form of a dove. Also four *fleurs-de-lis* were embedded between the branches of the cross and rays of sunlight chiseled in as though the Holy Spirit were sending out His power. Actually back then, each cross was a little different.

"We do not know for sure, but perhaps the reason this cross is so similar to the medal of honor was so the Protestants had a piece of jewelry that symbolized their faith but was not offensive to the king or to the Catholic church. So the goldsmith created a cross that had certain familiar points that reminded its wearers of the forbidden medal. Some believe it was the Huguenots' way of saying to the select group of calvary, 'You aren't the only ones who have the Holy Spirit! God has promised it to all who believe in Him.' "

Mr. Auguste was talking animatedly now, and Gabriella sensed a personal pride in his voice as he continued. "However, during the time of the Huguenot persecution, not many of these crosses were worn. You must remember," he paused and held out the cross in his palm, "that most of the Huguenots were poor villagers and mountain people who did not wear jewelry.

"It was most likely the more affluent city-dwelling Protestants who owned a Huguenot cross. There are records showing that those who abdicated their faith during the time of persecution in the seventeenth and eighteenth centuries were forced to sell their Huguenot crosses as proof."

Gabriella was fascinated by the jeweler's knowledge. "And now? It is very popular?"

"Oh, yes, *Mademoiselle*. Very popular, of course, among Protestants. It is really only in the last century that it has become so sought-after. Yours is especially beautiful. Eighteen-carat gold, and see how the cross has been chiseled on both sides. A very nice one."

"Mother Griolet said she bought it here, many years ago."

The goldsmith nodded politely. "Yes, Mother Griolet." He furrowed his brow, then slapped the counter with his hand. "Of course! I remember now. Yes, it was a bit strange—this dear little Catholic nun buying a Huguenot cross. I had completely forgotten the incident, though I know Mother Griolet well." He shrugged. "Of course, people can do what they want." He stared at Gabriella. "And how do you happen to have this cross?"

"My mother gave it to me. I only recently found out that she had received it as a gift from Mother Griolet." Involuntarily Gabriella shivered. "I'm afraid we must be going now. Thank you for your help."

"My pleasure, *Mademoiselle*. Your chain will be ready Friday. Shall I keep the cross with it?"

"Yes, that will be fine. *Merci*."

"*Je vous en prie. Bonne journée.*"

Ophélie turned from the counter, looking relieved, and took Gabriella's hand. "I thought we would never go," she confided. "And I am starving."

"Of course you are. *Allons-y*. You may pick whatever you want."

* * *

By five-thirty, the Comedie was a mass of cars and pedestrians, mingled into a slow-moving stream between the majestic buildings that outlined the square.

From their perch atop the fountain, the Three Graces looked down upon the chaotic scene with the peace and calm befitting the seductive symbols of love.

Jean-Claude was perched on the steps by the statue along with several students, and from this vantage point he could see most of the moving human traffic. He was watching a striking young woman with dark skin and bright pink lipstick, admiring her legs that protruded from her short skirt. The flash of red hair further across the square escaped his notice at first. Then he saw it. *Red hair. Lots of it. Walking toward the avenue that leads to the train station.* He hopped down from the statue and made his way across the Comedie, increasing his gait as he went. Soon he was trotting quickly through the crowd, his eyes riveted on the red-haired woman a hundred yards away.

The crowd thinned as it fanned off from the Comedie. Jean-Claude caught a full view of the woman. It was the one! He laughed out loud, fumbling for the camera in his leather bag. The zoom lens on, he inspected the woman and clicked a picture. Running, he clicked another and knocked into an elderly woman who was pulling a wheeled cart behind her.

"Pardon!" Jean-Claude called back, sidestepping another woman. He stopped to focus and cursed happily. A small child was with the red-haired girl. A small child that he knew very well. "Ophélie Duchemin," he snickered. Two more pictures as the little girl turned around and pointed toward a man playing the clarinette. Jean-Claude caught both of their faces in the shot.

The camera went back into his leather case. Jean-Claude jogged closer to the pair, then slowed to a walk. Coming up behind them, he touched the woman on the sleeve. "Excuse me, *Mademoiselle.*"

She glanced back but continued walking. "Whatever

you are selling, I'm not interested."

This time he grabbed her arm and held it tight. Still his voice was calm. "*Mademoiselle*. We have met before, *non?*"

She stopped to look at him, her face suspicious. Suddenly she recognized him. "Oh, yes, you are right. We have met before. Aigues-Mortes, right?"

"Precisely. How very nice to see you again. I see you have recovered from your fall."

The woman blushed. "Yes, I'm fine now. What brings you to Montpellier?"

"Business. And you, *Mademoiselle?*"

"Me? Oh, I live nearby. Not far at all."

Jean-Claude had pretended not to see the child. Now he glanced at her and exclaimed, "*Non!* Can it be? Ophélie Duchemin? Do you remember me?"

He picked the startled child up in his arms and kissed her on the cheek. "My, you have gotten big! Why, the last time I saw you was a year ago in Algeria. Imagine finding you here in France." He put Ophélie back down. She cowered close to the woman.

"Ophélie? Do you know this man?" The woman bent down to the child's level.

Ophélie nodded, a smile playing on her lips. Her big eyes gazed up at Jean-Claude. "Yes, Gabriella." Then she whispered, "He was my mama's friend."

Jean-Claude cleared his throat. "Excuse me, *Mademoiselle*. Allow me to introduce myself. I am Jean-Claude Gachon. I don't believe I know your name."

"It is Gabriella!" Ophélie volunteered happily.

Jean-Claude patted the child's head and smiled. The woman frowned at Ophélie, but Jean-Claude did not show that he noticed. He continued. "Gabriella? I may call you by your name?"

"If you wish," she said flatly.

"May I offer you a drink? The last time I offered, I believe you said you were with a friend. But do join me today. It would be an honor to have a drink with two such lovely young ladies."

"I'm afraid we have a bus to catch."

"Please, Gabriella, please!" Ophélie begged. "Maybe he knows about Mama! Please let us talk with Mr. Jean-Claude."

Gabriella nodded uncomfortably. "Well, all right. But just for a moment."

Jean-Claude led them to a table at the edge of the Comedie. He quickly ordered them three glasses of *sirop*, which arrived in tall glasses with thin, bright straws sticking out of the top.

His manner was smooth, polished, even kind as he addressed the child. "Little Ophélie, whatever brings you here to Montpellier? Is your mother here? It was quite a shame that we lost contact." He directed his gaze at Gabriella. "Do you know Anne-Marie? I mean, you must. A very dear friend of mine."

"Mama went away," Ophélie stated. "You do not know where she is, Mr. Jean-Claude? It was some bad men that took her." She started to cry.

Jean-Claude looked shocked. "Took her? What do you mean?" He held Ophélie's hands in his. "What kind of men took her? Did you know them?"

"I . . . I think so. It is hard to remember. I didn't really see them." She wiped her eyes. "Please won't you help me find Mama?"

Gabriella squirmed in her chair. "Ophélie, *cherie*. This man doesn't have any idea—"

"I would be most glad to help you," Jean-Claude interrupted. "I will do anything I can. But you must tell me where you live, so I may reach you, dear."

"I live by the church!" Ophélie blurted out.

"Ophélie, please! Let me talk to the man . . . to Jean-Claude," Gabriella scolded.

He sat back in his chair and ran his fingers through his thick brown hair. "Excuse me, Miss Gabriella. I did not mean to intrude. It is just . . . such a shock to see Ophélie here. I had lost touch, you know, with the war going on in Algeria. I do not mean to invade your privacy. It is only that if I could help in any way, I would be more than happy to do so."

He removed a pen and piece of paper from his shirt pocket and he quickly scribbled a number. "I live in Marseilles, but I travel a bit. Give me a call. Perhaps I could have your number. In case something turns up?"

Again Gabriella hesitated. "It is just that we do not have a private line. It might be hard to get through."

"But Bribri! There is a phone in the office. I have seen it."

Gabriella glared at Ophélie. "Yes, dear, there is, but I do not know the number. Listen, *Monsieur.* I will call you back next week. Will that be all right?"

"That will be fine. Just fine," Jean-Claude said. "Why don't we say next Tuesday night? A week from today? That would be the fifth of December, I believe."

"Yes, that sounds okay. Now I'm afraid we really must be going. Thank you for the drinks." She stood up and reached out her hand, which he took and squeezed.

"The pleasure was all mine, I assure you. May I accompany you home?" He had picked up Ophélie again and was tickling her neck.

"No, that isn't necessary. But thank you all the same."

He took out a ten-franc piece and handed it to Ophélie. "Here, my child. Go buy yourself a pastry with this. From *Tonton* Jean-Claude."

"Oh, *merci!*" Ophelie laughed and hugged his neck.

"And I hope we will have the chance to see each other again too," he said softly to Gabriella.

He watched the woman and child walk to the bus stop far down the road. He did not move from the *café*, but pulled his binoculars out of his bag. "Bus 11," he mumbled when Gabriella and Ophélie climbed aboard. "Bus 11 leads to the east side of town. And little Ophélie lives by a church. That shouldn't be hard to find. Not hard at all."

It was well after dark when Jean-Claude caught the train back to Marseilles, satisfied with the bit of luck he had run into on la Place de la Comedie.

Chapter Eighteen

David Hoffmann did not leave the classroom after he finished his lecture on the morning of the 4th of December. Instead he stared aimlessly out the window from the second story into the courtyard. The orphans were at recess. Many were playing tag, squealing as they chased each other around the garden.

Several children wandered alone on the outskirts of the game. The Arab boy was one of these. He was too old for the orphanage, too tall, his skin too dark. Although he withdrew from play, everything about him called attention to the fact that he did not even fit in among the misfits.

In sharp contrast, the little girl he had stumbled upon in Paris seemed to feel right at home. He smiled, seeing her dash about the courtyard in pursuit of a playmate. He liked to watch her from his window, although he was careful that she never saw him. He preferred that she think the benevolent stranger in Paris had disappeared as quickly as he had come. He did not have time to involve himself with another social case. The child had found a kind of home, and that was something positive to think about.

But the rest of his work left him numb. He no longer looked forward to class as he had for the past year and a half. Then, there had been the challenge of impressing and puzzling the young ladies. Of baiting them in an innocent game of cat-and-mouse. There had been the satisfaction of knowing he held a certain power of presence over his class.

That need for power had waned during the fall with the coming of Gabriella. She answered his deep-felt need to dig deeper into the human soul. She had been willing to go on the journey with him, even if her philosophy of life seemed diametrically opposed to his. All the better for the battle of the minds.

It had been a pleasant detour for David, taking his mind off the weighty matters of the war. A companion and an unwitting accomplice. But now he dared not try to gain back the friendship that had budded. It wasn't just pride that kept him away from Miss Gabriella Madison. He was sure he could win her over, if he tried.

But David knew that his silence came from more than pride. It came from respect. He cared for her. He cared that she was safe, that no other men would chase her through some crowded *marché*. Not love—the word made him laugh cynically. That was not the feeling. Respect, and perhaps friendship, but certainly not love. He could not afford to feel love again. There was enough trouble for him still from the first time.

* * *

Gabriella stood in the hallway in front of David's open door for a full five minutes. His back was turned toward her as he looked out the window. When finally he turned around to retrieve his briefcase from his desk, she reluctantly knocked on the door.

He looked up, startled. Seeing Gabriella, he frowned. "Yes?"

Gabriella felt her heartbeat accelerate. She almost turned to go. There he stood, ever confident and cynical, while she trembled before him. "May I come in?"

"Of course," he said with a curt smile.

"You aren't going to make this easy for me, are you?" she accused.

"I don't know what *this* is, Miss Madison."

She felt as if a wall stood between them. Taking a deep breath, she began, "I came to say I'm sorry."

"To ask forgiveness, is that it?" His tone was cutting. "If I remember correctly, that was the subject of our last conversation."

"I knew I shouldn't have bothered. Never mind." She turned to leave.

"Wait! Gabby, please." He came around his desk and touched her sleeve. "Please wait."

They regarded each other in silence. David cleared his throat and motioned to a chair. "Please. Sit down."

Gabriella obeyed without a word. She did not take her eyes off him.

David ran his fingers through his short black hair. His face was a dark shade of crimson as he sat on his desk and shrugged. "I don't know what to say." He rubbed his eyes with his hands. "Untrue. There are many things I could say, but it would just be a game. You're not here for that." His hands were beside him, grasping the rim of the desk. He raised his eyebrows quizzically. "I would like to know why you are here, Gabby."

"I will tell you on one condition," she answered.

"What is that?"

"That you listen, really listen before you say a word."

He grinned an almost boyish, sheepish grin. There

was a dimple in his left cheek that she'd never noticed before. "Agreed."

He looked vulnerable—a posture not typical of David Hoffmann—and Gabriella wanted to hug him.

She sighed and began talking. "You probably have not wanted an explanation for my aloofness the past month, but certain recent circumstances have convinced me that you deserve one." She twisted her hands nervously. "I have heard it said that there is a fine line between love and hate. I suppose I decided that it was much safer to hate you than . . . than the alternative." Her face was flushed.

Gabriella continued, "I am sorry that I got so mad over what you said about forgiveness and revenge. You have every right to believe whatever you want to believe. It is none of my business. It is true that I hoped to convince you otherwise, but that was only because—" She struggled for the words. "That was only because I felt compassion for you, a caring." Her blue eyes were shining with tears.

David wrinkled his brow, his dark eyes intense, but didn't speak.

"It was ridiculous of me to think that you cared for me too. I mean, beyond a casual friendship. I'm sorry that I've made things awkward between us." She closed her eyes for a moment, trying to regain her composure.

He looked as if he would like to hop down from the desk and come to her, so she hurried on. "One other thing. I'm almost through." She blinked back the tears.

"You were right. There is a death of the soul that makes life a living hell. A memory that is bitter and haunting. And perhaps it takes a very long time to forgive. Perhaps the pain will swallow me up whole until there is nothing left to forgive. Perhaps that is what you meant. I did not understand then, but now . . ." She stopped and buried her face in her hands, shaking her head. "Stupid girl," she whispered. "I promised myself I wouldn't cry. I will go. That is all I had to say." She fumbled in her purse to find a Kleenex and stood up.

Then David was at her side, pulling her toward him, his strong arms holding her against his chest. Neither breathed or moved, but it seemed to Gabriella that everything was racing madly. His hand stroked her hair, carefully, cautiously.

Gabriella did not dare to look up. "Please, David, don't . . . don't care too much. I didn't come here for this. I can't."

David stepped back from her, his hands resting lightly on her shoulders. "I'm sorry. You are right. There is too much that separates us, Gabby." He breathed heavily. "But there is something that has broken you, my friend," he pronounced the last word with caution. "Let me walk with you to Mme. Leclerc's. I promise I will listen."

Gabriella nodded as he wiped a tear from her cheek.

They passed Mme. Leclerc's apartment, walking through the center of Castelnau and out into the countryside beyond the village. The frost of the morning dissipated under the sun's warm regard as Gabriella related her memory of the rape, her nightmares, her anger with Mother Griolet. David interrupted occasionally to ask a question, but otherwise he was quiet.

"I cannot understand why Mother did not tell me before I came. It was as if she knew I would find out, but she didn't want to be the one to reveal it. That is so unlike her. She is not afraid to confront the truth."

"But you said that neither she nor Mother Griolet knew you had witnessed the rape," David interjected. "Perhaps she was not worried that you would remember; perhaps it was only so painful for her to know you were returning to this place."

"Perhaps," Gabriella said thoughtfully. "But Mother Griolet? She sent me to the mission house with her blessing."

"You would have preferred her to sit you down and tell you about the rape, the pregnancy, and Ericka? I don't know if she felt it was her place."

"Oh, David, maybe you are right. I do not know. All I know is that something is dead in me. In a different way from when Ericka died. And every night I hear a voice inside my head that says, 'It's your fault! Why didn't you scream, little girl?' I know that it is not God's voice accusing. Excuse me—I realize you do not believe. But God is not the accuser. It is another who accuses." Her voice was barely audible.

"And then everything gets confused. I should have screamed. Then there would have been no rape. But that means no Ericka. No pain and no joy. And I am so angry!"

"Have you written your mother?"

"I tried several times, but I always sound accusing and harsh. And what good will it do her to know I am dying in my soul? She will only worry."

"I suppose she would want to pray for you," he said softly.

Gabriella stopped walking and stared at him in disbelief.

"I am only trying to see as you see. Perhaps it would be of some comfort to your mother if she felt she could pray for you. Isn't prayer supposed to bring comfort? A conversation with the Almighty?"

"Something like that, yes. I don't feel like talking about it anymore. I'm too tired." She rubbed her forehead, feeling suddenly drained. David was ready to talk about prayer, and she had no energy for it.

She changed the subject. "There is something that has

been bothering me ever since you came to eat at Mme. Leclerc's. The *lapereau*, the rabbit. You aren't allergic, are you? It was something else."

David grimaced. "A very bad memory from the past. I don't wish to talk of it now." He glanced over at Gabriella and took her hand. "Someday, perhaps."

"Won't you tell me anything about yourself, David? Why you can't forgive? What wakes you in the middle of the night?"

"I have already told you, Gabby. It is too painful to rehash all the details. I am a half Jew, and I lost my mother and sister in the camps. I was the guilty little boy who stood by and said nothing."

"But what could a little boy say? You are not guilty!" Gabriella was adamant.

"And then neither are you, my dear. Neither are you."

By the time they returned to Castelnau it was noon.

David left her at the door leading up to Mme. Leclerc's apartment. "Dare I ask you for something, Gabby?"

"Yes, ask."

"Come with me to Les Baux on Saturday. As my friend. It is beautiful there. It will get you away from the memories."

"Oh, David. I can't." She smiled as he looked at her questioningly. "I promised someone I would not run after danger anymore."

"And I am danger? Surely not. There is business there, but no danger. Please?" His dark eyes were soft, like a puppy's, hopeful for play.

Gabriella said nothing. She closed her eyes.

"What are you doing?" David asked suspiciously.

"I am praying," she retorted. "I am sure it sounds silly to you, but I am praying for the strength to say no.

Can't you understand?"

He took her hands. "No, I don't understand, Gabby. I only know that I have missed you. Our talks. Your wit. Does your God forbid friendship? What would be the intrigue of a life spent only with people who think just as you do? Please, please don't tell me your religion forbids friendship. Don't tell me you are afraid to be with someone who makes you think. No, Gabby. You are too smart for something that narrow."

In her mind she heard the word *friendship*. It was, after all, only a friendship. *Ye are the light of the world,* she heard. *Ye are the salt of the earth.* "Oh, why must you confuse everything? Of course my God does not forbid friendship with…with…um…atheists."

David laughed. "You say the word as if I am some sort of despicable enemy!" He bent down to look her in the eye. "I am your friend. Only your friend."

"Good-bye, David," she said. "Thank you for listening to me." She turned her key in the lock and pushed open the heavy door. Without looking back, she added, "I'll go on Saturday."

"Thank you, too, Gabby," he called after her. "You have a lot of guts. You're going to be okay."

* * *

Ophélie huddled on the bottom bunk at rest time. Anne-Sophie was asleep next to her, snuggling contentedly with the teddy that had been lost and was now found. On the bunk overhead, Marine whispered with Lorène. Most of the other girls slept. But rest time was Ophélie's time alone. And what a wonderful time it was, now that she could read. Every day she pulled out Mama's letter. It had taken her three weeks to get through the first page, sounding out the words in a whisper. Then she would reread each sentence again and again until she had practically memorized it.

Once in a while she could not figure a word out, no matter how hard she tried. Then she would copy it carefully in her *cahier de lecture* to show to Gabriella the next day. One word at a time and Bribri had never seemed suspicious.

Finally she was on the last page. Page one was all about how much Mama loved her and how she never wanted to leave Ophélie. And something about the war and helping other mommies and children. And Mr. Gady. Ophélie frowned, remembering how she had cried when she read that part.

The second page was about the cross, the cross of Papy and how when she wore it, she would be safe. Ophélie had not taken the cross off since she had read that page last week. Now she turned to the third page, and with difficulty, began sounding out each letter, as Mother Griolet had taught her to do in class.

"I m ... mu ... st, I must tell you one m ... more t ... th ... thing. I h ... have never talk ... talked to you of your fa ... fat ... father." Ophélie gasped. *Father!* That was the word, she was sure. Somehow, she had never imagined that she had a father.

She wanted to read faster now, before the bell rang and ended rest time. "I do not know w ... whe ... where he is, but Ophélie, he is a good man." She frowned. So Mama didn't know where her father was.

"He does not know he has a dau ... daugh ..." She struggled with the word for several minutes. "Daughter!" she said out loud.

Marine peered down from the top bunk and giggled. "You are talking to yourself, Ophélie."

Ophélie said nothing, waiting for Marine to start whispering again with Lorène.

"I c ... cou ... could not tell him. Please forgive your

mama. But he is a good man who h ... hel ... helped me
w ... whe ... when we were bot ... both very young and
living in Al ... Alg ...." It must be Algeria. The country
with the war.

"Per ... perhaps some ... some day you will be able
to f ... find him ..."

The shrill clanging of the bell startled Ophélie. She
pushed the letter under her pillow as the other little
girls scurried off their bunks and out the door. One
more look! Just one more look!

She pulled the letter out and quickly found her place
at the bottom of page three. She would not have time to
finish it all. But maybe one more line. "He is an Ame ...
Amer ...." She threw down the paper in frustration.
Another word she could not read! Sister Rosaline would
be coming at any minute to check for her. Just one more
line. She skipped the big word and continued reading.
"Very hand ... handsome and smart. His name is Da ...
Dav ... David ...." *David!* Like the shepherd boy in the
Bible. She had read the story in class yesterday. The boy
who killed the giant. Her daddy had the same name!

She stared at the letter again. Another word came
after *David,* but it was long and complicated, too. "Ho ...
Hoff ..."

"*Coucou,* Ophélie!" It was Sister Rosaline's high-
pitched voice. "Come, now. Time for afternoon class!"

Silently Ophélie stuffed the letter into the tights and
closed the middle drawer. She jumped off the bed and
bounded into the courtyard, screeching to a halt behind
little Christophe, who was pulling Anne-Sophie's pigtails
and giggling.

A father, she thought all through the afternoon. *A
father named David.* She felt happy with the knowledge.
A secret from her mother. But how in the world would
she find him? She could not even find her mother, and

she knew just what she looked like. How could she find her father who, for the moment, was only a name written on a pink piece of paper in Mama's hand?

* * *

Afternoon class was over for the orphans. They filed outside into the chilly December afternoon. The sky was already growing dark. Gabriella waited for Mother Griolet to come back through the hall.

"Can we talk for a moment?" she asked the nun.

"Of course, my dear. Do you wish to come to my office?"

"Yes, yes ... that will be fine." Gabriella disliked the awkward distance she felt with the nun. They walked to the ground floor without talking.

Mother Griolet unlocked the office door and motioned for Gabriella to enter. When they both were seated, Gabriella fiddled with her hair, twirling it absently around her fingers. She did not know how to start.

"Well, I am sure you realize why I've come to see you," she said finally. "It is my conscience. Today is my day to say I'm sorry. I'm not very good at it, but. . . ." she sat up in the chair. "I need to apologize for my anger the other day. I am sure you did not wish to see me hurt. I am sorry that I accused you."

"Thank you, *ma fille*. I know it is not easy. And your anger is normal," Mother Griolet reassured her.

"Have you ever felt like you were dying inside?"

"Yes. I have known that pain before."

"And how did you find the courage to forgive? I have already forgiven once for what happened to Ericka. Now it seems I must back up and start over ... only it is even more painful. I know in my head that it was not my fault. But I feel responsible."

"It is often that way. Gabriella, I do not mean to

sound like a distant doctor who has all the answers. It is simply that I deal often with children and adults who have been abused—physically, psychologically, emotionally. The grieving period can be long. You must be patient with yourself."

"And in the meantime what do I do?"

"You keep living. And talking out your feelings. Actually your outrage of last week was very good. A necessary step. I have prayed you would not feel embarrassed to come back. It is too hard to carry your anger alone."

"Do you think we can forgive *anything*, Mother Griolet? The worst of offenses? Do you think it is possible?"

"Forgiveness is not just for the offender," the nun stated, compassion in her eyes. "You are innocent, yes. But you are a victim, and until you forgive, you will always be a victim, locked in your hurt and bitterness. Forgiveness frees."

She paused for a moment, then continued. "How big is your God, Gabriella? Mine turns tragedy into triumph. A rape and a precious daughter born."

"But she died!" Gabriella protested. "Why must Mother grieve twice for her? You said Mother died in her heart when Ericka was conceived. But then she looked past the awful pain and found love. Why did she have to die a second time, with Ericka? It wasn't fair!"

She held the cross in her hand. She had returned to Mr. Auguste's shop to retrieve it with its chain. She thought of Mother Griolet's words. *An intricate weaving of lives.* A Huguenot cross that a Catholic nun had given her Protestant mother to help her forgive an unknown Arab. A daughter born, only to be yanked away too soon. Gabriella closed her eyes. The story tormented her. How could a simple cross bring peace to such a tangled mess?

Her eyes still closed, Gabriella saw the image of Ophélie smiling before her. She whispered, "And now this same cross has brought another six-year-old into my life." She opened her eyes and looked at the nun, who seemed to be in prayer. "Tragedy to triumph, is that what you said, Mother Griolet? You said your God can bring triumph out of tragedy, *n'est-ce pas?*"

Mother Griolet lifted her head and nodded slowly.

Gabriella stood up quickly. "He is my God too. I have something to do now. I will try to keep living as you say. There are others I must keep living for."

* * *

The phone booth stood at the back of the small square in Castelnau where an olive tree rose from within the stones of the street. The small fountain beside it sprayed water into its moonlit pool, occasionally sending its spew toward the glass booth as a gust of wind rose and caught the water. Gabriella closed the sliding door behind her and felt in her pocket for the paper and franc piece. She squinted in the dark to read the number, slowly lifted the receiver from its hook, and dialed.

The phone rang once, twice, a third time. She was about to replace the earpiece in relief, when a man's voice answered on the line.

"*Allo? Oui, est-ce que c'est Jean-Claude?*" Her voice was shaking as she listened for the reply.

"Jean-Claude, this is the woman you met in Montpellier. Gabriella? You remember? . . . Yes, of course, you would. Well, I have promised the child, Ophélie, that I would call to see if you have any news . . . I am sorry to bother you . . ."

She nodded as he answered. "Yes, well that is good news indeed!" She listened, wrinkling her brow. "You want to meet us again?" Gabriella hesitated. "I really don't know. . . . This Saturday on the Comedie? I'm afraid not—I'm leaving town for the day." She felt annoyed at his persistence, afraid he was more interested in pursuing her than helping Ophélie. "No, it is impossible for Saturday, I assure you. . . . No, I already have a date. We're going to Les Baux-de-Provence. You've heard of it, of course? . . . Yes. So you see, I cannot meet you Saturday. I will call on Sunday then. If there is any way you could find an address where you think Anne-Marie is. . . . Anything would be most helpful. Ophélie will be thrilled that you have heard her mother is safe. Thank you. *Au revoir.*"

She hung up the phone and left the phone booth with an uneasy feeling. She wished he would have simply given her the information over the phone. He seemed nice enough. Perhaps it would not be so bad to go out with a green-eyed Frenchman. For Ophélie. But halfway back to Mme. Leclerc's house, she was not thinking of the young Frenchman, but of David Hoffmann and their brief embrace that morning.

* * *

Jean-Claude switched on the radio in his dingy kitchen, laughing to himself. The fair Gabriella had called after all. He had not been sure she would. A very clumsy girl, he reflected. Or perhaps she wanted him to follow her to Les Baux-de-Provence. Perhaps she had an inkling. Surely if she was "Hugo," she could not be thoughtless. "No, my little redhead. Ali will be happy to hear that I plan to visit Les Baux this Saturday."

He chuckled softly, running his fingers through his thick brown hair. "Les Baux-de-Provence! Now there's a place for an accident if ever there was. *Bon sang*, Gabriella. I'll meet you there on Saturday."

Chapter Nineteen

"I am glad you decided to come with me, Gabby." David glanced over at Gabriella, seated beside him in the *deux chevaux*.

"I only agreed because you promised no more secrets, David. You are sure there's nothing to tell me?"

"*Au contraire*, there is so much to tell you, my dear. We are driving through the countryside of Frédéric Mistral and Alphonse Daudet, the land ripe with olives and the best of its oil in all of France. Before you lies a scene from Van Gogh or Cezanne or Gaugin. This is where they painted, throughout this rich region of Provence. There is nothing like it anywhere on earth, Gabby. Nothing." He reached over and squeezed her hand, then immediately released it.

"David Hoffmann, you are so hard to resist! A walking history book, the king of culture. I have never known anyone like you. But also the Master of Silence, if you wish. Tell me then, please, about this magical land of Provence. I only hope your faithful little *baignol* will get us there." She lovingly patted the car's ripped upholstery.

"You can't get to les Baux by train; it must be discovered by car. It is only a hundred kilometers from Montpellier, and we've already come eighty. We'll make it. But I'm afraid we'll have a bit of wind up on the mountain. December isn't the ideal time to see les Baux, but ..." he let his voice trail off.

"But you had business to do in town," Gabriella finished his sentence with a mocking tone.

He laughed. "Yes, Gabby, something like that."

The sun was bright on the road. As they drove, Gabriella watched the wind whipping through the fields, checked only by rows of tall pointed cypress trees outlining the fields, leaning at a forty-five degree angle to the ground.

David commented, "Those trees are there precisely to protect the fields from the wind. Even on a calm day, they remain perpetually bent in adoration to the Mistral.

"We're coming closer. See the small chain of miniature mountains in the distance? They are called the *Alpilles*, the little Alps. All this region used to be marshes, from Arles to the Alpilles, until one of your Protestants, a Mr. Van Eys from Amsterdam, figured out how to successfully drain them and turn them into cornfields. Unfortunately, he had to rush back home for safety when the Edict of Nantes was revoked.

"The next little town, Fontvieille, is home to a famous windmill. In it is a strange kind of compass around the ceiling, marked with the names of the thirty-two different winds that blow through Provence."

"So all this wind isn't necessarily the fault of the Mistral?" Gabriella questioned.

"Today he's the guilty one, but for heaven's sake, no. There are many others. Now let me see, what have I told you of les Baux?"

"I think you said there are only ruins of the village

228

and castle. It was built into the mountain, right?"

"Yes, into the southern side of the Alpilles. It was one of the most powerful feudal houses in Provence in the Middle Ages. There used to be over four thousand inhabitants in the city. Now you have at best three hundred, most of whom gain their livelihood from the tourist industry." The road separated into a V, and David took the left branch, following the signs to les Baux-de-Provence. "We'll park down in the valley and hike up to the town."

"It's amazing that from back here you can't even tell there is a city up there," Gabriella commented as they approached the valley and stared up at the massive piece of granite before them.

"That way, they were protected against their enemies. A good strategy and successful for years. Les Baux was often in rebellion against the King of France, and lodged many a Huguenot during the sixteenth century. In 1632 Cardinal Richelieu, Louis XIII's minister, put an end to Les Baux as it had been. The castle and ramparts were destroyed." David pulled his car into the dirt driveway of an old farmhouse and parked in the grass.

"We'll get out here," he said, coming to her side of the car and opening the door. He offered Gabriella his hand.

"How noble," Gabriella laughed, taking his hand and stepping out of the *deux chevaux.*

They walked along a small paved road, enclosed on either side by the old stone walls of the farmhouse. As the wall ended, David took her arm, and they slipped into what looked to be a private garden.

"Oh, it's beautiful," Gabriella remarked, looking around at the perfectly groomed boxwood hedges. "I imagine it must be magnificent in the spring with all the flowers." In the corner of the garden stood a small stone pavilion. "What is this?"

"That, my dear, is the Renaissance Pavilion of the Queen Jeanne, erected in 1581, actually a hundred years after she died. Queen Jeanne was the wife of the Roi René—remember, we saw a statue of him in Aix? He gave les Baux to his wife in the fifteenth century after the dynasty died out." David stepped inside the pavilion. "Very good representation of Renaissance architecture, wouldn't you say?"

Gabriella stood outside, admiring the small stone structure that formed a hexagon in the corner of the garden. Three bay windows supported by seven fluted columns opened out onto the garden. Above the arches of the windows, the grotesque faces of gargoyles peered out from the otherwise serene hideaway. Two giant cypress trees flanked either side of the pavilion.

"It's since been given the name 'The Temple of Love' by the *fibrigues* poets of the last century." He raised his eyebrows, pulled her toward him, and softly kissed her cheek. With an exaggerated French accent, he said, "It is too bad that we are just friends, *ma cherie.*"

Gabriella giggled and walked out from under the pavilion, her cheeks red.

"*Allons-y!* We have many other points of interest to see today." Laughing, he caught up to Gabriella and led her out of the garden and down the road.

They walked in silence for ten minutes, winding behind farmhouses and a few elegant hotels that offered food and room to the wealthiest tourists. David took her arm and whispered, "Come this way." The road took a sudden turn, and the large stones that had seemed far above them were suddenly at their level.

"This, Gabriella, is the Val d'Enfer."

"The Valley of Hell, hmm. An interesting name." As she looked around her, she exclaimed, "And I see why. Look at those huge rocks! And that one there. Why, you'd think they were gigantic skulls."

He smiled. "Exactly." As they walked and climbed higher through the rocks, looking down on the large pieces of granite, she had the eerie impression that three or four cruel giants had been laid to rest in the valley and alas, this was all that remained of them now.

"Come on. We need to be getting up to the city. It's nearly lunch time. Don't want the *boulangerie* to close before we get there. I know a shortcut we can take."

David found an overgrown path that cut through the trees and vegetation, rocky and steep. Gabriella wished she had worn more comfortable walking shoes.

David caught her easily and held his arm around her waist as they continued climbing. "There is a fascinating story about the Viscount of les Baux, who lived here in the fourteenth century. He was called Raymond de Turennes—a real colorful character. Apparently, the way old Raymond got his kicks was to leave his mountain refuge with his band of warriors and ravage the country-side, kidnapping whomever he wished. He would take his prisoners up to the castle and demand a ransom. Of course, some of the peasants had no one to pay ransom for them. These unfortunates Raymond led to a window in the dungeon that gave a splendid view of the valley below, and *oop la!* He pushed them over the side. As they fell to their grisly death, he laughed until he cried."

"David! That's awful! Is it true?"

"Quite true. When we get to the top, I'll show you the very spot."

"I'm not sure I care to see, thanks all the same," Gabriella retorted.

They arrived, out of breath from the steep ascent, by a little sidestreet that led directly to the back entrance to the city.

"The south side of the city has been restored,"

David said, "and numerous merchants sell their wares to tourists in the summer. There are ónly a few shops open in the winter. But if we climb higher we can get into the ruins of the castle and the dungeon."

By now the wind was biting, and Gabriella tucked her hands inside the pockets of her pea coat. She was only half listening. "Hold on a minute, won't you?" she called after him. "I'm freezing. Let me just warm up inside this store." Before David could protest, Gabriella had already disappeared behind the open door of one of the boutiques.

Immediately she was greeted by a young gypsy-looking woman with thick black hair that fell in curls around her shoulders. She wore a white lace blouse with a full skirt made from provencial print.

"I may help you, yes?" She sang each word, adding another syllable to the end.

"*Merci.* I'm just looking." Gabriella was surrounded by provincial material, bold, bright patterns in reds, yellows, and blues. The store was perfumed with the scent of dried lavender mingled with sachets marked *herbes de provence.* Large bars of soap were arranged by color in wooden crates. Gabriella bent down to smell the fragrant aromas of *tilleul, vanille, romarin, cyprès, miel,* and *lavande.* She breathed deeply and shut her eyes, enjoying the blend of fragrances.

Along the back wall of the boutique stood a large assortment of clay figures. "These are the *santons* of Provence, *n'est-ce pas?*" Gabriella inquired.

The shopkeeper smiled broadly. "Yees, dey are all originals, handcrafted in dis region. You will see dey are marked wif the stamp of de artisan."

Gabriella admired the famous *santons* of Provence. She had heard much about the small clay figures that were created by provencial craftsmen to depict the people of Provence, each bringing his or her gift to the *crèche* of the baby Jesus. On one shelf a full nativity scene had been set up, complete with the Holy Family, a donkey, lamb, camel, and dozens of provencial villagers bringing their offerings to the Christ Child. Gabriella reached to touch the brightly painted clay figures. Some were only a few inches high, the larger ones stood a foot in height. These wore real provencial material: an old woman dressed in bright yellow and red with a bunch of lavender in her hands, a graying shepherd with cloak and staff and a lamb around his neck, a baker with his sack of long loaves in one hand and his white hat falling to the side, his mustache powdered with flour.

Ah, he is perfect! Gabriella thought. Without further thought, she took the clay figure from the shelf and placed it on the counter. "Could you wrap this, please?" she whispered, not wanting David to suddenly appear in the store and discover the treasure she had found for his Christmas gift. Eighty francs was expensive, but the urge to buy the figure for David was stronger than her practical reasoning.

"It's perfect," she laughed again to herself. "My dashing professor who loves the French bread, but always makes me buy it. Ah, David, someday I pray that you, too, will come to the *crèche* of our Lord Jesus and lay the loaves of your heart before Him." She was still imagining the scene when the gypsy woman handed her the well-wrapped box and the change from her purchase.

David had taken a seat further up the road and was waiting for Gabriella with a scowl on his face, his nose red from the cold.

"Shopping!" he muttered when he saw her package. "We must hurry. The store will close soon. I'm almost positive there's a *boulangerie* around the corner."

"That's fine, but could you put my package in your backpack first?" Gabriella asked. Grudgingly, he obliged her. But around the corner they found only another brightly colored store window advertising provencial prints and pottery. David cursed under his breath.

Gabriella continued up the street and turned onto the next side road. "Look, David," she called. "There's a *boulangerie* right here."

"Ah! Good, you found it." Relief spread across his handsome face. "Be a love and get me a *pain de seigle,* not too dark, mind you." He rummaged in his pocket for a five-franc piece and gave it to her.

Gabriella, her red hair shimmering in the high noon sun, narrowed her clear blue eyes and taunted, "Are you kidding? Me get the bread? Not on your life. Not after Aix. *You* get whatever kind of bread you want, David Hoffmann."

He shrugged his shoulders and slipped into the store.

* * *

Jean-Claude Gachon pulled his gray plaid wool scarf over his mouth and crept back into a corner of the narrow sidestreet as a lean man with powerful shoulders entered the *boulangerie* just within his view. He raised his eyebrows in surprise.

Jean-Claude waited as the young man rejoined his lovely red-haired companion outside the store and placed a loaf of bread in a small backpack. The couple continued up the tiny road. The man stood a good half-foot taller than the woman, and his hair was thick and black. Jean-Claude studied him carefully, snapping a photo of the two together.

"So, you are here after all, Mr. Hoffmann," he reflected out loud. "Of course! It would be you!" *Anne-Marie's old lover.* Yes, Jean-Claude remembered her confession when he had questioned her about the picture he had found of David Hoffmann over two years ago. So he was here. Jean-Claude frowned. Mr. Hoffmann might prove more difficult to deal with.

He followed them up the uneven street to where it was blocked by an iron barrier. An arrow on a sign indicated that tickets to visit the ruins of the castle and dungeon could be purchased in the building to their right. Five minutes after Gabriella and Mr. Hoffmann entered the building, they left out another door and continued their ascent. Jean-Claude stepped up to the window to buy his ticket.

He glanced briefly at the miniature reproduction of Les Baux-de-Provence as it would have appeared in the Middle Ages. He was not very interested in the history of the city, but he wasted time reading and studying maps and panels. At last he stepped out of the ancient stone refuge into the open air. A strong gust of the Mistral's power greeted him. He bent into the wind, climbing the hill until it opened before him onto a vast plateau. He saw the young couple, huddling together as they pushed against the force of the wind.

Suddenly the handsome Frenchman lost his calm composure and broke into a laugh. He knew a wonderful story about this mountain fortress. A story of a crazy viscount who pushed his victims from the dungeon onto the jagged rocks of the mountain, watching them fall to a gruesome death. The wind stung his eyes and tears formed, and he laughed again. The two young people walking a hundred yards in front didn't suspect a thing.

* * *

Gabriella was clinging to David's arm, her head bent down to protect it from the cold gale. Their progress was slow.

The ruins of the castle spread out before them, still hewn into the sides of the mountain. David headed them into a small cove of the first of a series of large rocks. There the stones protected them from the rushing wind.

"I hope you aren't planning on picnicking up here," Gabriella yelled over the wind's whistle.

David's face broke into a wide smile. "What could be better? To face our fate against the elements." Seeing that she remained unconvinced, he added, "We'll just have a look around. Then I'll take you back into the village for a piping hot bowl of their regional soup: *soupe de pistou.* It will stick to your bones and warm you up. But come along now. Be brave, fair princess!"

Gabriella screwed up her nose and retorted, "As long as you are not Raymond de Turennes, I shall follow you anywhere."

He led her to the side of the mountain. Before them the plains below spread out in every direction for miles. "There in the distance is Mont St. Victoire, the farthest peak you can see. And over there, the Camargue, and even further out, on a very clear day, you can see Aigues-Mortes. You can understand how at the time, the Baux family could control all the traffic on the roads from Aix to Arles. That was the ancient Roman Way, called Aurelia."

The Alpilles dotted the horizon, while directly below them lay dozens of fields outlined by the tall cypress trees. "If I weren't so cold, I'd love to stay here all day," Gabriella commented. "As it is, let's see these ruins and get back to warmth."

"Gabriella! I'm surprised at you. Where's your sense of adventure?" He took her hand and led her along the plateau. It was fifty feet wide, with either side walled in with the castle ruins. They stepped over a low wall of stones into the facade of what had been a large square room. Ducking their heads, they made their way through a doorway and down a short flight of stone steps into the skeleton of another room. Gabriella grabbed onto the stones as a gust of wind pushed her backwards.

"The Mistral must be nearly a hundred kilometers an hour," David calculated. "Fierce." But his eyes shone with pleasure, as if he would challenge the wind and conquer it.

Gabriella shivered beside him. "How can you be enjoying this? We're nuts to be out here. There's not a single soul up here besides us."

"Patience, Gabby. We'll just go to the end and climb up to the dungeon ruins. I don't want you to miss the view."

They pressed on, up narrow steps and down others, following the jagged outline of the fallen castle. At the farthest end of the ruins, David stopped. "I'll follow you up here." He pointed to a steep set of steps that led up to what had been the second story of the dungeon. A wrought-iron guardrail had been placed beside the steps for the tourists. Cautiously Gabriella mounted the steps, with David close behind. She clung to the rail for support against the force of the wind, then flattened herself against the wall and held onto the guardrail with one hand as David motioned her to follow him. They came around the corner where they could see the outer wall of the dungeon built into the mountain.

"Look below!" David shouted, for the screaming wind made it virtually impossible to hear. "This is where Raymond did his deed."

Gabriella peered down, barely daring to look. But indeed the wall ended abruptly, and all that was left was a deep abyss below.

"Horrible!" she screamed back. "Let's leave."

* * *

Jean-Claude had watched the progress of the two young people like a hawk contemplating its prey. He stayed forty feet behind them, hidden within the ruins. As they rounded the corner of the dungeon, slipping out of sight, he gleefully scaled to the top of the cliff and perched ten feet above David and Gabriella. He waited for her to peer over the ledge and he laughed. "You are perhaps with me in this little game, David Hoffmann, *non?*" The position was perfect. Eyes blazing, he rubbed his hands together in a frenzy, as if he were Raymond de Turennes' ghost come back to haunt the castle.

I will hardly have to throw the rock, he thought, kicking his foot against a loose stone the size of a soccer ball. *The wind will do it for me. "Cruel Mistral wind blows red-haired foreign girl to her death in the same spot that Raymond de Turennes did his devious deeds centuries before,"* the papers would boast. The people would shake their heads and murmur, "Tragic."

Jean-Claude moved closer to the couple, the large stone now in his hands. Gabriella stood to the right of David, clutching the rail as she peered into the valley. She let go momentarily. Jean-Claude stepped out of hiding, and with an unheard grunt, threw the stone forcefully at Gabriella's feet. It hit her hard and bounced off into the ravine. Jean-Claude waited to hear the woman's chilling scream above the fury of the Mistral, then he raced to the top of the dungeon wall and hid in its shelter, laughing while tears ran down his face.

* * *

Gabriella had just turned to retrace her steps when a large rock hit her hard in the shin. She screamed as she stumbled and slipped. David lurched toward her outstretched hand, but she had fallen through the railing, past his grasp.

"David!" she shrieked, grabbing the jagged stones of a narrow ledge leading to the precipice. Dust blew into her eyes as she hung awkwardly on the ledge. Heart pounding, she managed to pull her chest onto the rock. Her feet dangled in the air. One shoe came off and fell into nothingness.

It was no use to cry out. She could not be heard. David was bending down from above, reaching toward her. She thought of the strength in his hands. Yet he had nothing to grab onto himself. Before them the whole valley stretched like an opened mouth, ready to swallow them whole. David was on his stomach, reaching, leaning across the pale yellow boulder. He wedged one foot into a split in the rock. It was all there was to hold him in place.

Gabriella watched his hand, terror in her eyes. The wind blew as if it was in a battle with David for her life. It pushed against her with the brute power it had gained running across the plain. She felt her hands sweating in the freezing air, slipping from the jagged rock. Her eyes met David's, and for that moment she read his thoughts louder than the howling wind. *Hold on!*

With a heave he pulled her up against the craggy, pointed rocks that ripped deep into her coat and legs. She fell onto the narrow ledge and lay breathless beside him. The roaring wind stung her eyes, bringing tears and drying them in the same effort. She was planted on the ledge in fear, not daring to move. David's arms gripped her tightly, pulling her against him, so that his back sheltered her from the wind.

"Can you get up, Gabby?" She felt his hot breath against the back of her neck as he spoke in gasps. "I will hold you. Only a few feet and you'll have the railing. Can you grab it now?"

He loosened his grasp and she slid through his arms,

forcing her body over the short distance to grab hold of the railing. Her head swam. She felt dizzy with fear.

David had raised himself from the ledge, gently pushing her up to safety. As she sat, clinging to the railing, he pulled himself beside her. They inched their way around the corner of the castle and rested their backs against the wall. The Mistral buffeted them in its fury, but they did not move. Nor did they see a lone figure running across the plateau, swept along by the wind like a dustball in a ghost town.

* * *

The way back was much easier as the wind pushed them along, back across the plateau. David held Gabriella in his arms. She did not protest. He felt her body shiver against him, felt the low sobs that racked her fragile frame. Her coat was torn and her stockings full of runs. Blood held them against her legs. He looked at her left foot and felt a shudder rip through his soul. Somewhere at the bottom of the ravine lay a woman's low-heeled tan pump where once the bones of less fortunate victims had rested.

It did not make sense to David. He had glimpsed the rock that hit her before it fell over the mountain. Even the bitter wind could not dislodge such a rock. It was as if something, someone had thrown it. But the place was barren except for them.

He let himself out the iron gate that led back into the village. Two hundred yards down the cobblestoned road he set Gabriella down on a curb.

"Here, we're at the restaurant. Do you want to go in?" She looked up at him with her chapped, tear-stained face. Her hair was a mass of red tangles. "We can go on to the car if you'd rather. I only thought you might like a place to wash up."

She nodded slowly. "Yes, let's go in."

They entered the small restaurant, which smelled of thick soups and strong cheeses. Its empty tables were covered with bright blue provincial print, and warmth hung in the air. A young, stocky woman with short brown hair greeted them with a smile. Then she noticed Gabriella's disarray. "*Mademoiselle* is hurt?" she asked.

"An accident, yes," David whispered. "Could you show her to the *toilettes, s'il vous plaît?* And would you have a towel or cloth she could wash up with?"

"*Bien sur*, of course," the woman replied, taking Gabriella by the arm. "You may come into my apartment. It is just here, behind the restaurant." David watched Gabriella limp along beside her and disappear behind a bright red curtain.

He ran his hands through his hair. He removed the backpack from his back, but his shoulders still sagged under some unseen weight. He thought back to Aix and the young man he had knocked out with a wine bottle. The man had had no identification on him. Just a camera.

And today, David had been sure no one was around. He had been so careful. For ten minutes, his eyes stared blankly at the menu, but his mind wandered.

Gabriella came back through the curtains. Her face was washed and her hair brushed. She wore slippers on her feet and carried her coat and shoe in her arms. "*Merci. Merci, mille fois,*" she said, smiling at the young woman who accompanied her to the table.

"Shall I bring you two bowls of *la soupe au pistou?* It is delicious, potatoes and vegetables and cheese."

David and Gabriella nodded simultaneously, and something in that small gesture made them both laugh. As the waitress left their table, they looked at each other. David took her hands. "Gabby, I am so sorry. Forgive me, will you? I never dreamed.... It was foolish of me to take you up there, in this wind."

"I must admit, we had quite an adventure. Enough to last me a while!" She thought for a moment, then said, "Enough to cover last week's nightmares over with the fear of today."

"Are you all right? Not hurt?"

"One lost shoe, a pair of ruined hose, and numerous scrapes and bruises. Nothing very exciting to show for what I've been through."

"The lost shoe is the proof," he said, smiling, but immediately his face clouded. "Gabby, it is time I explained a few things to you. Do you want to know? You are not afraid?"

"I *have* to know, David. Surely whatever this secret business of yours is can't be more dangerous than the little accident I've just had."

"Yes, you are right. But I cannot tell you here." He covered her hand with his.

The young woman brought them two earthen bowls of thick, steaming soup. They ate in silence.

* * *

They rode back toward Montpellier with the wind whistling outside the car. David kept glancing in the rearview mirror. No one was following them.

He cleared his throat awkwardly. "Gabby, dear, I'm not quite sure how to start. I ... I'm afraid that somehow what happened today wasn't an accident."

"I knew you were thinking that."

"I'm sure you suspected the same. Every time we've gone somewhere, there's been trouble. In Aigues-Mortes you sprained your ankle, in Aix there was the man following you, and now ..."

"But David! That is crazy. Aigues-Mortes was just an accident. I was clumsy, and then Jean-Claude helped

242

me." She looked up at David, sudden recognition in her eyes. "Jean-Claude! He knew I was coming here today. I didn't see what harm it would do ... He knew!"

"Hold on, Gabby. Just who is Jean-Claude?"

"He's the young man I met in the Tower of Constance at Aigues-Mortes. I ran into him again in Montpellier the other day with Ophélie—the new orphan. I think I told you about her?" David nodded. "He used to know her mother, and he said he could help us find her, and I was supposed to call him back. When I did, he wanted to meet me today, but I told him I couldn't because I would be in les Baux."

"You told him you were coming here?"

Gabriella blushed. "Yes. I know I talk too much."

"Never mind that now. Tell me what this Jean-Claude looks like."

"He is maybe five-feet-ten, thick brownish hair. Quite handsome really. And green eyes. I ... I notice eyes. Their color, I mean." Her face reddened again.

"He is the man who followed you at Aix, too."

"How do you know that?"

"Because I knocked him over the head with a wine bottle."

"You what?"

"Believe me, it was to protect you. I didn't see what good it would do to tell you afterward."

"David, do you think Jean-Claude is trying to hurt me? That he was somehow here today? But why?"

"I think he is indeed after you. But he should be after me. It is a case of mistaken identity." David sighed deeply and turned his piercing eyes on Gabriella.

"I cannot tell you everything, Gabby. It is a long story, a story of war and innocent victims. You do not need to know. But the bread. The bread, you have guessed, got you into trouble in Aix." He reached behind him and placed the backpack in Gabriella's lap. "Go ahead. Take out the bread."

She did so hesitantly.

"Break it in two and pull out the center part."

Gabriella obeyed. As she broke the loaf, a small piece of paper wrapped in plastic fell into her hands. Gabriella stared at David, bewildered.

"It is *this* that I find in the bread. My instructions. You see? Do you understand?"

She nodded, trembling. "I see ... I see."

He reached for her hand. "Gabby, please. Hear me out."

"You are frightening me, David. Perhaps I shouldn't know. You mean when I went to get the bread, this man was watching me? And you knew it?"

"No, of course I didn't know. I am afraid someone has talked. It is too complicated to explain it all now. But you deserve to know. Because I am sure you are in danger. It is my fault. I am sorry."

"David, my heart is still racing from the fall. I am scared! And now what do I do? Walk back out into the wind and wait for some sadist to kill me? Now I will be looking over my shoulder until I leave France."

"No, Gabby. No. You will stay safe in Castelnau. The next time, he will come after me. I will make sure of it."

She did not reply, but placed the plastic-covered paper on the dashboard.

"You must say nothing about this, Gabby."

Her eyes were sad, void of any blue sparkle. "Whom would I tell, David?"

"You will help me then?"

She answered softly. "I will help you, David. Do I have a choice, after all?"

Chapter Twenty

Ali Boudani sat in his room, impatient and brooding. There was no time to finish his little work with the demands of Ben Bella and the rest of the FLN on his back, sure of victory in the near future. Ali very much wanted victory for Algeria. But first he wanted revenge.

The office where he worked in the Casbah was a tiny cubicle with a single window that looked onto a polluted alley. Lined up across his desk were old framed photographs of himself: in one he was a child, standing beside a man in military uniform and a young woman with long, thick black hair; in other pictures he was older, posed with first one, then two, and eventually six other siblings. Still the young mother smiled out of every picture, seemingly pleased with her growing family.

Finally there was a large framed photograph of Ali as a young man in military dress, standing tall and proud beside the older man he so closely resembled. Ali let his eyes fall on this picture and smiled briefly. "Father," he whispered.

He stood up and walked to the cement block wall,

running his fingers over the cool stones. Taped to a dingy whitewashed wall was a yellowed newspaper clipping with the picture of a group of soldiers, dressed neatly in uniform. Ali's father stood in the back row, looking confident. Around his head, a bright blue circle had been drawn. A dozen other men's heads were circled, not in blue but red, and several of these circles had a red X drawn through the middle, virtually hiding the face of the soldier beneath.

A small caption below the photograph read: "Paris, France. The Scout Platoon of the Thirteenth Battalion of the North African Army has made quite a name for itself in several major battles of 1943. This platoon, made up primarily of Algerians and *pied-noirs*, has been decorated now for its bravery. The platoon is led by Lieutenant Mohemmed Boudani under the Battalion leader, Captain Maxime Duchemin."

Ali spat at a face in the picture. "Captain Duchemin! You traitor. I will find your daughter and granddaughter, and then I can draw the line through your family, as I have done for the others. They will join you in an empty grave, debris from the war. No one will remember them. My father will be avenged."

He touched the face of his father and whispered, "It will take more time, but I will win. I have been foolish to wait to kill the woman. But you see, Father, many are gone. The whole family. Slain. Only a few have escaped to France. Even there they are not safe. In the end we will wipe out the families of those *pied-noir* and *harki* traitors who left you to die. Then I will know revenge! Then I will enjoy a free Algeria, rid of swine!"

Another clipping had been taped next to the picture of the soldiers. Underlined in the same red ink was one paragraph: "In what has been called one of the ironic tragedies of this war, French forces, on the brink of victory, raided a German campsite in the middle of the night of April 5, 1945. Thirty-seven men of the Scout Platoon of the Thirteenth Battalion from the North African Army, made up primarily of *pied-noirs* and Algerians, inflicted heavy casualties on the German battalion. The North African platoon suffered only one casualty. The Algerian lieutenant, Mohemmed Boudani, highly decorated for his bravery during the two previous battles, became the scapegoat for his platoon. His body was later found, hanging from the rafters of a delapidated barn, with evidence of extreme torture."

Beside the newspaper clipping, Ali had posted a piece of paper, numbered in vertical fashion from 1 to 37. He had written names by the first twenty-two spaces. Four of these names, including his father's, had been crossed out with the words *died in war* written beside them. A red line had been drawn through the names of eleven other men. He peered at the list now and chuckled. "You see, Father, how many of these cowards have died. Died to avenge your death. These men and their families. The *harkis* and the *pied-noirs*. Do not worry. I am not finished yet. Somewhere I will find the names of the others. I will find their families. And they will suffer as we have suffered."

* * *

Anne-Marie unfolded a crumpled sheet of paper. "It is no use, Moustafa. I cannot remember everyone. You have warned these families?" She pointed to a half-dozen names scratched on the paper.

"They are warned, the ones who are in Algiers. The *Capitaine* will sail tomorrow night with four children to Marseilles. I have arranged it all. Ali will not murder any more innocent children."

Anne-Marie rubbed her forehead and sighed. "It is

all my fault. Oh, God, I hate this life. It is as if I reached out a gun and shot them myself."

Moustafa took her hand, squeezing it tightly. "You were forced to talk! No one judges you! Certainly not I. We are here now because I, too, was weak. Every night I wonder if the other children escaped to France, or if they were found because I talked." He closed his eyes briefly, remembering the cruel laughter of Ali as Moustafa had writhed in pain. He gritted his teeth, then opened his eyes to shut out the memory.

He continued talking, his voice etched with emotion. "I think of Rajib—such a fine young boy. Is he safe in France? And Hakim? I am only glad I did not know more. Only dates and cities." He stroked her face. "And I knew where you were, Anne-Marie. It is all my fault that you are here. I am so sorry."

Anne-Marie placed a finger over his lips and shook her head. "Don't, Moustafa. Don't think of it now. You could not help it."

His eyes flashed. "If I let them, these thoughts would pull me down and smother me in their hopelessness. But I must not! We must not give in to self-pity. You have forgiven me, Anne-Marie, for my weakness?"

"Of course, Moustafa. You know I have." Her eyes were liquid and sad as she answered him. "But can I forgive myself? For the families I betrayed to Jean-Claude? For my own daughter, who is living another nightmare because of me?"

He grabbed Anne-Marie's shoulders, his voice a passionate whisper. "We are in a war of madness, and we are dealing with a madman. Do not live in guilt. We can help." He looked at her lovingly. "Do you wish to leave now, Anne-Marie? There is room on the boat for you."

She shook her head immediately. "No, I will stay with you here. If they have brought Ophélie to Ali, she is somewhere in this town. And we will keep searching. You will go again tonight?"

"I will go."

She reached out for his hand, and he pulled her against his chest. "Moustafa," she whispered, coughing. "You are right. It is all madness. Why must Ali hate so? Our fathers did not leave his father to die. It was an accident of war. How can he believe otherwise? After all these years. If he will only leave us alone, we will be trampled underfoot in this war anyway.

"Look what he has done to us! He is the one I will never forgive! I do not hate the Arabs, you know it well. I love your people. But him, I hate. And his sadistic friends. These I will never forgive."

She buried her face in his shirt. Moustafa stroked her hair. Anne-Marie continued, "It wasn't supposed to be this way. He murdered my parents. Your father too! He is pure evil." She was hugging Moustafa, unconsciously driving her clenched fist into his back.

Moustafa waited for a moment to speak. "Anne-Marie, my love. I have been thinking. It grows more dangerous daily for all the children trapped in this war. We must continue to use this operation, even after the ones Ali seeks are safe. This is why we are still here. We will find Ophélie and make sure she is safe. But I must stay and help. Algeria will fall apart before our eyes. It will explode in this final clash of power and blood. Marcus tells me what the OAS plots. I must stay. Tell me you will stay with me."

She was still holding onto him. "Moustafa, it is madness. Our love is madness. There will be no place for us. We have been friends, but there is no place in the world for a *harki* and a *pied-noir* who are in love."

"Then stay with me here, Anne-Marie. For now no one says a thing. For now we are alone in the eye of the storm. Stay with me here." He cradled her soft, delicate face in his hands. "You are so beautiful, my love. Do not worry, not for now."

He kissed her carefully, as if to bring a spark of life back into her eyes, a flame of passion when she looked at him. He kissed her again and again, until she answered back hungrily. Until for a moment they forgot how impossible indeed was their love.

* * *

Gabriella left her room as the doorbell to Mme. Leclerc's apartment sounded. She pulled on her coat and looped a green scarf around her neck.

"A date on Sunday night?" Caroline teased, stepping out of her room. "Don't stay out too late, Gab. Remember there's school tomorrow."

"Don't worry," Gabriella retorted, forcing a smile on her face.

Mme. Leclerc had opened the door and was chatting politely with David.

The smile still plastered on her face, Gabriella kissed the landlady softly on the cheek. "I won't be late. But don't wait up. I have my key."

"*Ooh la la, ma chére!* I will long since be asleep. You just have fun." She winked at her boarder.

David took Gabriella's arm and escorted her out the door. "I'll take good care of her, Mme. Leclerc," he laughed.

They walked casually down the steps and out into the deserted street. The moon was full. The air smelled of smoke as all around town, the black vapor wisped and twirled out of chimneys.

Gabriella could see her breath as she spoke. "Where shall we go?"

"Do you have the phone number?"

Gabriella reached into her pocket and withdrew a piece of paper.

"Good," David said. He looked over at Gabriella. "Are you okay?"

"Scared stiff," she replied with a shiver.

David put his arm around her shoulders and gave her a playful hug. "You'll do great, my dear."

She broke away from him, walking ahead. "I get the feeling this is all a little game to you, David. Cat and mouse, is that it? I am not laughing, I hope you notice. I am trembling inside my boots. I am not a spy. My training is in literature and art, you may recall. I've studied under a very distinguished professor."

He caught up to her, grabbed her arm, and pulled her around to face him. "Listen to me, Gabriella Madison. You have every right to be mad. But what's done is done. You said Jean-Claude expects your call. This is our chance. Shake him up a little. It is the only way to get the heat off of you and onto me." He stamped his boots on the street impatiently.

Gabriella looked at the ground. "David, I can't. For all we know, he thinks I'm lying dead at the bottom of les Baux. Why prove to him that I am alive and well? I'm too scared. And ..." She turned her blue eyes up toward his. "And I don't want you to take the heat either."

"You're too sweet, Gabby. Much too sweet. Don't worry about me. Come on. I guarantee you he will not just wait around thinking you're dead. He'll be up to something. This is our chance."

The phone booth was hidden behind a row of small family-owned stores, their neon signs extinguished. Gabriella stepped into the booth, and David followed. He towered over her as she dialed the number with a quivering hand. She listened for a ring and cleared her throat. On the third ring, a voice answered.

"*Allo?* Jean-Claude, this is Gabriella." There was a long pause before he responded.

"Yes, how are you?" she answered. "Fine? Good. Well, I'm just calling to let you know that we have had good news about Ophélie's mom. Thank you for your help, but I think we'll be arranging a get-together soon ourselves." She let her words soak in.

"Can we see each other? Well, thank you for the offer, but actually I am already seeing someone. It was nice meeting you anyway, and again, thank you for trying to help. *Au revoir.*"

She hung up the receiver and fell into David's arms, eyes shining. "Whew! I did it! He believed me!"

He hugged her lightly, then let her go and stepped out of the booth. "That is fine, Gabby. Let's celebrate. Can I get you a coffee?"

Gabriella hesitated. "A coffee," she teased. "I'm sure that is not how you normally celebrate."

David laughed loudly. "I won't touch that with a ten-foot pole, Miss Madison. No comment." He brushed his fingers through her hair and said, "There's only one *café* open on Sunday night anyway. We better at least make an appearance to keep the town gossips happy."

* * *

Jean-Claude hung up the phone with a snarl. "She knows something," he thought. Too bad the red-haired tramp had escaped injury. It was really too bad. But Jean-Claude was not deterred. He scratched a quick note to Ali:

"Found Gabriella in les Baux as planned. She was with an old friend of ours, David Hoffmann. It makes perfect sense that he is here. He is linked with his old lover, I am sure.

I had hoped to rid you of the redhead at les Baux.

The wind was on my side, but alas. Awaiting further instructions. Your faithful friend, J-C."

Another roll of film, another letter to Algiers. Another day to wait. "You don't frighten me, Gabriella. Nor you, David Hoffmann. Not one little bit."

* * *

They entered the *café*, which was empty except for the barman and two old men huddled at the bar. David chose a table in the back of the small room. He ordered a coffee for himself.

"*Un chocolat, s'il vous plait,*" Gabriella said.

A soft love song played in the background, its melody drowned out occasionally by a burst of laughter from the men at the bar. The *café* smelled of smoke and strong liquor. David reached out to touch Gabriella's hand. His black eyes were piercing, yet tender. "So, tell me, favorite student, what is going on inside that red head of yours?"

She blushed with a quick smile, pulled her hand away from his, and nibbled a fingernail absentmindedly. "Too much is going on in my head. Too much."

"Tell me."

She felt the power of his presence, even as he whispered. She closed her eyes, afraid to meet his gaze. "I feel trapped, David." She glanced up at him. The music in the background grew louder. A man's voice crooned, "*I love you. I love you. Never gonna forget you.*" David did not move or speak.

"I'm afraid. Mother Griolet said the best way to get past the hurt and anger is to keep living. And to be honest about what I am feeling. So I tried.

"But now . . . now, I am trapped not only in my mind, but in some awful little war game of yours. I don't want to know what it is, and yet . . . I wonder . . . I wonder who you are." She was fumbling with a white cloth napkin. "I wonder what you are doing." Her eyes met his. "And I don't know what I'll do when I find out."

The waiter placed the hot drinks on the table. Steam rose and twisted enticingly between Gabriella and David as they held each other's gaze. No one spoke.

Finally David broke the silence, lifting his hand to touch the cross around her neck. "The Huguenot cross, Gabby. Such a strange cross."

Again she felt his power over her and drew back. "That is what everyone says," she whispered. The haunting music stopped. Gabriella shook herself out of her lethargy. "You know, David," her voice was composed again. "It was this cross that interested Jean-Claude at first, in Aigues-Mortes. At least that is what he said."

David smiled. "Of course. That makes perfect sense."

"What do you mean?"

He unbuttoned a little pocket inside his blazer and pulled out a piece of paper. "You did not want to see it yesterday. But this is what was in the bread." He held it carefully in his hand for Gabriella to inspect. In the center of the paper were written the words *jeudi21 16h30SNCF.* In the top left-hand corner was scribbled the picture of a Huguenot cross.

Gabriella touched her cross as another love song floated across the *café*. She glanced briefly at David, then down at the paper. "I see," she mumbled. "I see."

* * *

Moustafa waited until midnight to start back through the slums of Bab el Oued and pass under the arches that led into the Casbah. His heart raced as he walked briskly through the labyrinth of streets, but by now he knew his way well. After a month of nighttime wanderings, he was beginning to feel at home in the

Casbah. The thought made him shudder. At home in the neighborhood that plotted his extinction and that of all the French loyalists.

Since Rachid's death, Moustafa had observed Ali's frantic gait, like that of a captured stallion. He was not as careful as before. The room that had been Moustafa's prison with Anne-Marie now was used for Ali's weekly midnight meetings with the few trusted men needed to carry out his revenge.

Moustafa perched himself on the roof of the adjoining building, concealed in the pitch of night, and peered through the small window. The men were there, as they were every Saturday night.

Ali was pacing the floor, talking in hushed tones. The men nodded and focused their attention on the screen at the front of the room. Straining to hear through the open window, Moustafa watched as a slide of a woman with long red hair appeared on the screen. Ali was talking.

"We have recently received more slides from Jean-Claude. You remember this lovely woman that Jean-Claude has bumped into several times. He has found her again. A student in Montpellier." Another slide flashed before them, a crowded square with the back of the red-haired woman to the screen.

Another slide showed her closer up. "And please notice the small girl at her side!" Ali cried triumphantly. "None other than Ophélie Duchemin."

Only the murmurs of approval from the men in the room covered Moustafa's gasp. "Ophélie!" he whispered.

Ali was crooning on. "Jean-Claude met them here in Montpellier. The child, of course, remembered him as a dear friend of her mother's. She did not know of Jean-Claude's way of convincing Anne-Marie to talk." He laughed cruelly. "The child begged this woman, Gabriella she is called, to have drinks with Jean-Claude and see if he could help them find her mother." He chuckled.

"Of course, Jean-Claude was happy to comply. This Gabriella has contacted him once, and Jean-Claude has planned to meet her not far from Marseilles. In fact, I believe the appointment was for yesterday. Things are shaping up, you see. We are confident that this Gabriella is behind the operation. She is the one they call Hugo. We will get rid of her and have the child. The rest of the information will come quickly. In the meantime, there are still three *pied-noir* families here in Algiers who must be done away with. On with you now."

Moustafa scrambled up the roof and hid himself behind the arch of the two adjoining buildings. Six men filed out of the basement and parted silently down the streets of the Casbah. He waited for fifteen minutes before springing to the ground like a cat and tracing his way back through the night to the little apartment of Marcus Cirou.

* * *

The nightmare woke her with a start. Anne-Marie's nightshirt was covered with sweat as she sat straight up in bed, breathing loudly. *Only a dream*, she sighed. Only a dream of her past. Only a vivid picture of another haunted night.

She saw him before her, laughing as he reached out to her with the red hot iron. The hazel eyes she had thought so warm and inviting during their last night's passion now gleamed at her with a wild power. Somewhere Ophélie cried out for her mother.

"I don't know anything else. What can I know? I was his daughter, not his officer."

Enraged, Jean-Claude touched the hot iron to her right arm. Her screams filled the night. Twice more he burned her, laughing as he watched her writhe with pain. Then he grabbed her long hair and jerked back her neck. "You will find the list of names, Anne-Marie. Thirty-seven names. You will find them before next Friday when I come back. The next time, it will be your daughter screaming, and not from hunger either."

She looked at the black skies. Moustafa was not back yet. Anne-Marie's gaunt frame trembled under her oversized T-shirt. She switched on the lamp that sat on the floor by her mattress. A crumpled piece of paper lay beside the lamp, and Anne-Marie picked it up. Rubbing the sleep from her eyes, she studied the names scrawled on the sheet. Twenty-five were listed. She closed her eyes and tried to picture the list she had copied so carefully and placed in the blue bag so many months ago. But she could not remember another name.

At the top of the page she had written in capital letters "Scout Platoon of the Thirteenth Battalion." Underneath she had printed the name of her father, and after it, the words "murdered along with his wife by Ali." Beside other names was written either "killed in battle" or "murdered by Ali Boudani," with details about the members of each soldier's family.

"I don't want to remember anymore," she groaned.

The door to the room opened and Anne-Marie saw Moustafa, bathed in the light of the moon, standing before her. His eyes glowed as he rushed to her and picked her up in his arms.

"It has been all lies, Anne-Marie! Wonderful lies! Ali does not have Ophélie. She is in the south of France in Montpellier with a young woman. Jean-Claude has seen her, but she is not with him."

Anne-Marie pulled herself out of Moustafa's embrace. "You are sure?" She touched her forehead, suddenly feeling dizzy. Moustafa caught her again.

"Yes, sure! I saw the slides of her with this woman. A woman named Gabriella who wears a Huguenot cross. They say she is Hugo. Unbelievable! Do you know her?"

"No, I have never heard of her. She has Ophélie? How do we know that she will not harm her?"

"In their voices, I could tell. They know Ophélie is safe with this woman."

Anne-Marie wrung her hands together nervously. "If this woman is working for us, then she will help. She will protect Ophélie."

"Yes, of course. Now sleep, dear one. Go to sleep. I will join you later." Moustafa slipped out of the room.

Anne-Marie lay awake for a long time, staring into the blackness of the room. "If this woman is Hugo," she whispered to herself, "then where are you? Where are you, David Hoffmann? Are you there too? And do you know that Ophélie is your child? Do you know? Do you even care?"

Her eyes were closed, but she was still wide awake when Moustafa entered the room and lay down on the mattress beside her.

* * *

Gabriella could not sleep. She flipped through her Bible, from one page to another, reading underlined passages to herself. "I will not fail thee, nor forsake thee. . . . the Lord shall preserve thy going out and thy coming in from this time forth, and even for evermore. . . . I am the Vine, ye are the branches; He that abideth in Me, and I in him, the same bringeth forth much fruit: for without Me ye can do nothing. . . ."

She spoke the words in the verses with emotion, as if she could pull God out of the black book and into the room with her.

"You are here, Father. Lord, You have promised to

258

be here." Her voice was a faint whisper, a feeble cry. "I need You! I am so confused. I am so scared." Sobs escaped as she spoke to the air. "Lord, I did not mean to get into this. It is too much for me. I am scared and tired. Please. I need help. Someone to show me what to do."

The cross dangled before her. "Oh, God! Forgive me! Forgive me for hating a memory that has ripped me apart. This is too heavy!" She moaned softly, wiping her eyes with the sleeve of her gown.

"And forgive me, Lord, for loving a man who is not Yours. He is pulling me along with him, and now I cannot get away. Now I am trapped. Forgive me." She buried her face in her pillow and cried, a low soul-wrenching cry. "Oh, God, who is he? Who is David Hoffmann?"

* * *

It was the middle of the night as Ophélie tossed in her bed. Her mind was racing. *Somewhere Mama called out for her. She ran toward her mother when suddenly her mother's voice turned into piercing screams. Ophélie tried to open the door, but it was locked. The screams quieted and the door opened. Jean-Claude stood in the doorway, his eyes bright.* Ophélie screamed and woke herself up.

"Mama! Mama! He isn't your friend after all. Now I remember. He isn't your friend."

Ophélie cradled her pillow in her arms. She heard the wind rattling the windows, and she stared at the shadows that flickered across the wall. She thought about her mother for a long time, picturing her thin, beautiful face and sad eyes. Then Ophélie Duchemin closed her eyes and thought about her father. In her mind there was only a black void. She saw nothing.

"Father," she whispered. "David Hoffmann. Who are you?" She turned over and went back to sleep.

Chapter Twenty-One

Monique Pons paused in a narrow street of Castelnau to rest. The ten-kilo turkey she had just purchased weighed down her straw basket. She breathed heavily. In the daytime, the Christmas lights that had been attached across the road were not blinking. But everywhere the air spoke of Christmas.

"Monique! There you are. *Coucou!*"

Yvette Leclerc caught up with her friend. Her cheeks were rosy red, and she laughed heartily. "Let me help you with that turkey. *Ooh la!*"

Together the two women walked across the busy square to Monique's apartment. Together they carried the turkey up the flight of stairs and into the kitchen. Then Yvette hurried back down the steps to retrieve her basket of fruits and vegetables from the *marché*.

"Do we have everything now for the meal? It is only two days away." Monique's eyes sparkled.

"And such a meal we will have!" They had decided to celebrate the midnight Christmas Eve meal together, with their boarders, since it seemed that two of them were a couple again. What could be more appropriate?

"Let's see. We have the *foie gras*. We have the *pâté*, and the *saumon fumé*, and the olives for the *entrée*. We have turkey and chestnuts, and you are making the *gratin dauphinois*. The green beans I will get tomorrow."

"And I will make the *bûche de Noël* on the 24th. The girls will love it. Americans are always enamored with the Christmas log for dessert. Yes, everything will be just perfect!"

They looked at each other and burst into happy giggling, like two schoolgirls sharing a secret. "A midnight meal for Christmas," said Yvette. "And I believe Gabriella has a gift for your Mr. Hoffmann. *Ooh la!*"

"It will be just perfect. Mr. Hoffmann will find something for his young lady too. A great surprise, no doubt."

* * *

Mother Griolet closed her grammar book and smiled out at the twenty-five children seated before her. "So there, *mes enfants*, school is over for the holidays. No work for ten days."

The children broke into a loud cheer, laughing as they put their books into the wooden desks.

Mother Griolet spoke again. *"Attention!* Children! Listen up, please will you. As with every other year, we will have our special Christmas meal in the cafeteria on Christmas Eve. And you will all bring one shoe up to my den to leave by the tree, *n'est-ce pas?*"

The children nodded eagerly. Mother Griolet saw the perplexed look on Ophélie's face. "We have two children who were not with us last year, Hakim and Ophélie." She smiled at the tall, dark-skinned boy who brooded in the back row. "It is our Christmas tradition at St. Joseph's for each child to leave a shoe under my tree for *Père Noël*. Yes, old as I am, Father Christmas still comes to see me every year! And oh, my! Such goodies he leaves for all the children."

They nodded their heads gleefully.

"It's true!" piped in little Christophe. "He brings the goodies while we are eating our Christmas meal. Then we can come and sing around the tree. We stay up very late on Christmas Eve!"

"Oh, *oui, oui!* Last year every girl got a different dolly. Every one of us," volunteered Anne-Sophie.

The schoolroom had erupted into excited chatter when Gabriella entered the class. Mother Griolet clapped her hands together. *"Les enfants!* Children! Please, calm down. Gabriella has asked me if she could bring you a present today, something for each of you from her." Immediately the children grew silent, anticipation in their eyes.

Gabriella came to the front of the class. She smiled. "Who can tell me what is so important about Christmas?" she questioned.

Several little hands flew into the air.

"André, yes, go ahead."

The shy six-year-old stood up and grinned nervously. He looked down at the floor. "It's when baby Jesus was born." He sat down, his thin face red.

"Exactly! Thank you, André," Gabriella said. "So here are your gifts. No use grabbing; they are all the same. A present from me to you. So you can read for yourselves about the greatest story in the world." She hefted a large basket onto Mother Griolet's desk.

The nun smiled. "May the children open the gifts now, Gabriella?" she asked.

"Yes, yes, of course."

Mother Griolet came before the children. "There is just one more thing I need to say before we continue." She cleared her throat. "Today we shall be receiving four new children to the orphanage. One boy and three girls. Isn't that a nice Christmas present?"

The children nodded.

"I expect you to welcome them warmly, just as you always do. That is all. You may go ahead, Gabriella."

As the young woman began calling out the children's names, one by one they filed foward to receive their gifts. Mother Griolet smiled as she observed the way they tore open the bright, shiny paper and proudly held up their books for others to see. A children's New Testament. The nun left the room as the children raced foward to embrace Gabriella.

She is going to make it, Lord, this Gabriella. She is learning the secret: to get past your pain, you give to others who hurt. Thank You, Lord, for her example.

She climbed the steps to the ground floor, entered her apartment, and went into her office. She walked around her desk and stood at the window staring out into the empty courtyard. "Four more children, Lord. I do not know them, but You do. You see and know all. And I am sure You will provide everything we need to take care of them. As You did in the other war. As You did in Your Word, with the little boy and his loaves and fishes. I think I am ready, but only in Your strength. Only in You can I do it."

She watched the pansies in the courtyard below, their petals fluttering with winter wind. "Delicate and strong," she murmured. "Even in the coldest months, they keep their smiling faces. Blown by your Spirit, O Father, may I do the same."

* * *

Gabriella met Mother Griolet in her den. Her face was radiant. "It is so much fun to be with the children. They love me, you know. I feel as though they need me,

263

even if my life is a mess."

"I understand how you feel, my child," replied the old nun. "It is a rewarding work. Hard but rewarding."

"My dear," Mother Griolet paused awkwardly. "I am afraid I must ask you to do me a favor."

"Yes, of course. What is it?"

"I was hoping you could go into Montpellier this afternoon to meet these new children. Mr. Vidal had offered, but he is unable to get away."

"The children are coming by train?"

"Yes, it is a long story. They are refugees from the war."

"From Algeria?"

"Yes, that is it. They need shelter here in France." She smiled weakly. "This is a bit of a secret, my dear. If you would not talk about it, I would be most grateful. If you do not wish to go, I will find someone else."

"No, it is not that." Gabriella spoke in a far-off manner. "It is not that. I will go. You tell me where to meet these children, and I will go."

* * *

Ophélie jumped at the chance to ride the bus into town with Gabriella. As they pulled into the train station, she clasped her teacher's hand tightly.

"Thank you, Bribri! For the bus ride and the beautiful book. The Bible with pictures. Thank you!"

Gabriella patted the child's hand as they descended the steps from the bus. "Let's see now. Mother Griolet said it arrives at 4:30." She searched the large board that announced the arriving trains. "There it is. It will be at *quai* number two in just a few minutes. Come along."

People were milling about the station, stringy-haired students with their backpacks, somber men in business suits. Gabriella watched Ophélie's exuberance.

264

Suddenly the child's face clouded. "Bribri," she said. "I had a dream. I remembered something scary."

They had arrived at the *quai*, and the train approached slowly in the distance.

"I don't think Mr. Jean-Claude is good. I think he was one time mama's friend, but then he turned bad and made her scream."

Gabriella put her arm around the child. They shivered together as the train screeched to a halt before them. "Oh, Ophélie. I am so sorry. But don't you worry. He doesn't know where we live. We will never see him again."

* * *

Four silent, wide-eyed children followed Gabriella and Ophélie out of the train station. They carried nothing with them; their clothes were filthy and their eyes hungry. Two were Arabs, Gabriella was sure. The other two looked French.

"Tell me your names, please," she said softly as they waited for the Bus 11. "We will just ride the bus to the church. Mother Griolet will have a nice supper ready for you when we get there."

The children remained silent. The youngest child, who was about five, began to cry. Her sister put an arm around her. The bus appoached.

"This is it, children. Let's climb on."

* * *

"Have you seen Gabriella, Mother Griolet?" David asked as he met the nun in the stairwell of the parsonage.

"Oh, hello, Mr. Hoffmann," the old nun replied, guarding her space. "Yes, I believe she took Ophélie into town this afternoon."

"I see." David frowned. "You are sure?"

Mother Griolet nodded.

"Thank you. Thank you very much."

David hurried out of the parsonage grumbling to himself. "To town! I told her to lie low. Whatever is she doing in town? Today of all days! Unless ..." He cursed angrily and trotted down the street to where his *deux chevaux* awaited him at the curb.

* * *

Jean-Claude had followed the children from Marseilles. Again Ali's information had been right. Four scraggly kids. Kids that Ali wanted dead. Jean-Claude had jumped on the train to Montpellier. Now he scowled as he watched the woman, Gabriella, herd her little flock onto Bus 11. He ran toward the bus as the doors closed, and the bus veered into the busy street.

"Taxi! Taxi!" he called.

A young man puffing on a cigarette pulled up in an old BMW taxi, and Jean Claude hopped in.

"Where to, *monsieur?*"

"I have just missed the bus there, number 11. I was to meet some friends at the station, and they have just gotten on the bus. Please, if you could follow them." He flashed a quick smile as the taxi driver took off in pursuit of Bus 11.

* * *

Ophélie screamed as the bus doors closed. Gabriella, who was busy comforting the refugees, turned.

"What in the world, Ophélie? What is the matter?"

"It is him! I saw him. Mr. Jean-Claude. He is following us. He is trying to get us."

"Ophélie! Are you sure? Perhaps you are just imagining it because you are afraid."

But Ophélie was adamant. "I am sure, Bribri." Other passengers looked questioningly at the child.

Gabriella led Ophélie to a seat; then she cautiously looked out the window. They were well past the train station, and she saw no one. Peering out the back of the bus, she noticed a taxi following them, but she could not make out the person sitting in the back.

Through each intersection, the taxi kept close to the bus. At each stop, as people got on and off, Gabriella watched the taxi until she was sure that Jean-Claude Gachon sat in the back seat.

At any moment Gabriella expected Jean-Claude to jump out of the taxi and onto the bus, a pistol in hand, ready to shoot them all. But he did not. Gabriella sat, frozen with fear, until the bus passed the Castelnau stop. She could not let him know where they lived. They would stay put for now, she decided, until she could think of what to do.

"Children," she said, trying to sound cheery. "Children, I must go up front and ask the bus driver directions. Please just sit tight." She caught Ophélie's eyes. The child sat perfectly still, her eyes wide with fear.

Gabriella made her way to the front of the bus. "Please, *Monsieur*," she began, trembling. "I have a ... a problem. Someone is following me and my children. In the taxi. He must not find us. Could you please change your route?"

The bus driver glared at her. "What are you saying, *mademoiselle?* I cannot outrun a taxi. I am sorry."

"No, of course not," she agreed.

"If you are going to stay on the bus to go back through town, it'll cost you another ticket, for you and the kids."

"Yes, of course ... of course." She fiddled in her purse, bringing out a handful of change and paying the bus driver.

"*Merci, Monsieur*," Gabriella stammered, as she

swayed with the turning bus and found her seat again.

* * *

Jean-Claude grew impatient waiting inside the taxi. He was certain that Gabriella, Ophélie, and the children were on the bus. It wound slowly in and out of town, like a giant centipede. Still they did not get off. "She saw me," he muttered to himself. "Ophélie saw me."

He fought to control his urge to leave the taxi and jump on the bus. But Jean-Claude had received explicit instructions from Ali, admonishing him for the accident at les Baux. "See to it that you draw no more attention to yourself," the hastily scrawled letter had read. "Your task is simply to find out where these children are being housed and how this Gabriella and Mr. Hoffmann receive information. Later you will get the list from Ophélie Duchemin. Be patient. She must still believe you are a friend of her mother's. Slow down!"

Jean-Claude did not like to be told to slow down. He was an athletic man, trained for action. But he knew how to wait. He could wait all night if he needed to, until the red-haired woman thought the coast was clear and led him straight to where Ophélie Duchemin was hiding.

* * *

When David arrived at the train station, it was well past 5:00. A quick search of the building revealed what he feared. No one. Gabriella was not there waiting on a late train as he had hoped. Angrily he pushed his *deux chevaux* in gear and drove back toward Castelnau. He was sure Mother Griolet had sent her to pick up the orphans. A mistake. A terrible mistake if anyone was watching for a woman with red hair.

David slowed down, passing a Bus 11 as he drove to the east side of Montpellier. He scanned the faces in the

268

near empty bus. No Gabriella.

As he headed into Castelnau, another Bus 11 was leaving the village, going back towards Montpellier. He glanced at it, saw a shock of red hair, and the bus was gone. Quickly he turned the *deux chevaux* into a side street and backed around. If indeed it was Gabriella, why was she going back to town, he mused. He caught sight of the bus again, fifty meters in front of his car. David pulled up closer to the bus, behind an old BMW taxi. Then he saw the reason Gabriella had not gotten off in Castelnau. Jean-Claude Gachon rode in the back seat of the taxi, his gaze fixed on Bus 11.

* * *

By six Mother Griolet was trying to suppress the panic rising inside her. Gabriella had not returned with the children. "Dear me, what have I done? I should never have sent that child." Twice she had called the train station to make sure the train from Marseilles had not been delayed. Twice she had been assured that it had arrived on schedule. She could not imagine what had happened. She waited and prayed.

Now she walked through the girls' dormitory, making sure the three beds were made up for the new children. Sister Rosaline had made sure that the small chest of drawers for each new child had been filled with the appropriate clothes.

Preoccupied with thoughts of Gabriella, Mother Griolet opened a drawer. The long sleeved blouses and wool skirts were there, the panties and tights, the barrettes and brush and comb. And the doll. Sister Rosaline loved to prepare the drawers for the new orphans. The clothes always smelled sweet and fresh, even if they were used. The doll had on a bright new dress, crocheted by Sister Rosaline herself. Even as

Mother Griolet contemplated her fellow-worker, the short, plump woman came in the room.

"There you are, *Mère Griolet*," she exclaimed happily. "And the children have not arrived yet? Miss Gabriella is not back with them?"

"No, I am afraid not, Sister Rosaline."

"Don't you worry, now," the Sister added. "That Gabriella is a smart girl. She'll have them here in no time. Anyway, I have a few more drawers to fill for the last new little girl. I'm afraid there aren't enough tights." She scratched her head as she hurried to the last bunk and opened a drawer.

"What would you think of taking a pair from one of the other girls? Half of them don't wear them, anyway. That little Ophélie, for instance. She only wears her white tights. I wash them three times a week, I'll bet."

Mother Griolet was hardly paying attention. "Well, then, go ahead and take the blue pair, if you wish. I'll explain it to her later. I'm sure she won't care a bit."

Sister Rosaline scurried to Ophélie's bed and opened the second drawer in her small bureau. She grabbed up the blue tights and closed the drawer.

"Now what in the world has that child put inside these tights?" she fretted. She wiggled her broad hand down the tights and pulled out a small, blue velvet bag.

"A child's treasure, no doubt," the Sister concluded. "No wonder she never put these on."

Mother Griolet frowned for a moment, coming out of her reverie. "May I see that bag?" she asked.

"Why, sure," Sister Rosaline answered, smiling as she handed her the sack.

The small nun took the velvet bag into her hands. "Yes, I'm sure this contains her only treasures. Never mind. Just leave the tights here."

"Fine, Mother, just fine," Sister Rosaline patted her

lightly on the back before leaving the room. "I'm off to check on the clothes for the boy. We don't have much for a twelve-year-old." She scampered out, calling back over her shoulder, "Don't you worry about the kids! Miss Gabriella will get them here just fine."

* * *

Mother Griolet did not like to snoop in the personal belongings of others, not even the smallest child's. She held the blue bag in her hands for a moment, considering what to do. She looked at her watch again. Six-thirty. "Whatever is keeping them?" she whispered.

She pulled open the little bag, letting the contents fall on the bunk bed. There was a tiny photograph of Ophélie with what had to be her mother, a lovely dark-haired woman with large, sad eyes. Two small pink envelopes, wrinkled and folded, were the only other contents. Mother Griolet picked up one envelope. "Mr. Gady" was written on the outside. The seal had not been broken. She carefully opened it and removed several pieces of stationery. The first two pages were a personal letter to the man, Mr. Gady. The last two pages were typed, a list of names, apparently soldiers. Their family members' names were typed beside the soldiers', then their addresses and by some names, the words "murdered" or "killed in war." Mother Griolet gaped at the list. Then she read the letter.

Dear Mr. Gady,

I send you my daughter, my treasure. I know you will care for her as we have arranged. If you have this letter, it is because I have been forced to flee for Ophélie's safety. You now have the only complete list of the Scout Platoon of the Thirteenth Battalion—the list Ali wants. I have marked the families whose names he already knows with a red

271

X. You will note, too, that others have already been murdered.

Hugo awaits your news. Moustafa has already arranged for trips through October. Send these names to the following addresses. Hugo will answer you with further instructions as soon as you contact him. Assume that I can no longer help. I will do my best to get back to you soon. Until then, keep close contact with Hugo. Tell him that you have another child who must come to him. He must not know she is my own.

Please, please take care of Ophélie. She is my life.

Thank you for all your help,
Anne-Marie Duchemin

Four addresses were written underneath Anne-Marie's signature, with arrows drawn back to the names of different children on the list. There was another address, a post office box, beside the name "Hugo."

Mother Griolet shook her head and sighed, setting the papers on the bunk. Slowly she picked up the other envelope, which had already been opened. "Ophélie" was written across its front. The old woman took out three thin pieces of stationery. "A letter from her mother," Mother Griolet sighed. "This is why you were so eager to learn to read, Ophélie."

She read the letter silently to herself:

Dear Ophélie,

My treasure! How I love you, my dear. You must always know that I am with you, even if you can-not see me now. I never wanted for us to be apart. But for now, it is necessary. It is hard for you to understand, but I will try to explain.

There is a war in Algeria, you know. When we lived there, I made friends with people whom I thought were kind. But they turned out to be mean and only wanted to hurt innocent people. So we had to leave Algeria to get away from them.

Now I am trying to help other children and friends like Moustafa get out of Algeria, so they will not be hurt. The other papers in this bag are very important. Mr. Gady will know what to do with them. They will help other people be safe.

I want you to keep this cross that my father gave me. He said it will bring hope and faith. Remember how much Mama loves you. The cross is also important. When you wear it, good people will know you need to be protected. You will always be safe with the cross. Mr. Gady will take you to a safe place.

Mother Griolet paused, reflecting out loud. "The Huguenot cross. So there is a reason she wears it. It was there to tell me all along, and I did not know." She continued reading the letter.

I do not know when I will see you again. But I must leave so that no one will find you. It is because I love you that we are separated now. I know it is hard for you to understand, my jewel.

I must tell you one more thing. I have never talked to you of your father. I do not know where he is, but Ophélie, he is a good man. He does not know he has a daughter. I could not tell him. Please forgive your mama. But he is a good man who helped me when we were both very young and living in Algeria. Perhaps someday you will be able to find him. He is an American, very handsome and smart. His name is David Hoffmann.

Mama was very foolish and young when she loved him, but I know he would take care of you.

He would be proud to have a daughter like you.

*I must go now, my love. Someday I will see you
again. I am holding you tight in the arms of my
soul. Be brave, little Ophélie. You are special. The
God of Papy be with you.*

I love you,
Mama

Mother Griolet put down the letter, tears trickling
down her lined face. Forgotten were the orphans and
the hour. All she saw was a beautiful child with a secret
she could not share.

She shook her head again and again. "Mr. Hoffmann,
her father! It is impossible. It is crazy. He cannot know.
Or perhaps he knows and says nothing because he fears
for this child's safety. Dear Lord, I am confused. Who in
the world is this David Hoffmann?"

With one hand on her temple and the other still
holding the letter, Mother Griolet sighed heavily. An
unexpected piece of a puzzle she never meant to put
together lay in her hands. "I'm being pulled deeper into
this secret, Lord. I am not sure whom to trust. But I
trust You." She returned the letters to the blue bag,
slipped the bag into the leg of the tights, and placed
them back into Ophélie's drawer. "Keep your treasures,
little girl. For a while longer, you keep them." Mother
Griolet walked back to her apartment to wait.

* * *

David Hoffmann parked his car on the side of the
street just in front of the bus stop. He quickly mingled
with the other pedestrians awaiting Bus 11, hunching
down to hide himself from view. A moment later, the
bus pulled into the stop and he got on.

He walked to the back of the bus where Gabriella,
Ophélie, and four other children sat, looking fearful.

Gabriella gasped. "How did you get here? How did you find us?"

"A bit of luck, Gabby. How long have you been riding around town on this bus?" He sounded amused.

"Over an hour, maybe two. Have you seen who is following us?"

"Oh, yes. Our old friend is running up quite a bill in that taxi."

"I was petrified he would come on the bus and shoot us all," Gabriella whispered. "So I talked to the bus driver and he let us stay on."

"You've done just fine, Gabby. Except I thought I told you to lay low for awhile."

"Mother Griolet asked me to pick up some children arriving at the train station today. At 4:30. Refugees from Algeria." She eyed him suspiciously. "You knew about this, didn't you? That was what the instructions meant on the paper you found in the bread."

"Yes, dear, children. War orphans," David replied.

"From Algeria?" She was dumbfounded.

Again David nodded.

"You are helping to save children? That is it? At St. Joseph's. Hakim? And Ophélie?"

David raised his eyebrows. "You have guessed it. I'm afraid it's rather complicated. And Mother Griolet has no idea that I'm involved. She must not know, Gabriella." His tone was stern.

"Why not?" Gabriella was incredulous.

"To protect her. The less she knows, the safer she is."

"But after today, the children will surely say something to her."

"I'm sure with your lively imagination, you can make up a good excuse for my sudden appearance." He winked at her.

Gabriella felt suddenly relieved and squeezed his

hand tightly. "So this is what you do, David Hoffmann? This is your secret! Saving children." She could not contain her excitement. "It is a wonderful secret. This secret, David, I can live with. I will help you."

He shook his head. "I'm glad you approve, my dear, but right now you are in a bit of hot water. A nut is on your trail. So listen to what I'm going to do. It will be simple. It's all a question of timing."

* * *

Nearing the Place de la Comedie, Bus 11 pulled into its stop in front of the train station. Jean-Claude saw Gabriella descend the steps with the children.

"*Arretez!*" Jean-Claude commanded as he thrust a wad of bills into the surprised taxi driver's hand and leapt from the taxi. Instantly a tall man blocked his way. As Jean-Claude tried to step around him, he felt a crashing blow to his chin. The last thing Jean-Claude remembered was people all around shouting, "A doctor. Get a doctor!"

* * *

David Hoffmann left Jean-Claude on the sidewalk, surrounded by a group of curious pedestrians. He raced toward the Comedie. When he was a safe distance away, he stopped and turned around. From this perspective, he watched Gabriella climb back onto the same waiting bus, five children trailing obediently behind her. A moment later, the bus took off down the road toward the east side of town. Jean-Claude still lay on the sidewalk surrounded by curious pedestrians.

David shook his head and muttered, "That was a little too close for comfort." He lost himself in the back streets of the *centre ville* and did not head back to Castelnau until well after dark.

Chapter Twenty-Two

December 24 in Algiers came and went like every other day during that long fall of 1961: filled with fear. The streets were empty of people by dusk. Somewhere a plastic bomb exploded in the Casbah as the OAS unloaded its fury. The graves of innocent victims littered the countryside, but the terrorists on both sides paid little heed.

An old man with a turban around his head knocked softly on a door on the second floor of an old apartment building in Bab el Oued. The woman who opened the door eyed him suspiciously.

"A letter for you and your children, from Moustafa," he urged as the woman took an envelope from him. "He said it is most urgent. Something about leaving Algiers. Instructions from Hugo."

A spark of relief lit up the woman's eyes. "Thank you, sir. Thank you." She closed the door behind her. The old man with the turban walked down the hall, pausing only long enough to hear the woman calling, "François, Emilie, *venez ici!* We have news. Come."

The turbaned man was almost to the steps when he

heard the explosion. Gazing back at the apartment, he saw smoke escaping from under the door. He nodded slowly and murmured, "Merry Christmas. Merry Christmas to you from Ali."

* * *

The Christmas Eve meal ended at midnight. Mme. Pons and Mme. Leclerc glowed with pleasure as the young people crowded around the long dining room table at Mme. Pons' house. Stephanie and Caroline were chatting about how much they had eaten. They begged Mme. Leclerc for her recipe for the *bûche de Nöel*.

Gabriella and David were in deep discussion about a French poet. The conversation around the table had been lively all night, Mme. Leclerc thought with satisfaction. Much better than the fiasco two months ago.

Candles flickered by the window. She could tell that the students did not want to leave. Stephanie was terribly homesick, and Caroline seemed simply bored with classes out.

"Girls, will you go to Mass tomorrow?" the old woman inquired.

"I doubt it," Caroline replied casually. "Sleep late. Then I'm gonna get together with a few other girls."

"And you, Gabriella. What are your plans?" Mme. Leclerc asked.

Gabriella looked around, her face red with embarrassment. "I don't know. I mean, I haven't made plans. Church, of course," she stammered.

David took her hand in his and interrupted, "I'm afraid Miss Madison will be quite busy all day." He eyed her seductively. "*N'est-ce pas*, my dear?"

Mme. Leclerc clapped her hands together. "Marvelous! Busy on Christmas, even so far away from your family. That is just right. I don't want my girls to feel too homesick. That is all."

She bustled into the kitchen to meet Monique, who was clearing off plates and humming to herself.

"Did you hear that, Monique! Did you hear what Mr. Hoffmann said? Miss Madison is going to be quite busy. All day tomorrow she will be. *Ooh la!*"

"It has been a wonderful success, Yvette, our Christmas meal. We can leave in the morning *tranquilles* to see our families. Our boarders will be having a delightful time of their own." She laughed loudly and rolled her eyes. The two widows giggled for a long time before they composed themselves and joined the young people in the *salon*.

It was almost two A.M. when the little party broke up. Mme. Leclerc started back to her apartment with Caroline, Stephanie, and Gabriella. David caught Gabriella's hand before she left.

"I will pick you up at ten. Is that too early? We can go to church together, and then you can come here for lunch. Mme. Pons is leaving me all the leftovers."

"You mean it?" Gabriella furrowed her brow. "You want to go to church with me?"

"Of course. It is Christmas."

* * *

The *Eglise Reformée* in Montpellier was tucked behind the Place de la Comedie on a small side street. One of two Protestant churches in the city, the congregation was nonetheless sparse on Christmas morn as Gabriella and David stepped into the sanctuary. "Thank you for coming with me," she whispered.

Throughout the worship service David sat, respectful and pensive, with Gabriella beside him. He sang along with the familiar Christmas hymns. At the end of the service, as the pastor pronounced the benediction and people rose to leave, he took her hand.

"I need to go back to Mme. Leclerc's for a moment," she said. "Will you come with me?"

"Of course." They walked to where the *deux chevaux* waited patiently behind the large, open square. David drove through the deserted streets back to Castelnau, stopping in front of Mme. Leclerc's apartment.

Gabriella left him in the dark stairwell as she rushed up the stairs and into the apartment. In her room, she retrieved two brightly wrapped packages, placed them in a plastic sack, and left the room.

"What have you got there?" David questioned her as she joined him on the stairs.

Suddenly Gabriella felt foolish and blushed. "Nothing much. Just a gift for Christmas."

"I thought everyone exchanged gifts last night at Mother Griolet's."

"Oh, yes, that was for the children and the students, but...but you weren't there."

He put his arm around her shoulder and held her close as they walked through the town. "You are sweet, Gabby. Too sweet."

* * *

Mme. Pons' apartment was dark and empty, and at once Gabriella felt awkward. David turned on the light in the *salon* and took Gabriella's coat.

"Can I get you something to drink, Miss Madison?" he teased. "A *pastis* perhaps or a *muscat*? For Christmas."

"I'll try a *muscat*. You say it is really good."

"That's right, you never got to taste it in Aix. Would you like to hear a little Christmas music from the good old USA?"

"You have some?" she asked, delighted.

He brought their drinks and sat across from her, raising his glass. "A toast to us, Gabby. Friends." He tipped his glass against hers.

"Friends," she murmured.

He disappeared into his room, emerging moments later with a record album in its folder. He held it out for her to inspect. *50 Favorite Christmas Songs*, it read.

"This is great. Where did you find it?"

"I have connections," he quipped. He placed the record on the phonograph and put the needle down, and "Rudolph the Red-Nosed Reindeer" began to play.

"Would you like to open your present now?" she asked. She handed him a small, rectangular box.

He raised his eyebrows as he took it from her. "You shouldn't have gotten me anything."

"It is nothing. It is just . . . symbolic."

"Symbolic of what?"

"Just open it," she laughed.

Carefully he unwrapped the paper, laying it on the floor. In the background Bing Crosby was serenading them. "*I'm dreaming of a white Christmas . . .*" David opened the box and reached inside, withdrawing the foot-sized statue of the baker.

"A *santon!*" He laughed heartily, obviously pleased. "A *boulanger!*" He raised it in his hands and admired the clay figurine. "It is perfect." Turning to look at Gabriella, he added, "Thank you."

"I found it at les Baux, before all the problems. He reminded me of you. A lover of French bread." Her eyes were shining with excitement. "I couldn't resist it, and now . . . well, now that I know what you are up to, it seems even more perfect." Her palms were wet, and her left foot was jiggling nervously.

"Gabby," he brushed her face. "I have never known someone so thoughtful, so determined to find something that is right."

"I'm glad you like it." She glanced down at the other package that lay at her feet. "There is something else, too."

"Another! This is my richest Christmas yet."

"You're teasing."

"Well, let's just say that my dad and I never really celebrated the holiday."

He ripped off the paper on the second present, uncovering a thick, black leather-bound book. "A Bible?" he said, sounding confused. He ran his fingers over the new leather. "It is a very handsome volume, but Gabby ..."

"I know you don't read it," she interrupted quickly. "But I just thought ... it might remind you of me some-day ... of our friendship."

"Yes, indeed it will." He was quiet for a moment. "I have read it, you know. Parts of it I know by heart. There is some very beautiful literature in the Bible. And some pretty far-fetched stuff, too, you have to admit."

She did not reply. A chorus harmonized on "Silent Night." *Sleep in heavenly pea—eace. Slee—eep in heavenly peace.*

"I'm sorry, Gabby. I don't want to spoil your holi-day. I know it is an important day for you. Your Savior's birth. Thank you for the Bible. And I'll read it again. Just for you. How's that?" He patted her hand.

"That would be really nice," she answered. "Start with the Gospels, why don't you? Perhaps you are not as familiar with the New Testament?"

"Why do you say that?"

"You are Jewish, aren't you?"

"Half Jewish, my dear. Jewish enough to be put in a camp, but not enough to follow the Old Testament teachings. Not without a mother ..."

"I'm sorry to bring it up."

"Don't be, Gabby. You seem to be finding out a lot of other things about me." David suddenly seemed eager to talk. "You might as well know. My mother was a devout Jew, a God-fearing woman. I still remember her praying by my bed at night, singing to me from the psalms. But when you are only six and you watch your mother die, something happens. Afterward her sweet melody was replaced by discordant hate and cruelty. Everything changed.

"After the camp, I could not find anything to bring back the joy in life. And I was only a little boy! My father and I lived a tense, miserable existence, hating the sight of each other because it reminded us of the family we once were.

"By the time I was ten, I was sure that there could be no God. I have never been able to see as you see. To believe. The hate is too strong. And Gabby, I am afraid to forgive."

She watched him holding his head in his hands, and she felt pity for him. "Why?" she asked quietly.

"Why? Because I do not want to be reconciled with my past. I want to flee it . . . and yet somehow I keep finding it staring me right in the face." He stood up and walked over to a window.

"I wish I knew what to say to you, David, but I do not. Only that in walking on through the pain, not avoiding it, there is a certain freedom over your past. At least, that is what I am finding."

"Your freedom is found within the confines of your religion, Gabby. I don't want that kind of confinement." But there was no anger in his voice, no accusation.

"I understand why you think religion is confining, but I am not really talking about a religion, you know. I am talking about a Person. My faith centers around a Person."

The music swelled. *Christ our Saviour is bo-orn; Chri-ist our Saviour is born.*

The record turned silently round and round. David walked over to the phonograph, flipping the disk over to the other side.

"Excuse me for a minute," he said as he slipped into his room.

Gabriella walked around the den. It still smelled of the delicacies from the previous night. She felt a quick pang of homesickness and a sudden desire to be alone.

Then David reappeared, grinning sheepishly, the same vulnerable boyish grin she had seen once before. "I have something for you, too."

Gabriella could not hide her surprise or pleasure. "For me? You do?"

He smirked. "You're not the only one who likes symbolism, remember." He handed her a thin square package.

Unwrapping it, she found a gold-framed print of Monet's painting of the poppies. A card with her name on it was taped to the glass.

"Should I open this now?" she asked haltingly.

"Yes, why don't you?" His voice was soft, tender, his eyes filled with quiet admiration.

She took the card from its envelope and opened it. The inside was filled with David's script.

*A wildflower, bright and red
exuberance that softly spread
to capture fields of dreams and hearts
a silent splendor stops and starts
and I found pleasure in the touch
and smell of such
a wild and happy
crimson-coated poppy.
David*

Gabriella's eyes brimmed with tears. She bit her lip, then looked up at him, a smile on her face. "It's beautiful. The print and the poem. Thank you. I . . . I don't know what to say."

He was smiling too. "Funny how sometimes it is through pictures and poems that we paint and write what we cannot say." The record played softly on as the young people gazed silently at each other.

* * *

They had eaten the leftovers and listened to the record three times. The afternoon was waning. David took Gabriella's hand and led her to the couch, and they sat down together. He put his arm around her.

"Somehow it seems that we are more than friends," Gabriella whispered, leaning against his shoulder.

"Am I making you uncomfortable?"

"No, not exactly. Only confused."

He rested his head on the back of the couch, and spoke slowly. "You are wondering if we should be more than friends?" He turned his head toward Gabriella and winked. "If our attraction is not merely platonic, but romantic? Why do I not kiss you? How we can share so intimately and yet remove the physical? And you are fighting with yourself, because you don't want to want what you want."

Gabriella's face turned red. "Something like that, yes."

"And do you want to be my girlfriend?"

She did not know what to say to his blunt question, and he respected her silence. "Gabriella, I would like to explain something to you. I think you will understand. I have enjoyed the presence of many women. I'm sure you are not shocked. Brief encounters to bandage a deeper hurt. But I have rarely found a soul mate.

Someone who looks deeper and feels. Someone who makes me question and care." He stroked her hair.

"And then you came along, a welcome surprise for this old cynic. A safe bet, an unwitting accomplice on my secret mission. I found you delightful. And off limits.

"The friendship was possible, but our moral and spiritual outlook differed so. . . ." He played with her hair. "An angel and a devil."

She squirmed away from him, feeling vulnerable.

"I would not mind a romantic fling, Gabby, if that is what you were after. But I know better. You want a meeting of souls, a sharing that encompasses the whole being, physical, emotional, spiritual.

"And I cannot give you my whole being. I do not own it yet." He rubbed his forehead with his hand. "How can I explain it? Perhaps you will not believe me, but the fact is that I respect you too much to pull you into an affair that would leave you heartbroken and guilty. After all, I am not wooing you away from another man. It is a God, a jealous God, who demands your total devotion. I cannot fight that, Gabby. I will not."

He moved closer to her again. He gently put his hand under her chin and lifted her head so that she met his eyes. Hers were brimming with tears.

"Dear Gabby, you do not want me. Ours is an impossible love. Something Shelley or Keats would write about with heavy hearts. Please, don't cry. Forgive me for speaking so bluntly." He offered her a white handkerchief.

She blew her nose loudly and dabbed her eyes. "You are right, David. You have seen my heart and my questions. But it doesn't seem fair. Aren't you afraid that you will go through the rest of your life and always wonder, if only? If only we had given it a chance?"

He grinned, turning up one side of his mouth.

"Sure, I'll wonder. I'll think about you in ten years and hope you aren't married to a boring old pastor who preaches hellfire and brimstone but puts you to sleep in bed." He raised his eyebrows mischievously, and Gabriella laughed.

"So I'm doomed," she stated. "I can't be a disobedient child even if I want to. You'll hold me back. You, my tempter, will protect my purity." Her eyes were sparkling again.

"Innocent and chaste, I used to picture you. But I'm afraid I've at least destroyed the first stereotype. You're in the thick of things with me now."

"Yes," Gabriella said, happy to change subjects. "I want to know more about this secret mission of yours. Why, David? Why are you helping bring kids out of Algeria?" Before he could answer, she continued, "And don't give me that bit about revenge and minorities. Maybe it's true. But there has to be a deeper reason. Something has made you feel strongly enough about this war that you are here in lowly Castelnau, smuggling orphans into France."

He sighed, shifting his frame to another position on the couch so that they were facing each other, no longer touching hands. "You really want to know?"

The way he regarded her made Gabriella's heart skip a beat. If she was merely David's friend, he could care about another.

"Yes, of course I want to know."

"Mother Griolet told you that I once lived in Algeria." She nodded.

"I made friends during that year, just before the war started. It was 1953. And one of those friends is now in trouble. This friend wrote me about a need, a desperate need to get children out of Algeria. Children who were in danger of death. I had just graduated from

287

Princeton and had some time on my hands, so I decided to see how I could help."

"You must have cared a lot about this friend to come here," Gabriella stated, a sly play in her voice.

David smiled and shook his head. "Yes, I suppose I did, at one time. But that was a long time ago. And now . . . now I am involved in this operation and I find it . . . compelling."

"And the cross?" Gabriella had removed her cross from under her blouse and now held it in her palm.

"The cross is our symbol, a symbol of our operation. Nothing religious. It was a reminder of the past. It seemed to fit. Quite a coincidence that you wear the same one."

"Yes, a coincidence, David. A simple coincidence."

The sun was peeping behind the red tiles of the houses facing the apartment. "I should take you back, *non?* I have a few things to do, and perhaps you will be seeing Miss Thrasher and Miss Harland?"

"Yes, I suppose I should get back."

He helped her with her coat, and they left the apartment, walking out into the dusk of Christmas day. The streets were empty. Gabriella thought of a hundred things she wanted to say to him, but she could not bring herself to say any of them. *"Don't leave me alone tonight. I want to stay with you. Just a while longer."*

He stopped at the entrance to Mme. Leclerc's apartment. "Listen, Gabby. I'll be leaving for about ten days—until school starts back up. Please remember what I have said. Lie low. Jean-Claude won't come here. You will be okay?"

"I'll be okay. I have four new orphans to look after." She did not meet his eyes, for hers were filled with tears. "Thank you for a lovely day, David. The lunch, the print, the poem. I will not forget this Christmas, David Hoffmann." She stood on tiptoe and kissed him softly on the cheek.

"Nor shall I, Miss Madison," he whispered.

* * *

It was late on December twenty-fifth when Moustafa brought back the grim news to Anne-Marie. His face was haggard, his shoulders sagged. "I am so sorry. No one saw a thing. It was at six P.M. when the bomb went off. Mme. Santier and her two children, killed."

"Murderer!" Anne-Marie cried out. "He is a cruel and systematic murderer." She was sobbing. "They were so close. Two weeks and they would be gone. Now this. Now nothing. Now only three more names to cross off the list. And somewhere in the Casbah, a madman rubs his hands together and dances a sadistic tango with death. Somewhere in the middle of hell itself."

* * *

The Christmas record played softly in the background as David packed his suitcase. He hummed along with "Silent Night," reliving the afternoon with Gabriella. *She knows too much now*, he thought. But there was nothing to be changed. Ten days on the road. He hoped that Jean-Claude Gachon would decide to stay away from Montpellier for a while, after what happened last week. But nothing was sure. Quickly he scribbled a note on a scrap of paper. Before placing it in an envelope, he sketched a rough drawing of the Huguenot cross in the left-hand corner.

The *santon* stood on the chipped desk. "Gabby," he said aloud, recalling the sparkle in her eyes as she had explained the symbolism of the clay baker. He sighed and shook his head. *Get her out of your mind. You've explained things to her clearly. She agrees. Get her out of your mind.*

The black leather Bible sat beside the *santon*. David leafed through its thin gold-lined pages. The words were in French. He closed it, then opened it again. Gabriella's handwriting adorned the inside cover. He paused to read the inscription.

Dear David,

Wise professor! Shakespeare memorized it, John Donne preached on it, Victor Hugo quoted it. Throughout the centuries, God has drawn man to His Word to read and be transformed. You who can so eloquently transmit the deeper meaning of works written by mere mortals, tarry a moment on these immortal pages. May you find there, as I have, the Bread of Life for your hungry soul. If not, at least you will have dared to seek an answer to its heavy questions.

Thank you for being my friend,
Gabriella   *December 25, 1961*

Underneath her note, she had written a verse: "For everyone that asketh, receiveth; and he that seeketh findeth; and to him that knocketh, it shall be opened." Luke 11:10. A Huguenot cross was sketched underneath the verse.

David remembered his promise to her, *I will read it for you, then,* and put the book into his suitcase. He left his room and stretched out on the couch, listening to the familiar melodies of Christmas carols, the tinkle of a bell, the soothing violins, the triumphant trumpet. *O come let us adore Him, Chri—ist the Lord.* The record ended, again turning silently on its table. David did not move to stop it. He fell asleep, still hearing the refrain of the last hymn in his mind.

Chapter Twenty-Three

The plane trees in Castelnau, which offered shade in the heat of summer, had been cut far back so that they appeared like armless men, thrusting their knobby appendages toward the magnificent blue sky. Early January shone bright and full of promise, Gabriella reflected, as she hurried through town. She had been right after all. The ten days without David had passed swiftly, taken up with the children and their games and cares.

She had agreed to sleep in Sister Rosaline's quarters by the dormitory while the nun took a week off to be with her family in the north of France. Ophélie had especially taken advantage of the extra hours with "Bribri." Gabriella smiled to herself, thinking of the child. What was it that Mother Griolet had said? Tragedy to triumph? Sometimes, when the six-year-old lay curled on Gabriella's temporary bunk, the young woman would smell the child's clean hair and remember Ericka cuddling up beside her in Senegal, squeaky clean after her bath in the iron tub behind their hut.

Then it took an extreme effort for Gabriella to pull herself back to the present and into the life of the bright-eyed girl lying at her feet. Every time that Ophélie shared a story or a new discovery, Gabriella would think, *So this is what comes after six. This is what she would have seen.* The thought haunted her when she was alone, an aching, joyous hurt.

At night, alone on her cot in Sister Rosaline's room, Gabriella felt a crushing weight of sadness. Often she drifted off to sleep crying out softly to her mother. But when she woke the next morning, the heaviness would be gone, replaced by a chorus of happy children. Hearing their voices, Gabriella felt she could go on.

The four new orphans began to shed their masks of fear, warming up to the merry laughter of the other children. Mireille and Julie were sisters, five and eight, who told Gabriella of the terrible night their mother was beaten to death in their apartment. The girls had escaped out a window and fled to a cousin's house. Elima was thirteen, on the verge of puberty, shy, reserved and distrustful, a beautiful Arab girl. Gabriella did not know her story. Youssef, the twelve-year-old Arab boy, had found an immediate friendship with Hakim. They laughed and played and planned together.

But Mother Griolet seemed distant and disturbed. Gabriella approached her this morning with care.

"Mother Griolet," she began softly, as the nun met her in the hall of the basement by the classrooms.

"Yes, my dear. What may I do for you?"

"It is only that you seem . . . concerned. I know you have such responsibilities, but you are not yourself. I am wondering if it is something I have done."

The little woman's face broke into a smile. "For goodness' sakes, no. No, Gabriella. Here, come into my apartment."

Gabriella followed Mother Griolet into her den.

"*Au contraire,* I don't know what I'd do without you! I suppose I am feeling my way through a new adventure. There are quite a few concerns, with these children from Algeria. You see, for now it is quite clandestine ... and no one knows how long this war will go on or how many more children will come." She paused for breath. "Dear me, I am going on and on. I'm forgetting who is in charge. He surely knows what is coming.

"There's a verse I learned years ago, during the Second World War. It jumped out at me, and I grabbed it and used it for all it was worth." She chuckled. "It is from the psalms: 'Lord, my heart is not haughty, nor mine eyes lofty: neither do I exercise myself in great matters, or in things too high for me.' I keep reminding the Lord of this verse."

Gabriella sat on the sofa watching the old woman. "I think you are an amazing lady. Look at all you've done for these children and hundreds of others. And yet you just keep going, without taking any credit. You're my heroine, Mother Griolet. I hope you don't mind. I want to be like you someday."

"*Ooh la,* Gabriella. Watch out, now! You can see me as a role model, if you wish. But be careful! It is so easy to admire men and put our hope and glory in simple humans. I don't want that. I don't need it. And I'm sure to disappoint you." She winked at Gabriella. "Glory is a dangerous thing, linked with that enemy, pride. No, sweet child, give the glory to the Lord. He is the only One who deserves it." She bustled out of the den and into the courtyard, calling to the children. "Lunchtime in ten minutes. Yoohoo, children!"

Gabriella watched the nun disappear behind the door. She rose to leave, too, with a feeling of fresh anticipation. Today, David Hoffmann would be coming home.

* * *

Pierre Cabrol arrived at work at three A.M., just as he had done for the past thirty-five years. He flicked on the light in the *boulangerie* and pulled a stained white apron over his head, tying it around his trim waist. Thirty-five years of baking bread had not gone to his middle, he was proud to say. Often, among his buddies, he smirked and added that there were plenty of other things that had gone there, but not too much bread.

Pierre loved his work. He relished the early black hours before dawn alone in his kitchen, preparing the dough, letting it rise, smelling the first whiff of cooked bread as it baked in the ovens. He enjoyed creating the pastries, with their creams and the chocolate fillings. He especially liked the special orders for parties and weddings. That was when he could let all of his creativity go and prepare a *pièce montée,* stacks of pastry puffs filled with cream and mounted into an elaborate mountain of sugar.

His wife would sometimes roll her eyes and tease him in the midst of one of his creations. "Pure genius, Pierre. Pure genius, *mon mari.*"

He would pat her bottom and shoo her out of the kitchen to the waiting customers in the front of the store. That had been their life for all these years. And neither could complain. Even in the World War when flour was so scarce, he had kept the store open, handing out loaves to the famished villagers who came by. Pierre, the Prince, they had called him. That had made him grin foolishly, proud, until his wife had told him that he would pop off the buttons on his shirt and she did not have any more thread to sew them back.

But Pierre's favorite memory was not of handing out bread to starving people. It was even better, more delicious, like the first bite of a *brioche,* fresh from the oven. It was that memory that held him this black morning, as he rolled the dough and felt it seep slowly up through the openings between his fingers.

Loaf after long, raw loaf he placed in the metal racks that he could then wheel into the huge oven. *Baguettes* and *gros pains, pain complet* and *pain de campagne.* Then as he rolled out the dough for his loaves of *pain de seigle,* he laughed a jolly laugh.

"Oh, yes! Oh, yes, Pierre," he sang to himself in the stillness of the room. "You are not young anymore, but you remember! Remember the knives you hid in the bread. Baked them right in the dough and off they went! Remember the papers and the names of those imprisoned. The secret information! Ah, yes, those were the days, my boy!" He hummed to himself in happy recall. "And so, again you can play this game of hide-and-seek! Another war. Not the Resistance, *mais non!* But another little game. Another way to help. Pierre, *Le Prince!"*

He reached into the pocket of his heavy gray trousers and pulled out a small piece of paper. He had received it yesterday in the delivery from Marseilles, hidden in a bag of flour. A piece of paper, which he now rolled into a thin cylinder and placed in a tube of plastic.

"And *oop la!* In she goes," he sang, as he embedded the plastic tubing in the middle of the dough in one of the *pain de seigle.* On this loaf he added no fancy cuts to bake up into crisp little ridges. It was a simple omission. No one else ever noticed. But he knew. And he would be ready when the right person came into the store, asking for a *pain de seigle.*

* * *

Jean-Louis Vidal passed up the *café-bar* on his way through town. Tomorrow classes resumed. His thin lips were pressed together in a forced smile as he toddled along the cobblestones, turning down a side street and into a *boulangerie*. Jean-Louis spat quickly before entering the store. The aroma of fresh bread hung thick and succulent around him.

"*Bonjour,* Jean-Louis," called out an aging baker from behind the counter. "*Alors, quoi de neuf?*"

"Nothing much up today, Pierre," the broad-bellied professor answered. "Only thought I might be tasting a bit of your bread. That's all. *Pain de seigle*, if you don't mind."

The baker's mouth opened into a delighted bellow. "*Pain de seigle,* Jean-Louis. *Mais bien sûr!* Of course. I have one just for you." He handed the little man a hot loaf, winking at him. The store was empty. "Just like in the old days, *n'est-ce pas, mon ami?* I've not seen so much fun in almost twenty years. Was a lot sprier then. We both were, as I recall."

The two men grinned, and Jean-Louis paid for his bread. As he left the store, he added, "Keep the change."

* * *

The afternoon sun shone through the windows of Mother Griolet's office. She did not notice the flirting rays as she tapped her foot nervously under her desk. A note lay before her, with a Huguenot cross drawn in the corner. She had received it ten days ago and reread it now.

> *Someone is seeking information about the new orphan named Ophélie. Potentially dangerous for the operation. Watch the child carefully. Do not let her leave premises. Answer no questions.*
> *Hugo*

Mother Griolet had worried over the note all week, unable to forget the letters Sister Rosaline had found concealed in Ophélie's tights. This child was an important link with what was happening in Algeria. That list of names was no coincidence.

But how could she protect Ophélie? Thankfully Mr. Hoffmann had been gone for the past ten days. Mother Griolet feared him the most. But surely he would not betray his own child! Or did he even know she was his child? The letter said that Ophélie's mom had never told him. And Ophélie seemed to have no idea that her father was nearby, either. Mother Griolet sat in the office, perplexed. She needed to confront the child with the facts.

The nun folded the note and tucked it into a pocket in her robes. She left her apartment and walked out into the crisp, clear afternoon air. Quickly she entered the girls' dormitory and found Ophélie's bed. Opening the second drawer, she retrieved the pair of blue tights and pulled the blue bag out. The two small envelopes appeared to have been untouched.

Mother Griolet took out the letter to Mr. Gady. Carefully she copied every word into her small spiral notebook. Then she took the other pieces of paper and began copying the names and addresses listed there. Her hand was shaking as she wrote, quickly yet precisely.

"Dear Lord, forgive me if this qualifies me for a spy." The thought made her laugh to herself. "A seventy-two-year-old nun spying on a six-year-old orphan. Your sense of humor, Father, indeed. But the child will not be bothered. She will continue in a state of blissful ignorance. This, I think, is best."

The bell rang loudly, announcing the end of classes. Mother Griolet slipped the envelopes back into the blue bag, then tucked the bag far down into the leg of the blue tights, and placed them neatly in the second drawer. She reviewed her work. "Not bad for an old nun," she concluded, and walked briskly out of the dormitory as the children burst out through the basement doors into the courtyard.

* * *

There were thirty-two churches in Montpellier, and Jean-Claude had visited twenty-three of them. At first he had limited himself to those on the east side of the city, but when that search turned up empty, he decided to include all of the churches, Catholic and Protestant. But so far, he had found none that housed children.

Three days recuperating from a concussion had been a waste of time, he contemplated angrily, furious at the thought of the man who had struck him. He was sure it was David Hoffmann. "You pig! You are always showing up unexpectedly."

Now it was January 10, and he needed to get news to Ali. He came to the parish of St. Pierre on the Quai de Verdançon. A kind-looking priest opened the door to his knock and straightened his clerical collar. *"Oui, Monsieur?"*

Jean-Claude cleared his throat and spoke with the same gentle, flowing words he had used when talking to twenty-three other priests. *"Bonjour, Mon Père."* He inclined his head. "I am looking for a child, an orphan. She is a *pied-noir.*" He produced a picture of Ophélie. "Her mother was killed in the war, and I am her uncle. The child has been lost, but the last word we received was that she was living in a church in Montpellier. I have visited most of the parishes now, with no success. I am desperate for news. Would you perhaps know of this child?"

The priest shook his head, rubbing his chin as he thought. *"Non,* I am sorry. We do not house children." Then he smiled. "Ah, but perhaps you have not tried the communities around Montpellier. Have you been to Castelnau? There is an orphanage there. It's been run for

years by an old renegade nun." He stopped himself, looking embarrassed. "Forgive me, I mean a kindly Sister has
run the orphanage for years. Perhaps she would have
some information."

Jean-Claude kept calm. "That is a good idea.
Castelnau, did you say?"

The priest nodded.

"And what is the name of this church, if I may ask?"

"It is called the Church of St. Joseph."

"*Merci. Merci beaucoup,*" Jean-Claude said.

"*De rien,*" the priest called out, as Jean-Claude
skipped down the stone steps. "God be with you."

* * *

Jean-Louis Vidal finished his afternoon history class
on January eleventh and watched the girls file out of
the room. He liked to observe the legs of Miss Caroline
Harland when she wore her skirt high above her knee.
Not such a bad profession, this teaching of American
girls. Even if it was hard to get inspired after two weeks
of vacation. Ah, but the legs of Miss Harland could at
least make his heart beat faster!

Jean-Louis removed his worn leather coat from the
back of the chair, retrieved his battered briefcase and
papers, then closed the classroom door and locked it.

His disheveled appearance contrasted with the neat
Ivy League attire of Mr. Hoffmann, he knew, but it did not
matter. Why throw a coat away if it still kept him warm?
Why indeed, when there was no money to buy another.

He paused as he came to the ground floor, and
knocked lightly on the door to Mother Griolet's apartment. The nun opened the door after a moment.

"*Entrez!* Mr. Vidal, it's you. Good. Come in, please."

They stepped into her office, and Jean-Louis pulled
the door closed. "Jeanette," he said softly. "You are fine?"

His red eyes were tender. "You look tired, *mon amie.*"

"Oh, Jean-Louis, I am tired. I have told the Lord I will not worry, but there seems much to worry about. A daily battle in the mind." She sighed. "I have something for you. You will know how to get it where it needs to go, I am sure." She flashed him a smile.

"Of course. And I have something for you too." They exchanged papers silently, briefly touching fingers. "Jeanette?"

"Yes?"

Jean-Louis cleared his throat. "You are doing a good job, Jeanette." He said it quickly, flushing under the red veins in his cheeks.

"Thank you, Jean-Louis," she replied, and she looked grateful. "You are sure we are not too old for this, now?"

Jean-Louis' eyes twinkled. "Jeanette Griolet," he scolded playfully. "Was it not you who told me that the Lord takes care of His own? That He gives strength to the weary? Something about mounting up with wings as eagles? Dear woman, you will not stop now?"

"Of course not, Jean-Louis. As long as the sun shines and the rains fall, O Lord, I will follow You."

They caught each other's gaze and giggled suddenly.

"Your eyes are still as bright as they were in the other war, Jeanette. Don't tell me that you are tired of your work. I know you love it."

"You are right, old man," she teased. "Now off with you. We both have work to do."

Jean-Louis left her office, shaking his head as Mother Griolet called after him, "Go easy on the *pastis* this afternoon, will you?"

* * *

Jean-Claude took Bus 11 from the center of town to Castelnau. He chuckled to himself. After six weeks of hunting, surely this church of St. Joseph's was where Ophélie Duchemin was living.

The town was small, its main road cobbled. The bus let him off in the middle of the village, across the street from a small square where a fountain sprayed. People were milling about in the late morning. Jean-Claude stopped a pedestrian and asked for the directions to the church. The woman nodded and pointed to her right. "It's just down the street there. You can't miss it."

He turned a corner, and the stone church came into view. It was small, with a wrought-iron spire and bell on top of the steeple. The side door to the chapel was ajar. He stepped down into the cold, deserted chapel. His shoes echoed on the stones. *"Allo?"* he said softly, but no one replied.

Leaving the chapel, he walked around the side to where another building joined the church. He knocked loudly on the door. There was no answer. He knocked again, banging his fist on the large wooden door. From within, he heard a woman's voice calling, *"J'arrive.* I'm coming. Just a moment."

"Take your time," Jean-Claude muttered to himself. "Take your time. I am in no hurry now."

* * *

Mother Griolet opened the parsonage door, panting for breath. "Excuse me," she huffed, greeting the young man who stood before her. "I am sorry to make you wait. What may I do for you?"

The man looked about twenty-eight or thirty. He was muscular and handsome, with thick brown hair and a disarming smile. Mother Griolet was sure she had never seen him before.

"Bonjour, Soeur," he began, his voice soft and respectful. "I am searching for my niece, a *pied-noir*

301

orphan whose parents were killed in the war. Most recently we have heard that the child is being housed in a church in Montpellier. I have visited most of them with no luck. I am desperate for news. A priest in the city told me of your orphanage, and I have come hoping you will be able to help me. The child's name is Ophélie Duchemin." He pulled out a picture from his shirt pocket and handed it to Mother Griolet.

The old nun had placed her hand on the door to steady her balance. A cold chill ran through her, and suddenly the man was transformed before her into a German SS officer. She remembered the terror of that encounter. *Compose yourself, Jeannette,* she rebuked herself silently, still keeping the same smile on her face. *Lord Jesus, help me. You have promised to give the words in the appropriate time.*

She cleared her throat as she stared at the picture of Ophélie. "I am sorry, but we are a very small orphanage. We only have room for thirty children. Most have been with us for a few years. It is difficult to place them." She lowered her voice to a whisper. "The priest perhaps told you?"

The young man leaned forward to catch every word, eager anticipation on his face. "No, he only said it was an orphanage."

"Ah, yes ..." Mother Griolet paused and gazed up at the billowing clouds. "Sometimes they don't like to mention it. The children are handicapped. You understand?" She tapped her head with her fingers. "Nothing inside. Poor ones." Then she feigned a surprised look. "Oh dear, I have been rude. Is this child, is this child ... handicapped?"

For a moment he stared at her, stupefied. "Handicapped? Ophélie? No, no of course not."

Mother Griolet shook her head slowly. "Well, I'm

afraid she will never be sent here then. We are, shall I say, selective. I would invite you in, sir, but I am afraid the corridors smell rather bad. I was just cleaning up an accident."

The man looked horrified. "Yes, how terrible for you."

Mother Griolet was crying now. "It is so sad, so sad. But *Monsieur*. Excuse me, I do not know your name."

"It is ...I am called Philippe," he replied nervously.

"Well, Mr. Philippe, I will tell you there is another orphanage in town. It is actually further out, past Assas. St. Bauzille-de-Montmel. You have heard of it?"

"No, no, never." His eyes had narrowed. "And can you get to it by bus?"

"By bus?" Mother Griolet paused. *"Oui!"* she brightened. "Yes, the same bus that brought you here. Number 11, is it?"

He nodded.

"Well, take it till you get to Teyran. There you must change. I am not sure of the number, but the driver can tell you."

The young man shifted his weight on the steps, his hands fidgeting in his pockets. *Perhaps he has a gun,* she thought. *He will shoot me right here and barge in and have a look for himself. And he will find the child.* But after a moment, he turned slowly away.

"Merci," he said. "St. Bauzille-de-Montmel, you said."

"Yes, exactly. Good luck, Mr. Philippe. God be with you."

She waited until he was out of sight before she closed the door. Slowly she made her way to her office and sunk into the large leather chair. Her hands were trembling uncontrollably, and she could hear the beating of her heart. She rested her head in her shaking hands. "Lord, he will be back. I know it. And what will I tell him then?"

* * *

David Hoffmann had returned to Castelnau the day before. Now he peered out the window of the language lab on the second floor of the parsonage, watching Jean-Claude Gachon retreating down the road. He sighed with relief and wiped his face with his long fingers.

Somehow Mother Griolet had convinced Jean-Claude that what he was searching for was not here at St. Joseph's. For now. But he would be back, David was sure. And what would she tell him then?

Chapter Twenty-Four

If ever there were a confused place on earth, Anne-Marie was sure it was in Algiers. A tangled web of terrorism, counterterrorism, espionage, and counterespionage threatened to trip up every citizen—Arab, *pied-noir*, French soldier, and mercenary—during the month of January 1962. While President de Gaulle worked on compromise with the FLN, three separate branches of the French secret service prowled about, seeking to stop the OAS's brutality. Everyone belonged to some clandestine movement. Anne-Marie reminded herself that she, too, had belonged to several. But protecting children from a vengeful Ali was not recognized by anyone else.

She slipped out of Marcus Cirou's apartment late in the afternoon of January eighteenth. Moustafa was at her side. The real terror in Algiers occurred between dark and dawn, when most of the bombings by the FLN, OAS, and now the new secret police took place.

Moustafa pushed Anne-Marie along. "We must deliver the information. There is no other way. Ali has the names of these last two families. If we can get them out, I am sure he will not know the rest. Go on, now, love. I will meet you back at the apartment at dusk."

She traced her way along the narrow streets. On every wall there was a painted slogan. OAS had been painted one night, only to be painted over the next morning with the French secret service initials MCP. She walked past a shopkeeper who was sweeping out his store from the debris of a predawn bombing. She did not stop to stare.

She found a dingy apartment building called La Fillette. Clothes hung from every balcony, refusing to dry in the cold, humid air. She entered the stairwell, which was littered with beer cans and cigarette butts. The stench of urine hung in the air.

On the third floor she searched for apartment thirty-six. She waited to make sure no one was following her on the steps. All was silent. Anne-Marie knocked lightly on the door.

"Who is there?" A woman's voice called out from the apartment.

"It is Anne-Marie Duchemin."

The door opened a crack, and a gray-haired woman peeped out. "Come in," she whispered.

Anne-Marie stepped into the apartment. Some type of meat was roasting on the kitchen stove. "How are you, Mme. Bousquet?"

"We are all right, Miss Duchemin. Thank you. Do you bring news?"

"Yes. The boat will leave on the 25th. The children must be at the dock at midnight to catch the boat. We will pick them up in the alleyway behind your apartment building at 11:30. You understand? But it is not safe for you to remain here. Ali Boudani has your address. Is there anywhere else you could go for a week?"

The woman's eyes showed fear and fatigue. She

306

breathed in deeply. "Yes, I can go to my cousin's home outside the city. But what of Mme. el Gharbi? You will go to her? You will warn her? She is beside herself with grief. Her husband was murdered two days ago. His throat was slit—the *harki* punishment. She is terrified for the children. Please, Miss Duchemin. Please! Take our children with you. Hide them for us. I am an old widow. If I die, it will hurt no one. But the children. They deserve another life. A chance to escape before it is too late." She lowered her head. "Too late as it is for Mme. Sentier and her children." She wiped her brow.

Anne-Marie reached out and squeezed the woman's hand. "Mme. Bousquet, we are doing our best. If there is no one to meet the children in France, it is not better. We must be careful. If we can get the children any sooner, I will tell you. Otherwise, they must be ready on the 25th. Do not worry for Mme. el Gharbi. I will let her know."

"Thank you, child. Thank you." The aging woman glanced to the sky and crossed herself. "God be with us. God spare us."

"Yes, it is as you say." Anne-Marie closed the door behind her, tiptoed down the steps, and stepped back out into the streets of Algiers.

* * *

"What is the link between literature and art, then?" David questioned his students as he concluded his lecture. "That is the topic of tomorrow's discussion. And on Friday we will take the morning to visit the Musée Fabre in Montpellier. There are many great works in the museum, most notably, of course, those of Frédéric Bazille, the great painter from Castelnau, a contemporary of Monet.

"Please don't forget that your papers on André Gide are also due Friday." Several girls groaned at the reminder. "That is all. You are dismissed, ladies."

The young teacher closed his briefcase. When the other students had left, he joined Gabriella, who was staring out the window. They watched the children playing in the courtyard. Ophélie was chasing the new orphan, Mireille, their high-pitched squeals reaching up to David's classroom.

"Your Frenchman came to St. Joseph's last week," David said.

Gabriella gasped and looked up at him. "Jean-Claude? Came here? Why didn't you tell me before?"

He ignored her question. "He is looking for you and the child. For Ophélie. I'm sure he will be back. You must be ready."

"What do you mean?" Gabriella's voice was agitated.

"You must never answer the door to the parsonage. Watch your steps, and Ophélie's. And find a place to hide with the child in case he shows up. You must not be seen, either of you. We will be receiving more orphans next week. He cannot know, or the whole plan will backfire. You must help me, Gabby." Fatigue showed on his face.

"I have said I will help. But you are worried about something else, David. What is it? What is wrong?"

"Everything, Gabby. Everything and nothing. 'The world is too much with us, late and soon.' "

Gabriella smiled. "Does quoting Wordsworth help you relax?"

"Perhaps," he answered absently. "Perhaps it is like reading the Scriptures for you." He brushed a wisp of hair away from his eyes. "Will you come with me for a drink? Just here in town."

"Of course." She beamed up at him.

Dear Gabby, he thought as they left the room. *What shall I tell you?*

They trotted through the town to the old *café-bar.* Several older men were seated at the tables enjoying a late morning *aperitif.*

"Excuse the ambiance," David whispered as they found the same table in the back of the *café* where they sat after the phone call to Jean-Claude in early December. This time, the music was louder, the laughter more raucous, and a chilly gust of wind swept through the room each time the door was opened. Gabriella huddled over the table. "May I take your coat?" David asked.

"No, thanks. I'm freezing," she retorted.

He ordered two hot chocolates and waited for them to appear before speaking. "Gabby, I have received some more information about the work. It will take me a while to sort it out with my contacts in Algeria. It has been so long, you see, since I have actually heard from them. But when it is all worked out, St. Joseph's may be flooded with kids. And Mother Griolet will need someone to help her. I mean, to get the children, to deliver messages. It will be quite time consuming. But I need you to be that person."

She sighed as he took her hand. "David, you know I want to help. I have no choice, really."

"I may be gone for a while, dear. I'm convinced there will be more peace talks going on between de Gaulle and the FLN, to try to settle this Algerian question. Things will start happening fast, Gabby, and we must be ready. Ready for something bigger than we bargained for."

"And if Jean-Claude finds us? What will we do then?"

"You will contact me. I will leave an address and check in every few days. But, Gabby, he must not know. Not yet. He works for an Algerian, high in the FLN. A man with a grudge from another war. This man seeks to wipe out whole families through cold-blooded, premeditated murder.

"But I have a feeling that when Algeria is independent, it will all break up. If we can hold on a few more weeks, a couple of months, this danger will be over—and another, different one will come."

Gabriella's eyes glistened. "War and danger and secrets and spies. I never expected this from little Castelnau." She gave him a wry look. "I never expected cruel memories of my past either. But I will try to help. Tell me what to do, and I will try."

He stroked her fingers. "You are beautiful and brave, my Gabby. You will tell me the inner strength comes from your God. I am reading the Gospels as I promised you. I do not know if it is from God, or simply from an amazing woman's drive, but I know you will do it."

"And Mother Griolet? She will not grow suspicious if you go away again?"

David chuckled. "My dear, she is already suspicious. Very suspicious. She dislikes me. But Mr. Vidal will take my classes. She will not protest."

"When will you go?" Gabriella sounded desperate.

"Next week. Sometime after the 25th."

* * *

They drank their hot chocolate; then David scooted his chair back and stretched out his long legs under the round Formica table. He folded his arms across his chest and smiled as he stared at Gabriella.

"Have you ever been in love before, Gabby?" he asked suddenly.

Months ago she would not have dared to answer his question, afraid of a snide remark. She was sure that she was blushing again. She could feel the heat of embarrassment on her face. *What I really want to say, dear David, is that I'm in love with you.* But she could not.

The silence was broken by her one word reply. "Once."

310

David did not question her further, but in his eyes she read his hunger for a few details, and so she continued. "I was fifteen; he was seventeen. His name was Dimby. A brave, strong, kind man. We grew up side by side; we were like sister and brother. We didn't mean to fall in love. I learned African customs from his sisters. I spent many hours at his home. His family was the first in the whole region to accept our God.

"Dimby thought about deep things. We could talk and laugh and . . . and suddenly we were in love," she finished quietly, unable to explain the depth of emotion that had passed between them.

"You mean you were in love with an African? He was black?" David asked increduously.

"Correct on both counts." A slightly defensive edge crept into Gabriella's voice.

"And what did your parents say? Surely they forbade it! A white missionary kid from the States in love with a black man from a tribal village in Africa!" His voice was full of wonder.

"No, they did not forbid me to love him. My parents also liked Dimby very much. Perhaps they were strange. I don't think they saw black and white when they looked at people. They saw hearts and souls and hurts. They didn't discourage me, but they knew that our love would not work."

"What do you mean?"

"Dimby was promised to a young girl in a nearby village. The fathers had arranged it years ago. To break this tradition would create distrust and hatred toward us as missionaries."

"Surely Dimby realized this. Why did he pursue you? How? How did you do it?" His question was unfocused, but she understood his meaning.

"We cried and whispered our love. He brought me a

wreath of African lilies—a sign of commitment in his tribe. He held them out for me to smell, and the sweet scent curled up between us. Love! Then we burned the flowers and scattered the ashes, as is their custom when someone very cherished dies. We never touched, never kissed, never held each other in an embrace, but in our hearts we knew. We had loved. He left that night and soon after was married to his promised bride. I never saw him again. He lived in a hut a half mile from my home, but never again did our eyes meet. His tribe was known for its discipline. For honor and family respect, they would never go against family."

"But he loved you! And he was not really one of them anymore. You said he was a convert."

"There are things we cannot understand. We must accept. I did not think it was wrong that he leave. It had not been wrong to love him, but it was not wrong to lose him. This was life—their custom."

"And your mother. What did she say to you?"

"She said: 'I will lift up mine eyes unto the hills, from whence cometh my help. My help cometh from the Lord, which made heaven and earth. He will not suffer thy foot to be moved: He that keepeth thee will not slumber. Behold He that keepeth Israel shall neither slumber nor sleep.' And she hugged me. I cried for a long time. A long, long time, but still she held me. Finally Mother said, 'He does not make mistakes, Gabby. Someday you will see, our God does not make mistakes.' "

David reached over and tenderly took her hand. "I am sorry, truly."

She did not meet his searching, compassionate gaze. Instead she asked, "And you, David, have you ever been in love before?"

Still holding onto her hand, he replied, "I don't know. I don't know." His voice was soft but tormented.

"Is it so hard to know whether you are in love?"

His eyes caught hers in a moment of recognition. The eyes that were so often dark and brooding now carried a spark of something. What was it, Gabriella wondered. At once she knew. Like the faraway gleam of a lighthouse promising safety to the weary, wind-tossed vessel, his eyes carried the light of hope. Just a flicker, but nonetheless, hope.

In that moment, he took her other hand, squeezing them both softly in his and whispered, "Perhaps, my dear Gabby, it is not so hard at all to know when you are in love."

* * *

Ali Boudani did not notice the stench of rotting fruit that seeped in the window of his apartment as he read the paper on the morning of January twentieth. He was quite pleased with the headlines. In Paris on the eighteenth, the OAS had set off numerous explosions and killed none of their intended victims. In Algiers, however, two of the prime men with the OAS had been assassinated from within their own ranks. Surely the brutality of this desperate operation would benefit the FLN, as the French were divided amongst themselves. Surely de Gaulle would give in to the FLN's demands before long, and a free Algeria would come about.

He stood up from his delapidated desk and reread the names listed on the wall. Mme. Sentier and her children had perished soon after her husband's neck was slit. That was good. Another *harki* family dead. But two remained in Algiers. Mohemmed had more information about Mme. el Gharbi, whose husband had been murdered last week. The family was in hiding, but Mohemmed had news. They would be the next target, Ali decided. Tomorrow night, if possible. Then there would

313

be only Mme. Bousquet and her grandchildren.

Ali contemplated this possibility as he picked up a slide he had recently received from Jean-Claude. He held it to the light. "David Hoffmann, you are elusive. But it is good to know you are back in France. So it has been you all along. How foolish of us not to have guessed this sooner." Ali closed his eyes and saw the young man in his mind as a strapping teenager.

Anne-Marie was introducing David to Ali. "This is Ali Boudani. His father was in my father's division in the war. An excellent soldier." Anne-Marie turned her cherubic adolescent face toward Ali. "David's father is here in Algiers working in the American Embassy. I am showing his son around the city." Her melodious laughter rang out as she bade Ali farewell, holding onto David Hoffmann's hand. It had been a five-minute encounter, but now Ali recalled it vividly.

"Of course, you were here before the war broke out. In 1953 and '54. You stole Anne-Marie away. She has paid time and again for her foolishness. She will pay again. And so will you."

A young Arab boy entered Ali's room after knocking lightly on the door. "Hello, Hussein, my boy. Do you have news for me?" Ali asked.

"Yessir, Ali. Good news!" The boy grinned, his eyes shining with excitement.

"Let me hear it then," Ali growled.

"It is the woman. I have seen the woman you search for. She went into La Fillette apartments in Bab el Oued. She talked to an old woman. I was quiet, quiet as a mouse. She did not see me. She said the children must be at the docks at midnight on January twenty-fifth."

Ali patted the boy's thin shoulders. "You have done well, Hussein." He dropped a few shiny coins into the boy's dirty hands. "And did you see where this woman lives? Did you follow her to her house?"

The young boy's face fell. "No, Ali, I did not see. I tried to follow, but an Arab met her. He had a gun with him, and I was afraid. I followed as far as rue Tripoli. Then I lost them."

"It is good enough for now. Out with you, Hussein. Keep looking, my son. Keep looking."

The boy nodded and dashed out of the room. Ali sat back in his chair, lit a cigarette, and took a slow drag. "Midnight on the twenty-fifth at the docks. We will be waiting."

* * *

It was late afternoon on January twenty-second when Mother Griolet climbed the steps from the basement and opened the door to her apartment. She was glad for a moment of silence, for her mind was racing. There were more children arriving on the twenty-seventh. She unfolded the note that Jean-Louis had handed her ten days ago, checking to make sure of the date and time. Jean-Louis would meet the children as they arrived by boat in Marseilles. This time there would be five children. Mother Griolet sighed as she thought through the logistics of lodging five more children. There were exactly five free beds left in the dormitories, one in the girls' and four in the boys'.

A smile erased the worried expression on her face. Hadn't Jean-Louis said there would be one girl and four boys coming? "You always provide just what we need in the right time, Lord." She sank onto the brown couch in her small den and slowly bent to unlace her black leather shoes. She propped up her feet on the coffee table. Her ankles were swollen under her thick hose.

She could not forget the handsome young man at her door last week, asking for information about

Ophélie. Nor could she forget the letter from Ophélie's mother with her revelation about David Hoffmann.

Something else bothered her about Mr. Hoffmann. It was only a faint memory, but as she dwelled on it, she felt a sharp panic rising within her. Quickly she went to an old file cabinet in the back corner of the office and pulled out the bottom drawer. She leafed through the files and found several dated 1943. She pulled them out and cursorily perused the contents. Her eyes fell on one short paragraph. She read it over twice, then sighed heavily. Slowly she replaced each file.

"Whom can I talk to about these things, Lord? Whom shall I trust?" She thought of her old friend, Jean-Louis, with his bloodshot eyes and ruddy cheeks. Did he remember as well? But it was not Jean-Louis who needed to know.

Then she thought of Gabriella. "She is young and strong, Lord. But she is already dealing with a lot of pain from her past. And she loves David Hoffmann. In spite of herself, she loves him." She closed her eyes and did not move from the couch for half an hour. When she rose again to her feet, she felt confident. "I will talk to her, Lord. I will tell her the secrets she does not know about two people she loves very much."

* * *

Ophélie grabbed Gabriella's hand as they left the schoolroom following afternoon classes. "When can we go to ride the train, Bribri? When will we take the bus again to town?"

Gabriella hugged the child tightly, and kneeling down, looked her in the eyes. "We cannot leave the church for a while, Ophélie. We do not want to meet Mr. Jean-Claude again, you know."

Ophélie shook her head and frowned. "But I have

only ridden a train once. It was so much fun, when that nice man brought me here from another place."

"You mean when you came down to St. Joseph's?" Gabriella asked.

"Yes, I came with that nice *maître*. He never talks to me, but he is the one. I am sure. I have seen him at the school."

"You mean Mr. Hoffmann?" Gabriella asked, surprised. "Mr. Hoffmann brought you to St. Joseph's?"

Ophélie's face went pale. "I . . . I do not know his name." Her eyes were wide. "He is the tall man who likes you."

Gabriella laughed. "Yes, Mr. Hoffmann and I are friends."

Ophélie looked as if she might cry.

"What is it, sweetie?" Gabriella was still kneeling beside her. "Is something wrong?"

"No, nothing. I don't think." Ophelie furrowed her brow. "What did you say his name is?"

"His name? It is David Hoffmann."

The little girl let out a low cry and broke away from Gabriella's grasp. She ran through the courtyard toward the dormitory. Gabriella followed after, calling out to her. When they reached the dormitory, Ophélie turned on her heels and gazed up at Gabriella. Her brown eyes were filled with tears. "Please, Bribri. I want to be alone," she said softly.

"You are sure, Ophélie? I cannot help you? I am sorry if I upset you."

"It is okay," she replied and ran to her bunk. She waited until she saw Gabriella walk back across the courtyard, stopping to play with Christophe and Anne-Sophie. Then Ophélie opened her drawer and brought out the tights. She reached inside and found the blue bag and pulled it out. Carefully she unfolded her mother's pink pages on the bed. She stared down at the words on page three. "He is an American, very handsome and smart. His name is David Hoffmann." She was sure that those words meant David Hoffmann, the same man that Gabriella said was the tall teacher.

Ophélie began to tremble. Soon she was crying as she cuddled the letter to her heart like a soft teddy bear. "Oh, Mama. I do not understand. If that man is my father, why does he not talk to me? Why does he pretend I am an orphan? Why didn't he tell me who he was? Maybe he doesn't love me. Maybe he is very mad that I am his little girl." She cried into her pillow as the other children giggled and played outside. When the bell sounded for dinner, Ophélie stuffed the letter and the blue bag into the tights. Her stomach was in knots as she replaced them in her drawer. "Daddy?" she whispered. "Please come to me, Daddy. Please love me."

She remembered something Gabriella had taught her. Dropping to her knees, she folded her hands across her bed and closed her eyes. "Dear God. Bribri says that You love little children. That You listen when they talk to You. Please make my daddy like me." She could not think of what else to say. Then she added, "And please take care of Mama. And someday, God, can we all be together? As a family. Someday, please?"

She wiped her eyes with the sleeve of her navy sweater and left the dormitory, pulling her coat around her shoulders. It was dark outside as she walked the short distance to the dining hall. Ophélie was not sure if the butterflies dancing in her stomach were from excitement or from fear. But at least now when she thought of her father, she had a picture of him in her mind. It was the picture of a tall, kind man leaning down to cradle a screaming child by the bridge in a city that had erupted into madness.

Chapter Twenty-Five

Gabriella woke on the morning of January twenty-fifth with a dark feeling. She opened her Bible to the Book of Psalms, where she had been reading for the past month, and continued her devotions. A gnawing question was in her mind. Ophélie was upset about something that had to do with David. What was it? And David had left last night. She thought back to their last conversation in the *café*.

He says we are only friends, Lord. But he loves me. I know he does. I can read it in those dark eyes of his.

If only he would admit it. But he did not want to love her, of that she was sure. Gabriella closed her eyes and prayed the same prayer she had prayed for four months now. "Lord, I'm stuck here with a man I love. I can't deny my feelings. But I want to do what is right. Most of the time, anyway. So won't you please take away these awful yearnings for him? Please. Otherwise I will give in to a strange man who has covered up his heart."

She thought for a moment and added, "But would it be so bad, Lord, if he loved me and I loved him?

Wouldn't that be good? Make him Yours. Amen."

She left her room with a lighter heart and joined Stephanie, Caroline, and Mme. Leclerc in the kitchen for breakfast.

"Too bad Mr. Hoffmann will be gone for a while," Stephanie teased. "We'll all be snoozing away with Mr. Vidal twice a day!"

Gabriella laughed and nodded. Yes, it was too bad that David Hoffmann had left town for a while.

* * *

Following morning classes, Gabriella sat in Mother Griolet's office. The old nun bustled in and took her chair.

"Thank you, dear, for sparing me a few minutes of your time. How are you today? *Ça va?*"

"Oh, *oui. Ça va.* Everything is all right, I guess."

"You are not too overworked with the children? I am afraid I am asking a lot of you these days."

Gabriella shrugged her shoulders. "It is good for me, Mother Griolet. I like to think too much. To analyze and run ahead of the Lord and plan my own endings." She blushed. "So you see, it is good for you to keep me busy."

Mother Griolet folded her hands on the desk and regarded Gabriella kindly. "My dear one, I am afraid I have something else to talk to you about." She cleared her throat. "I know that you have a great affection for Ophélie..."

Gabriella nodded.

"...and for Mr. Hoffmann, also."

Gabriella shot her a surprised look. "Yes. I have told you about my feelings for him before."

"Yes, um, yes, you have." The old nun wiped her brow with her hand, then ran a finger around her mouth. "I don't really know how to begin."

320

She absentmindedly rummaged through a stack of papers on her desk. "Recently I came across some very puzzling and astounding information. I feel it is best to share this with you."

Gabriella scooted toward the edge of her chair, listening intently. Mother Griolet's usually serene face was outlined with worry. The wind outside knocked on the heavy wooden shutters, begging to come into the warm office. Again Mother Griolet cleared her throat.

"Perhaps if you would come with me, I could explain things better." The old nun got slowly to her feet, hesitating before she came around her desk and left the office. Gabriella followed obediently after her through the hall and den, out into the courtyard, across the sparse lawn, and into the girls' dormitory. The room seemed silent and somber without the chatter of little girls. Mother Griolet went to Ophélie's bed and opened the chest of drawers.

"We found this quite by accident when Sister Rosaline was preparing for the last orphans' arrival." She produced a pair of tights and slipped her wrinkled hand down one leg. "I don't suppose you have ever seen this before?" She held up the blue velvet bag.

Gabriella shook her head, wondering.

"There were several surprising items in this bag. But I think this letter from Ophélie's mother will interest you most." She handed Gabriella three thin sheets of pink paper. Gabriella met her eyes with a questioning look.

"I . . . I have the feeling that I am about to find out some more bad news, Mother Griolet."

"It is not bad news, my dear. But quite unexpected. And important for you to know."

Gabriella sat down on Ophélie's bed, bending her head so as not to bump it on the top bunk. Mother

Griolet stood beside her. Silently Gabriella perused the letter, her eyes brimming with tears as she read about a mother's love for her child.

"This is why Ophélie wanted to learn to read so desperately. Look . . . here are the words she could not understand. She asked me about them." She glanced up at Mother Griolet.

"Yes, Gabriella. Read on."

There was not a sound in the room except the gentle rustling of paper as Gabriella turned from the second to the third pink page of paper. Suddenly she let out a sharp cry. "No! No! It can't be!" She dropped the pages and stood up too quickly, bumping her head on the bunk.

"Ouch!" she moaned and fell back across the bed, sobbing.

"Gabriella," Mother Griolet touched her shoulder, but Gabriella pushed her hand away.

"It is nothing. I am all right." She turned her distraught face to the nun. "At least, my head is all right. But my heart . . . It can't be! How could David be Ophélie's father? He has no idea."

Suddenly she remembered Ophélie's reaction when she had mentioned David's name. So this was why.

"Poor little Ophélie. She has no one she trusts. She has been betrayed too often." Gabriella picked up the last page of the letter and stared at it again. "Thank you for showing this to me, Mother Griolet. It was the right thing to do, I assure you."

"I am afraid it may be hard on you, dear."

Gabriella smiled. "I am finding that there are many hard things in life. I have a lot to learn." She forced a smile on her face. "Give me a few days to digest this, and I'll be fine."

Mother Griolet reached up and placed her worn hands on the freckled face of Gabriella, then kissed her softly on each cheek. *"Que Dieu soit avec toi, ma chère. God be with you."* She patted her lightly on the back. "Go on with you now. I'll put this back. Go on home and have some lunch."

"Yes. That is a good idea, Mother Griolet. *À bientôt."*

* * *

It took every ounce of strength Gabriella could muster to walk through town with her head held high. Inside she felt sick and betrayed. She argued with herself all the way to Mme. Leclerc's apartment. *What is David up to? What cruel game is he playing?* Mostly, she felt a burning jealousy of Anne-Marie Duchemin. Years ago he had loved her, and they had conceived Ophélie. But perhaps he truly did not know he had a daughter.

"But you came to France for her mother," Gabriella whispered as she climbed the steps, not bothering to press the orange button in the stairwell. "You are here because you love Anne-Marie. You want to help her."

Again the sick, angry emotions choked her. Gabriella went into her room, setting down her backpack on the floor with a thud. She leaned back across her bed and stared at the ceiling, noticing the uneven plaster. Water stains from an old leak showed through the paint. In the corner a spider web hung, abandoned, covered with dust.

She reached in her mind for the sticky web. It was tangled, tangled. Everything was running together in her head, like a mass of dusty webs.

I hate you, David. I hate this mess you have pulled me into. I hate caring about you. Oh, God, if only I could rip out this heart and replace it. Then I could smile for a family reunited.

She closed her eyes and imagined David embracing Ophélie, and a beautiful young woman running to hold them both. David turned and let his head fall back in ecstasy. He kissed her as they laughed and wept while Ophélie shouted, "Mama!"

"Oh God, this is how the story should end. It is only right." She clenched her fists. "But I will just be honest with You, because there is no one else I can tell. I hate it. It isn't fair. It seems as if you dropped these people into my life for me to love, for me to bring together. And now You will rip them away. They are not mine. I know it! I hate myself for caring so much. But I *do* care. I need them!" She hit her fist on the bed.

"And You, God! You are asking too much this time. It isn't fair." Suddenly another thought came to her. *Perhaps she's dead. No one knows if Anne-Marie is really alive or not.* Gabriella felt a twinge of twisted hope, immediately followed by guilt. *How can I think that? How can I wish Ophélie's mother dead? Oh, Gabriella, you are really mixed up.*

Without knocking, Stephanie came into the room and sat down beside her. "Gosh, Gab, you look awful. What's up?"

Gabriella sat up quickly and turned a remorseful face toward Stephanie. *I wish I could be like Stephanie,* Gabriella thought, without speaking. *She just is. She doesn't think past the fun of the moment. She doesn't complicate life. But she seems happy enough.* "Sometimes life is a mess," Gabriella said sullenly.

"Oh, come on, Gab. You've got a professor who is wild about you, you're traveling all over France, you're smart as a whip, and you're pretty. Why would you say life is a mess?" She laughed her hearty, husky laugh as they headed to the dining room for lunch.

Gabriella shook her head and marveled. She even let out a silly, childish laugh in spite of herself. "You're right, Steph, I'm sure. I'm sure you're right."

* * *

Jean-Claude Gachon opened the white envelope with an Algiers postmark. He laughed as he read Ali's brief note.

"Last known children to be eliminated here on 25th. Find the list. What is taking you so long? Find the woman and child. Better yet, find David Hoffmann. He will know."

Jean-Claude glanced at the calendar on the wall of his kitchen. Today was the day. January 25th. "I salute you, Ali Boudani!" he guffawed, suddenly rising to his feet and standing at attention like a regimented soldier. "I salute you, sir, for your good deeds of slaughter. Yessir!" He stamped his foot loudly on the floor. Then he cleared his throat, still feigning allegiance to his unseen boss.

"About the woman and child. I am sorry to say that they are not being lodged at the forty-two different churches of Montpellier and surrounding areas. But I have a good lead." At this, he lost his serious composure and broke again into hysterical laughter. Eyes brimming with tears, he danced around his kitchen in sock feet. "Imagine this, Ali. They are hiding out at an orphanage for cuckoos. A nuthouse! I will go back soon. A nut goes into a nuthouse, and what does he find? Nuts, of course." He threw back his head and guffawed, delighted with his joke.

* * *

Anne-Marie watched the orange ball of fire slowly descend across the horizon. The clock on the wall in Marcus Cirou's kitchen showed 5:30 in the afternoon. In five hours she would leave for the docks, waiting for the children to join her in the tiny alleyway at the edge of Bab el Oued. She bit her lip anxiously, wringing her hands. Moustafa would be coming soon.

She was not sure what to tell him. She did not know

how to break the news that she was leaving with the children. She had wrestled with the idea all through the night. It had to be so. There on the other side of the Mediterranean she would find Ophélie.

She knew Moustafa would not protest. He would nod and agree. But leaving Algeria now meant that she would not come back. She felt sick to her stomach to think of Moustafa left behind, alone without her. The thought tormented her. But the longing to see Ophélie, to hold her, to know she was safe . . . the mother love was stronger. Anne-Marie could not imagine life without Moustafa near her, but Ophélie deserved her mother. Right now, she could not have both of them. She wondered if it would ever be possible.

She thought of another she might meet in France. Somewhere, she was sure, there was a brilliant young American who had loved an adolescent *pied-noir*. She shivered to think of meeting David again. The man who had given up a career in the States to help her launch a desperate mission. What would she see in his eyes?

The kitchen door opened, and Moustafa walked in. He was thin and haggard, his curly black hair tousled by the wind. "It seems everything is working as planned," he said, grinning wearily at Anne-Marie. "This is good."

"Moustafa," Anne-Marie said. She came to his side and put her arms around his neck. "Moustafa, I must tell you something."

His brow wrinkled as he held her close. "What is it, *ma chère?*"

She saw in his eyes that he knew, even before she spoke the words. "I must go with them tonight. I must see Ophélie. I must be sure. I am sorry. I do not want to abandon you." She held his unshaven face in her hands, tracing his three-day-old beard with her fingers. "You could come too, Moustafa. We could make a life there. We will have rescued all of the families that Ali knows about. We have done our best. Please."

"Do not beg me, Anne-Marie. I have already deserted my people once."

"But you are not deserting. You are helping. You have saved lives. I am sure there will be work to do in France. David will know—" As she pronounced David's name, she stopped short. Moustafa released her. "I am sorry. But you know, Moustafa, that he is somewhere helping."

"Of course, I know. We set it up this way two years ago. It is only that I am afraid of losing you. Losing you to the father of your child."

"Then come, Moustafa! Stay with me tonight. David Hoffmann is not the man I love. It is you. Please come with me tonight."

He held her again and kissed her softly. He ran his fingers through her thick hair and sighed. "You must go tonight, Anne-Marie. You are right to go."

* * *

A light-skinned young Arab man slipped out of the Casbah at 9 P.M. He was well built, muscular, with close-cropped black hair. In his right arm he carried a machine gun.

Ali's instructions had been explicit. Midnight on the docks. Children boarding a boat. Get there at least two hours in advance and watch. There are many docks, so watch well. Watch and wait. And kill. Ali wanted nothing left. Nothing but bloodstains for the mourners, if they dared turn out to mourn in this city of creeping death.

No one roamed the streets of Algiers at this hour. No one except men on a mission, like himself. He was not afraid. He had killed before. The FLN called him their little terrorist. He was good. With bombs, *plastiquages,* and especially a machine gun.

By the time he reached the port, the moon was high. The sound of the sea lapping against the body of the boats lulled his racing heart. The smell of fish hung pungent in the air. Nothing moved. The young Arab crouched beside a long sailboat and waited.

* * *

Five children clung to their mothers in a narrow alley of Bab el Oued, huddling behind heaping barrels of trash. It had started to drizzle. One woman, an Arab, wore a white lace scarf over her head. The other, a *pied-noir*, drew a dingy raincoat over her graying hair. The children watched wide-eyed in the dark.

Anne-Marie whispered, "It is time." Silently, the buxom Arab mother pulled three small boys to her breast and wept. The *pied-noir* woman crossed herself and kissed a young girl on the forehead, then embraced the smaller brother. Anne-Marie took the women's hands and squeezed them. She read the fear in their eyes.

For a moment, she thought it was unfair that she should leave with these women's children. She remembered her last sight of Ophélie, running through the streets of Paris. She prayed a silent prayer to an unknown god and left the two women, weeping and clinging to each other.

* * *

Moustafa crept out of Marcus Cirou's apartment at 11 P.M. He had to have one last glimpse of Anne-Marie. Her kisses were still fresh on his lips; he could still smell the fragrance of her hair and soft olive skin. She had cried for two hours before leaving to meet the children. He would not let her see him again, but he must have one last look. He must know that she was safe with the children.

He made his way through the empty streets of Bab el Oued until he came out onto the wide boulevard in front of the sea. All was black. He hid himself behind several fishing tugs and waited.

* * *

There was a light breeze in the frigid air as the children crawled along the dock on their bellies. The boards creaked under the movement of the tide. Anne-Marie's heart raced. She crouched in the shadow of a yacht, watching the five children slithering ahead of her like a procession of snakes. One by one, they reached the small sailboats that floated unobtrusively between several larger vessels. One by one they crawled toward the outstretched shadow of a man aboard the *Capitaine*. As Anne-Marie observed their progress, she glanced behind her to make sure no one else was there. It had become a habit. But no one had followed them.

Suddenly, from behind a tug, a man sprang out onto the dock across from her, pointing a heavy machine gun in the direction of the crawling children. Anne-Marie jumped to her feet and screamed, throwing her weight into the man and knocking him off balance. With a curse, the young man swung the gun at her head. It crashed on her skull as he heaved her into the waters. She hit the ice-cold water, still conscious, falling down, deeper down. She heard the ricochet of bullets popping through the water as she scrambled helplessly to pull herself up for air. Her legs stung with pain. All was dark.

She bumped her head against the hull of a ship and swam panicked to the side, desperate for air. Her legs felt like dead weight, dragging her down. She fought to maintain consciousness, grabbing frantically for something, anything. A ladder! Under the dock she pulled herself up the rungs of a mussel-covered ladder until her head was above water. She tried to control her gasping lungs as she intertwined her arms between two rungs of the ladder, wedging herself against it. Somewhere in the water below her legs dangled with no feeling at all, and then she fainted.

* * *

It had happened so fast that Moustafa had not had time to think. *React! His* senses told him as Anne-Marie fell into the water. The shadowman turned his gun to the waters and sprayed the surface with bullets. He rose to aim again at the children, and Moustafa drew the gun he always carried inside his belt. Rachid's gun. He fired once, then twice as the man cried out and turned. Another shot rang out. The machine gun spat a round of bullets into the air, and the man fell with a crash and lay silent.

In the distance, Moustafa watched panicked children diving into the boat as it cast off from shore without a sound. He threw himself into the water where Anne-Marie had fallen. "Anne-Marie. Anne-Marie," he cried in a hoarse whisper. "It is me! It is Moustafa." A thick dread stabbed at his heart in the icy black waters. He swam around boats, underneath them, and back to the docks. When he resurfaced, panting, he listened. A dripping somewhere. He swam towards the faint noise. Anne-Marie's arms were pinned through the bars of a ladder. She hung there in shock.

Carefully he pulled her to him. Her body had gone limp. With Anne-Marie in front of him, he lifted her rung by rung up the ladder. Two feet, four feet, six ... until her upper torso collapsed on the dock. Moustafa shimmied up beside her. He pulled off his sopping coat and wrapped it around her still body. Then, he left her side and ran to where the young Arab man lay lifeless on the dock. Quickly Moustafa dragged the body to the edge of the dock and shoved it into the water. Picking Anne-Marie up, he carried her across the dock, stopping only to retrieve the machine gun that lay beside a puddle of wet blood.

Moustafa ran through the death-ridden streets of Algiers. His thick wet hair spilled drops of the sea onto his face, and they mingled with his tears. "I am here, Anne-Marie. *Ma chère*. Hold on. Hold on."

* * *

Jean-Louis Vidal gulped down a last *pastis* as he waited for a sailboat to dock in the port of Marseilles. A fog horn sounded, and a little drizzle fell outside. The *café-bar* was crowded and smoky. Jean-Louis glanced at his watch. It was 7 A.M. on January 27th. If the boat had set sail from Algiers at midnight on the 25th, it should be here by now, he reasoned. The sky was dark with clouds. He pulled his *casquette* over his head and left the bar, an umbrella in his hand.

"It is likely that you will not be alone," David Hoffmann had warned him last week. Now Jean-Louis watched out of the corner of his eye for a handsome brown-haired Frenchman, tall and muscular. The docks were quiet. Row after row of boats floated peacefully in their place in the morning mist. The *Capitaine*, David had said. Black with white trim. Every boat looked black in the pre-dawn light. For thirty minutes, the round-bellied history professor walked the docks nonchalantly. In the distance a boat crept silently into harbor. Jean-Louis watched its approach thirty-five feet away. Squinting, he could make out the name *Capitaine* on the side.

* * *

Anne-Marie breathed shallowly in Marcus Cirou's bedroom. Her legs were wrapped in thick gauze, and a large bandage covered her skull. Her eyes were closed. Moustafa held her hand as he sat beside the bed, stroking her fingers.

Every few minutes her eyelids would flutter and almost open. She moaned softly. "Ophélie." She opened her eyes and stared at Moustafa. Sad, brown eyes. He touched her face.

"He came ... from ... nowhere," Anne-Marie whispered feebly.

"Shh, my dear. Save your strength. You are safe now."

She closed her eyes but continued talking, "I am sorry, Moustafa. I do not know ... I do not know about ... the chil ..." she began to cry.

"Do not worry about the children, Anne-Marie. They got away. None of them were hurt. It is okay."

"Okay, yes." She smiled weakly, squeezed his hand, and fell back asleep.

Moustafa bent over her and kissed her forehead. "I am so sorry that you are still here. But I will care for you, my beautiful one. We will survive."

Chapter Twenty-Six

Mother Griolet leaned on her desk as she looked out at the thirty-four children seated before her in the basement classroom. Their eyes were riveted on her in anticipation. Soft brown eyes in pale white faces. Black eyes surrounded by dark olive skin. French eyes, *pied-noir* eyes, Arab eyes.

"*Bonjour, mes enfants*," she began. "Today we are happy to welcome the five new children to class who arrived at St. Joseph's on Saturday. Most of you have already met them, but I would like to introduce them to you again."

She came around the desk and walked to the first row of children. Smiling down at a little girl, she said, "This is Rachel and her little brother, Guy. Welcome to St. Joseph's." The children stared up at her with fearful eyes.

Mother Griolet felt a pang of pity for them. She tried to imagine the scene that Jean-Louis had described to her, the details he had himself just heard from the captain of the boat. The children had barely escaped death as a man had opened fire on them while they were boarding. The young woman who was accompanying the children had been thrown into the sea by the assailant, and then, miraculously, another man had shot down the first man as the children scrambled onto the boat.

The terror was still in the children's eyes when they arrived at St. Joseph's, so Mother Griolet had ordered three days of rest and games and good food. No classes for the new children until Thursday.

"I want you to meet the three brothers who have come to us, Yacin, Hamid, and Amar," she continued. "We are very happy to have you here with us." The other children clapped their hands loudly, enthusiastically, giggling together.

"*Les enfants!*" Mother Griolet reproached them. "*Un peu de calme. S'il vous plait!* Please calm down.

"I need to remind you of something. There are times to have fun and times to be serious. I have told you this before. And you remember our little play of last week. One day you will perform it for real. You must be ready. Remember? We thank God for our healthy bodies. What would we be like if it were not so?"

Immediately, twenty-nine children went limp on their desks, while the new children stared at them wide-eyed. Christophe and André slapped spastically at each other. Anne-Sophie stood up with her eyes closed and felt about her desk, bumping into another chair. Hakim moaned softly in the corner, crouching on the floor. Lorène and Marine rolled their eyes and let their tongues hang out of their mouths. Ophélie ran to the back of the room and hid in a broom closet.

"Children, please behave," Mother Griolet said sternly. They acted as if they did not hear her. "Children!" she raised her voice, but still the children ignored her. Then quietly she whispered, "Thank God for our healthy bodies." Immediately the children returned to their desks, sat straight and attentive and were silent.

"Very good, children. Excellent. Now please get out your math books." As they took out their workbooks, Mother Griolet muttered under her breath, "I think we are ready now, Lord."

* * *

The open market bustled with people in the old part of Aix-en-Provence. Mme. de Saléon busied herself squeezing avocados, picking through endives, apples, and heads of lettuce.

"*Coucou!* David," she called, waving a thick bunch of radishes his way.

David Hoffman looked up from where he had been examining green and black olives, and approached his friend.

"What do you think? These will be heavenly for lunch, *n'est-ce pas?*"

"Of course, Madeleine, they will be delicious with some soft butter. And a good glass of *rouge*." He winked at her. "Will you excuse me for a moment? I am going to fetch the bread. I'll meet you at the apartment."

"*Impeccable, mon ami,*" Mme. de Saléon agreed.

David wound his way through the twisting, narrow, cobblestoned streets of Aix. He came to the small street directly behind the Cours Mirabeau. Quickly he found the *boulangerie* and let himself in the door. There was a line of customers in front of him. The *boulanger* saw him enter and lifted his eyebrows, still talking merrily with a pretty young woman who was paying for her purchase.

When the store was empty of other customers, the baker smiled at David. "*Alors, mon pote,* what's up with you?"

"A *baguette* and a *gros pain* will do me fine today,

Gilbert. I suppose that is no trouble?"

"No trouble at all," replied the short, stocky baker. The store remained deserted except for the two men.

"And your friend, the redhead?" Gilbert asked quietly.

David shook his head. "My friend, the redhead, poor woman. She has her hands full."

"Nice woman," Gilbert commented, raising his eyebrows and winking. "You should keep her out of trouble, *mon pote*. Take care of your women. I have a nice little place in the mountains with a fireplace and a double bed. You work too much, Mr. David."

David laughed heartily as a stooped woman with a straw basket teeming with fruits and vegetables puffed her way into the *boulangerie*.

"Thanks for the advice, Gilbert. I might take you up on it someday." David picked up the two loaves of bread and his change and left the *boulangerie*.

* * *

Mme. de Saléon brought a plateful of radishes to her elegantly set table and sat down across from David. "So tell me, my friend. How are you? The last time we talked, you had just sent your girlfriend off unexpectedly to Montpellier." She looked at David with tender gray eyes.

David shifted his weight in his chair and began buttering a radish. "I am doing pretty well, Madeleine. But there are some problems back in Montpellier. How much longer do you give the war? Another month? Six?"

Mme. de Saléon's eyes sparkled. "We never tried to guess in the other war, David. We just kept doing what there was to do each day."

"I know. Each little man has his part to play. Keep quiet, and the others will be safe. I know."

"David, do you have the 'information' you need?"

"We had brought all that we could . . . until now. Now I have some more work ahead. A lot more."

"When will you go back to Montpellier, then?"

"Two days, maybe three. I still have a visit to make in Aigues-Mortes."

"And your girl, Gabriella, she enjoys this line of work too?"

David chuckled. "If you asked her, she would say she has no choice. She's got the guts and brains for it, but she's so blasted religious. She looks at life in a strange way, Madeleine."

"Religious!" Madeleine clapped her hands together enthusiastically. "Why, that is just fine. Religion has its place, you know. Look at your orphanage in Castelnau. If it weren't for religion, where would you keep your 'information'?" She prodded him playfully.

"True, but Gabriella is more than devout. She really believes that a God up there is directing her life. It makes her untouchable!" He wiped his mouth and laid down his napkin on the table.

"Untouchable, and so all the more desirable. Is that your problem?"

David's eyes flashed. "Who knows, Madeleine. Maybe. Or maybe it's because I know it just can't work. You remember, I've seen firsthand what happened to a woman who loved God and fell in love with a man who did not."

Mme. de Saléon's face clouded. "David, you exaggerate."

He raised his voice. "No, Madeleine! I do not. Mother's love for Father was passionate and pure. And he abandoned her. He abandoned us."

"David! It isn't true. Why must you insist on this? Do you forget that I was there? I would not be sitting here now if your mother had not stayed in Paris. Yes, there was a risk involved, but your mother and father were in agreement. And she had an American passport. He had no idea it would turn out as it did." She paused, a mist in her eyes. "He had no idea that she, that you all, would be taken."

David said nothing, his dark eyes brooding. He picked up the last radish, buttered it, and bit into the raw vegetable. "Anyway, it is of no use. Gabriella loves another. I've never been very lucky at fighting with the gods." He smiled wryly.

Madeleine shrugged, stood up, and hurried off to the kitchen for the main course.

* * *

Jean-Claude Gachon stepped off the train in the Montpellier train station with a wide grin on his face. He carried a small sports bag over his shoulder and marched quickly across the street to the long line of waiting buses. Bus 11 sat behind two others. Jean-Claude hopped on and paid his fare.

He could barely control himself as he took a seat near the back of the bus and removed a newspaper from his bag. Every once in a while, the stillness on the bus was punctuated by his sharp laugh.

He leafed through the paper, dated February 5, 1962, reading of the fourteen *barbouzes* who had been killed the week before in Algiers when their hideout exploded. The French secret army had taken a beating that night, he chuckled.

The bus pulled away from the curb and headed toward east Montpellier. Jean-Claude reached his hand into the sports bag and patted a small, cold revolver. He was sure to have his information today. "Be patient, Ali, sir. *Un peu de patience,* and you will have everything you need." He snickered to himself and pretended to be oblivious to the stares he received from several passengers.

* * *

Gabriella let out a loud sigh as Mr. Vidal concluded his lecture on Gustave Flaubert. Stephanie had been right. Two classes a day with the alcoholic history prof was unbearable. Gabriella wished David would come back. She wanted to rush into his arms and cry and tell him that she loved him. But she did not let herself dwell on that image.

She knew what she would have to do when David returned. She had rehearsed her lines for the past ten days. She would act casual and a little removed. Then she would say, "I need to tell you something. Ophélie Duchemin is your child. You know, the little orphan you brought here on the train. Your daughter!" While he looked on amazed, she would produce Ophélie's letter from her mother.

Gabriella had reached the basement, lost in her thoughts. She did not feel a desire to be with the orphans right now, but Mother Griolet was counting on her more and more. The new children were terrified of everything. Mother Griolet looked tired and almost feeble lately. And to make matters worse, several children had broken out with the chicken pox.

Gabriella wanted to help. But every time she saw Ophélie, she felt a prick of pain in her heart. *I need to tell you, too, dear little friend. I need you to know that I know.* But Gabriella had not felt strong enough to be able to hug Ophélie and act thrilled with the news that David Hoffmann was her father.

She walked into the classroom, poised and seemingly carefree. Mother Griolet was just finishing up the reading lesson. From above, the doorbell sounded loudly. The nun gave Gabriella a grateful nod. Gabriella whispered to her, "You get the door and then rest a bit. I'll watch them until lunch. Go on." Mother Griolet bustled into the hall, patting Gabriella on the shoulder as she left the room.

"Hey, kids!" Gabriella shouted, for they had erupted into chatter. "Listen please! You've got a few minutes till recess. I'd like a drawing of the sea and every kind of thing you can think of that you find in the sea." Several children grimaced in protest. Jérémy shook his head vehemently. His face was still covered with scabs from his recent bout with chicken pox, and Anne-Sophie and André looked much the same.

"Go on, kids," Gabriella added crossly. "Get to work."

She stepped out into the hall and listened. Gabriella could hear Mother Griolet talking excitedly, her voice agitated. "Yes, I understand, Mr. Philippe. You are desperate for the child, but as I told you before, she is not here. I am afraid I can do nothing for you."

Gabriella could make out Jean-Claude's voice laughing, threatening.

"Yes, of course you may look around." Mother Griolet was talking quickly, loudly. "Of course. Follow me."

Immediately Gabriella raced back into the classroom. Trying to sound composed, she whispered, "Kids! It's time for the play to begin. Wad up your papers! Quick. Thank God for our healthy bodies. What would it be like if it were not so?"

The children, delighted, began wading up their papers, tossing them in the air, grunting and spitting as they played. Gabriella grabbed Ophélie's hand and motioned to the Arab children to follow her down the hall to the large storage closet at the end of the hall. She rattled the key and unlocked the door, pulling

Ophélie and the other children in after her. With the same key, she locked the door from the inside.

Ophélie stood silent beside her. "It's going to be fine, children," Gabriella whispered. "We mustn't make a sound."

She led them to the back of the closet. They squatted behind boxes of cleaning supplies and old brooms. In the darkness, Gabriella listened for Mother Griolet's voice. But all she heard was a low moan coming from Ophélie. "Mama. I want my mama." Gabriella put her arms around the child, and they waited.

* * *

Mother Griolet's hands were trembling as she opened the door to the basement classroom. She sent up a silent prayer of thanksgiving at the sight before her. Some of the children were babbling, some throwing wads of paper at each other, while a few crouched in the corner, drooling. Mr. Philippe stood beside her, observing the scene.

"Children! Children! Be quiet. We have a guest." This only caused the children to increase their wild behavior. Mother Griolet, looking harried, turned to Mr. Philippe. "I am sorry, it is hard to control them."

"I can control them if I have to," he menaced, striding into the classroom.

Mother Griolet cleared her throat. "Mr. Philippe, excuse me, but I must warn you that several of the children have chicken pox. It is quite contagious. I'm sure you've had it?"

He wheeled around angrily. "Never mind. I'm not afraid." He glared at the children with scabby faces.

"No, of course not. It is only, as I am sure you realize, that it is quite dangerous for adult males to catch the disease." She lowered her eyes. "You know what I mean?"

"What?" He cursed impatiently. Then understanding

341

flashed across his face. "Go on then," he snarled. "Show me around this place."

"As you wish," she replied calmly. "You will excuse me. I must call one of the Sisters to stay with the children. Here, step out into the courtyard with me." She rushed him past the storage closet and into the frosty February air.

"*Cuckoo!* Sister Rosaline! Sister Isabelle!" After a brief wait, Sister Rosaline appeared, her cheeks flushed.

"Yes, Mother Griolet?" she questioned, eying the athletic man with suspicion.

"Sister Rosaline, could you please watch the children for me? This nice young man would like to have a look around the facilities. I'm afraid the children are a bit wild today." She emphasized the word wild, and Sister Rosaline nodded and let herself in the basement door.

"Now if you'll follow me, I'll show you the dormitories."

He caught Mother Griolet roughly by the shoulders. "I'll look around myself," he spat. "I want to check things out real well."

Mother Griolet followed him into the dormitories, saying calmly, "As you wish, *Monsieur*. But I assure you, we do not have your niece here with us." She sat down on a bunk bed in the boys' dormitory and watched the frenzied man at work, looking under beds, in closets, rest rooms. All the time, Mother Griolet kept repeating silently to herself, *I will lift up mine eyes unto the hills, from whence cometh my help. My help cometh from the Lord, which made heaven and earth. The Lord is thy keeper. The Lord shall preserve thee from all evil....* The strong, *beau* Frenchman never stopped his search long enough to see how violently Mother Griolet's hands were shaking in her lap.

* * *

Jean-Claude Gachon searched through every room of the church and orphanage of St. Joseph's. An hour passed, and still the children played loudly in the courtyard and threw food in the dining hall as Jean-Claude looked on in disgust. "Nuts. Real nuts," he muttered angrily. But no little Ophélie Duchemin, and no redhead named Gabriella.

He felt a slow rage building inside as the wind whipped and banged the shutters of the school building. He walked into the basement from the garden with the nun following behind. Jean-Claude turned to his left and pointed to another door. "What is in here?"

"Supplies," the nun answered. "Have a look if you wish." He tried the door, but it was locked.

"Oh, I'm sorry. I keep it locked because of the children. You never know what the little savages might get into. Just hold on a minute, and I'll fetch the key."

"Forget it," he said impatiently. Jean-Claude was angry that he could not frighten the old woman. *She must be nutty too*, he deduced as she answered each of his questions with quiet composure. But she was getting tired, he could tell. If he could simply keep her talking for a while longer, perhaps she would reveal something.

"I am sorry to have disturbed you, Sister. You have been most kind to show me around. I am afraid I will have to keep looking. Please give my best to Mr. Hoffmann when you see him." He let the phrase dangle before her like bait for a fish.

The nun looked at him, perplexed. "Excuse me, but I don't know a Mr. Hoffmann. Are you quite sure you are all right, Mr. Philippe?"

"Yes, I'm just fine. I'll be going now."

"As you wish, sir." They walked up the stairs to the ground level together, and the nun opened the door for Jean-Claude. Once again he looked around furtively.

"Au revoir," he mumbled over his shoulder. He walked briskly to the center of town, cursing to himself. "A house of nuts. A real house of nuts."

* * *

"Dear God," Mother Griolet cried, collapsing against the heavy wooden door. "He is gone. Thank You, dear God. Forgive me, Lord, if You disapprove of our little scheme. Somehow it seems that You do not." Slowly she descended the stairs into the basement and hobbled along the hall to the end. She knocked softly on the door to the storage closet.

"Gabriella? Gabriella? You can come out. God has given us healthy bodies."

A shuffling noise came from inside the closet as some-one fumbled with a key. Then the door swung open, and seven children escaped into the hall. Gabriella exited last, looking exhausted. She fell into Mother Griolet's arms, and they embraced each other tightly.

"I was sure he would come in," Gabriella confessed.

"It was the Lord who put the idea in my head: act as if you would be happy to show him the closet. I am glad that man could not see that everything inside of me was shaking. I don't know how he didn't see," the nun said increduously.

"Oh yes, you do," said Gabriella, with a tired smile on her face. She glanced upward.

"You are right. Our God can blind the eyes of the enemy."

The children still huddled around the two women, not moving. "Come children," Gabriella cried. "The game's over. Let's go get some lunch. I'm starving." The Arab children eagerly ran after her to the dining hall. Ophélie stayed near Mother Griolet.

"What is it, Ophélie? You are afraid, is that it?"

Ophélie nodded.

Mother Griolet hugged her to her breast. "There is nothing to be afraid of anymore. Everything is all right. You will see."

"I want my mama," the child replied. "I am asking Jesus to please give me back my mama ... and my daddy, soon." She stared at Mother Griolet with hopeful eyes.

The old nun patted the child's head. "This is a good prayer, little Ophélie. This is good."

* * *

David Hoffmann left the town of Aigues-Mortes on the 7th of February, following the beach road in the direction of Montpellier. Within an hour, he would be back at St. Joseph's. He was glad to be heading there after two weeks of traveling. He watched the wind play through the marshes, dividing them like a comb parting hair.

Gabriella. He was anxious to see her again. Suddenly, he turned his car off on a dirt road leading toward the sea. He parked it in the dry shrubs and got out.

He walked in the direction of the beach, kicking the sand with his black loafers. He pulled his leather jacket together and buttoned it. Two weeks of working out details for the operation made his head feel clogged and thick. He had visited contacts in Marsailles, in Aix, in Aigues-Mortes. He had written letters to Algeria. Now he waited for a response. The waiting was long.

David inhaled the sea air and stretched out his long arms, swinging them in large circles to the side of his body. A few lonely gulls cawed out to him, reprimanding the tall stranger who interrupted their peaceful habitation. He paid no attention.

He walked out to the sea and took off his shoes and socks, leaving them in the sand. He rolled his pants above his shins and splashed his feet in the freezing water.

"Feel it, David! Feel something," he said softly to himself. Then again, this time yelling, "Feel something!"

He welcomed the frothy sea rushing over his feet. It stung him at first, but after a few minutes, his feet grew numb. He left the water and lay down on the beach, letting the fine, dusty sand sweep over him. Lying on his back, he raised his arms to the sky. He began to laugh, a slow, mocking laugh.

"Gabriella claims that you are up there, God. Prove it then! Just prove it! Open up your heavens and drench me with rain. Still I won't believe. Life is not ordered by a god. It is coincidence and fate. I have read some of your book, as I promised Gabriella. Your Gospels that promise life and peace and forgiveness." He rolled over onto his stomach and began writing with his finger in the sand.

"You don't seem to understand," David argued out loud to the deserted beach. "I am not going to forgive." He spat out the word like a rotten piece of fruit. "Dear Gabby, I will never forgive them. And so, I suppose, I shall never be forgiven."

A verse from a poem by Donne flashed across his mind.

Wilt Thou forgive that sin where I begun
which is my sin, though it were done before?
Wilt Thou forgive that sin through which I run,
And do run still, though still I do deplore?

He had questioned, David reasoned. And had found something. But what?

"There was someone once, Gabby." He closed his eyes and imagined Anne-Marie coming toward him, laughing, an adolescent shimmering with beauty. "There was someone I cared for once." He spoke now to his memory of Anne-Marie. "You needed me then, all those years ago. You saw the war coming, as your

346

father predicted. But you would not leave with me! And so I sent you a hundred unanswered letters from America. And then, out of the blue, you needed me again. You knew I would come to help."

Absently he drew in the sand again. "You would be surprised to know that I am afraid. Afraid for you. Afraid for the children. And others." He thought of Mother Griolet, her green eyes twinkling as she spoke to the American girls. Then he thought of Gabriella. It hurt to think of her.

David pulled out a folded piece of paper from his leather jacket. He studied the list of names scribbled there with addresses. "Anne-Marie, now you have heard from me. Answer me back! Someone please answer."

He rose to his knees and brushed the sand from his coat and hair. Standing, he looked down at what he had drawn. A cloud passed overhead, obscuring the image momentarily. Then the bright sun broke through and illuminated a crude sketch of the Huguenot cross.

"Someone please answer," David repeated and walked back toward his car.

Chapter Twenty-Seven

It was Saturday, the tenth of February, when David asked Gabriella to join him for a drink. She knew she wanted to be with him, and yet she felt scared. There was so much she needed to tell him.

They entered the crowded *café* in the beach town of Palavas, unnoticed by the men and women engrossed in lighthearted conversation. The last color of the sunset, an orange-pink hue, was leaving the Mediterranean sky. The *café* smelled of coffee and whisky mixed with the stench of sweat and cigarette smoke. Spoons clanked against saucers as waiters yelled orders across the counter.

The waiter hurried them to a round metal table. With a swish of his rag, he wiped away a puddle of liquor with several flies hovering above it. "What will it be?" he barked impatiently.

"A Coke," Gabriella stammered. David, completely collected, ordered a *pastis*.

"So, my beautiful Gabby, how have you been? Really. Tell me about the adventures of the past two weeks at St. Joseph's." He was smiling.

She wondered if, after all, they would only make small talk. David seemed cool and removed from any sign of emotion. She could not meet his dark, penetrating eyes as she held her hands together in her lap to keep them from trembling. The waiter approached with their drinks.

Here I am with this man I care terribly about, but I cannot tell him. David looked up, as if sensing her pain. Silently, he slipped his strong hand over her trembling one. *I know what I need to say.* The pain was agonizing, that sickly fear of leaving it unsaid. The words that had flowed so easily and unhindered in the past stuck dry in her mouth. *I must tell him. I must.*

With a deep breath, she squeezed his hand and met his gaze. "Jean-Claude came back," she said, biting her lip.

"When?"

"Two days ago." She closed her eyes as if to blot out the memory. "I suppose it would have seemed comical if we hadn't been so completely terrified. You would have been proud of the kids." She caught his gaze and told him the whole story.

David shook his head, looking amazed.

"It was a miracle that we weren't found, David!" Her eyes were shining, the blue set off by her turquoise blouse. Then her face fell. "It was so frightening. The Arab children are still terrified, especially the five who arrived on the twenty-seventh. Did you hear about their trip?"

Again David shook his head.

"Something awful happened at the port in Algiers. A man started shooting at the children as they were getting on the boat. Then a woman who was with the kids tried to stop the man, and he pushed her into the sea and shot her. Another man then shot the first guy, and the kids escaped. The stuff a spy novel is made of, huh?"

"The stuff of war," David muttered.

Gabriella paused and took a long sip of coke. She tossed her red hair over her shoulders and pulled it into one thick strand. Then she released it, and it tumbled across her shoulders again. "Ophélie is scared, too."

"Hmm," David nodded, but he seemed lost in other thoughts.

Gabriella cleared her throat. *Now you must tell him.* The room swirled about her, the noise of the waiters' screaming seemed amplified. Beads of perspiration broke out on her forehead. "David?"

"Yes?"

"David, could we go outside for a bit? I ... I'm not feeling too well."

"Of course." He got up quickly and came to her side. "What's the matter?"

"Nothing, nothing that a little fresh air won't help."

David left the change for the drinks on the table and followed Gabriella out of the *café*.

* * *

They walked for ten minutes in silence. The beach air was cold and pure. Gabriella thrust her hands into the pockets of her jacket. She stared at the sand as she walked, almost dragging her feet. David took his long strides in slow motion, not passing hers, but he did not speak.

Gabriella suddenly stopped, turned to face David, and took his hands. "I've got to tell you something, David. And I don't know how." Her eyes brimmed with tears. "I need you to help me with this one."

David raised his eyebrows, perplexed. "Sure, Gabby. I'm all ears." She did not speak. Gently, he touched her chin with his hand and looked into her eyes. She bit her lip to try to control her tears.

350

"This is so wrong. I shouldn't ...be ...crying. It is
...I think ...I think you will find ...that it is good
news." She was wiping her eyes with her fingers.

"Okay," she sniffed. "I'm going to try again. But I
can't look at you." They started walking.

"Mother Griolet found some information in
Ophélie's drawer ...some papers from her mother. One
was a letter." There was an awkward pause. "In the letter, she told Ophélie about the father the child had never
met." Gabriella reached out and took David's hand.
"Ophélie's mother's name is Anne-Marie Duchemin and
...and her father's name is ...David." She stopped and
looked up at him. "It is you."

A hundred expressions washed over David
Hoffmann's face as Gabriella regarded him with teary
eyes. "Me?" he whispered in amazement. "What? Me?
Ophélie's father?" He ran his hands through his hair. He
stood transfixed, watching the waves lap onto the shore.

Gabriella wanted him to deny it, to wonder how it
was possible, to ask to see the letter. But he did not. He
slowly shook his head, and as if she were not even
there, he said, "Of course. Of course. That is why you
never answered my letters. And why so suddenly you
asked me for help. Ophélie...my daughter."

Gabriella backed away from him, feeling unfit to
share this private moment of revelation. *I am an
intruder in this story. Nothing but a bumbling intruder.*
She watched David in this moment of surprise. Still he
stood straight, composed, a tall tower. Silent and
strong. She knew he was reliving something from his
past, and she was jealous of his memories.

Can't you see that this is stabbing me? But why?
Why should he see? And how? The reasoning made her
head throb. She felt dirty, ugly. *If only you saw how
deeply I care for you, for Ophélie. If only you saw how*

351

afraid I am that you will not need me anymore. I am sorry I cannot smile for you, David. It is wrong, I know.

He left the water's edge and came to her side. "Gabby. Dear Gabby. Thank you for telling me. As you can imagine, this is quite a shock. It is unbelievable that my daughter has been with me. I have watched her play day after day. And I never knew."

"It was you who brought her to St. Joseph's," she said.

"Yes, I found her in Paris on that crazy—" He stopped mid-sentence. "Ophélie knows who I am? That I am her father?"

"She just recently found out. She did not know your name, and when I mentioned it, she went white. Then Mother Griolet showed me the letter, and we realized the child had been trying to read it for all these months."

"And she never said a thing?"

"No. Even now she has no idea that Mother Griolet and I know." She hesitated. "And now you."

"I must see her! I must tell her. What will I say?" He was pacing the beach.

"We will figure out a way to tell her. Don't worry."

"Gabby, it is such strange, good news. I have never thought of myself as a father. Never felt the least bit interested. But now ... suddenly I am."

"She is very worried about her mother," Gabriella broke in.

"Yes, I'm sure she is. For Anne-Marie. I am worried, too." He looked at her sympathetically, the cynical eyes caring.

He started to speak, so she quickly said, "And I hope you find her."

For a moment, his gaze was quizzical, pained, even confused. She could say no more; the courage to speak had drained her. She relaxed her fierce grip on his hand and let the breeze run through her hair.

But David did not relax his hold on her, and with his black eyes intent on Gabriella's face, he whispered, "Dear Gabby, don't you know that I *have* found her."

* * *

David Hoffmann had wanted to be many things during his twenty-four years of life. A professor, a writer, a poet, a spy, a diplomat, an explorer. But he had never wanted to be a father. The mention of the word left a bad taste in his mouth. For him, the word connoted all that he despised in humanity: anger, abandonment, prejudice, betrayal. Yet as he lay on his bed at Mme. Pons' apartment and thought of being father to Ophélie, he felt a sudden warmth.

"How will I learn to be your father?" he whispered into the night. "Who will teach me the lessons I have not learned? I never saw Anne-Marie's round belly. I never held you as an infant or knew when you took your first steps. I don't even know what I missed. So how will I learn to love you the way a good father should?"

A phrase flashed through his mind. *Like a father pitieth his children* . . . Somewhere in the Bible that Gabriella had given him, he had read that verse. He remembered laughing at the idea that a father would have compassion on his children. But now he desired to read more.

He picked up the large leather book and flipped through its pages. He was sure he had not read it in the Gospels. But he had read it. The Psalms! Last week, he had read through the Psalms. Some he knew by heart from his childhood. And this one was there in the webs of his memory. He came to Psalm 103 and began reading out loud: "Bless the Lord, O my soul; and all that is within me bless His holy name. . . . Who forgiveth all thine iniquities; who healeth all thy diseases; who redeemeth thy life from destruction." His voice caught for a moment. Then he read on until he came to the verse, "Like as a father pitieth his children, so the Lord pitieth them that fear Him."

"I have a daughter now," he said as he finished the psalm and closed the book. "Perhaps the God of Gabriella will teach me how to be a father. Perhaps."

David Hoffmann turned out the light in his room and watched the crescent moon cupping a piece of the sky in its hand. He saw the beautiful face of Ophélie in his mind. "I saved your life once, little one." He laughed at the irony as he relived the night of October 17 with the wounded child. "By the bridge I found you. By the bridge where I was to meet Emile Torrès." He thought back to the note he had received those months ago. "He had 'information' for me. Was it you? Was it you he had for me? And by a wild providence, we are here together."

He rubbed his eyes with his long, bony fingers and sighed. "I do not know where you are, Anne-Marie. I only hope with all my heart that you do not lie dead in the waters of the port in Algiers. But Ophélie is safe with me. I will keep her safe for you, until you come back. I promise. I will be her father. I am ready now."

* * *

The sliver of a moon cradled a lone star in the black Algerian night. Anne-Marie's breathing came in gasps. Her eyes were glazed. A wet rag lay on her forehead as Moustafa desperately tried to bring down her raging fever. He cursed himself for not having taken her to the hospital. Hospitals were not safe in Algiers. A whole ward of *pied-noirs* had been murdered in one a few months ago. Equally gruesome stories were reported weekly.

But now he feared he had been wrong to try to care

for her himself. Both legs had become infected from the bullet wounds. A thick yellow puss oozed from below her right knee. She did not speak coherently. Marcus Cirou came in the room, wringing his hands and begging Moustafa to take her to the hospital.

"She is dying here," he commented wryly. "She cannot do worse there."

They drove through the night to the Santa Maria, a Catholic hospital on the outskirts of Bab el Oued. The French nurses greeted Moustafa with a suspicious air. "Let me take care of this," Marcus ordered. "You cannot help her now."

Moustafa waited outside in the cold night air, stamping his feet and cursing the moon. He tried to think of something besides Anne-Marie's gaunt, pale face.

The list of names had appeared miraculously in the mail last week. This was good news. Ophélie must have given the list to the redhead, he supposed, and she had mailed it. It didn't matter who had sent it. The important thing was that now the operation could continue.

But Anne-Marie had seemed indifferent to the long sought-after list. She had only cried out feebly for Ophélie, staring blankly into space. Then she had gotten the fever and the infection. Now Moustafa had no stomach to continue his work. Not if Anne-Marie died.

"Live!" he cried out to the moon.

He was not sure how much time passed before he felt Marcus' hand on his shoulder. He wheeled around to face him, fearful to read the verdict in Marcus's eyes.

"She is stabilized. They said we got her here in time. Just in time." They walked to the car in silence.

* * *

Normally the aging history professor and the dashing young American teacher did not meet for drinks on a

Sunday afternoon. But this afternoon they sat like old friends sipping a *pastis* while the Mistral howled outside.

"He is still in Marseilles, I am sure," Jean-Louis commented. "He didn't bother us at the port as you had feared, when I picked up the kids. But when he came calling at St. Joseph's last Wednesday, I followed him back home." A smile crept across his face.

"Good job, Jean-Louis! And what did you find?"

"Here is his address, right in the middle of the slums. No surprise. He's got a screw loose, that man. At first glance he appears perfectly normal, but there's something not right about him." He lowered his voice. "I'd be getting rid of that one as soon as I could, if I were you." And he grinned like a shy schoolboy. "I am glad I can leave the dirty work to someone younger."

"Thanks," David scowled.

"You should not waste time, David. I am not sure what he would have done if he had found Miss Madison and the children. He looks capable of just about anything."

"I'll be leaving again then. Tomorrow morning," David agreed reluctantly. He thought of Ophélie. He did not want to leave now. "What did George tell you about the *Capitaine* incident?"

"Pretty messy. The kids were real torn up about the whole thing. Apparently the lady who was with them was shot and pushed into the water. Another guy killed Ali's boy, and the kids got away. George didn't waste any time waiting around to see what happened, you understand. He took off with the kids."

"I'll make the rounds again. Aix, Aigues-Mortes, and les Baux. You talk to Pierre. I'll be back as soon as I have news." David scratched his head. "You don't mind handling my class again, *mon pote*?"

"No problem for me, David. It's just your girls. They

can't seem to stay awake for me." Jean-Louis chuckled.

"Women." David rolled his eyes. "Listen, I was just thinking . . . second quarter exams are scheduled for the first full week in March, right?"

"*Oui, bien sûr,*" Jean-Louis agreed.

"Then you can start a review for them. Of both quarters. I'll leave all my notes. I hope I won't be gone long. I have a lot of things I need to be doing here." The two men nodded, touched glasses, and stood up.

"*À bientôt,*" David said and they parted ways.

* * *

David knocked lightly on the door to the parsonage. After a moment's wait, a voice asked from within, "Who is it?"

"It is Mr. Hoffmann."

The door opened slowly. The nun looked surprised to see him. "Mr. Hoffmann? How may I help you? You don't look well at all."

"Mother Griolet, I am sorry to bother you at this time of night. I must talk to you."

"Yes?" Her expression was worried, reserved. "Come in." She showed him into the office and offered him a chair.

"I know you are not fond of me, and for that I am truly sorry. You are . . . you are a fine woman." He hesitated. "I admire your work with the orphans . . ." He looked her straight in the eyes. ". . . And with the *pied-noir* and *harki* children."

Mother Griolet raised her eyebrows. "Exactly why did you come to see me tonight, Mr. Hoffmann?" she asked.

"Because it is time that you know. Things are becoming more confused, and I think it best that you understand . . . in case anything happens to me."

"What do you mean?" She sounded alarmed, almost angry.

"I mean, Mother Griolet, that I am Hugo." He met her eyes again, and they were filled with surprise. "I am sorry to announce it to you in such a way, but I must. For a long time, I thought you were safer not knowing. But now there are so many other reasons, and the war will soon be over. There will be more refugees, many more."

Mother Griolet was sitting forward now. "You, David Hoffmann, are Hugo? You are behind this operation?"

"Yes."

For a moment she looked bewildered. Then her face broke into a wide smile, and she clapped her hands together. "It is impossible! I mean, excuse me, but I would never have guessed. Amazing." She shook her head from side to side in disbelief. "Why, this is wonderful news!" Impulsively she came around her desk and kissed him on both cheeks.

David's face turned crimson, and he stuttered, "I am indeed glad that you find it so good. I was afraid you would be concerned . . . about the future of the operation."

"Oh, yes, of course. I *am* concerned about the future and the dear *pied-noir* and *harki* children. But the wonderful news is that I was wrong! Wrong about you, Mr. Hoffmann! How I disliked you! I was sure you were working against us. And then when I found out about the young child." She stopped short. "But perhaps you do not know?"

"Yes, I know. Gabby told me yesterday. It was this that made me realize I must have you on my side. For Ophélie's sake. My daughter's." He pronounced the word with an air of wonder. "Forgive me, Mother Griolet. It is all so new and strange. I had no idea I was a father." For a moment they smiled at each other in

358

compassionate silence.

"It is ironic, you know. The whole idea of the Huguenot cross came from her mother, Anne-Marie. She wore the cross, a gift from her father who was Protestant. I met Captain Duchemin years ago in Algeria. He was a respected and much decorated *pied-noir* from World War II."

"You know that Ophélie now wears her grandfather's cross?" Mother Griolet added softly.

"Really?" David exclaimed. "No, I have not been close enough to her to notice ... yet." He paused, looked away, and then continued.

"I also met the captain's beautiful daughter. We were rebellious adolescents, but she gave me hope for the first time in years. Then I left Algeria for my studies in Princeton, and we lost contact. The letters I sent her were never answered."

David stopped himself and apologized, "I am sorry to bore you with my past."

Mother Griolet shook her head quickly, *"Au contraire!* I am fascinated. Please continue."

David stepped back into his reverie. "Then out of the blue Anne-Marie wrote me, a desperate sort of letter. It was December of 1959. She was begging for help. She claimed that a madman named Ali, who was with the FLN, had a personal vendetta to eliminate all the soldiers and their families with whom his father served in World War II. This man blamed his father's platoon for leaving his father, the lieutenant of the platoon, to be murdered by the Nazis. And he blamed Anne-Marie's father, the battalion captain, for setting up the raid that cost his father his life."

He paused again. Mother Griolet waited, intent on every word. "Anne-Marie's parents were killed in a bombing in Algiers in 1958. Afterward, she was tricked into disclosing the names of some of the men in this platoon. Ali then began systematically to eliminate these men and their families, disguised, of course, in the realm of terrorism and a war that killed at random.

"That is when Anne-Marie begged my help, to get these families out of Algeria—especially the children. And so I devised this little operation.

"The cross I remembered was the jewelry of a persecuted minority, the Huguenots. I am from a persecuted minority too." He cleared his throat and did not try to hide the pain in his eyes.

"Yes, I have not forgotten after all these years." Mother Griolet smiled compassionately at David. "It came back to me not long ago. You were here with us for a few months, *n'est-ce pas?* A Jewish orphan?"

"Yes." For a moment, neither could speak. When David broke the silence, it was only with a hoarse whisper. "You gave me life, Mother Griolet, in this orphanage. I did not remember it was you, but the only happy memory of my childhood after Mother was taken from me is of a warm, smiling woman in black rocking me in her arms." His voice caught, and he swallowed hard.

"There were so many orphans here at that time. I had completely forgotten your name," Mother Griolet replied softly. "I only realized that you had been here last week. Then I was really confused," she winked. "But now I am beginning to understand."

David rubbed his forehead with his hand. "I did a bit of research after receiving Anne-Marie's letter, and found out that St. Joseph's was still here. I figured this part of France would be a good contact point. And I was sure there would still be some members of the Resistance around who would help me."

Mother Griolet's eyes twinkled. "Dear Jean-Louis. So you are the one who got him back into this!"

360

David shrugged. "Jean-Louis and several others. So I came back. To help another persecuted minority. And I hoped in the process to find Anne-Marie. I knew she would be in danger. I have not heard from her directly now for months. I do not know where she is, or if she is even still alive. And now things have ... changed. I have a daughter...." He looked away, past Mother Griolet, out the window. "And I am in love with another ... with a Raphaelite angel who also wears a Huguenot cross."

He took a deep breath and turned toward Mother Griolet with a new composure. He spoke in a professional, controlled tone. "It is good news, Mother Griolet, but there is also much danger for Ophélie and Gabby. It is my fault. This Ali is determined to have his revenge. You have already met one of his assistants—Jean-Claude Gachon."

Mother Griolet nodded. "Yes. He calls himself Philippe. I am afraid I have perhaps been unwise. I did not know how to keep him away. Thank the Lord I received a note, from you perhaps, warning me of him."

"Yes. You have done fine. Gabriella has told me about the incident. It seems that Jean-Claude is determined to have Gabby and Ophélie. That is why I must become more visible—so he will chase me instead. He suspects I am around, and I will give him more bait."

Now David regarded Mother Griolet, pleading with his eyes. "I need you to watch over my daughter ... and Gabby. I fear you must keep them hidden with the *harki* children, until I know that it will be safe for them again. Until I can convince Ali and his friends that they have no use for them."

"You will sign your death warrant then?"

"I hope not, dear Mother Griolet. I have made a mistake in letting the suspicion fall on innocent shoulders. I will not let it continue. I must go now. You will help?"

"Yes, I will help." As he turned to go, she added, "Be careful, Mr. Hoffmann. God be with you."

Again his dark eyes met hers, intense in their message. "Pray for me. I would consider it a privilege to have your prayers."

* * *

Mother Griolet walked David Hoffmann to the door of the parsonage. She closed it softly behind him and leaned against the heavy oak door. Bowing her head, she whispered, "Dear God, be with him. I have misjudged the man. Bring him back so that I can know him better. Bring him back for the girls."

* * *

A woman screamed at a pudgy toddler who had escaped into the narrow street in front of a row of buildings piled on top of each other in the Casbah. The child squealed in protest as his mother grabbed him by the arm and dragged him inside. Ali Boudani paid no attention to the scene playing out before him. He fingered a letter that he had received from France that lay still unopened in his pocket.

The afternoon sun was low in the sky, but Ali did not turn on the light as he entered his basement apartment. Yesterday's paper still lay across the desk, with the date visible: Tuesday, February 13.

Ali smiled as he read of the eight victims who had been killed as anti-OAS demonstrators had clashed with police in a metro station in Paris on the 8th. Today hundreds of thousands of working-class Parisians came to mourn them, the largest turnout of the public since the Liberation. The French were killing the French. This was very good.

But Ali was most pleased by the news his turbaned

362

friend, Mohemmed, had brought him earlier that day. Mme. Jacqueline Bousquet was buried Thursday after her apartment burned to the ground on Tuesday. She was trapped inside. No other bodies were found....

Ali snarled, "Fool, woman! You did not think you would join your grandchildren in France." He spat on the floor, then glanced at the list of names he had pasted on the wall. He drew an X through the name of Mr. et Mme. Guy Bousquet. Then he scribbled beside the names, *children escaped to France.*

There was no word from his young terrorist. Ali knew what it meant. Somewhere amid the boats in the port, a body had sunk to touch the bottom of the sea. And somewhere in the south of France, five children were free. Their freedom angered him more than the news of the French slayings brought him pleasure.

Bringing it out of his pocket, Ali tore open the letter with a Marseilles postmark. It was dated February 7. "No more leads on woman and child. Searched suspected orphanage. Not there. Have not seen Mr. Hoffmann again. Await further instructions. Respectfully yours, Jean-Claude."

Ali threw the paper down with a curse. "Bumbling idiot. You will pay! You will all pay."

His eyes shone as he laughed his wicked laugh. "It is only a matter of time until we are free. *Algérie indépendante!* Death to *pied-noirs*, death to *harkis*, death to you, Mr. Hoffmann. It is only a matter of time."

Chapter Twenty-Eight

Gabriella stopped to admire a large chocolate heart in the window of the *pâtisserie* across the street from Mme. Leclerc's apartment. It sat, rich and inviting, on a bright red doily that sparkled and shimmered as the afternoon sun caught its reflection in the window. She pulled her coat around her, fumbling with the buttons. But it was not the chill of the February morn that made her shiver.

February 14. The day for lovers. The holiday was unknown in Senegal, yet every year, her parents had celebrated. Gabriella remembered helping to confect an elaborate chocolate heart for her mother to present to her husband by the light of a candle after the girls had been shooed out of the hut. Gabriella had longed for such a valentine all her life.

But today there would be no valentine from the cocky American teacher. He was off on another adventure, leaving her once again to straighten out the details of his life.

She caught a glimpse of herself in the window of the *pâtisserie*. She was pale and thin, tucked inside her pea coat. She looked hard into her eyes. They stared back at her with an emptiness that angered Gabriella. Her eyes had always been her favorite feature. Not the unruly hair that everyone either hated or loved, but her eyes. She liked the way they sparkled and danced. She liked how she could meet another's eyes without fear, and peer into the soul. She liked their bright blue color. But today they looked dull.

She turned away from the store and dragged her feet along the cobblestones, listening to the barking of a small gray poodle that pulled furiously on its leash beside the heels of its owner.

Gabriella did not want to reach the church so quickly or let herself into the parsonage with such ease. There was no bounce to her step as she descended the staircase into the basement and walked down the hall and out into the courtyard. She watched the children laughing, running, playing.

Ophélie squealed with delight as she caught up with André, tagged him, and turned to flee in the other direction. "You're it!" she called after him, giggling.

Waiting until the little girl had stopped running and stood watching the other children, Gabriella approached the child. "Ophélie," she said.

"Bribri!" exclaimed Ophélie. "I didn't see you. Come play with us!"

Gabriella smiled. "Actually, I was wondering if I might borrow you for a moment. Do you think the others can get along without you?"

Ophélie giggled. "Of course." She grabbed her teacher's hand, and together they entered the girls' dormitory.

Gabriella sat down on Ophélie's bed and motioned for the child to join her. Then carefully, she opened the second drawer of Ophélie's chest and removed a dark blue pair of tights.

Ophélie regarded Gabriella wide-eyed. She let out a small whimper of protest as Gabriella reached into the tights and pulled out a little blue velvet bag.

"How did you find it?" Ophélie whispered.

"Quite by accident," Gabriella assured her with a hug. "You are very smart, Ophélie. A very clever hiding place. Sister Rosaline found it when she was preparing for the new orphans. It was Mother Griolet who read the letters and showed them to me."

Ophélie stretched out on the bed, away from Gabriella, and buried her head in her arms.

Gabriella pretended not to notice. "I was so surprised to learn that Mr. Hoffmann is your father. I could hardly believe it! But you know who was even more surprised than I was?"

Ophélie shook her head but did not look around.

"Mr. Hoffmann! I told him a few days ago, and well, he was just speechless." Gabriella stretched out on her stomach beside Ophélie. "He was delighted, overwhelmed. Very, very happy."

A hint of a smile curled onto Ophélie's lips. At once she frowned again. "Then why doesn't he come to see me?"

"He will! Oh, he will! It is only that he has had to go away for a few days. But when he gets back, we will have a party. A celebration."

The child rolled over onto her back, letting her long, brown hair trail over the side of the bed. Gabriella imitated the child's move, sweeping her curly mane behind her. She met Ophélie's eyes and they giggled.

"Gabriella, why did my father not know about me? Why was Mama afraid to tell him that he was my daddy?"

Gabriella grimaced, searching for the right words. "That is a good question. I cannot say for sure. But your mother was very young when you were born. And your father was living far away in America. He was going to school. I think your mother did not want to make him come back to Algeria. She knew he would want to see you, but somehow she thought that it would not be fair."

Ophélie furrowed her brow. "I do not understand. Wouldn't my father want to be with my mama and me? Why did he leave her in the first place?"

"I do not know, sweetheart. Someday your mama will tell you. All I know is that both your mama and your father love you very much. And your father does want to see you."

"He saved me once, you know, Bribri. He told me to tell no one about it, but since you know he is my father, and since he likes you so much, I'm sure he wouldn't mind." She beamed at Gabriella.

"It was when we lived in another city. Paris. And I went with Malika to march for freedom. That is what she told me. Only it wasn't like that at all. The police shot people, and everyone was running and screaming. And Malika fell, and then something hurt my leg. I was so scared. More scared even than when the bad men would come and see Mama.

"I was scared like . . . like when we hid in the closet from Mr. Jean-Claude. Only it was worse because my leg hurt so bad. And then this nice man, Mr. Hoffmann . . . I mean, my father, picked me up and took me to his room and helped me get better." Ophélie's words were tumbling out faster than she could talk.

"I begged him not to take me to the police because they were killing people. I saw it. And I couldn't go to see Mr. Gady anymore because . . . because he was . . . dead." She scrunched up her nose and looked at Gabriella with sorrowful eyes.

"So he brought me on a train, and another man

came to get me—you know, the fat man with the red eyes who comes to St. Joseph's. And then ... and then I met Mother Griolet, and then you had the same cross."

Gabriella placed her arm around Ophélie and squeezed her tight. "That is a very remarkable story. Your daddy saved you, and he didn't even know that you were his daughter."

"And now he must love me even more, right?"

"You are right. Yes, you are right."

Ophélie said nothing for a moment. Then she asked, "What will happen to me, Bribri, if my father marries you?"

Gabriella laughed loudly and blushed. "Mr. Hoffmann is not going to marry me, Ophélie."

"Oh," she said quietly. "But he likes you."

"Yes, but we are only friends."

"Then will he marry my mama? Will she come back, and will he marry her?"

Gabriella cleared her throat. "Would you like for that to happen, Ophélie?"

"Oh, yes! Then I would have a mama and a father together. I would like that very much!"

"Yes, that would be good for you, Ophélie. That would be very good for you."

Gabriella turned onto her side, propping herself up on her elbow. The Huguenot cross slipped out from her blouse and dangled in the air from her neck.

"It is such a beautiful cross, Bribri," said Ophélie, pulling her own cross out and holding it in her small hand. "Mama was right. She said that I would be protected if I wore this cross. Soon everything is going to be just right."

She leaned over and kissed Gabriella on the cheek. Gabriella brushed Ophélie's hair with her fingers and smiled through the mist in her eyes.

"You are a wonderful little girl. A very brave, wonderful little girl." She replaced the velvet bag and the tights in the drawer. Hands intertwined, the two walked back out into the sunshine together.

* * *

The slums of Marseilles sat, squalid and run-down, in the heart of the city by the Vieux Port. Cement apartment buildings rose into the sky. The view of the Mediterranean was no compensation for the stench in the corridors, David reflected, as he climbed to the fourth floor of a dingy gray building. He sat down on the steps of the top floor and waited. Doors slammed, dogs barked, babies screamed. Occasionally he could make out the sounds of a fight in the street below.

The repugnant smells of urine and trash mingled and clashed. David rubbed his eyes, which were red from lack of sleep. He listened for footsteps in the stairwell. He knew what he must do if Jean-Claude Gachon showed up. He touched a small bottle in his pocket, but he did not relish the thought of using it.

He dozed off and on, leaning his head against the white stuccoed wall. *Ophélie was laughing and calling out "Daddy!," running to him with outstretched arms. A woman shyly approached from the shadows. She wore a white robe. He could not see her face. "Look who is here with us, Daddy." Ophélie laughed, taking his hand. He squinted to see the woman, but she was hidden by the bright glare coming from the cross she wore around her neck....*

David shook himself out of his dream. Someone was climbing the stairs. He peered down from the balcony as the footsteps stopped on the third floor. A key rattled in the door. David leaned far over the bannister and caught a glimpse of the back of a man's head disappearing into an apartment. The door closed.

David crept down the flight of steps, took the bottle from his pocket and dabbed a liquid on the door front with a thick rag. He rang the doorbell and hurried down the stairwell and out into the street.

"Welcome home, Jean-Claude," he whispered. "I've been waiting for you."

* * *

The old *concierge* shuffled to the door, muttering to himself. "You don't pay rent, you get evicted. It's the sixteenth of February, *punaise!* Three weeks late, and you expect to stay. And now you expect me to answer your door for you. *C'est fini*, Mr. Philippe."

The *concierge* opened the door and glanced into the hallway. It was empty. He reached down to retrieve an old rag that lay by the door. A sharp odor stung his eyes. He grasped at his throat, gasping for air.

"*Aidez-moi*," he called out, choking. "Help me!" He sank to the floor and lay still.

* * *

It was after dark when Jean-Claude returned to Marseilles on February sixteenth. As he entered the stairwell of his apartment building, a young woman dressed in a tight low-cut black dress greeted him.

"*Ooh la la, monsieur*," she said gesticulating wildly. "The *concierge*, he has been poisoned. In your apartment. The police are searching for you." She rubbed her body invitingly against him. "If you like, I can help you find a place to hide."

Jean-Claude eyed the woman with interest. "And what do you know of this tragic accident, *ma chère?*"

"I know the old man will live. Mme. Olivier heard him cry out and called the ambulance." She smiled, revealing a row of cracked teeth. Her strong perfume drifted up to entice Jean-Claude. "And I know that a stranger has been hanging around these parts. Do you care to know more, *Monsieur?*"

"Of course," Jean-Claude cackled. He pulled the woman behind the steps, wrapping his arms around her waist. "Tell me everything."

"You will pay?" She raised her eyebrows.

Jean-Claude removed a wad of bills from his leather sack and held them before her. "I will pay for everything you give me, lovely lady. Everything."

She took the money and led him through an alleyway and across the street. "A tall man, very handsome and strong. He has been here two days now, watching your building. He was nearby when the *concierge* was poisoned." Her eyes shined brightly. "You know this man?"

Jean-Claude threw back his head and howled with laughter. "Oh, *oui!* I know this man. Where is he now?"

The woman shrugged. "I do not know. He left when the police showed up. But I am sure I can find him for you."

"It is good. He is around. I will look for him later. Right now, I need a place to spend the night. I won't be going back to my apartment, you understand." He touched her ear and played with the earring.

"I understand perfectly, *Monsieur.* Follow me."

* * *

Moustafa held the thin sheets of paper in his hand, reading carefully the list of names and addresses. They were all there. Thirty-seven of them. He compared the list he had received in the mail last week with the crumpled sheets on which Anne-Marie had scribbled names for the past three months. Twenty-two families had been taken care of, one way or another, he thought to himself grimly.

He cursed as he read the names: Rajib Karel, Marie
Sentier and children, Jacqueline Bousquet, Mme. el
Gharbi. Lost. Lost with their *harki* husbands and
fathers. Now there were fifteen other names, new names
to contact. He felt confident the *pied-noir* families would
leave anyway, as soon as the war ended. They would
flee to France and find shelter from Ali. They need only
be warned.

But the *harki* families. His stomach turned and he
felt sick as he thought of his father, thrown out on the
street like a piece of trash, his throat slit from ear to
ear. Five *harki* families still needed to escape before the
war ended.

Moustafa spoke out loud in Marcus Cirou's empty
apartment. "But what will you find in France, my brothers and sisters? Only angry stares and hatred. Unless
you wear a badge proclaiming your father fought with
the French, no one will understand. They will reject you!
They will reject us."

He carried the new list of names to the kitchen table
and sat down, an angry glare on his face. His thoughts
turned to Anne-Marie. "David Hoffmann, I know you
are waiting for her. She will come too, when she can.
For now she is only hanging on day by day.

"And so am I! I will not let you have her. Not yet.
Not until I lie dead like my father in some forgotten
street of Algiers. Until then, David Hoffmann, we will
work together, but in our hearts, we will be enemies. It
must be so."

* * *

Jean-Claude Gachon was not coming back to his
apartment in Marseilles. Of that David was sure. Three
days had passed since the ambulance had come to the

building. Nor was he lying in a hospital recovering from a near-fatal accidental poisoning. That was the *concierge,* David reminded himself disgustedly of his mistake.

But Jean-Claude was still in town. David had paid handsomely to have the information from the pretty little prostitute who hung around the neighborhood beside the Vieux Port. David would not leave Marseilles until he had found him. There was a good chance it would be soon.

His hotel room was cramped and dingy. An orange bedspread, torn and stained, covered a rotting mattress. David spread out his briefcase on the bed and examined his papers. "Ophélie," he whispered.

He took out a piece of beige stationery and began writing.

You must think that your father doesn't care, but it is not true. It is only that you are not safe until I find this bad man. Then I will come. Then we will buy the biggest religieuse *that Pierre's* boulangerie *will sell us. You see, I know you like them. Gabriella has told me. It will not be long now.*

He twirled the pencil in his hand. How should he sign the note? *Sincerely, Your father.* No. That was terrible. *Your loving father.* Still too formal. He thought back to the letters from his father. Cold, distant, unfeeling. He must communicate something different in the first letter to his daughter.

What did I always want to hear? he asked himself. He knew the answer before the pen touched the paper. He wrote the words slowly, carefully, as if he were climbing into the pen and spilling himself out onto the sheet.

He held the letter up to read and smiled when he came to the signature. "I love you, Ophélie—Daddy."

* * *

373

The pansies in the courtyard of St. Joseph's tossed their heads impatiently in the wind, their petals folding in and out like the hands of coy maidens, reluctant to reveal their velvet faces. Gabriella studied the flowers from the basement doorway of the parsonage. The yellow and white pansies had flourished in the winter months, yet several of the dark purple and amber flowers had died out.

"What makes some of them stronger than the others?" she questioned Mother Griolet, who had joined her. "You bought them at the same nursery, and we planted them at the same time. Why did the purple ones die? They seemed to be the strongest. The frilly, delicate ones are those that have thrived."

"It's like that every year, Gabriella. The yellow and white pansies beat out the others. I suppose they have what it takes to withstand the winter."

Gabriella stepped into the courtyard and walked toward the flowers. "Do you think I have what it takes to make it through the winter?" she asked, bending down beside a bed of flowers.

Mother Giolet stood above the young woman, placing her hand on Gabriella's shoulder. "I'm sure you do."

Gabriella fingered a yellow pansy, moving her fingers over the smooth texture of the petals. Beside the flower, the withered root of another lay. Quickly Gabriella pulled the remains of the flower out of the dirt. She stood up, holding the roots and dried petals out for Mother Griolet to observe. "This one didn't make it. See."

"No, you are right," the old nun sighed. "My dear child, it sounds like you need a good cup of hot chocolate in my den. Come along."

Gabriella let the dead flower fall to the ground and gently took hold of Mother Griolet's arm.

* * *

"I know you can't possibly understand the feeling," Gabriella stated, frustrated. "It is the most awful thing. I'm jealous. I'm jealous that he loved her at one time. That he fathered her child. It is far in the past, but I am so jealous." She struck out her hand in exasperation and knocked over her half-filled cup of hot chocolate. A curse escaped her lips. Immediately Gabriella blushed. "Excuse me. I didn't mean to say that."

Mother Griolet chuckled. "I've heard much worse. Just a moment, I'll fetch a rag." She hurried out of the den, returning a moment later with an old kitchen towel. Gabriella sopped up the liquid on the coffee table.

"Continue, child," Mother Griolet said softly.

Gabriella remained silent for a while, thinking. "I'm . . . I'm jealous because he has every right to love her again. And he won't love me because I'm too . . . too something. Religious, maybe. Or naive. And I know it is for the best, I guess, but it makes me furious. And now it just seems like God is punishing me for ever loving David Hoffmann." Her words were gaining momentum, rushing ahead of her.

"But really I didn't mean to care about him, and he's the one who dragged me into this whole thing, and now he's going to take Ophélie away from me. And I know she's not even mine to keep. It's the most awful feeling. I just want to leave this whole mess."

Mother Griolet leaned back on her worn couch and propped one leg on the coffee table with difficulty. She closed her eyes momentarily before she spoke. "It sounds as though you are more angry than jealous. Angry with a lot of people. Maybe even God. Am I right?"

Gabriella fidgeted with her hair. "Probably," she answered sulkily.

"Why do you think God is punishing you, Gabriella?"

"I don't know. Some sort of discipline because in my mind I'm straying from the straight and narrow. I don't know."

"Do you think He is more interested in our circumstances or what we learn from them?" the nun prodded.

Gabriella did not answer. She could not think of anything worthwhile to say, and wondered why she felt such a need to reveal her thoughts to this old woman. But Mother Griolet did not seem to mind her silence.

"Years ago, I loved a man."

Gabriella perked up, startled at the nun's revelation.

"He was a fine man. I met him here in Castelnau. I considered leaving my calling for him."

She had closed her eyes again, and Gabriella watched them flicker underneath the wrinkled skin. She had never noticed how wrinkled the skin was, nor the numerous brown splotches on the nun's face. Suddenly she seemed very, very old, and very vulnerable. Gabriella almost spoke, to stop Mother Griolet from sharing something Gabriella had no right to hear. But when she opened her mouth to speak, no sound came out.

Mother Griolet seemed not to notice; her eyes were still closed. "But then the first war came along, and he left. It was only four months later that I received word of his death.

"But you know, Gabriella, I never thought God was punishing me for some sin of loving a man. Nor did I think He caused this man's death so that I would not leave my calling.

"God is bigger than our simplistic or most complicated reasoning. I could not box Him in." She paused, and the silence made Gabriella shiver.

Presently the small woman, who suddenly seemed fragile, spoke again. "I learned, though. I learned many things. How much it hurts to love, and how deep a soul can ache with missing another. And how unfair life can be. I learned how to grieve, and I found God was there in a much deeper way than I'd ever known before.

"Of course I was angry and crushed. It was part of the grieving. But I am not sorry for these painful lessons. I use them every day of my life."

She rubbed her eyes lightly and opened them to stare at Gabriella with the same compassionate gaze that she often wore on her face like a gentle emblem of empathy.

Gabriella rose to leave. "Thank you," she murmured. "Thank you for sharing."

"You will be all right, my child. You will see."

* * *

David Hoffmann stood alone on the beach near Marseilles. The dark sky was interrupted occasionally with brief flashes of heat lightning far in the distance, and it struck him that if he were a painter, this scene would be paradise. A tranquil tide lapped lazily at his feet, but farther out in the Mediterranean, tiny white-caps of water rose and fell, dotting the sea like the stars above in the black sky.

"It's beautiful," David said out loud. "Beautiful and vast and eternal. Like You, God of Gabriella. I do not believe in You. I do not believe an ultimate being of good exists. There is too much misery around.

"But she does. She believes it. If You were a man, I know I could win. I have always won. I can charm with intellect.

"But God of Gabriella, I do not know how to fight against You! In her mind, you are bigger and better than man. You understand the questions we are afraid to ask. And she believes You love. She believes You love and forgive." He kicked at the sand and cursed.

"Ah, forgive! Who would talk about that impossible

word if they knew! Can I forgive my mother's and sister's murderers? Can I forgive my proud and guilty father? No, God of Gabriella, I cannot. And can I forgive You? God of the Jews, who watched silently as they were slaughtered by the millions. I will not forgive You, God! You will never be my God."

He raised his clenched fists to the quiet sky and screamed in anguish as the water gently touched his feet and the lightning flitted around.

"You are not here, God! You can't be. For if You were, then she would be right, and all I have done in life is a hopeless waste." He lowered his arms till they hung loosely by his side and slowly unclenched his fingers. He stared at the living painting before him. The breeze felt unexpectedly chilly on his face, and he realized that it was because of his own tears mixed with the night air. He had not cried in many years. He remembered all too well the last time he had.

They stood still in the frozen camp of Dachau, awaiting roll call on an early December morning. The year was 1943. His mother was in front and his younger sister, Greta, behind him. Suddenly a rabbit appeared from behind the barracks, scampering in front of them toward safety. An officer laughed, raised his gun, and fired. The little beast burst into fragments before the weary onlookers. But Greta cried out "No!" in the innocent voice of a three-year-old and began running toward the lifeless rabbit. "You shot the bunny. You shot the bunny!"

In a flash, his mother was running after Greta, crying, "Come back, dear, quickly! It does not matter." But it was too late. Far away from the tower, a shot rang out, and Greta fell. His mother screamed in horror and ran to grab her fallen daughter.

"Leave her there!" an officer shouted.

But Mother did not hear. Did not move.

378

"Leave her there!" The only sound in the quiet of that tragic dawn was of Mother's sobbing. Then one more shot. And all was still again.

David's tears ran down his cheeks, uncontrolled and unnoticed as he relived the past. He saw himself as a child of six. *Greta had run, his mother had run, but he stood riveted in his place, dying in his own silence.*

Roll call continued, and then this hopeless mass of humankind turned their dull eyes down and walked back to the barracks, past the remains of the rabbit and the small body of Greta and the bleeding body of Mother. Only David stared as he walked by and he whispered, "Good-bye, Greta. Good-bye, Mama. Good-bye, life."

That night, sandwiched on his bunk between other women and children, he could not stop the tears from flowing. He sobbed into the filth of the torn blanket for hours. And when he could cry no more, he lay awake with the eyes of an old man in the face of a child and said, "And so, I am alone."

* * *

Much later, David turned to walk back toward the town. He felt weak and spent. For two hours he had wrestled with the God of Gabriella and the nightmare of his past. How could the two be reconciled? Forgiveness. It had worked for her. Could it work for him?

"You cannot exist, God. But Gabby is real. And to be with her is to taste eternity. She brings hope. To love her I must love You. And yet that will never work, she says. It has to be from the heart. What heart? But You must exist." David placed a hand on his throbbing head.

"I give up, God of Gabriella. You are too strong for me, and I have no strength at all tonight. Forgive me, God of Gabriella, for hating. For wanting revenge. If You exist, then take me if You want me. Take me, as Gabby says, and see what You can do. Tonight David Hoffmann is tired of being alone."

Suddenly he was on his knees, not noticing the wet sand beneath him until, reaching down, he scraped the damp earth into his hand and held it up toward the flashing heavens. "Here I am, with nothing to offer you but a hardened heart and a handful of sand. Here, God of Gabriella, take it and be my God too."

Chapter Twenty-Nine

The bedroom in Marcus Cirou's apartment that Anne-Marie now occupied was dark, the shutters drawn to keep out any sunlight. Anne-Marie dozed fitfully in the bed. Her frame was but a skeleton under the sheets. The effort of reaching for a glass of water beside the bed exhausted her.

Her body was slow to heal. She needed the care of nurses, but Anne-Marie refused to return to the hospital. Three weeks there had been enough almost to kill her, she had explained weakly to Moustafa. It was not a safe place. She would not go back.

Moustafa came to her side and gently wiped her forehead with a cool rag. "I will bring you some soup, *ma chère*," he whispered.

"Yes, that will be good. Soup will be good."

When he came back in the room, Anne-Marie turned her haggard face to him. "What is the news today?"

"It is more of the same. Rumors that the cease-fire will come soon. Dear . . ." he began. "I must get you to France. You will be better there. You will get stronger as soon as you see Ophélie. Please, drink this soup."

He lifted her head off the pillow and slowly brought the spoon of hot soup to her mouth.

"Thank you," she rasped. "Yes, if I could only get to France. You will take me to the *Capitaine*, Moustafa? You will come with me?"

He stood up and walked to the window, staring at the peeling paint on the inside of the shutters. "You know I cannot leave yet, Anne-Marie. But do not worry, dear. I will get you there safe." He came back to the bed and sat down beside her. "You must concentrate on getting stronger. I will do the rest." He stroked her head.

Anne-Marie forced a feeble smile. "The doctor said I would walk again. The bullets were taken out. I cannot understand why it is taking so long to heal."

"We nearly lost you twice, you know. It takes time. In another week you will walk. It will be March then. You will spend springtime in France, Anne-Marie, with Ophélie. This you will do." He kissed her softly on the cheek.

"Thank you, Moustafa. *Merci*."

* * *

It had started as the chicken pox. All the children got the chicken pox in February, Mother Griolet reassured Gabriella. It was the same every year.

But Gabriella did not feel peaceful. For five days Ophélie's fever had raged at 104. February was coming to a close. The other children were healthy and strong, but Ophélie was confined to Sister Rosaline's room, on the cot. Gabriella took turns with the Sisters sponging her off, holding a cool rag on her head, trying to relieve the itching. The child was covered with scabs, and some had become infected. The doctor ordered antibiotics to be taken orally. Still the fever hung on.

"Why doesn't Daddy come? If only he would come to see me, I know I would be well." At times Ophélie yelled out, delirious, "Daddy! Daddy! Mama! Come now!"

Gabriella did not know why David had not come back. His absence of a week had slipped into over two. She fought to control her anger. "Don't you care, David? Don't you care about your daughter? Please don't abandon her, too. Don't lock her out of your life."

Gabriella closed the door to Sister Rosaline's room and walked down the corridor toward the girls' dormitory. Coming to Ophélie's bed, she fell heavily to her knees and cried, "Oh, Lord. She must get better. The doctor says there is nothing to do but wait and try to get the fever down. He doesn't even know why the medicine isn't working. But You do, Lord. What does she need?"

Suddenly she saw her mother, exhausted and red-eyed beside the bedside of little Ericka. Gabriella could almost smell the stench of death and see the yellow tint of Ericka's skin.

"Oh, God, please. Daddy never made it back to see Ericka alive. Please, Holy God, may it not be so for David. Bring him home. Bring him home to meet his daughter. And let her live to know her dad."

Sister Isabelle startled Gabriella, touching her on the shoulder as she prayed. "Miss Madison. Excuse me, Miss Madison. But something has just arrived in the mail today for Ophélie."

Quickly Gabriella got off her knees and stood up, taking an envelope from Sister Isabelle. She recognized the handwriting. David's.

"Thank you, Sister Isabelle. Thank you. Perhaps this will be just what little Ophélie needs."

Sister Isabelle grinned, and looking heavenward, she whispered, "Yes, maybe it is just what the Doctor ordered."

As the nun left the dormitory, Gabriella opened the envelope, her fingers shaking as she struggled with the seal. For only a moment, she imagined what it would be like to get a letter from David. A letter filled with his words for her.

How many times had she reread the poem he had penned for her? How many times had she stared at the print of the poppies that hung on the wall of her room and wondered? And that last little phrase he had spoken to her, as he held her hand on the beach. *"Dear Gabby, don't you know that I have found her."* What did he mean? *Please, please tell me, David. I am afraid to guess. You love me. Was that it? You love me. You cannot say the words, but you want me to know.*

And yet his silent response after that brief awakening brought waves of doubt to her mind. At first they lapped gently at her feet like the lazy tide of the Mediterranean. But gradually the doubts rose and swelled in magnitude before her, crashing into every part of her thoughts and destroying her concentration.

Exams were four days away. Surely he would return for exams. Until then, she was left to play the childish game of "He loves me—he loves me not" as she silently picked off the petals of her memories of the past six months.

Somewhere even further back in her mind, she huddled against her mother's breast and found comfort in the words, "Somehow, Gabriella, you will learn that our God does not make mistakes."

Gabriella shook herself back to the present. This was Ophélie's letter. A letter the child desperately needed. It was simply a waste of time to imagine anything else.

Gabriella read over the page-long note, a soft expression on her face. It was the tender side of David Hoffmann revealed, and a tingle ran through her. It was too deep to describe...the joy of a distant man struggling to express his feelings for a little girl. Gabriella knew it had not been easy for David to write the note. His handwriting was clear and measured, as if he was writing slowly, instead of the hurried script he wrote on the blackboard in class. These words had mattered to him.

"You are a kind man after all, David Hoffmann. Underneath it all, you are a kind man."

She walked back to Sister Rosaline's room and peered through the doorway. Ophélie's eyes were closed. "Ophélie? Sweetheart? May I come back in? I have a surprise for you."

Ophélie turned her head weakly toward Gabriella. "*Oui.* Come in, Bribri."

Gabriella perched on the end of the cot. "A letter has just come for you in the mail." Ophélie's expression did not change. "It is a letter from your father, from David."

With extreme effort, Ophélie raised her head off the pillow. "Really?" she asked, a wisp of eagerness in her faint voice. "Really, Bribri? Daddy wrote to me?"

"Yes, dear. See? Shall I read it to you?"

"*Oui, oui.* Please, Bribri. Please read it." She let her head fall back on the pillow.

Gabriella read:

Dear little Ophélie,

My daughter. You must think your father doesn't care for you. But it is not true. I do care! It is only that you are not safe until I find this bad man. Then I will come to you. Then we will buy the biggest religieuse *that Pierre's* boulangerie *will sell us. You see, I know you like them. Gabriella has told me all about you. It will not be long until we are together.*

Soon I will be with you, and we can make up for all the years we have lost. For all the years we

never knew about each other. You will see, Ophélie.
I will be back soon. Until then, I know you are in
good hands with Gabriella.
   I love you, Ophélie
      Daddy

Gabriella watched as Ophélie placed her hand on
the cross around her neck. She fingered the jewelry,
smiling weakly. "You were right, Bribri. You were
right. Daddy does love me. He said so. I will get better
now. Your God will protect me, and I will be all well
when Daddy comes back. He said it will be soon."

* * *

Rosie Lecharde was not beautiful or rich, but she was
smart. She had grown up on the streets of Marseilles,
and she was not afraid of anyone. She laughed at the
slimy little men who pawed her body in the raunchy hotel
rooms in the slums of Marseilles. She always got an extra
tip before they left, she thought smugly, remembering
how easy it had been to take the bills from her last customer's wallet.

And Rosie knew that the handsome young Frenchman could bring her more money. He was hungry for
many things, this man. And she could give him everything he needed. Ten days with him had already provided her with more money than she had seen in a year.

She preferred the lanky gentleman with the black
eyes, the one who had poisoned the *concierge*. But he
was not as hungry. He was more careful. She laughed to
herself, wondering how to lure him along. Careful and
smart, he was. And maybe desperate?

The streets behind the hotel were silent. She pulled
her tattered shawl around her shoulders. At least she
would sleep well tonight. Jean-Claude was a madman,
but at least he kept her warm. She pranced into the

lobby, her high heels clicking on the crackled linoleum.

"Room thirty-two," she said, winking at the desk clerk.

"He is waiting for you," the young man mumbled.

Rosie pinched her cheeks and rubbed her hands up and down her arms. Jean-Claude would not like to see that she was cold. She spread a thick coat of bright pink lipstick across her lips, checking her work in the mirror of her compact. She slipped it back into her purse and knocked on the door of room thirty-two.

"Come in," Jean-Claude crooned from within.

He sat in the room's lone chair smoking a cigarette, a half dozen empty bottles of cheap red table wine at his feet.

"Well?" he growled at Rosie.

"I found your tall friend. I told him I might be able to work something out with you. He'll come. You say when, and he'll be there."

Jean-Claude nodded approvingly. He stood up and stumbled over to Rosie, a wild gleam in his eyes. "Very good, my little tramp."

He slapped her hard across the face. Rosie cried out as she fell across the bed. Jean-Claude leaned down over her, looking worried.

"Are you hurt, little Rosie?" His words were slurred. "I didn't mean to hurt you, little Rosie. *Au contraire, ma petite pute.* Of course not. We have every reason to celebrate tonight, *n'est-ce pas?*"

He pressed his body down on top of hers. Rosie closed her eyes, trying to ignore his putrid breath as he fumbled with the buttons on her blouse.

"Every reason to celebrate," he said again. Rosie Lecharde did not struggle. She let the drunken Frenchman paw while she thought of money and freedom. Rosie Lecharde was smart.

* * *

David didn't look any different to himself as he shaved in the bathroom of his one-star hotel room in the slums of Marseilles. The same long, thin face with deep-set black eyes and thick eyebrows stared back at him in the mirror, much as it had in the past. But something felt different, David mused, as the razor slid smoothly through the white foam on his face.

"Hope," he said suddenly and laughed. Yes, that was it. Today there was hope. Never before had he awaked with the excitement that he had felt during the past week. Ever since the night on the beach. Hope.

He shook his head. It almost sounded, well, fabricated, shallow. That would be his response to anyone who tried to explain what he was feeling. That had been his response to Gabriella. But he could not deny the deep sense of hope that he carried.

He grinned in the mirror. He wished he could tell Gabriella. He wished he could see the expression on her face when he said, "I've done it."

But he could not return to Montpellier and Castelnau now that he had the information from the prostitute. Not yet.

He rinsed his face and dabbed it with a towel. The sun was peeping in between the slats in the rotting wooden shutters. David pushed them open, welcoming the cold air on his freshly shaven face. He returned to his bed and spread out the briefcase on it. Mr. Vidal would be waiting for his exam. Tomorrow was the first of March. Exams were only four days away.

He had explained to Mr. Vidal where to find last year's exam, which lay in his desk at Mme. Pons' apartment, in case he did not have time to write another. That would be the simplest way.

He pictured Gabby waiting for him, coming hope-

"And these days, Yvette? What is going on inside her fiery little head?"

"She is losing hope, Monique. She picks at the food. Poor child. And not a thing I can say. Poor foolish child."

* * *

Hussein looked no more than ten years old, when in fact, he was fourteen. He wished adolescence would hurry up. He wished for the fuzz his friends had underneath their noses. He wished for a sudden growth spurt. He wished that the young Muslim girls would lift their eyebrows and flirt with him as they did with others.

But at least he had something to do in Algiers. At least Ali paid him a few coins for his eyes. At least, until now, no one had turned a gun on him and shot him in the middle of the day, in the middle of the street. He was still alive, and that, on this first day of March, 1962, was something to be thankful for indeed.

His mother wrung her hands together and worried when he left the apartment each day.

"Don't you understand, Hussein? They kill anyone. Anyone. A boy. What is a boy to the OAS? Especially if he is Muslim. Just another empty can to be knocked down in the street while everyone watches. Please, Hussein, be careful."

It was true. Yesterday he had walked by the *café* at noon. It was sunny and people were out, happy to think of spring coming. The people sat and smoked and sipped their cognacs and whiskey. Then a shot came from somewhere around the corner, out of sight. And Hussein had seen a young man groan and fall to the ground, slipping out of his chair like a stuffed dummy. Dead. Right there at the table in the *café*. A newspaper was placed on his face. An ambulance eventually hauled off his body. Later the firemen hosed off the bloodstains. And still the people ate and pretended that nothing had happened. Pretended that their lives were not falling apart.

Thirty or more murders a day. Innocent civilians. Muslim and *pied-noir*. Masked, silent fear is what Hussein could almost taste in the air. But he had work to do, and it helped him ignore the tight little knot in his stomach as he walked through the neighborhood of Bab el Oued, flashing a picture of a lovely *pied-noir* woman and a young Muslim with curly hair at shop owners along the street. He had seen the woman one time. Surely, surely, she would step out into the sun someday and lead him to her apartment. The rest would be up to Ali. And Hussein would have more change jingling in his pocket.

* * *

Ali smoked and spat, smoked and spat. The February negotiations for cease-fire had failed. But rumor from the top of the FLN was that they would not fail in March. The mail was no longer delivered in Algiers. Five postmen had been slaughtered by the OAS. Life was shutting down.

Ali thrust his stub on the floor and crushed it with his shoe. "So we will crush you, slimy French. You think we are afraid of your terrorism. Who after all did you learn it from?" He chuckled softly. "Who indeed but from us? Seven years of this war, and you are at last catching on. Power comes through fear. Go ahead and try to hold on to Algeria. It is useless."

The last news from the nutty Jean-Claude had sounded promising. Ali smirked to think of the illustrious Mr. Hoffmann poisoning the wrong man. And now a sleazy little prostitute was keeping Jean-Claude warm and well-informed. That was fine.

His last instructions to Jean-Claude had been very

clear. "Do not eliminate Mr. Hoffmann. Not until he has led you to the child and the woman. Then you are sure to have the right information. Then you may do whatever you please with the whole lot. And do it quickly."

Meanwhile, through the littered back alleys of Bab el Oued, hiding behind overflowing trash cans, stepping on slimy orange peels, listening in *cafés* where students congregated, was a small, smart Arab boy. Ali liked to imagine Hussein at work. "Someday, you will be like me. You will be powerful, Hussein. If you develop sharp eyes and a quick mind."

Ali Boudani was not a man to give up hope in his cause. Not for Algeria. Certainly not. Victory was sweet. It hung on the tip of his tongue. And he would not give up hope for revenge. *For revenge,* thought Ali Boudani, *revenge is much sweeter still.*

Chapter Thirty

Rosie Lecharde wore sunglasses for her meeting with David Hoffmann. There was no use in showing him the ugly bruise across her eye. She had a feeling he might somehow care, this strapping young man, and she did not want David Hoffmann to care. She only wanted him to talk. Five hundred francs Jean-Claude had given her, with five hundred more if she could lead him to Mr. Hoffmann.

There was a shaft of sunlight peeking through the billowing clouds. She clicked her heels and wiggled her hips as if it were any other day in the world. She wished that she could go with the smart American. Jean-Claude was beginning to frighten her. *Don't think of it, Rosie. Don't even think.*

She had turned onto the Canebière, the busy main street in Marseilles. He had said to meet him where the rue de Rome joined the Canebière. Imagine. It was where the whole world sat and watched. The black-skinned sailors and blond-haired cadets, the buxom, white-teethed women from Martinique, and the tourists in bold, hot colors waiting for the next trip to the Chateau d'If. Everyone was there. But that was what he said.

The whole world is here, thought Rosie, *and so no one will even bother to look*. That would suit Mr. Hoffmann just fine. As if on cue, he stepped out of the shadows of some side street before she reached the rue de Rome. He grabbed her arm and yanked her back into the hidden street while the rest of the world teemed by, jostling and hurrying to and from the great port.

Rosie gasped as he swung her around. "Is he with you? Where have you left him, little lady?" He shook her hard, and Rosie was surprised by the strength in the American's arms and the anger in his black eyes.

"I...I am alone," she stammered.

He shook her again and laughed. "You lie well!" She thought he would strike her, as Jean-Claude had done, but suddenly his grip relaxed. "So?"

Rosie straightened up and looked him in the eye, feeling stronger behind her sunglasses. "So!" she spat. "It won't do you any good to bully me, Mr. Hoffmann. I only do as I am told."

"And who is telling you, Rosie?" he snarled. His grip tightened again. The terrible strength in his hands!

She did not shrink at the pain. "Whoever pays most is who tells me what to do, Mr. Hoffmann. Whoever pays most, and right now, you are not the one."

She wriggled up close to him, pressing her curves against his hard chest. "I am very friendly with those who pay. Do not worry. All is fair."

The tall American pushed her away, a disgusted look on his face. "You are lying, Rosie dear. Lying." He pulled out a brown envelope, thick with French bills. "Will this do? Will this appease you, Rosie?"

Quickly she counted nine, ten, eleven, twelve hundred francs. She smiled up at him, her wide lips parting. "This is adequate. Yes, adequate."

"So?"

"So he stays at the Hotel Poseidon," she said. "A real trash heap near the Vieux Port. It is not hard to find. Not far from the apartment where he used to live . . . before the accident." She eyed him through her sunglasses and thought for one moment that he squirmed.

"Room thirty-two. I will have him there waiting at 11:30 tomorrow night." She smiled again, batting her lashes out of habit, though he could not see them under the glasses. "But in the meantime . . . since you have been so generous . . . I have a few hours to spare, if you wish?"

He laughed outright, deep and angry, so that Rosie backed away from him. "No thanks, Rosie. I haven't got time for such an offer. Not today." He softened his tone. "Get yourself a good meal, and stay away from Jean-Claude for a day." He reached over and pulled off her glasses, and touched the ugly bruise on her eye. "You realize that he can be most unpleasant."

Rosie stared at him, again batting her lashes, thick with black mascara. She took back her glasses, touching his fingers invitingly before she put the glasses back on. "I will be going then, Mr. Hoffmann. Tomorrow night. I will be ready, and the madman will not suspect a thing."

She wheeled around and left him standing in the shadows as she stepped back onto the Canebière, where the whole world watched and shrugged.

* * *

Moustafa's hand trembled as he held the pen above a blank piece of paper. The note had to be written, but he did not know how to begin.

"Sir," he wrote and erased it immediately. Sir could mean anyone. This note must be specific.

"Mr. Hoffmann," he scribbled. "I must stay in

Algeria. For now. While there is hope. But Anne-Marie cannot. She has been badly hurt. She is dying here. I cannot send her alone with the orphans. Come get her, Mr. Hoffmann."

He put the pen down. David Hoffmann was used to getting his notes, Moustafa reflected. He only hoped David Hoffmann still cared enough about his old lover to respond quickly. Immediately, he knew what to say, even if it broke Anne-Marie's confidence. *"You must never mention to him about Ophélie, Moustafa. He has no idea."*

"Anne-Marie has a daughter. Ophélie. I am sure she is there with you. If only Anne-Marie could see her child, I know she would get well. You must take her back. I cannot leave now. Not yet." He hesitated and then carefully penned the address of a store two streets away in Bab el Oued. "Come soon, to this address. Someone will know where we are. Come soon, please, if you wish for her to see her daughter again. It is the only hope." He signed the note, rolled it carefully into a cylinder, and taped it shut. Then he wrapped a pile of old newspapers around it.

Hope, thought Moustafa. *What a strange little word*. He hoped that David Hoffmann cared enough to save Anne-Marie. But he also hoped that Mr. Hoffmann did not care enough to take her away from him forever. It was a risk that Moustafa decided he must take. Otherwise there would be no Anne-Marie left to love at all.

* * *

The store had absolutely nothing to draw attention to it, huddled on the corner of rue Michel and rue Estanov in Bab el Oued.

Moustafa paused outside to touch a potato and finger several onions, peeling off their flaking skins.

The broad-shouldered, ruggedly handsome *pied-noir* who ran the market gave him a wide smile as he entered the store. "Yes? What do you have?" his eyes were low.

"Another bit of news to go, Marc," Moustafa said, lowering his voice. He nodded to the newspapers in his hands. "Is it possible? The mail has stopped."

Marc let out a soft chuckle. "The mail has stopped, *oui*. Do you blame them, when the postmen are murdered one by one? Never mind. The boats are still leaving port. Our boat. Your cargo is still going?"

Moustafa nodded. "Yes. And this. It is urgent. It must go directly, with the cargo."

"This is not a problem," Marc insisted as Moustafa handed him the bundle of old papers. He stuffed a fish inside the newspapers and smiled. "Do not worry so. It will leave tomorrow night, Moustafa. I am on time. Have I ever been late for you yet?"

Moustafa tossed a handful of change onto the counter and nodded his head. The young shopkeeper placed the papers in a small box behind him. Moustafa watched the street from the shop window. It seemed clear. He did not like to be out in the day. Someone could see. Someone had seen before. For that Anne-Marie lay so sickly, so pale and haunting. But today no one was about. Hanging in the shadows of the yellowed buildings, he slipped out onto the sidewalks stained with dogs' urine and birds' droppings, and even, Moustafa thought wryly, yes, even the blood of humans.

* * *

Hussein crouched in the alleyway between two larger streets of Bab el Oued. Here he had seen the woman disappear with the Arab the last time. That was almost six weeks ago, and he had not seen them since. But he hung out in the alleyway nonetheless, at least an hour a day. There was always the possibility.

He crept in the shadows toward rue Estanov. The sun was blinking down on the smelly road, but it had not peeped into the alley. Someone walked by. Hussein's heart skipped a beat as he peered around the corner. Yes! There, on the other side of the street, in the shadows. Walking briskly. A young Arab man with tightly curled black hair.

Hussein did not need to look at the photograph Ali had given him. He had memorized it by now. It was the same man.

Hussein stepped into the street cautiously, blinking in the sunlight. Not a sound, not a sound, he reprimanded himself, as his shoe scuffed on the pavement. The young man, walking so swiftly ahead, did not turn back. Hussein started to cross the street, to the side with the shadows, but he was afraid. Calmly he tiptoed, yes, tiptoed fifty feet behind the young man. Now he was turning, turning up another street and disappearing from view.

In a flash, Hussein was safely in the shadows of the sidewalk of rue Estanove. He ran hard to the corner and peered around, but there was no one.

Impossible. His eyes scanned the street. No movement, no sound. No one. He whispered an oath, then regretted it. The man must be nearby. He was perhaps the one spying now.

The adolescent kicked at the pavement and turned his head down. He milled in the streets for ten minutes. He walked up rue Cambriole. Nothing. Hussein decided that he could wait too. He could outwait the Arab. He slipped into another alleyway with a view of rue Cambriole. The sun blinked and flickered, but Hussein stood perfectly still.

* * *

It was a whim, and David was not used to acting on
whims. But he could not get the thought of her out of his
mind. *Today Gabriella will sit down in my class and
take the exam. She will wonder why I am not there,
and then she will read the first question.* He smiled at
the thought of it. He wanted to be there to see, to hold
her, to at last say, "Yes!" Only that one word, and then
he would race back to Marseilles. Then he would sneak
through the putrid back streets of the Vieux Port and to
the room of Jean-Claude Gachon. Then . . . he did not
think any further. "What then, God. What then?" He
started to curse, stopped himself and smiled. Gabriella.

It was barely dawn. Two hours on the train, two
hours in Castelnau, two hours back to Marseilles. It
was all the time in the world. He grabbed his jacket and
briefcase and locked the door behind him.

It was only a ten-minute walk to St. Charles station
and the first train left for Montpellier at 7:15.

* * *

When David Hoffmann stepped into the street in the
predawn gray, Rosie Lecharde laughed out loud. She
shivered, standing up and shaking the crumbs of a *crois-
sant* from her shawl. *I did right to be here early. I did
right,* she congratulated herself. The long hours yesterday, hiding and following him to his hotel, would pay off
today. Mr. Hoffmann was in a hurry to get somewhere.

The streets were vacant and calm, and even the
noises at the Old Port were dulled in the early morn.
The Canebière lay long and wide, like a silent river, its
cafés closed, its banks and shops locked behind a jail of
bars. David Hoffmann darted across the street. The
stream of cars was thin but fast. Rosie followed.

Five minutes later the train station, massive and

glimmering as the first streaks of sun touched its dome, came into view, perched high on a hill. A long row of steps led up to the station. Rosie hurriedly climbed them, pausing only as David Hoffmann entered the doors and walked toward a *guichet*. He waited impatiently behind a wild-looking student at the only open window. The train station had long since awaked, and the lobby was brimming with well-dressed businessmen, waiting behind their copies of *Le Monde*. A train screeched on the *quai*.

Rosie watched, breathless, as he purchased a ticket and moved quickly toward *Quai* number three. *Where is he going?* She glanced at the large tumbling billboard as it rattled forth, changing trains and destinations. Avignon 6:43; Aix-en-Provence 7:05; Nîmes 7:15. Nîmes! Then on to Montpellier. Yes, that must be it! He lived in Montpellier. Jean-Claude had said it so. Montpellier.

Rosie raced to the *guichet* and panted, "My friend, the tall dark-haired man. He was just here? Did he buy one or two tickets for Nîmes?"

The woman, without looking up, replied, "One."

"Ah, dear! Then give me another. To Montpellier."

"Fifty-two francs, please. Train leaves at *quai* number three at 7:15."

The thrill of a race enchanted Rosie as she ran down the steps and halted abruptly before walking onto the *quai*. David Hoffmann was just disappearing into the third car. She waited five long minutes before she stepped quickly onto the *quai* and walked in the opposite direction, letting herself into the next to last car. When the train groaned and bellowed and screeched its way forward at 7:15, Rosie Lecharde was sure the American did not suspect a thing.

* * *

Gabriella climbed the steps to the second floor of the parsonage with a fleeting hope that David would be there to smile back at her, to hand out the exams—anything, just so that she at least knew he was still alive. But when she walked into his classroom, Mr. Vidal sat in the chair, pudgy and morose behind the desk.

Hope fell in her breast even as she glared solemnly at the room. She took her seat, her mind still racing. She could not decide if she was angry or worried or disappointed. All of the above. Multiple choice, and she felt all three. Was he lying dead in some alley in Marseilles? News. To have some news.

The bells in the tower chimed nine o'clock as Stephanie slipped into the desk beside her. She rolled her eyes at Gabriella and mouthed the words, "Did you study?"

Gabriella shook her fiery locks. "Not much." It was true. She had tried to study, but all she could hear with every page she turned was *Don't you know, dear Gabby? Don't you know?* John Donne preached it, Shakespeare scribbled it across the page in iambic pentameter. Monet splashed it onto a blank canvas, and suddenly it was vivid with color. *"Don't you know?"*

But she did not know.

"Excuse me, class," Mr. Vidal stood up, clearing his throat. His face was pure apology. "Mr. Hoffmann has asked me to give out the exam, reminding you that you have two hours to complete it. He urges you to use your time wisely. There are twenty identifications of quotes, then one poem to analyze. Afterward I will be showing slides for identification. And there are two essay questions. He wants you to reserve the last forty-five minutes for these. You may begin as soon as you get the exam."

He handed Gabriella five pages stapled neatly in the top left corner. Five pages written in David's bold script. Her heart raced. His hand! But he was not here.

Gabriella picked up her pen and wrote her name across the top of the first page. She read the directions for the first exercise. "Identify the quote by work and author."

She glanced at the first quotation. "Sole judge of truth, in endless error hurled; the glory, jest and riddle of the world!" She almost said it out loud. *Why, it's Alexander Pope's "Essay on Man"!* She heard herself pronounce the words, months and lifetimes ago. It had been the first time she had looked into David Hoffmann's eyes. "I didn't know you then," she whispered to herself as she wrote in the information.

The next quote was Donne. *Meditation XVII.* Familiar. The one from which came "for whom the bell tolls" and "no man is an island." But David had chosen the last sentence of the meditation to quote. *How odd,* she thought.

"...But this bell that tells me of his affliction digs out and applies that gold to me, if by this consideration of another's danger I take my own into contemplation and so secure myself by making my recourse to my God, who is our only security."

Strange that you would cite that, David, she thought. And she remembered that second day of class when he had challenged her to speak on Donne, and she had met him square on. *She was the one who had quoted the end of the meditation!* Now Gabriella felt her cheeks burning, as if David were yelling to the whole class, "Remember, I prithee, Miss Madison. Miss Gabriella Madison."

But none of the other girls seemed to notice in the least. There were a few groans and one flat-out protest of "This is impossible" from Stephanie. The class giggled. But no one said what Gabriella felt. "He wrote this exam for you."

There was a quote from Milton's *Paradise Lost*. But such a quote! "Henceforth I learn that to obey is best/and love with fear the only God, to walk/as in his presence ever to observe/his providence and on him sole depend."

No one else was seeing anything at all. They were simply racking their pretty little brains to think of something, anything to put down. *How could they not see,* she wondered. But Gabriella saw. It was a statement, some wild statement of faith that she read in quote after quote. It could not be coincidence that she could take the first nine quotes and read them almost as a thesis and argument for faith.

He was clever, David! And she found herself laughing. Then she stared at the tenth quote, and her heart skipped. "The Lord shall preserve me from all evil: He shall preserve my soul. The Lord shall preserve my going out and my coming in from this time forth, and for evermore."

Psalm 121! But he had misquoted it, replacing the thee and thy with the first person pronoun. *Why in the world,* she wondered. Then it came to her, drifting up as if out of a dream. *You will wait a very long time if you hope to hear me claim it as my own prayer....* He was mocking her during their first visit to the Place de la Comedie. And yet here in the exam, David was doing just what he said he would never do. He had changed the pronouns so she would know, without a doubt, it was his prayer.

David Hoffmann believed. Somewhere between the *café* of two weeks ago and the classroom of this morning, somewhere, David had believed. She felt a tear sting her eye and swept it away.

The next quote came from an early poem of Shakespeare: "Oh Mistress Mine where are you roaming?/Oh stay and hear your true love's coming,/that can sing both high and low./Trip no further, pretty sweeting,/journey's end in lover's meeting."

She gasped and blushed, her head hot with sweat. Now what was he saying? Now what? Journey's end in lover's meeting? *No,* she scolded herself. *You are reading too much into it. It is just a poem we studied in class. It is not a declaration of David's love for you.*

She focused on the next quote, trying to forget the last one. It was Coleridge's love poem to Sara, who would later become his wife. Gabriella laughed out loud to read the lines that David had chosen: "But thy more serious eye of a mild reproof/Darts, O beloved Woman! nor such thoughts/Dim and unhallowed dost thou not reject,/And biddest me walk humbly with my God./Meek daughter in the family of Christ!"

She shook her head in amazement, recalling how David had teased her with this poem, claiming that she would wish him to write such a thing to her. And now, in a sense, he had.

And then a quote by D.H. Lawrence. "The pain of loving you/Is almost more than I can bear." So simple, so direct. He had said it. She felt dizzy and confused. Surely he was not saying this to *her.* Were the other girls wondering if it was perhaps intended for them? But none of them looked embarrassed or anything other than frustrated with a difficult exam.

He told her with Wordsworth and Keats and T.S. Eliot, and then switching to prose and French, he said it again with Hugo and Flaubert. *I love you.*

She tried not to cry as she scribbled out a response to the poem she was analyzing. But it was Matthew Arnold's "Dover Beach," and "Dover Beach" always made her cry. He knew. David knew it.

Finally Mr. Vidal's slow, placid voice broke her thoughts as he announced the time for identification of slides. He turned off the lights, and Gabriella felt safe, despite her wet face. She was still writing about "Dover Beach" when the first slide came onto the screen. As she glanced up at the slide, she felt a piercing, stabbing pain of deep, pure joy. The poets would understand it. For there across the screen was Monet's *Poppies Near Argenteuil*. There was not a shadow of doubt now.

* * *

Gabriella wrote furiously, freely, happily. She barely noticed the other girls standing, turning in their exams and leaving the classroom. *How could they be done already?* she mused. There was so much more to say, to write. By the time the two hours were up, Gabriella was the only woman left in the room. Mr. Vidal cleared his throat apologetically.

"Miss Madison, I'm afraid time is up."

She flashed him a smile. "Yes, sorry. I'm almost done." She buried her head in her paper again. Five minutes later, she came out of her dreams as she heard, "Miss Madison."

It took Gabriella a moment to react. Only a moment to realize that this time, it had not been Mr. Vidal's voice at all. She gasped and looked up. David Hoffmann stood in the doorway of the classroom with the strangest expression on his face.

He moved toward her quickly, whispering, "Miss Madison. It is time."

Head swirling, Gabriella only saw that the room was empty, empty except for the very real presence of David. She dropped her pen and gaped at him, getting awkwardly to her feet. "David," she mumbled.

He was beside her, picking her up in his strong arms, swinging her around, squeezing her tightly, tightly as he laughed, "Gabby, my dear Gabby!"

And then he put her down, holding her against his chest. She heard his heart, thumping, thumping. He gently reached down, cradling her chin in his hand and turning her face up to meet his eyes.

"Gabby. Gabby, do you understand now? Do you know?"

She nodded, feeling her eyes fill with tears. She could not speak.

He leaned toward her, and the simple gesture seemed to take moments or hours, before at last his lips reached hers. They touched hers softly, and she shivered with pleasure.

He lifted his head and smiled. Then he reached down once more, pulling her against him and kissing her again. Softly, convincingly. She folded her arms around his neck. Kissing, laughing. It was something, a blossoming, a deep, luxurious feeling that she had waited, it seemed, all of her life to know.

Later Gabriella could not remember how long they had stood and held each other and kissed in the middle of the classroom on the second floor of the parsonage at St. Joseph's. She could only remember her desperate desire to keep David there forever and not step out into the hallway where life must resume.

But presently David took her hand and entwined his long fingers with hers. He placed his other hand on top of hers and patted it. "This is how we should be, Gabby. After all, we are right for each other."

It was a statement, and she knew he meant it. Yet she read something else in his eyes. Before he pronounced the first word, she read it. *But*...That terrible little word with the strength to change a destiny.

And then he spoke, confirming her fears. "But Gabby. I can't stay. Not right now. I came on a whim. Because I had to...I had to see you." He stared down at her with enchantment in his eyes, and Gabriella felt her legs wobble.

"But I must leave soon. I have found him, Jea ..."

Immediately Gabriella put a finger to his lips. "No. Don't say that name. Don't bring it here, to destroy this. You and me."

"Of course," whispered David, kissing her again. He held her face in his hands and peered at her. "Dear, dear, beautiful Gabby. Can it be?"

Gabriella smiled. "I think it can." She rested her head on his chest for a moment, but her mind was suddenly racing, full of questions.

"David?"

"Mmm?"

"How did it happen? How did you come to believe?"

He sighed deeply. "You, my dear, could explain it much better than I. It is quite a mystery, and yet it is suddenly so clear. I read, I read a lot. As you said. The Gospels. The epistles. The psalms. And I argued a lot with your God." He was playing with Gabriella's hair, watching the red strands, thick and curly between his fingers.

"In the end it came to the cross. And forgiveness." He chuckled, as he touched the gold chain around Gabriella's neck. "How very ironic, *n'est-ce pas?* It had been here all along to remind me." His voice caught, and he spoke, barely audible. "Of Someone who suffered a whole lot more than I had. The very hardest thing: forgiveness."

They stood at the doorway of the classroom, David's head resting on Gabriella's, locked in a sweet embrace. She did not move, but asked again, "And the rest? How did you know the *other* part?"

He chuckled again, softly. "The *other* part, as you say, Gabby, was wonderfully easy. It was just admitting it that was hard." He held her away from him and looked her full in the face. His eyes were deep, shining, sincere. "I have always known that I love you, Gabby. For the longest time, I have known."

When he leaned down to kiss her again, she met him eagerly, and once more, time ran by unnoticed.

* * *

At last David turned the key to lock the door of the classroom. "You have my exam?" Gabriella giggled.

"Yes, of course," he said, patting his briefcase.

"It was a bit embarrassing, the exam. I was sure the other girls must have understood, too. But apparently not."

David laughed. "The other ladies could not decipher a code if it were spelled out for them. But you needn't have worried. Except for the slides, their exam was completely different from yours." He was grinning.

"Why...how in the world?"

"Mr. Vidal used my exam from last year. I sent him a different one for you."

"Well, aren't you clever?" Gabriella mocked. "And now Mr. Vidal knows all about our love, I suppose."

David let his head fall back and roared with laughter. "My dear Gabby, Mr. Vidal knows a lot more than that. You would be surprised at just what he knows!"

Gabriella wrinkled her nose in feigned disgust, but did not question him further.

They stood poised for a long minute at the top of the stairs. Then David led her down the steps until they stood outside the parsonage. "And Ophélie? May I see her, quickly?"

Gabriella hesitated. "David...she's been very sick."
"Sick?"

"Yes, but she is much better now. Your letter was

just what she needed. But if you are only going to pop in and out today, I think that would be unwise. She might become even more upset. You understand?"

"Yes . . . I suppose." He looked lost in thought. "Listen, Gabby. Listen carefully. This is what I want you to do. I want you to meet me at the Pont-du-Gard with Ophélie."

He talked swiftly, before Gabriella had a chance to protest. "Today is the sixth. Will she be strong enough to come on the twelfth? That's almost a week."

"I . . . I don't know," Gabriella stammered.

"No, don't worry. By the twelfth all will be finished in Marseilles. It will give me time to check back in Aix and Aigues-Mortes. Take the train to Nîmes. Then the bus from Nîmes to the Pont-du-Gard. Bring a picnic, and we'll go to the beach. It will be perfect. No one will be there at this time of year."

Gabriella was not convinced. "Can't you just come back here, David?"

"No, not yet. That would be unwise. But I must see her. I must. The Pont-du-Gard on the twelfth." He was whispering excitedly now. "Take the 10:40 train to Nîmes. The bus leaves there at 11:35. I'll meet you at the bus stop."

"But, David. You are making me afraid." She was suddenly clutching his coat, as he turned to go. "Please. Please stay here with me."

He smiled and caught her up in his arms, pulling her behind the corner of the church out of view. He kissed her forcefully, passionately.

"If there is any problem, I will let you know. Don't worry, dear. I will get word to you if I need to. Only pray for me, sweet Gabby. Do not worry. Only pray." He gave her one last kiss and was off.

Gabriella touched her lips, which still stung with the

thrill of the touch of passion, of love. She walked back through the parsonage, dazed. Little explosions of joy were dancing through what must be her heart, and she found herself breathing deeply, deeply to regain her breath. David Hoffmann loved God. And David Hoffmann loved her. It was some strange miracle, blowing in from above to warm her in every part of her being. Gabriella smiled and, turning her eyes upward, she whispered, "Thank You. Thank You and please, keep him safe."

* * *

Rosie Lecharde stepped out of the small side door to the chapel. Such a convenient place to hide! So much news to hear! She was in no hurry to catch the train back to Marseilles. She laughed aloud as she watched David Hoffmann rushing along the cobblestones, out of Castelnau.

No, he could hurry home to meet Jean-Claude if he so desired. He would find a surprise or two waiting there, no doubt. But Rosie Lecharde laughed gleefully. She was going to take the bus in town to the Comedie. Her wallet was full, and she could sip *verveine* all day at a little *café*. Perhaps later in the afternoon she could find some interesting work in Montpellier. No rush. She would take the midnight train to Marseilles. She had all the time in the world to get back to Jean-Claude and tell him who would be visiting the Pont-du-Gard on March the twelfth.

Chapter Thirty-One

Eleven-thirty at night in the slums of Marseilles was a lively time. Taunting shouts and fistfights and gunshots. Action. Rosie Lecharde had been right. It was not hard to find the Hotel Poseidon. It sat in the heart of the city, next to the Vieux Port, not far away from Jean-Claude's previous apartment. *What a stupid mistake.* David winced with the thought.

There was absolutely nothing in him that wanted to go into room thirty-two and face a lunatic. Rosie's information had come too easily, he reasoned. Twelve hundred francs too easy. Or perhaps he was simply scared. Suddenly it mattered a great deal that he was alive. Someone cared. Two people cared about him very much. Not for what he could get them. Not as a leader of a cause. They cared about him. They needed him. And, he admitted to himself, he needed them. Ophélie and Gabby. Eighteen years had elapsed since he last let himself need someone. Since Mother.

He shook himself back to the present. It irritated him that he hesitated so. This was no time to feel distracted. No time to listen to his heart.

But there was something else, too. He could not explain the feeling, but it was there. Like a red siren turning on a police car far away. A persistent warning. He could not quite hear it, but he knew.

He did not go inside the hotel, but hung in the shadows beside the overturned garbage bin with its rotting fruit and broken bottles. Above him the windows from the rooms on the north side of the hotel looked out into the filthy alleyway. Thirty minutes passed. Music blared from a nearby bar that welcomed its clients with a bright flashing neon sign. A cat rubbed against David's leg, causing him to jump. The cat leaped onto the garbage bin and disappeared. But no one came out of the hotel.

He could not afford to lose track of Jean-Claude again. In two days he was due in Aix, and soon afterward, the Pont-du-Gard. He slouched down and leaned against the garbage can, ignoring the reeking smells. One o'clock came and went. David remembered seeing the hand approaching two before he drifted off.

* * *

He awoke with a start. He heard a muffled cry coming from a window above him. It was still dark outside, but the bar across the street was closed and its neon sign turned off. He could not read his watch. Another sharp cry. Probably nothing. David crept to the front of the hotel. The door was not locked. The reception desk was empty and the lounge black. A clock hung on the wall and he read the time at four-thirty, by the dim light shining in the corridor.

David stepped into the hall. The first room was number twelve on the right. Then number twenty-two. He crept softly past to the next door. Thirty-two. He stopped and listened by the door.

A woman moaned softly. "I don't know why he didn't show. I promise. Please . . . it is good information. Please . . ."

There was a cry and a shot. "Oh, my God, no," cursed David, instinctively pushing against the door. It was locked. He rammed it with his shoulder. It did not budge. He kicked it hard with his foot, and it swung inward.

Rosie Lecharde lay on the floor with a bullet through her head. He felt for her pulse. There was none. The window was open. David ran to it and looked down the back alley. No one. He jumped through the window and landed amidst the rubbish on the ground below, cautiously searching up and down the alley. Soon he heard the sound of a siren. He ran through the alleyway and out onto a deserted thoroughfare. Jean-Claude was nowhere in sight.

And if there is one thing I can be sure of, David thought grimly, *he won't be coming back to Hotel Poseidon and room 32.*

He walked slowly toward his hotel. Rosie was dead because he did not show. The bullet would have surely been his. And Jean-Claude was roaming the streets again, like a raving mad hyena.

"Oh, God, I don't know what to do," he whispered, climbing the winding wooden staircase that groaned loudly with each step. He collapsed on the ripped orange bedspread in his room and slept.

* * *

The orphans were singing grace before the evening meal. The faint melody caught Gabriella's attention as she wandered down the hall of the basement in the parsonage. Drifting as if in a trance out into the courtyard, she found herself humming along softly with the children. *"Pour ce repas, pour toute joie, nous te louons, Seigneur."*

Oh, yes. As the blessing said, she had so much to be thankful for. So many reasons to praise Him. She sat in Mother Griolet's wicker chair and studied the sky. It was not yet dark, and streaks of crimson and periwinkle blue sat for one last moment poised behind the bell tower of the church. The air was almost balmy in sharp contrast with the cold of last week. *"Rain is coming. A big storm,"* Sister Isabelle had told her earlier, pointing to the sky. *"You can smell it in the air."*

As for Gabriella, she smelled spring. Renewal. New birth. Hope. No more storms. She knew she was grinning foolishly as she thought of David. He was a romantic after all. She closed her eyes and remembered every quote in the exam. Declared love. Her heart began to race, just as it had when she first understood what he was saying to her. She relived the scene with pure pleasure. His voice behind her. She, startled, standing awkwardly to greet him. And then in his arms. And the kiss...

It was like something in the movies. Or a Broadway play. But so much better. So much better because it was happening, it *had happened* to her. No doubt, no day-dream. Three days ago he had kissed her and told her that he loved her. And in only three more days, they would be together again. The short week in between was like a brief intermission, a moment to step outside and collect her thoughts and be sure of her lines before rushing back in for the final act. She was glad to have this time to think and remember.

It had only been seven months since she left Dakar. It could have been seven years. She laughed. Maybe seven lifetimes, and she, like a cat, was entitled to two more. Nothing had been as she expected. Absolutely nothing. Except...

Yes, she thought. *You, Lord, have been the same*

yesterday, today, and tomorrow. Your love has not failed me. You have not left me alone, even when I was sure there was nothing left to hope for. She heard the children's laughter from inside the dining hall, but she saw only Ericka before her, spinning around, delighted with her sister's attention.

Ericka had known what joy was. The thought suddenly brought to Grabriella an overwhelming peace. In her short life, Ericka had known joy. Conceived by hate and brought forth in sorrow, she had still known joy.

It was a comfort. Mother Griolet was right. Life was not fair. But there was hope. And what had David said? Forgiveness? He had said the word! She laughed out loud. He had found forgiveness from above, and he had also forgiven.

She was suddenly on her knees in front of the wicker chair, the cool, damp earth soaking through her hose. She touched the cross around her neck. "Lord," she whispered. "Lord Jesus. Forgive me for hating. For hating because I could not make sense of so many things." She paused, thinking of Ericka and then Ophélie. "I forgive them. The one who did it to Mother. The ones who did not come. Daddy for being away. I forgive Mother for never telling me about the rape, and Mother Griolet . . ." She was sobbing now, but as she cried, she felt it physically. Someone was pulling a weight, like a huge, overstuffed backpack, off of her.

She rose from the ground, light-headed, free. It was a step. Another step in the process that Mother Griolet had described. Grieving. There would be others, she knew. But Gabriella did not want to think ahead tonight. Not anymore. She just wanted to be. "To abide," she said and pictured the vineyards bright with color as she and David had driven by them in the late fall.

She heard a slight rustling behind her and turned

416

around. Mother Griolet was approaching her, silhouetted against the light coming from the dining hall.

"My dear child," she began softly. "I didn't know you were still here. Are you not eating at Mme. Leclerc's?"

"Oh, yes, yes I am. I was just enjoying this evening . . . and thinking of some things you said to me."

"I said?" Mother Griolet laughed, surprised.

"Yes. Thinking of forgiveness and . . . and what comes after." Gently, Gabriella locked arms with Mother Griolet and they began to stroll around the courtyard.

Gabriella talked excitedly about what was bubbling inside her as the old nun listened thoughtfully. Then before she could stop herself, Gabriella told her about David.

"He believes, Mother Griolet. David believes."

The nun pursed her lips. "He believes? What do you mean?"

"He believes in God. In Christ. In forgiveness."

Mother Griolet gave a high-pitched chortle. "*Ce n'est pas possible! Dieu merci.*" She clasped her hands together. "This Mr. Hoffmann is full of surprises lately. Full of wonderful surprises. He is quite a different character from what I suspected."

Then she frowned suddenly. "And how do you know this? It is recent news? Is Mr. Hoffmann back?"

Gabriella blushed. "Not exactly. Well, he came back, briefly." She nibbled her fingernail as Mother Griolet raised her eyebrows.

"Briefly?"

"Yes, very briefly. He came back to tell me . . . to tell me about . . . believing. And . . ." she stopped herself, flustered.

"He came back to make sure you and Ophélie were well. Something like that?" Mother Griolet volunteered with a gleam in her eye.

"Yes, something like that." They walked for a few minutes in silence. Gabriella cleared her throat. She began again, "Mother Griolet?"

"*Oui, ma chére?*"

"You said you were in love once."

"Yes, that is true."

"Do you mind . . . I mean, excuse me for asking. But—"

"Gabriella, child. Do not be afraid to love. If this is right for you, you will know it. I have thought perhaps wrongly of Mr. Hoffmann for many reasons. I think you know what I mean?"

"Yes, he has told you then?"

"He has told me about his part with the orphans. Quite amazing. I have seen the tender side of this man. But Gabriella, you must decide. I cannot say what is sure. It is between you and him . . . and your God." She pressed her fingers softly around Gabriella's arm.

"I know. I have been so confused, but you are right," the young woman grinned. "I think I know."

Mother Griolet nodded. "I believe you know quite a lot. You have been helping Mr. Hoffmann, and now he wants you and Ophélie to stay put."

"Yes, and what about Mr. Vidal? David said he knows something too."

Mother Griolet smiled. "Dear Jean-Louis." She looked at Gabriella. "Mr. Vidal has been a friend of mine for a very long time. You see, it was his brother whom I loved."

"Really?"

"Yes. And Jean-Louis was a great comfort to me after his death. He gave me something else to do. Jean-Louis was the one involved in the Resistance. He started the whole thing with the Jewish orphans. I could never have done it without him."

Gabriella gave a low whistle. "Well, I would have never thought it of *him*." She reddened. "I mean ... he is so ..."

"Yes," the nun chuckled. "He is definitely inconspicuous. So you see, we have been friends for a long time. And now he helps us again. Mr. Hoffmann and he are very careful."

Gabriella was still thinking about Mother Griolet's lost lover. "I am sorry about Mr. Vidal's brother. I am very sorry for you."

The nun's green eyes clouded for a moment. She brushed a wisp of silver hair back under her black habit. "God has filled up my life in so many ways. I live with sadness, at times. But not regret. There has been too much else. Our God, remember, is in the business of bringing good out of bad. Never forget it."

"I won't," Gabriella assured her. "I have learned it myself." The wind picked up as the bells chimed eight o'clock. "Oh, my. I am late for dinner."

"Hurry on with you, then. *Ma fille.* Go on."

Gabriella hugged the old nun quickly and left the courtyard running.

* * *

The scabs were gone and the fever too. Ophélie looked at her face in the mirror. A few shallow pock marks lined her forehead. She wrinkled her brow.

"I look ugly. Papa will think I am so ugly."

Gabriella came to her side and brushed back Ophélie's thick, touseled hair with her fingers. "Nonsense! You are beautiful. You are only a little pale from being inside for so long. But you are well now, and the doctor has said you can sit in the courtyard for a while. In two days you will be feeling stronger. Then we will see your papa. And he will be so pleased."

Ophélie turned her face towards Gabriella. "Do you think he will really be glad to see me?"

Gabriella shook her head, grinning. "No, not glad." She winked at Ophélie. "He will be absolutely delighted."

Ophélie hugged Gabriella. "What shall I bring him? What would Papa like? I must have something to give him."

Gabriella did not reply immediately, and Ophélie began reciting possible gifts. "A piece of candy, maybe? Does he like candy? Or a picture? Yes, I could draw him a picture."

"A picture is a wonderful idea. Color it and sign your name, and he will be the proudest papa in the world."

Ophélie was laughing now. "Come with me, Bribri. Come with me to the classroom. I'll get my colored pencils from my desk, and paper too. Can we go right now? Hurry."

Ophélie dashed out of the dormitory and danced into the courtyard. She held her arms high above her head, twirling around in circles. Soon she felt dizzy and collapsed into Gabriella's arms, giggling.

"Ophélie, sweetheart! Calm down. You must not overdo it on your first day up."

"But, Bribri. You don't understand," the child panted. "I am just so, so happy. I am well, and I am going to see my papa very soon. I have to dance. I just can't help it." She broke away from the young woman and skipped around in the brown grass. She looked at the menacing gray clouds above and shivered in the cool air, enjoying the tingling feeling that engulfed her as she planned the picture she would draw. "Ponies running. Lots of bright colored ponies galloping in a field. Free and happy. Running away from the dark clouds to the sun."

Satisfied with her idea, she waited by the door to the basement of the parsonage for Gabriella to let her in.

* * *

David sipped a coffee on the Cours Mirabeau in Aix-en-Provence. A storm was brewing, and the first drop of rain landed neatly on the scrap of paper in his hand. His face was emotionless as he stared at the latest messages that Gilbert's bread had revealed. There was the usual one about the children. This time nine children would be arriving in Marseilles on the 18th. Nine children. David felt thankful to know that someone had gotten the list, Ophélie's list, that he had sent to Algiers. The remaining *harki* and *pied-noir* children threatened by Ali would be rescued. But the other note that lay before him brought different news.

"Not now," he said to himself, shaking his head. "Oh Anne-Marie, not now." He chuckled softly. "You have always picked the strangest times, my dear." He fingered an old photo that lay before him on the round *café* table. Then he put it inside his jacket before the rain could stain the lovely woman's face that smiled out at him. "You know I have never been able to turn you down, beautiful woman."

He picked up the note from Moustafa and read it again. Then he sighed heavily, letting the coffee cup rattle in the saucer as he set it down. He was relieved that Anne-Marie was alive. This was good news. For Ophélie. For the operation. For him. Yes, of course, he was glad. "After all, I came here for you, my dear." He was thinking out loud again, as he left a handful of change on the table and rose to leave the *café*.

"It is only such an inconvenient time to go to Algiers," he reasoned and then laughed. "Just a tad bit inconvenient with the war and cease-fire imminent. But, of course, I will come. Of course I will bring you back to see Ophélie. Your daughter . . . our daughter." He scribbled a note, drawing the Huguenot cross in the left corner of the paper and then tucked it in his pocket.

The rain fell freely now. He walked halfway across the Cours and stood at the base of the smiling statue of Roi René, holding his muscat grapes. "Gabriella," he mumbled.

Then angrily, David crossed the broad avenue and walked behind the Cours, into the small side streets of Aix. He kicked at the curb, cursing to himself.

Suddenly the voice of Gabriella floated up to him, removed as if from ages past. *"I cannot prove that prayers are answered or that God is above if you do not want to believe it . . . but that is not my business. Ask Him to prove Himself to you. I dare you to ask Him."*

"And what am I supposed to pray, anyway?" he begged to the cobblestones, cynically. "You figure this one out, God of Gabriella. Figure it out, if you will."

He stopped outside a child's clothing store. A bright pink stuffed pony was in the window front. Impulsively he stepped inside the store and purchased it. The saleswoman wrapped it in bright pink paper and put a pink bow on the package. He paid for the gift and left the store. A smile was barely visible on his lips.

"You see, God," he continued his argument. "I'm in love with this woman. You know her well. And I have discovered I am the father of Ophélie. A precious child. And now her mother needs me to rescue her from the jaws of a wild Arab. And so I will go. I will go to the mother of my child and perhaps I will find that . . . that this is what you want. A reunion. A family.

"But then what will happen to Gabby, God? Excuse me for saying it, but it does not seem quite fair." He laughed at himself, talking to the wind and the rain. "It is, if you remember, this woman that I love." He laughed again, a cynical, hard laugh. "Well, there You have it, God. A rather unorthodox prayer as I stroll through the back streets of Aix. I hope it will do. I certainly hope it will do."

* * *

The French would say it was raining ropes, Gabriella reflected as she watched the torrential downpour. Cold, damp, and gray, the winds gusted outside her window. She snuggled into her comforter, bringing her knees to her chest and wrapping her arms around them. She relished the sound of the rain pelting against the window and the olive tree twisting and blowing in the storm. A flash flood, the radio in Mme. Leclerc's kitchen announced as they had crowded around it after lunch.

Gabriella could not help smiling. She felt warm and safe. Monet's print of the field of poppies hung on the wall in front of her. She stared at it and then closed her eyes. *David was bending toward her in an eternal second, and then she was tasting the sweetness of his lips against hers.* She blushed with the thought. "He loves me," she whispered. She remembered the exam. Line after poetic line with the same message: *I love you.*

"And he loves You, too, Father. Somehow. This is what makes all the rest possible."

Tomorrow, surely the skies would clear. Then she would bundle up Ophélie, gather up the picnic basket of goodies, and take the bus, the bus to the train station. The train to Nîmes. The bus to the Pont-du-Gard.

She had never seen the imposing Roman aqueduct, but she imagined it rising out of the trees and David Hoffmann standing in the middle of the bridge, waving slowly, like a Roman warrior, beckoning to his family to join him in another adventure.

"I will be ready," Gabriella said. "We will be there for you." The rain continued to shower the town with conviction. But Gabriella had her mind on other things.

Chapter Thirty-Two

It was with great difficulty that David Hoffmann put the note from Moustafa Dramchini out of his mind the next day as he drove to the Pont-du-Gard to meet Gabriella and Ophélie. A frown crossed his face when he thought of Jean-Claude Gachon, a lunatic murderer, still on the loose. But David had made sure that no one was following him. This would be a private reunion, away from the crazy business of the Algerian war.

A bright pink package sat beside him in the front seat of his *deux chevaux*. He felt a sudden, nervous twinge at the thought of seeing Ophélie. His daughter. *What if she doesn't like me?* He reminded himself that, although he had developed quite a reputation with young women, he had no reputation at all with little girls.

Then he remembered with great relief that Gabby would be there. Gabby would know what to do if things got awkward. *Gabby!* He relived their embrace after the exam. He was very pleased with himself. She had been surprised. That was the way it was supposed to be. A revelation of love, a surprise appearance by the lover, and a long, passionate kiss . . .

Today he would walk across the Pont-du-Gard, hand-in-hand with "his women." He laughed approvingly. Then he frowned. Only for today.

Afterward, somehow, he would tell them about Anne-Marie. Ophélie would let him go again, to find her mother. But Gabby. He shook his head. She would let him go, but . . .

All at once he was following signs to the Pont-du-Gard and pulling his car into the parking lot located two kilometers away. There were no other cars. He stepped out into the nippy March air. The sky was still gray from yesterday's flash floods.

His hands were suddenly sweaty at the thought of a bus approaching. He held the pink package under one arm and stuffed his hands in his pockets. He wished he smoked. It would give him something to do with his hands.

No bus came.

Five minutes passed, but to David it seemed more like five days. He rehearsed what he would do. Ophélie would be holding Gabriella's hand. Yes, of course. Hiding behind her, shyly. That was only to be expected. Children were usually shy around adults they did not know.

Then what would he do? Ah, yes. He would walk forward and shake the child's hand and then offer her the package. Maybe a kiss on the forehead.

No, no, no! It was all wrong. That is what his father had done after every trip when they were apart. Always a bright package and shake of the hand and a quick kiss on the forehead. So cold and mechanical.

A bus loomed ahead of him, coming from nowhere. He stepped back to let it pass and park. Yes, they were there! A little girl's nose was flattened against the window. Her eyes were bright, and she was smiling. *My, but you look like your mother,* he thought.

The bus stopped, and he walked briskly toward it. Ophélie scrambled off and broke into a run. David opened up his arms, dropping the package, to receive her embrace. He bent down and she was in his arms, laughing and hugging him tightly around the neck.

"Papa! Oh, Papa!" she cried.

It surprised him how quickly the tears came. How naturally he picked her up and kissed her. "Ophélie," he whispered, for his voice was choked with emotion. "Little Ophélie. You are such a beautiful girl. My daughter."

He held her at arms' length and stared as she stared back until they both burst into laughter. "Oh," he said quickly, as if coming out of a dream. "I brought you something." He reached behind him and retrieved the fallen package.

He handed it to her and said, "Ophélie, I didn't know what to get you. I mean, it is such a gift, such a wonderful gift to have you, and I ..."

Ophélie laughed, a carefree, childish laugh. "Oh, Papa. I did not know what to bring you either. I only hoped that you would be happy to see me."

He squeezed her again. "Oh, I am, my child. I am."

He looked up over Ophélie's shoulder and saw Gabriella for the first time, standing with a picnic hamper in her hands. Her red hair was swept back from her face in a French braid. Her blue eyes twinkled. He wiped his eyes and motioned for her to join them. She walked up behind Ophélie, smiling broadly. David pulled her close and kissed her gently.

Ophélie ripped open the bright paper. "A pony!" she exclaimed. "A pretty pink pony." She turned to David and threw her arms around his neck again. "Oh thank you, Papa! Thank you. How did you know?"

Without waiting for his reply, Ophélie pulled a

sealed envelope out from the picnic hamper and handed it to David. He held it softly, almost reverently.
"Papa" was written across the front in Ophélie's childish script. She had drawn large red hearts all around
the word. He felt the tears coming again.

Carefully David unsealed the envelope and took out
a piece of paper. Unfolding it, he smiled. Six brightly
colored ponies were running across a green field. The
sky above was dark gray, but in the right-hand corner,
a big yellow sun spilled out its rays. The ponies ran
toward it, a pink pony in the lead. In between the
ponies and the gray strip of sky, Ophélie had written *I
love you, Papa. Ophélie.*

"It is an extraordinary picture, Ophélie! Thank
you!" He caught her in his arms again. "Please explain
it to me."

Eagerly, she pointed to the drawing. "You see, the
ponies are all of us. I am the pink one. I am leading us
to Jesus. He is in the sky, in the sun. And the red pony
is Gabriella, because she has such long, pretty red hair.
And then after her comes Mother Griolet. She is the
gray pony, there see? And you are the black one. You
are catching up with us and running to the sun. And the
beautiful white pony with the black mane and tail, that
is Mama. She is far behind, but she is coming. She is
coming with the brown pony. That is Moustafa. They
are coming too. I am sure." Ophélie looked into David's
eyes. "How did you know? How did you know to get me
the pink pony?"

David glanced at Gabriella, who was blinking back
tears. He wiped his eyes again. Before he would have
said "coincidence." But now he took his child's soft,
smooth hands, enfolding them in his own. "Inspiration,"
he whispered, and Ophélie seemed to understand.

David replaced the drawing in its envelope, sliding

it back into the picnic hamper. Arm-in-arm the three walked leisurely toward the Pont-du-Gard.

* * *

As they rounded the corner, an enormous three-tiered aqueduct spread across the river before them. David sighed. "There it is." He admired again the elegant posture of the ancient bridge, which gracefully arched its way across the tempestuous waters.

"Magnificent," Gabriella said.

"Yes, isn't it?" David had lifted Ophélie onto his shoulders for a better view. "It's the tallest of all known Roman bridge aqueducts, you know. One hundred and sixty feet high. The three tiers are quite unusual. The bottom two have extremely wide arches—fifty to eighty feet. Surprising even for the Romans. And the upper tier has thirty-five smaller arches, you see. The top is covered with huge flagstones that are twelve feet wide. Although it is forbidden, many a tourist searching for a thrill has walked on the top."

"No thanks," said Gabby. "I had my thrill in Raymond's territory in les Baux."

"*Oh, non,* Papa! I would never want to walk up there! Never." Ophélie squeezed David's neck tightly, holding the stuffed pink pony behind him.

"I understand, *ma chérie.* Don't worry. It is, however, quite an impressive view."

Gabriella gasped. "Do you mean to say you've been up there? You've walked across on a stone slab one hundred and sixty feet up, with only the sky to catch you if you fell?"

David grinned. "Surely you aren't surprised, my Gabby. And not just the sky. The Gardon River welcomes you below. It is usually very peaceful and not too deep. But you see how high the waters are now, and violent

428

from the flash flood of yesterday. They call it a *gardon-nade*. It has calmed a bit now, but March is always a testy month. Never fear, though. The Pont-du-Gard has withstood many a flood. Quite ingenious, the way it was built. Some of those stones weigh over six tons. Imagine!"

"It is beautiful, Papa. And so big! One must feel so very tiny to walk on it."

"Ah, you will see how you feel, little jewel. We shall walk across the bottom tier. There is no danger there. And then you can climb to the top and walk through the actual aqueduct, where the water ran."

Both Gabriella and Ophélie looked at him suspiciously.

"Again, perfectly safe—you are completely enclosed," David assured them. He smiled and continued, "I am only afraid that we can't picnic down on the beach, as I'd hoped. With the floods, it has been totally covered. But there are many other spots in the woods. Come along."

It was well after one o'clock when they reached the base of the huge bridge. The overcast skies cleared, showing patches of blue interspersed between the frothy gray clouds.

"We may see the sun after all, girls," called David. He stepped onto the bottom tier of the bridge, motioning for Gabriella and Ophélie to follow. It was twenty feet wide, and on one side a road had been built. They walked across in silence, Ophélie clutching David's hand and Gabriella holding the other.

"We are about sixty feet up here. Amazing that this thing has withstood 2,000 years of use." He ran his fingers over the stones of one of the arches that rose up to form part of the second tier. "The stones are made of coarse limestone from the quarries near here. Imagine the feat of moving these rocks."

Gabriella walked near the edge of the bridge. "It is still dangerous, David. Anyone could just plunge right over, even here. There are no guardrails."

David laughed and pulled her back toward him, hugging her and kissing her softly on the forehead. "You and your vivid imagination, Gabby. Don't look down. Look out. Out at the green snake of a river, now so angry and loud, filled to her banks.

"Ask the silent bridge what she has seen, what secrets she knows from all the centuries of watching. Can't you just imagine the Romans walking across the waters on this masterpiece!"

Ophélie interrupted her father. *"Papa, j'ai faim.* Please, can we eat?"

There was not another soul about. "Is there any reason we shouldn't spread our blanket out here?" David inquired.

Gabriella shrugged. "Sounds okay to me." She spread Mme. Leclerc's plaid woolen afghan beside an arch and pulled out sandwiches and cheeses and yogurts and salads from the basket.

"A real feast, and I'm sure Mme. Pons helped plan it," David said, eying the wine bottle tucked into the straw basket. "What have you told those dear women anyway, Gabby?"

Gabriella giggled. "Nothing. I only said Ophélie and I were going to picnic, and we might meet someone else. Can I help it if they are always planning and scheming?"

Ophélie leaned back against her father, cuddling the stuffed pony, and sighed. "I am so happy to be here with you, Papa. And with you, Bribri. I can't ever remember being quite so happy in my whole life."

"I know just what you mean," replied Gabriella, beaming. She took David's hand. "It is wonderful indeed."

David stretched out his long legs and pulled Ophélie onto his lap. He began to tickle her, and her childish laughter echoed out above the noise of the busy river. She squirmed, but he held her tight. "You can't get away from me, girl. Not up here, you can't."

Gabriella watched them, the child and the father. Ophélie resembled the picture she had seen of Anne-Marie, it was true, but there was something of David there too. The way she tilted her head, the dark eyes that sparkled and flashed. Gabriella could not be sure. But there was something.

Looking at the two, snuggled happily by the enormous arch, Gabriella felt a rush of emotion. It was so simple after all. Just the three of them. Together. Finally. As if all the centuries were standing still, frozen in a gentle smile on the Pont-du-Gard at this precise moment. A father and child on an ancient bridge. And a woman with wild curly red hair who loves them both.

*   *   *

It was going to be simple, gloated Jean-Claude, crouched in the shrubs off the shore of the Gardon River. The trio had paused on the aqueduct to eat lunch. Good for Rosie, the little wench! She had been right. Today was a day to celebrate. To spray bullets onto the bridge and watch the fools scurry.

He aimed his rifle at the lowest tier, where the little girl sat in David Hoffmann's lap. He looked carefully through the telescopic sight until he had David's chest squarely in focus. His finger played with the trigger as he sang to himself in a wild frenzy. *Ali says get the names, the names, the names. Ali says get the little list of names before you kill, kill, kill.* He sang it as a child's nursery rhyme and then answered with the same tune. *But Jean-Claude cannot wait for the names, the names, the names. Jean-Claude cannot wait for the list of names before he kills, kills, kills.*

He fought with himself to control the rising hysteria, the mad, sickly taste that was overtaking him. *Go to the bridge and find them. They cannot get away. You have the rifle. Take them back to the little nuthouse with the old lying nun.*

He laughed and said it out loud. "Old lying nun." *Get the names, and then . . . Bang! Bang! Bang! Be done with them all. And take the pictures to prove it to Ali. Yes, yes. That was a good plan.*

"But Ali, kind sir. Brave soldier!" He spoke in mock adoration. "It is easier here. To take them away now. Easier. And the lying nun, well, she must know too. Or why does she lie?"

The finger trembled on the trigger for another instant. *Jean-Claude cannot wait to get the names*, he hummed to himself. Then he pressed the trigger and braced himself as it kicked back with force against his shoulder.

* * *

Gabriella was never sure afterward what had been the order of events in that wild moment. David had suggested that Gabriella ask a blessing for the food, which had pleased and surprised her. Then Ophélie had leaned forward out of David's lap to hold Gabriella's hand. Likewise, David had reached out to hold her other hand, and at the same instant a shot fired far off. At first Gabriella had looked toward the woods to see. It was a second's reflex. But when she glanced back around, Ophélie's eyes were wide, and a sickly expression covered her face. Instantly they both screamed. David collapsed by the arch, his hand clutching his shoulder. Fresh blood seeped through his fingers.

"David!" Gabriella screeched. "David!"

He groaned, "Get down. Get down. Flat on your stomach."

Another shot rang out, and a bullet scratched the stone arch and ricocheted off as they fell on their stomachs.

David was rasping for breath. "Gabby, crawl back across when I tell you. Crawl, and you'll find a path leading up to the top tier, over in the brush. Follow it. Climb the steps and hide there inside the aqueduct. Don't look at me like that. Do it! Ophélie, stay with Gabby. When I count to three." He took a breath. "One, two, three."

David stood to his knees and forced himself forward in the opposite direction. Gabriella saw him out of the corner of her eye as she pulled Ophélie along beside her.

"Dear God, oh dear God. Father. You will guard our going out—" She heard another shot and another, but she did not dare look back. The end of the bridge was forty yards away. They ran, crouching until they reached the relative safety of the thick underbrush. Gabriella pulled Ophélie up beside her, climbing the embankment, and scrambling over the rocks and loose stones. Ophélie dropped her stuffed pony and cried out as it bounced down the slope.

"Come on, sweetie. We'll get it later. We must hurry."

She saw Ophélie's strength fading, her face ashen with fear. It took only a few moments to reach the ancient stone steps leading to the aqueduct. She pushed Ophélie in front of her as they climbed the narrow circular stair that suddenly plunged them into darkness. Quietly they huddled in the narrow conduit. It was barely two feet wide and six feet high.

Only then did Ophélie speak. "Bribri," she sobbed.

"Papa's shot. He's bleeding. Will he die?"

Gabriella shook her head. "No, no of course not. He will be fine. We must wait here. He will come get us. He will tell us what to do."

Her voice sounded surprisingly calm, she noticed. But pure panic was rising steadily. David was shot. It was a nasty hit. And somewhere, somehow a madman with a rifle was waiting to shoot again.

Dear Lord, she prayed silently, *You alone can see. Oh, God. Protect us. Protect all three of us. And give me wisdom to know what to do.*

She sat with Ophélie for a moment. "Do you feel strong enough to walk, Ophélie?"

The child nodded.

"Then come. We will follow the aqueduct through the tunnel." They inched their way forward in the dark. Every thirty feet or so, an opening in the slats above let in a shaft of light. It was all the hope they had.

* * *

David was beginning to feel lightheaded as the blood poured from the wound in his shoulder. It could have been worse, he reasoned. It could have been his heart. He had reached the other side of the bridge and sat panting. Four bullets had missed. That was good. It had to be Jean-Claude. Jean-Claude, the sniper, was baiting him, he thought ruefully. Even now he was doubtless heading for the bridge to finish his work.

Head spinning, David fought to keep conscious. *Gabby and Ophélie.* When Jean-Claude did not find them on the bottom tier, he would surely search inside the old aqueduct. They would be easy prey.

Forcing himself through the thick foliage, he climbed ever up toward the second tier. There was no path on this side to help him, and he slid as he climbed.

434

Another fifty feet and he would be up at the end of the third tier that spilled over onto land by a wide stone-walled walkway. Back across the walkway he knew he could enter the aqueduct.

He paused, listening for the sound of twigs breaking. Nothing. *But he is not far behind,* David knew. He fell onto the stone walkway and lay there panting. Water. If only he could get to the water, he could stop the bleeding. Inside the dark aqueduct, he ducked his head to enter for it sloped down, allowing less than six feet of height. He heard the sound of footsteps inside the hollow chamber. He stopped.

God, he thought. *God of Gabriella. I do not know what to pray. Life. Please life. For us.* His heart jumped erratically. More footsteps. Far away, he heard Ophélie gasp.

"Someone is there," she whispered.

"It is Papa," David said with difficulty. "I am here. Wait. I will come to you."

The steps were running now. They met near the center of the aqueduct, and Gabriella caught him in her arms. "David! David, are you all right?"

He winced with pain, ignoring her question. "Gabby. He will come, but I do not know which way. When he comes, take Ophélie the opposite way. He will follow me." He nodded upward, where a hole was between the slabs.

Gabriella gasped. "On top? You can't. You are hurt!"

"Gabby, dear," and he managed to smile at her as the light flickered across her face. "Gabby. This is very serious. Go. Go to the buses. Get the police. You will be safe with them." He felt his head swimming.

"David!" Gabby's voice startled him back to consciousness.

He turned around. Jean-Claude Gachon stood outside the aqueduct forty feet away, laughing, his wild eyes gleaming.

"Run now," David whispered and watched as the woman and child turned and fled down the narrow dark corridor they had just come up.

The rifle was slung over Jean-Claude's shoulder. *A madman*, thought David. *I am dealing with a madman.* A thought resounded in his mind, as if heaven itself were screaming down to him. *Then make him mad.*

With a groan, he hoisted himself up through the hole in the slate, using his good arm for support. He called back to Jean-Claude. "You are not afraid of heights, I hope."

The young man laughed, a piercing, evil laugh. "Of course not." He, too, heaved himself onto the roof from outside the aqueduct, and suddenly the two men stood facing one another on the twelve-foot ledge on the top of the Pont-du-Gard.

Do not look down, David told himself, as Jean-Claude eased his muscular frame toward him. *Keep him moving, so he does not have time to aim.*

"You are hurt!" Jean-Claude howled, delight in his voice. "Blood! I can see it."

The height was dizzying. David crouched. Jean-Claude inched forward, a wild gleam in his eyes. The river, running high, tumbled past so far, far below. *Jump!* David thought. From his position in the center of the bridge, the river was directly below. Surely the water was high enough to break the fall. But he saw, with a sick feeling, that the lower tier of the bridge jutted out beyond the top one. One would have to jump out far to miss hitting it.

Jean-Claude inched closer and drew his rifle. He stood twenty feet away from David. "You are a pitiful sitting duck. A helpless hare."

Helpless hare! The words stung David's mind. Not

436

another helpless rabbit that would be blown to bits by an enemy rifle. Adrenelin pumped through his body. He moved toward Jean-Claude. The Frenchman stepped backward, laughing. "You have been smart, Jean-Claude," David whispered. "It was Rosie who told you, *n'est-ce pas?*"

"Yes, of course. You fool! Rosie, who followed you to your stinking orphanage. And now you will lie in your own blood even as she does."

David made a quick movement again, from his crouched position, like a lion waiting to pounce. Jean-Claude stepped back again, laughing. "I am not afraid of a maimed cat, you filth. I will blast you in a breath."

One more move backward, David thought, and Jean-Claude would back into a hole in the slate and lose his balance. He moved forward again and yelled, "You are nothing, Jean-Claude. Nothing! Just a simple pawn for Ali. He will forget you in the blink of an eye."

Enraged, Jean-Claude lifted the rifle. In that instant, David jumped toward him. The Frenchman stepped back into the hole in the slate, teetering precariously as he fought to regain his balance. He dropped the rifle as he grabbed the slab of stone. The rifle floated, momentarily suspended in time, until it hit the bridge below with a hollow thud.

For a brief second, Jean-Claude seemed to lose his concentration as he followed the path of the rifle with his eyes. He fell to his knees, grasping the two-foot ledge to the left of the opening in the slate. David lunged at him, and the two men struggled on the narrow ledge.

Grabbing out to David, Jean-Claude caught his shirt. But the movement caused him to lose his balance. "Fool," he screeched as he slipped. Terror replaced the mad gleam in his eyes. "Help me!"

The man clutched hopelessly at David's shirt as he

slipped, and David felt his weight pulling him down and over the edge. David grabbed onto the ledge with one arm, and a searing pain shot through his other shoulder.

"Help me!" Jean-Claude commanded again, but already his body was hanging precariously off the top of the bridge, and his grip on David's shirt was slipping. David struggled to pull his weight away from the edge.

"I will take you with me," Jean-Claude howled.

With a last grunt he yanked David in his clutch before his fingers lost their grip and he fell, tumbling far, far down. David saw it in a flash, out of the corner of his eye. The man's body struck the first tier of the bridge a hundred feet below. It was not a pretty sight.

David fought to pull himself back up on the ledge. It was no use. Now his legs hung out into the free air. He clung to the ledge of the slate with his good arm, but he was slipping. Two thoughts flashed through his mind. *I have too much to live for, God. And then, Kick out with your feet. Kick off the stones.* With all the strength of a man who had suddenly been given another chance to live, David Hoffmann forced his feet against the hard rock and shoved himself off the bridge with such force that he propelled his body out, far out. It seemed an agony of hours as he fell, struggling against the sky to straighten his torso, before he hit the river and sank beneath its feisty waters.

Chapter Thirty-Three

Victory was in the air, and Ali could taste it. Soon Algeria would be free. Huddled in dark rooms in Evian, France, the FLN met with de Gaulle's men at yet another attempt to resolve the fate of Algeria. The talks had dragged on now for a week. But Ali was confident of the outcome.

It was all he had hoped for, all his father had promised. For a brief moment, the sweet taste of a free state made him forget his own personal vendetta. But only briefly. He fingered a page from the *Midi Libre*, Southern France's daily paper. It had arrived by boat that morning along with the news of the Evian peace talks.

The caption read "Desperate Dive to Death." Ali took a long draw on his cigarette and then ground the butt in an overflowing ashtray. Slowly his eyes followed the print on the page: "Yesterday afternoon, March 12, authorities found the body of Jean-Claude Gachon, 31, on the first tier of the massive 2,000-year-old Pont-du-Gard. Witnesses Gabriella Madison and Ophélie Duchemin said Gachon had terrorized them as they picnicked on the ancient aqueduct with David Hoffmann. Gachon and Hoffmann apparently climbed to the top of the aqueduct, where Gachon lost his balance and fell 100 feet below to his death on the first tier.

"Miraculously, Hoffmann, who also fell from the top, landed in the Gardon River 160 feet below. The police attribute his survival to the fact that the waters were swollen far over the banks after Sunday's flash flood.

"Hoffmann, who managed to swim to shore 200 yards further down the river despite a bullet wound in his left shoulder, was later rescued by city police and taken to the hospital in Anduze.

"Authorities say that Gachon was wanted in Marseilles for the death of a prostitute, Rosaline Lecharde. He is suspected of involvement in the FLN. The reason for his attempt on the lives of the three picnickers is not yet clear."

Ali wadded the newspaper and threw it onto the floor, cursing loudly. "Fool. Idiot! Bumbling idiot!" His face clouded as he remembered learning of Rachid's death. Two of his most promising men, dead. "You were crazy, Jean-Claude." Now Ali had no information whatsoever, except that his quarries were alive. *You have been most lucky, Mr. Hoffmann. Most fortunate indeed.* He spat on the floor.

"And what news do you have for me?" he questioned Hussein, who hovered beside him, a scowl on his young face.

The boy straightened and spoke in his deepest voice. "No one has come from that street, sir, absolutely no one. I have watched and watched. But sometime they will. They have to. Give me another chance."

"Then go!"

The boy shuffled out of the grungy room.

Ali glanced at the newspaper clippings on the wall.

His little mission was not complete. His father not yet avenged. "But the war will be over soon, Father. Then we will have cause to celebrate. Then we will crush the *pied-noirs* and their filthy *harkis* like the butt of a cigarette. And then, those we seek will be swallowed up as well. I am sure, Father. It will all work out in the end."

* * *

Moustafa's hands trembled ever so slightly as he held the letter. He kissed it softly with his lips. He was coming. David Hoffmann was coming to take Anne-Marie back to France, back to Ophélie. It was not what he would have preferred, but at least she would live.

His face clouded. If the *Capitaine* could sail with the *harki* children on the 17th, David Hoffmann would come back with the boat from France. It would be in less than a week now. If the *Capitaine* could sail. The OAS was supervising closely the departure of *pieds-noirs* on airlines and steamships. But a small swift sail-boat, perhaps, could still slip out.

"To save your own children and those loyal to you," he whispered to some imaginary member of the OAS, "do not stop it."

Anne-Marie was sitting up in bed, sheets rumpled about her, as Moustafa entered the room. "You look better this afternoon," he said, bending down to kiss her forehead. "And I have news. News that will make you smile."

He unfolded the slip of paper and handed it to Anne-Marie. The Huguenot cross was drawn in the corner. She read it aloud. "Received message about *harki* children and AM. Will return on *Capitaine* on 19th to get AM. Ophélie is quite well. Hugo."

Moustafa saw tears form in Anne-Marie's eyes.

"Thank God, she is well. He says she is well." She

let her head fall back on the pillow.

"It will be only a few days, *ma chère*. So soon now. So eat. Be strong." He met her eyes. "I have more work to do to get ready for the children. I will be back later."

* * *

Ophélie's pink stuffed pony smelled of perfume. Mother Griolet had scrubbed off the mud from when it had fallen out of her arms at the Pont-du-Gard, and now it looked like new.

"A bath for the pony," Mother Griolet had chuckled.

They had all laughed that night. Nervous, worried laughter. Papa was alive. She closed her eyes and saw him falling down, down until he was swallowed up in the angry river. She remembered Gabriella screaming. From their perch it had been impossible to tell who had fallen first. Only later, when the police had found Jean-Claude's body on the bridge, had they dared to hope.

Three days had come and gone. Today she could see Papa. She stood outside the heavy, white-washed hospital door and cuddled her pony in her arms. Then she lifted a small hand and knocked lightly on the door.

"*Entrez,*" a low voice answered.

Ophélie peeped her head inside. Her father lay engulfed in white sheets. His face was covered with bruises, black and yellow, making his eyes look even deeper set. His left shoulder was bandaged awkwardly. She shrank back in fear.

"Come on in, sweetie. Don't be afraid. Papa is going to be fine." His voice sounded weak and sad.

She inched near his bed. "I brought you the picture of the ponies, Papa. I thought it would make you happy to have it on your wall."

He placed his good hand on her shoulder and smiled. "That will certainly help me feel better. Much better.

Pull up a chair, Ophélie."

She dragged a metal-framed chair up to the bed. Still holding the pony, she handed the drawing to him.

"You know everything is okay now, don't you?" he asked softly.

She stared at him, nodding hesitantly.

David continued. "The bad man is gone. He will not come again, dear. We are all safe." She watched him intently. He did not seem convinced.

"What is the matter then, Papa? Why do your eyes look so sad?"

David grinned, and she saw the faintest little dimple appear in his cheek. "Why are you smiling now, Papa?"

"I am smiling because you see. You understand too much. And I am sad because I will have to leave again soon. But don't worry. Not for long."

Ophélie turned her head down. She did not want to read anything else in his eyes. He was right. She understood too much. But he was whispering now.

"I am going to get Mama. Your mama. Moustafa has written to tell me where she is."

Ophélie's eyes grew round. "Mama? You will find her for me?"

"Yes, Ophélie. I am going to get her. To make sure she comes back to us safely. So you must be brave for a little while longer. And you must help Gabby. It will be very hard for her to let me go."

Ophélie frowned. "Because she loves you."

"Yes."

"And you love her, too. Right, Papa?" She peeked at him timidly, her lips curling up.

"Yes. Yes, I love her."

"And Mama? Did you ever love her?"

He cleared his throat, and she thought he looked sad again. "Yes, Ophélie. I loved your mother. A long time ago. And then I had to go away. I wrote her, but she did not write back. She did not want me to know about you."

"Why not?" She stuck her lip out into a pout.

"Because I think she knew I would come back to Algeria if I knew about you. And she knew that I was supposed to be doing other things."

Ophélie wrinkled her brow. "I don't understand." She spoke defensively, suddenly irritated at adults who always complicated things.

"I'm sure it seems ridiculous to you, dear. You must simply believe me when I say your mother was doing what she thought was right. She loves you so much." He squeezed her hand. "And I love you too."

That was good, she thought. That was what she longed to hear him say. But she still had one more question. "Will you ever love Mama again?"

His eyes looked very sad now, and she was sorry she had asked. He pulled her head onto his chest and held her tight. She could tell he was deeply troubled. When he spoke, his voice was muffled. "I don't know, Ophélie. I just don't know."

Ophélie thought hard. What could she say to make Papa feel better? Suddenly she knew. She took the cross out from under her blouse, touching it to his finger. "Mama gave it to me. She said it was protection. And Bribri says it too. If we believe in God's Son, He will protect us. You'll see, Papa. It will be okay."

David fingered the cross gently as it hung around his daughter's neck. "It is beautiful, Ophélie. You are right. God will protect me." He let go of the cross, and Ophélie tucked it back under her blouse. She squirmed up and placed her lips softly on his unshaven face. "I love you too, Papa."

* * *

444

The room was austere and white. David's coarse black hair contrasted starkly with the starched white pillow. A small clay pot filled with primroses sat in the window, their petals bright red with a splash of yellow in the middle. The clouds outside the window billowed, puffed and white. A beam of sun shone through the glass and blinded Gabriella for a moment. She watched David, arm bandaged, face bruised. He did not look strong.

"The doctor said it's more than a miracle you survived," she said.

David chuckled, "Thanks to the flash flood. I can't say I'd like to repeat the act." He studied her face. "Maybe it was a miracle. Your God ... *our* God saw fit to answer my prayer. I have a lot to live for now." He reached over, patting her arm. "Don't look so worried. I'm okay. We're all okay."

A knock came on the door, and Mother Griolet poked her head inside.

"Come in, come in," David invited. "Have a seat." He motioned to the free chair.

"Praise God, you are recovering," the nun exclaimed, and placed her hand on his. She kissed him on each cheek, laughing. "It is not my custom to greet young teachers in such a manner, but this is a special occasion. Dear Mr. Hoffmann." She shook her head from side to side, patting his hand.

"Please call me David."

"Well ... *bien sûr*. David. How glad we are to see you in one piece. How much longer will they keep you here?"

"Just till tomorrow. I've got to get out. There is still much to be done."

"Yes, we're receiving nine children on the seventeenth. Nine! Imagine. What shall we do?" She looked heavenward.

"How many more will come after that, David? Do you

have any idea?" Gabriella asked.

"I think this is the last of those at risk from Ali," he stated. "But when the war ends ..." He shrugged.

"And just who is Ali?" Gabriella blurted. "Could you please explain it to me from the beginning?"

David turned toward Gabriella and Mother Griolet. "You have both heard bits and pieces of the story. It is not a pretty one, but I will tell you. Are you ready to hear?"

Gabriella whispered a faint, "Yes."

Mother Griolet nodded.

"In 1936, the French government in Algeria voted against granting equal rights for Algerian war veterans. Lieutenant Mohemmed Boudani was enraged. He had fought well in the First World War.

"His son, Ali Boudani, was likewise furious with the ruling. He was twenty-one and a soldier loyal to his father, who had always been his hero. They were both in Hitler's war. The anger in their soul against this racism mounted as they fought beside the privileged *pied-noirs*, but they remained loyal to France. And Ali's father promised his son that someday Algerians would know equality.

"But in late 1945, Lieutenant Boudani was captured, tortured, and killed in a raid. When the details of his death became clear, Ali was delirious with rage. His father, the leader of this platoon, was the only man to be captured. And that platoon belonged to the battalion under Anne-Marie's father, Captain Maxime Duchemin."

"But how do you know all this?" Gabriella interrupted. "Do you know Ali?"

"I met him in 1953, when I was with Anne-Marie. But it was Anne-Marie who found this out later. Let me explain.

"Ali moved into hiding in the '50s, working with the

Friends of the Manifesto and Liberty. He became a leader in the FLN, determined to create a free Algeria. Still, the image of his dead father tortured him. The hatred grew. He was a genius at guerrilla warfare and very respected in the FLN.

"Then a small incident brought things to a head. In the spring of 1958, he saw Captain Duchemin at a political rally for the North African Army. Anne-Marie says it was then that he decided to kill her father. He was possessed by some twisted desire to avenge his father's death."

"But Anne-Marie's father didn't kill him!" Gabriella protested. "He wasn't even in the platoon, right? He was much higher up. Wasn't it the German army? The SS?"

David nodded. "Yes, but Ali could not get past the image of a sacrificial lamb. He was convinced Captain Duchemin sent his father in to be killed and that the members of his platoon stood by and did not try to rescue him. Of course, this is not true, but ..." he shrugged.

"He is a brilliant and methodical man. He decided that blood-thirsty revenge was the only way to appease his conscience. So the captain of the Thirteenth Battalion of the North African Army, Maxime Duchemin, was slaughtered, along with his wife, in May of '58.

"But it wasn't enough. The plan grew. In late 1958 Ali organized a group of six men to bring him all the information to do with his father's platoon in the war. Documents of that sort were hard to come by, if not impossible. He targeted Anne-Marie, the captain's only child. She was twenty-one at the time, and known to be politically involved in the war, for the *pied-noirs.*"

Suddenly David's voice grew quiet. He closed his eyes and remembered Anne-Marie's hysterical voice across the miles, crackling through the phone wires. He did not want to dwell on that part.

He spoke with a sterile, removed tone, like a doctor reporting a cancer. "In December of 1958, Ali and some of these men abducted and raped Anne-Marie."

Gabriella gave a soft moan and shook her head. For a moment David's eyes met hers before she looked down.

"That poor woman," Mother Griolet clucked. "That poor child."

"He is a sick man, Ali. After the rape, Ali sent his dashing French counterpart to rescue her—Jean-Claude Gachon. For several months Anne-Marie felt safe with him. Jean-Claude convinced her that Ali wanted to harm other families of the men in one of her father's platoons in World War II. So, at his suggestion, she began looking for the names of these families and gave him several.

"But Anne-Marie is not dumb. Gradually, she wondered what was happening. In October of 1959 she learned that two *harki* families had been murdered ruthlessly, and she grew scared."

David rubbed his eyes and lifted a glass of water to his lips. He winced with pain at the movement. "That is when she wrote me at Princeton. I hadn't heard from her at all, though I'd written her letter after letter, back in '54 and '55. I finally gave up, hoping her silence was merely indifference and not an omen of the war." He set the glass down.

"Now I know she was afraid to answer. Afraid to tell me about Ophélie.

"Anyway, in October of 1959 she wrote and then called me and begged me to help these children who were going to be systematically murdered by Ali. She knew, well, she hoped I would be able to come to France ... because of my past." He let the phrase dangle, and Mother Griolet shot him a sympathetic look.

"Mother Griolet, you explain that part, please." David rested his head back on the pillow and closed his eyes. From far off, he heard Mother Griolet's kind, soft voice continue his story.

"...and he arrived at the orphanage in 1944, alone. It took several months before his father located him. The man was sick with worry."

David heard the words and opened his eyes. "My father? Sick with worry?" He laughed.

"David! Of course he was. I will never forget it. He stood before me and wept, and kept repeating, 'It was all my fault. All my fault.' Your father was heartbroken, David. Crushed."

"He was not! He couldn't stand the sight of me. He left us in Paris with American passports. And then as Mama was hiding the Jews, her family, and so many others, they came. The SS came, and my father was nowhere to be found." David's voice had changed. He spoke loudly, angrily.

"David, please. Please stay calm," Gabriella touched his hand, then held it tightly.

He sighed. "That is another story altogether. It is something I will resolve in time, if God wills." A weak smile crossed his lips. But still he was lost in the words, *He wept*. David had never once seen his father shed a tear.

Mother Griolet was talking softly. "You see, Gabriella, when David sent in his references and wanted this job immediately, well, I was delighted. I needed a teacher, and it was obvious he was quite brilliant, even though he had barely finished college and had never taught before. I never made the connection with the time he spent here as a child. Not until recently." She chuckled. "Perhaps if I had, I would not have disliked you so much." She winked at David.

"It was better for a while that you disliked me, that you didn't suspect a thing. So you see, Gabby, when I came here in June of 1960, I had done my homework. I knew there were those in the region who had been involved in the Resistance during World War II. It did not take me long to make the right connections."

Gabriella smiled. "Mr. Vidal, right?"

David nodded. "Yes. He helped me set up this little project with Mother Griolet and several *boulangers* in the region. We called it Operation Hugo—short for Huguenot. I had often seen Anne-Marie's cross. It was my idea to have the cross be the symbol of the operation. Drawn on the slips of paper. Those escaping had the paper with the cross and the date and time of departure only. Moustafa sent other info to the *boulangers* in France, not only the cross and the date and time, but also how many children were coming. They received the messages and baked them in the bread, and at certain times, I was to pick them up.

"Which is where you fit in, my dear." He squeezed her hand. "You kept me quite protected from Jean-Claude for a while. The first child who was to come over from Algeria in September never showed up. Something happened to him. I knew then that someone was onto the operation. So when I met you, I felt you could help me keep my cover without having to be in on the whole thing." He sighed. "Foolish of me. I am sorry, Gabby. I don't think I ever asked you to forgive me."

Gabriella kissed him tenderly on the forehead. "I cannot complain. It has worked out so differently . . . but I cannot complain." She blushed. "And yes, I forgive you."

She continued, "But what was Anne-Marie doing? And how did she and Ophélie get to Paris? Wasn't she in Algeria?"

"I did not know until Ophélie told me this morning. Anne-Marie and Moustafa and Ophélie fled Algeria—

from the bad men, as Ophélie puts it. They were in Paris for eight months. Then Ophélie escaped out the window of her apartment and went to live with Mr. Gady, an old shopkeeper whom I later found dead. Apparently, he was a friend of Anne-Marie's who had promised to care for Ophélie should there be trouble." He paused for a breath.

"It is all quite confusing," chimed Mother Griolet. "I'm glad I didn't know any of this. It would have been too overwhelming."

"You're right, it is complicated," David agreed. "Ophélie said she was supposed to give Mr. Gady her little blue bag, but she was too afraid. So that's when all communication with us broke down. And Anne-Marie and Moustafa ended up back in Algeria. I doubt seriously they went back of their own free will.

"In mid-October, I received word that something was happening in Paris. When I went up there to find out, of course I had no idea I would return with Ophélie. Or how she fit in the puzzle. It appears the man I was supposed to meet there was a double spy.

"He was going to use Ophélie as bait, no doubt, to trap me. But the whole plan fell apart when the riot broke out. And, miraculously, I ended up with Ophélie. The informant ended up in the obituaries."

Gabriella interrupted him. "And when I got the wrong bread in Aix, were orphans supposed to be coming? I've been worrying about that."

"No. I checked with the *boulangeries* fairly often, if I had not had any news. That time, there would have been no message in the bread even if you had gotten the *pain de seigle*. But I didn't know it then. That is why I was so angry. I was such a jerk to you, Gabby. I'm so sorry." David squeezed her hand.

"You were pretty awful several times. But I just knew

there was something in you worth exploring." Gabriella smiled. "Although you had me wondering for the longest time. But now I know." Her eyes were soft and filled with admiration. "It was a selfless act, a huge sacrifice of your time—not to mention the danger—for you to set up this operation."

David reddened. "I suppose there were some decent intentions mixed in with the bad, but don't flatter me, Gabby. I have much to learn about selflessness." He turned to gaze out the window, and spoke with a catch in his voice. "There was something appealing, satisfying about saving innocent children who were being sought out to kill for no crime of their own. They just happened to be the wrong race." His eyes were misty as he turned to face the women. "I could understand their suffering. I had to help."

He rubbed his eyes. "But I've strayed from the story. For the longest time after Hakim came, I had no word from Moustafa. Hakim was the one you brought news of in Aigues-Mortes."

"And Aigues-Mortes is where Jean-Claude first saw me and made the connection," Gabriella interjected. "Did he follow me to the bread store?"

"I don't think so. I think it was just your cross. He somehow knew of the symbol of our operation, and he saw your cross."

Gabriella held the cross gently in her hand. "Mother would never have imagined how much trouble this cross would get me into." She gave Mother Griolet a smile. "I suppose it all goes back to you. You bought the cross. You gave it to Mother. You were even the reason David came back to St. Joseph's."

The nun raised her eyebrows. "I am quite sure it does not all come back to *me*, but to *Him*. He is the Master Weaver. He saw it all before. The cross draws

452

us to Him, first, and then it draws us together."

David met Gabriella's eyes and touched her cheek with his hand.

"If I hadn't worn the Huguenot cross, who knows if Ophélie would have opened up to me?" Gabriella said, wonder in her voice. "And now what, David?"

He had wanted to tell her alone, to break the news gently and kiss away the worry lines that he knew would appear on her forehead. But he had no choice. It was the moment to say it.

With difficulty he straightened up in the bed. "There is Anne-Marie. I have received word about her from this man, Moustafa. She is quite ill. He fears she will die, and she cannot travel alone." He cleared his throat. "He must stay in Algeria to help other families escape. Not just those threatened by Ali, but other *harki* families. He has asked me to return to Algiers to bring Anne-Marie back."

Gabriella pulled her hand away from his and gave a soft whimper.

David fought with himself to remain calm. He wanted to say the right words. "Gabby, my dear. I must go. For Ophélie. If I can bring her mother back to her, surely this is right?"

Gabriella was twisting her hands together, staring at the floor. Silently Mother Griolet stood up and looked at David. "I will go now. I will leave you."

David nodded. "Thank you, Mother Griolet. Thank you."

"God be with you, David." She paused for a moment, resting her hand on the bent head of Gabriella. "And with you, my child." She left the room.

David motioned for Gabriella to come closer. Carefully she sat down on the edge of the bed as he put his good arm around her. He kissed her tenderly. She was crying.

"Please, Gabby, please try to understand."

She laid her head on his chest. "I am trying. I am trying, David, but I can't. I can't understand why you must leave now. Now when things are so good. We are safe, we are together. Ophélie is here." Her blue eyes were shining with tears as she looked up at him. "Don't leave me now."

He breathed out slowly. "I must ... I must leave. But do not be afraid, Gabby. Do not be afraid of *her*. That was so long ago, and you are now. Now you know for sure that I love you."

She did not answer. David grappled for something to say. "What was it you told me, Gabby? Something your mother said. *He does not make mistakes. Someday you will see that our God does not make mistakes.*"

Chapter Thirty-Four

The news of the cease-fire agreements coming from Evian spread quickly across the city of Algiers on the morning of March 19. Effective at noon. The gray skies echoed the mood that many felt: the cease-fire was necessary, but there was no victory. A war that started with a handful of extremists on All Saints Day in 1954 had cost French and Algerians hundreds of thousands of lives over the past seven years. In three months the Algerians would hold a referendum to vote for independence. The agreement written up between the FLN and de Gaulle's men specified plenty of precautions for the *pied-noirs*, but Anne-Marie knew the outcome. The *pied-noirs* would leave—leave their homes, their land, their cities to go to an unfamiliar and perhaps even hostile country where they were citizens.

She had become aware of the negative sentiments of the French toward the *pied-noirs* during her months in Paris. It would not be easy. But she did not care. Nothing could be worse than the nightmare she had lived through in the past two years. And she would be with Ophélie. Tomorrow, perhaps, David Hoffmann would walk back into her life and carry her to France. She forced herself to stand and limped badly across the room. At least she was walking. The bandages that had surrounded her legs for six weeks like the bottom half of a mummy were finally removed.

Moustafa came into the room, falling onto the bed with a sigh. He shook his curly hair, eyes solemn. "Cease-fire, Anne-Marie. Thank God the last children are gone. Because now is when trouble really begins."

"Don't say it, Moustafa. Please. Surely now there will be peace!"

"And you think the OAS will sit placidly by and not lift a finger? Fireworks are coming. Plenty of them. And not as a celebration from the Arabs." He stood up quickly and grabbed Anne-Marie's hands. "But you will be gone from this mess, *ma chére*. You and Ophélie will be safe."

Anne-Marie frowned and said, "And when will you come to France?" His eyes looked dull, the chocolate brown without sheen. "Tell me when you will come, so I can hope. I will not leave without knowing."

He kissed her tenderly, and Anne-Marie closed her eyes. The kiss gave her strength. She felt a flash of passion, but suddenly Moustafa was holding her away. "We have known it is impossible. For these months I have had you, and knowing that, I have hoped. But Anne-Marie, I cannot tell you when or if I will come back to France. I know things ... and I am needed." His chocolate eyes regained their luster. He pulled her close to him, and Anne-Marie could feel his heart beating. "We have made it this far. We have shared a love I only hoped for months ago. Surely, somehow, it will carry us through. But I will not ask you to wait for me. I will only ask that you call out to the heavens and pray that the *harkis* be spared further loss.”

“Kiss me again, Moustafa,” she whispered. “As if it is for the last time, something I can remember and hold onto.” When he released her, she touched her lips as if to seal in the wonder—wonder that a war and another man she had once loved would not erase.

“Ophélie,” she said out loud. “Wait only a little longer. Mama is coming home.”

* * *

Papa was leaving tomorrow to get Mama in Algeria. Ophélie could not decipher her feelings. Fear, excitement, love, anger. They seemed to be colliding in her mind. Her hands behind her head, she stretched her small frame out the length of the bed. Something from her mother’s letter came to her. She quickly rolled over and opened the chest of drawers, taking out the blue bag. She cradled it in her hands, then carefully pulled apart the strings. Her small, delicate hand reached inside, as it had done so many times before, and pulled out the contents. Everything was there. She picked up Mama’s letter and read it again. There, on the first page, was the phrase she had remembered. *“I never wanted us to be apart, but for now, my love, it is necessary.”*

Mama had said it, and now Papa was saying it too. Just for a while. Then Papa would bring her back and they would be a family, like other families. Papa, Mama, Gabriella, and her.

Ophélie frowned. No, somehow that would never work. She sighed as she stared at the tiny photo of her with her mother. Why couldn’t Papa love Mama and Gabriella? Why did he have to choose?

She kissed her mother’s picture and whispered, “Mama, I can read and write, and I have found Papa. Everything is almost perfect. When you get back, then it will be like a fairy tale, and we will live happily ever after. I am sure."

She pulled out the top drawer where she had stored a few blank sheets of paper and colored pencils. She could write, and Mama needed to know she was waiting for her. Leaning on the top of the chest of drawers she wrote slowly in her best cursive. *"Je t'eme Mama. Vien me voir vite. Je t'attend. Ophélie."* She checked it over. Maybe there were a few spelling errors, but surely Mama would understand: I love you. Come see me soon. I am waiting for you. Over her words she drew a large rainbow, its many-colored arc filling the page.

She tucked the note in the pocket of her black wool skirt, kissed the little photo, and replaced the blue bag in the drawer. Now Mama would see for herself that she could write. And she would hurry to come here, to this place that had become Ophélie's home.

* * *

Mother Griolet had kindly insisted that good-byes be said in her apartment while she cared for the children in the basement. The little threesome sat in awkward silence, dreading the minutes that ruthlessly ticked by. David swallowed several times, for his throat felt closed and dry. He motioned to Ophélie, who was standing solemnly by the window. Slowly she walked over to her father.

Gabriella bit her lip. He read the pain in her eyes.

David held Ophélie in his arms tightly, rejoicing in the smell of her freshly washed hair and the feel of the soft skin, so young and alive and unblemished. "My dear, my daughter." His tone was gentle. The morning light seeped through the window and engulfed them.

"Ophélie, I will go now. I will go and find Mama. I will bring her back to you, to us." For a brief moment he glanced over to Gabriella, with all the love and hurt of the world in his eyes.

"You will not take me with you, Papa?" she begged.

"No, no. It is much too dangerous. You must stay here with Gabby. She will care for you." He turned to Gabriella, who was standing partially in the shadows. The sun tinted her hair, and it glistened thick and red, tumbling over her shoulders. He felt a hollow pain in his stomach. "You will care for Ophélie, won't you?"

"Of course I will." She motioned for the child to come to her, and Ophélie ran into her arms.

Ophélie reached into her pocket. "Papa? I have something for Mama. Will you take it to her for me?"

David took the folded paper. He was beside them at once, stroking Gabriella's hair and softly saying, "You have told me before. A God bigger than us is in control. I believe it now. Will you let me go?"

Gabriella nodded and turned her head down. He knew she was crying. He lifted her chin with his good hand. His eyes were piercing, then he softened. He contemplated kissing her. Instead, he put his warm, strong hand in hers and squeezed it hard. Ophélie held him tightly around the waist. He pulled them close to his chest and with a heavy sigh, whispered, "I love you both."

He could not say anything else, although he thought of a hundred different things he wanted to tell Gabriella. But they were things to be said by candlelight, nestled in the back of a charming little restaurant. He could not say them here.

Finally he broke the tortured silence. "I'd better go." He had no heart for small talk. He simply hugged Ophélie and Gabriella as tightly as he could manage with one arm. For a brief moment he pressed his lips against Gabriella's forehead.

Then he left the room.

* * *

From the window in the den, Gabriella and Ophélie watched David walk into the street below. He paused to wave back at them, looking almost vulnerable, with several wisps of black hair falling across his forehead and a half-smile crossing his face. The dimple was barely visible. And the eyes, the dark brooding eyes caught Gabriella's, and all she read was love. One arm of his leather jacket hung limply to the side, concealing the bandaged shoulder. The other clutched a small suitcase. The briefcase was under his arm. It was the picture of David that she would keep in her mind afterward.

"Bribri, are you all right?" Ophélie's face was shining with tears. "You love him so, Gabriella. And he loves you. I know it. You will not pray that Mama dies, will you?"

Gabriella frowned for a moment. Then she scooped Ophélie up in her arms. "I will never pray for that. There is a God bigger than us who sees our hearts and understands, just as your papa said. He has already worked everything out. You will see, precious child. We will see. I am sure."

* * *

The noise from the classroom was deafening as Mother Griolet entrusted the children to Sister Rosaline and Sister Isabelle. "It may be that lunch is late. Don't worry. Just try to calm them down now while I check out the bedrooms."

Her head was throbbing from the noise. Nine new children. Wild, terrified little *harki* children. Crying, screaming, clutching. "I know they should be here, Lord. But I don't know how to do it. I will need more help, more room." She was out of breath by the time she reached the dormitories. Two extra bunk beds had been squeezed into the girls' dorm, on loan from Mme. Lemoine for as long as Mother Griolet needed. "Thank You, Lord, for kind, simple women who don't ask too many questions," the nun said.

She paused for a moment, then walked into the boys' dorm. Two cots from the hospital were neatly made. "Bless you, Sister Rosaline. How that good woman found enough sheets, I have no idea. *Merci, Seigneur!*"

Satisfied that each child would have a place to sleep that night, she left the dormitories, walking back through the courtyard and the basement. The din from the classroom had quieted, and Sister Rosaline was very animatedly telling a story. "Bless you," Mother Griolet whispered again as she trotted through the hall and up the steps, letting herself into her apartment. Mr. Vidal sat in front of her desk.

"Jean-Louis, forgive me for keeping you waiting," she said, sitting down with a long sigh.

Mr. Vidal rose slightly and nodded. "You have seen the paper this morning? The cease-fire goes into effect at noon."

"*Dieu merci*, it is over. And the children got here safely." A smile crossed her lips. "Thank you, Jean-Louis. You had no problem in Marseilles?"

He laughed. "It went as smoothly as you could expect with nine little ones. I do believe I'm getting a little old for this." He rubbed his bloodshot eyes. "And you, Jeanette? You have everything you need?"

The old nun cleared her throat and clucked, "I need your prayers. Many prayers, Jean-Louis." She thought for a moment. "You are sure you can keep on with Mr. Hoffmann's class? Until he gets back?"

Jean-Louis grunted, "It's the least I can do. That poor man, going to Algeria at this time. You should have forbidden it, Jeanette. To keep him alive."

"God has provided me with another capable teacher," she said, winking at him. "And who am I to forbid what the Lord ordains? We must pray, simply pray."

"*C'est compris*," he said. "You've done a good job, dear woman."

"*Toi aussi, mon ami*, you too." Then almost timidly she asked, "Do you think ... do you think this is all of the children?"

He shuffled his feet and looked to the ground. "In my opinion, it will get a lot worse over there before it gets better. I don't think we're done. But as far as Hugo goes, mission accomplished." He grinned rather shyly. "I'll be going now. Oh, and you have two visitors in your den."

They touched hands lightly and left the office together. Mr. Vidal toddled slowly down the steps. She watched him go, then walked down the hall to her den.

Ophélie was sitting on Gabriella's lap, both of them staring out the window. Mother Griolet watched from a distance. The girl and the young woman were crying. Mother Griolet cleared her throat softly. "Excuse me for interrupting you."

Gabriella looked over her shoulder at the old nun. Her face was flushed, her eyes brimming.

"He has left?"

"He is leaving soon. Taking the bus to the train station."

"And you did not wish to see him off?"

Gabriella shrugged and nodded down toward Ophélie.

Understanding, Mother Griolet came beside them. "Ophélie will stay with me for a while. She will be fine. Won't you, dear?"

The child bit her lips, holding her pink pony close.

"You will see, children. Life goes on, and there is

462

hope." Suddenly Ophélie pulled the cross from around her neck. She offered it to Gabriella. "If you are going to Papa, take him my cross. Then he will be safe. He will understand."

The young woman took it and replied softly, "You know, Ophélie, that God will protect him, not because he wears a cross, but because David has the Lord in here." She pointed to her heart.

"I know. But still, it will help remind Papa of God... and of me. He must have it." She was adamant.

"Very well, then, I will take it to him." Gabriella unfastened the chain and slipped it over her hair. As she did so, a ray of sun came in, and Mother Griolet watched the splashes of light dance through the room. The crosses hung together, touching lightly.

"Two crosses," she said finally. "Two Huguenot crosses." No one said a word for several eternal seconds. "Go on with you now," Mother Griolet urged Gabriella. "Go on."

* * *

Once convinced, Gabriella raced down the steps of the parsonage and out into the cool, ethereal spring day. Her hair flying out behind her, she tripped on the cobblestones, regained her balance and dashed around the corner, past the olive tree that brushed against her window, past the fountain that sprayed gustily, to the bus stop. David stood with his back to her. Several older women sat with stone-faced expressions, waiting for Bus 11.

For a moment Gabriella hesitated. Then she called out, "David!"

He whirled around, catching sight of her, an expression of delight and surprise crossing his face.

"Gabby!" he laughed, picking her up with one arm and kissing her hard on the mouth. "I'm glad you came," he mumbled between kisses.

"We'll be the talk of the town now," she giggled.

David grinned. "It was bound to happen one way or another." He glanced at his watch. Taking her hand, he led her away from the bus stop, across the street and behind a row of stores.

"I have this for you," Gabriella stammered, taking the cross from around her neck. "Ophélie wanted you to wear it for her. So you will remember that God is protecting you. So you will remember her." Her voice caught, and a cool shiver ran down her spine. He was really going. The minutes were ticking by, and she suddenly realized that she had not given him anything at all.

"I wish I had something for you," she began, but he put a finger to her lips.

"Don't. Don't say it. Do you think I will forget you, beautiful Gabby? I have the Book you gave me. And now I have the cross. It is all I need."

His hand was on her shoulder as he looked down at her, his black eyes soft. "I will never forget all you have shared with me. Never."

She did not like the way he said *never*. "You are coming back, aren't you? You won't be gone too long?"

He touched her face, brushing her cheek with his fingers. "I'll be back. Pray for me, Gabby. I will come back." He fumbled with the lock on his briefcase. "I almost forgot to give this to you. I was going to mail it from Marseilles, but since you are here." He held out a white envelope. "Your exam." He winked. "You did very well, my dear."

He pulled her to him once more and kissed her for a long moment. It was a soft, passionate kiss. She knew he did not want to leave her. "I have to say good-bye now, Gabby." They held hands and crossed back toward the bus stop.

The bus was slowly crawling up the street.

"Good-bye, David." Her voice was choked with emotion. "I love you."

He looked back, poised forever on the step of the bus, his dark eyes studying her, his good arm clutching his black leather suitcase. He set it down and waved once. The doors closed, and he was gone.

* * *

Yvette Leclerc and Monique Pons were watching the young couple's good-bye from the window of Monique's apartment.

"*Ooh la la*. Young love is *difficile*," Mme. Leclerc sighed, sadly shaking her head.

"*Triste, oui, mais alors!* It is a beautiful story. They must be strong and brave. If fate and *le bon Dieu* are on their side, *alors* all will turn out fine," Mme. Pons reassured her friend.

"The good Lord, yes. Surely He is with them. And who knows? There may be a wedding yet, one of these days," Mme. Leclerc chuckled.

Monique Pons rolled her eyes and picked up a potato that she had been peeling. "You never know. Life is full of surprises, *n'est-ce pas?*"

* * *

Gabriella did not walk back to St. Joseph's immediately. She followed the road past Mme. Leclerc's and out toward the countryside. She remembered the time she had strolled this way with David in early December when their friendship had been reconciled. The vines had been naked then, but now tiny sprouts of green were appearing on the twisted branches.

She ripped open the envelope and removed four folded sheets of paper. They rustled in the breeze and she looked down to read them, but her eyes were blurred. She wiped them quickly. Across the top of the exam, David had scribbled, "Excellent work, Miss Madison." There was no grade. She felt an edgy disappointment. It looked as if he had made no other comment on the exam. She had hoped for a word, another phrase. Something she could keep from him.

Turning to the last page, she saw that there was something written at the very bottom. "I'm sitting in this hospital bed, barely able to write. I am thinking of you, Gabby. When you wonder, when you begin to question, read this exam again and know that I mean every word. *Je t'aime,* David."

She touched the words with her hand, then held the pages to her breast. Gabriella gazed out into the distance and said, with a soft confidence in her voice, "The Lord shall preserve thy going out and thy coming in from this time forth and even for evermore. Amen." Far across the field, she saw a lone poppy quiver in the early spring breeze, bending back and forth, holding its bright red face to the sun.

End of Book I

The Huguenot Cross

Protestantism began in France in the mid-sixteenth century. The first French Protestants were called Huguenots. Despite almost continual persecution from the Catholic church and the Kings of France, the Huguenots grew in number and influence. In 1598, Henri IV, King of France, granted Huguenots religious freedom under the Edict of Nantes. The ensuing persecutions forced hundreds of thousands of Huguenots to flee to England, Ireland, Scotland, Holland, Germany, Switzerland, Russia, and North America. Many thousands of Huguenots who remained in France were martyred for their faith. However, in 1685, this edict was revoked by Louis XIV.

The Huguenot cross is believed to have been created by a goldsmith in Nîmes around the year 1688. It is in the form of a Maltese cross and strongly resembles the military decoration called the Medal of the Order of the Holy Spirit, created in the late sixteenth century by King Henri III as a military distinction for excellent warriors.

The Huguenot cross comes in many different forms today. Originally it was made up of four equal, thick branches, each branch in the form of an arrow turned inward, with two little "balls" on the outer points of the arrow. Four fleur-de-lis were embedded in between the branches of the cross and a dove, symbolizing the Holy Spirit, hung with its head turned downward from the lowest branch.

The cross is very popular among Protestants in France today.